D1493632

AUTHOR'S NOTE

Yarmouth is an actual harbour town on the Isle of Wight. Some details of the geography of the town have been changed to suit the story. For example, if you visit, you won't find Harbour Close, nor Wight's, the gallery, the vet's or the hairdresser's, which are all completely fictitious and not based on any actual businesses. In the same way all the people in this story are completely fictitious.

Cowes, too, is a real place but the streets which feature in the novel are entirely made-up.

PROLOGUE
SATURDAY 18TH FEBRUARY 2017

I sat in darkness, my hand shaking as I held out the match and lit the black candle on the altar.

On a piece of paper, I wrote the name, 'Ruby Moore, born February 1987' and then pinned it onto the small doll, the voodoo doll. Twiggy legs and arms, blue silk dress. I'd attempted to take any sweetness away from it with its face, carving out hollow sightless eyes, and a thin cruel mouth.

Picking up the voodoo doll, I said the words, loud and firm, 'The pain you gave me will come back to you a hundred times worse. You are cursed.' I repeated the words, conjuring up as much hate as I could. A voice whispered at the back of my head, to stop, to step back, but I pushed it away. No, I had to concentrate: the more hate I released, the more effective the curse.

Slowly, I picked up black-headed pins and pushed them into the doll, then carefully placed the voodoo doll inside a black cardboard coffin, and sealed the lid. I wrapped the box in a piece of black silk, placed it in a drawer and locked it.

Sitting back, I slowed my breath, stared at the candle as the wax dripped down the side. Finally, I leant forward, placed my hands over the crystal bowl containing black salt, and closed my eyes. It was done.

1

SATURDAY 6TH MAY 2017

Nia sat out on the deck huddled in her seat, the sea breeze cold on her face, surrounded by excited children and harassed parents, holiday-makers heading to the island.

Although she was aware of their shouts competing with the gulls screaming above her, the smell of the sea mingled with the ferry's engine that was chugging, she felt strangely detached.

Her phone pinged a message; it was from her husband, Chris.

Glad the car is sorted, safe travels, miss you already

Nia stared at her phone. When her aunt, Gwen, had suggested she come and house-sit for a month, Nia had initially turned it down. The idea of going away on her own filled her with dread. In her twenty years of marriage, apart from the occasional night away, she'd always been with Chris. In any case, surely nothing could be solved by running away from her problems. However, Chris had agreed, in fact encouraged her, and she'd reluctantly said she'd go.

And so, she was sitting on the ferry with her dog, Romeo, and as much luggage as she could manage on her own. Nia leant forward, rested her chin on the head of her cocker spaniel, stroked his soft orange-white ears. 'It's me and you, Romeo. Just the two of us now.'

She looked ahead and slowly the island came more sharply into focus and she could see the town of Yarmouth and the harbour, shaped like a horseshoe, its arms waiting to embrace and welcome her.

'This is going to be our new home for a while,' she said to Romeo. 'Gwen said we'd enjoy the beaches and downs; we have a whole new island to explore.' There was something exciting about visiting an island, she had to admit. There were no bridges or tunnels between this island, the Isle of Wight, and the mainland. The only way to get here was by boat. If the weather was really bad, she could get completely cut off, and actually Nia found the idea rather appealing.

An announcement echoed around the ferry summoning passengers to prepare to leave. Nia quickly took out her make-up bag, checked her lashes, touched up her lipstick and smoothed down her black hair held tightly in a bun. She threw her rucksack onto her back, another bag over her shoulder and picked up the handle of her wheeled suitcase with one hand, the lead in her other. The plan had been to bring her car, but nothing in her life was going to plan lately. She let others rushing to cars and coaches go ahead of her and then gingerly made her way to the lift.

Nia had quickly researched the town, described as cosy, 'the town time forgot', with narrow streets leading to a square with a town hall, church, pubs, cafes and a small independent business. However today it was very busy, as cars streamed off the ferry, rows of cars queued to go on, and in the town people spilled onto the road from the narrow pavements.

From Gwen's directions Nia knew she didn't have far to walk and soon she arrived at Harbour Close: white, neat, clean terraced houses, tulips and daffodils standing proudly in the pots. Safe and snug as a cat lying in the sunshine. Taking a deep breath of sea air laced with Mediterranean smells of fish, garlic, and coffee, she could feel her shoulders drop, her jaw relax.

Gwen's house was one of the first buildings on her left; neat box hedges in planters stood either side of the light blue front door. Even though Nia knew Gwen had only left the day before, it had the air of a house that had been abandoned. Gwen was hundreds of miles away now in San Francisco with her daughter. Nia missed her, wished Gwen had been there – a hug and some home-baking were exactly what she needed right now.

But she had to get on. Gwen had told her to pick up the house keys from the hairdresser's opposite. Nia had smiled at that; it seemed like a sign.

Nia went over to 'Gems' but hesitated at the front door. It didn't have the edge of the grey and stone salon she used to work in back in Cardiff, but it was freshly painted, with neat bay trees standing guard either side of the front door. Glancing through the large windows, she saw it was free from old-fashioned posters favoured by more traditional salons in villages around the country.

Nia glanced at her reflection in the window, checked her hair again, tucked a stray strand behind her ear. Satisfied, she dumped her cases outside the salon, in a way she'd have probably thought twice about back home, and went in with Romeo. Music from a local radio station played; two hairdressers were working with clients. The smell of hair products, the gentle buzz, mirrors, gowns, flooded her with a deep sense of loss and reminded her of the clients and their families she'd left behind.

'Can I help you?' asked the woman with short, dyed white-blonde hair, fashionable joggers and trainers who came over to her, smiling.

She swallowed hard. 'I'm Nia. I've come for the keys to my aunt Gwen's house.' Suddenly she looked down at Romeo. 'Oh, sorry, I didn't want to leave him outside.'

'That's OK. Hello, sweetie. We love dogs, don't we?' Nia heard a gentle burr to the young woman's voice. She grinned at Nia. 'I'm Jade.' She nodded towards the other hairdresser. 'That's my sister, Ruby.'

Ruby gave a cursory smile but went back to cutting her client's hair. She looked a lot less fashionable than her sister, wearing a cotton flowered skirt and plain blouse, no make-up. However, she did have the most beautiful long blonde hair, falling like liquid sunshine, almost reaching her waist.

'I live in the flat above the salon,' continued Jade. 'Ruby's further up the close with her husband, Richie, at the art gallery. We are all under strict instructions from Gwen to make you feel at home.' Jade glanced out of the window at the abandoned luggage. 'You've got a lot of stuff. Didn't you bring a car over?'

'It was awful. My car broke down as I was going to drive onto the ferry.'

'Oh, God, no. What did you do?'

Jade crossed her arms, leant on a shelf, ready to listen.

'Well, my car was towed off to a garage in Southampton. I'll pick it up when it's fixed. Sorry. I don't want to hold you up,' said Nia, looking over at the client sitting in the chair. However, she was philosophically scrolling through her phone.

Jade grinned. 'Don't worry. You know, you are ever so like Gwen, what with that gorgeous Welsh accent and the black hair – you'd think you were her daughter.'

Nia blushed. 'Thank you. People often say that. I found it really hard when she left Cardiff.'

'I can imagine. She's settled in really well here; we are all very fond of her. I'd love to fly off to America, but not in a panic like Gwen.'

'I know, but of course her daughter, Ceri, needs her. The baby is not due for another two weeks, but Ceri is finding it hard going. She was desperate for Gwen to go out as soon as she could.'

'Ceri is lucky to have a mum like Gwen. You must let us know if you get any news.'

Jade glanced around the room, with a mixture of humility and pride. 'Gwen said you used to be a hairdresser. I'm sure your salon in Cardiff was a lot posher than this.'

'It's larger, but this is great.'

'Thank you. So, this is your first visit to the island. You'll have a good time, and so will this chap.' Jade stroked Romeo's head. 'Right, I'd better get you those keys.'

Jade disappeared to the back of the salon and Nia looked around again. Unusually, among the display of the sponsored hair products they sold, there was a selection of candles: red, white, and green, in beautiful shapes.

She was looking at them when Jade returned. 'I make those,' she explained. 'They are made of soya wax, all vegan, if you're interested.' She handed Nia the keys. 'That's the front door, back, windows, and the garage – do you need help? I can come over with you.'

'I'll be fine. Thank you for the offer though,' replied Nia and left.

Feeling rather like an intruder, Nia opened Gwen's front door. This opened directly into the living room, which contained enough furniture, books and general clutter for a room three times its size.

Nia pictured her house back in Cardiff: a modern, minimalist, executive home. They'd moved in ten years ago; it was Chris's dream house. She smiled as she looked around and had to admit this was more her style.

Nia opened the back door and held Romeo's collar as she checked for good strong fences all round.

It was a modest-sized garden: scruffy borders, a few small trees. To her left was the wall of the building that faced out onto the main road, to her right a lower fence that separated her from the neighbour's garden and down the bottom a high wall that gave them privacy from the street. All were secure or high enough to keep Romeo in, and so she let him go and he rushed around, sniffing his new territory.

Leaving Romeo to explore the garden, Nia returned to the kitchen. As she expected, this was far more organised than the living room. Gwen loved to bake.

Nia went upstairs. The main bedroom faced the street. There was the same mixture of furniture, but she did find space had been made in drawers for her things as well as half the wardrobe emptied. Nia started to unpack; she couldn't bear things in cases. As she hung up her pencil skirts, body-con dresses, tight jeans and neat blouses she saw the contrast with the riotous skirts and tops that still hung there. She smiled. There was a time when she'd worn clothes like those, but the neat, smart clothes she wore now were ones Chris liked, and she guessed slowly she'd changed her wardrobe to suit him.

She arranged her shoes: three pairs of heels, one pair of old trainers, the only casual shoes she had for walking Romeo and a pair of wellington boots. Chris liked her to wear heels, and so, even in a job where she was on her feet all day, she had grown used to wearing them most of the time.

Deciding she had to somehow make this place feel like her own, Nia took down an old suitcase from the wardrobe and started to fill it with stuff from around the room, then set out her own, few expensive cosmetics, a book and torch next to her bed. She took out her nightie, but as she did she held it close to her face. It smelt of home, of him. Tears burned her eyes: she was here, alone. She tried to remember when she'd last spent a night on her own. Nia had not been on a holiday without Chris for the twenty years of their married life. The most they had ever been apart was when she'd gone away with Safi for the odd night, or to visit her parents. But as for doing things entirely on her own, well, she couldn't remember ever staying alone in a hotel. She'd not even eaten in a restaurant or cafe on her own for years either.

Shaking off the sadness, Nia went downstairs to be greeted by Romeo running in from the garden. She opened one of the bags she'd brought, took out a bowl, filled it with water and put it on the kitchen floor.

Nia looked in the remaining bags. She'd had to leave a load of things in the car, including Romeo's bed, with her own bedding, as they were too bulky to carry.

'Me and you are going to make do and mend, as Mum would say, for a week,' she said to Romeo. 'Don't worry, I have your food and poo bags and soft piggy.'

Nia then spotted a note. As she started to read, she realised Gwen wrote as she talked, and she could hear her voice, each word coated with her smooth, warm tones.

Welcome! Make sure you treat this house as your own home. The appliances are all pretty self-explanatory. I've written a list of the boring stuff like bin days etc and left food basics in the fridge. I hope it helps you to have some time to yourself, look after yourself. I will try to keep in touch but what with the time difference it won't always be that easy. Email me if there are any problems. There are lots of walks and places to visit. I promise you the island will look after you. You can breathe here, I think, it's a magical place. On one of the book-shelves is a file where I jot down some walks, you might like to look at it sometime. Just one thing, if you get a chance to befriend Ruby from the hairdresser, I'd be grateful. I've mentioned her to you a few times as I knew her mum. I am sure there is something wrong, she seems very down. Maybe as an outsider you may be able to see things that have evaded me. The main thing however is for you to look after yourself. Take care, Gwen xxxxx

Nia thought about Ruby and her sister over at the hairdresser's. She wasn't sure how she was going to get to know Ruby; she looked quite shy. In fact, she wasn't sure how she was going to get to know anyone here, and guessed she was going to be spending a lot of time on her own.

However, she couldn't have been more wrong and at that moment she heard a knock at the door.

2

Nia found it odd and exposing to have a front door that led straight into her living room.

However, her visitor was completely unfazed, and greeted her with a wide smile. It was Jade from the hairdresser's, and she was holding up a bottle of red wine. 'A "welcome to your new home" present.'

Nia invited her in. 'That's kind. Would you like a drink?'

'Never say no. Glad I bought something decent now.' Jade followed her in.

Nia handed Jade a glass and they sat on separate armchairs.

'Is this your nipper?' asked Jade, taking in the photo of a young woman on the dresser.

Nia looked at her quizzically. 'Nipper?'

Jade laughed. 'Nipper is an island word for children. You'll hear it a lot over here.'

'Your accent sounds almost west country. Did your parents come from there?'

'No, visitors, or overners – that's another island word – they often think that. The island accent is a really soft burr.'

'I like it. Anyway, the nipper in that photo is my daughter, Safi.'

'What does she do?'

'She's travelling before going to university. She worked in a local supermarket, trying to save some money, and now has gone with her boyfriend, supposedly getting language experience in Spain ready for doing her degree. I'm not sure how much she's learning. She seems to be having a very good time.'

'Lucky girl. I wish I'd gone travelling. I hardly get to the mainland, let alone abroad. And do you have a husband or partner at home?'

'Yes, he's the headteacher of our local high school. He's very busy.'

'Wow, that sounds stressful.'

'It is. So tell me, Jade, have you and your sister been at the salon long?'

'Originally Ruby and I both worked in Sandown after we did our hairdressing courses at the college. Ruby moved over here with Richie when they got married six years ago. He took over the gallery and she was working with another hairdresser here. When she left Ruby asked me to join her. It's a good salon and I get the flat above.'

'Do you like living in Yarmouth?'

'It's a bit dull in the winter, but I like the holiday season, meeting new people. Do you know the island?'

'This is my first visit. I always meant to bring my daughter over to stay with Gwen, but we never got around to it. It's an interesting town. The streets are very narrow, aren't they? I've never lived in quite such close proximity to my neighbours before.'

'The houses are so close together, aren't they? Not much gets missed. If you're lucky, I'll be the first person you see in the morning and the last at night. I never shut my curtains and because I go to bed much earlier than Gwen, we have a standing joke that I can tell what time she goes to bed because I see her light come on. It always wakes me up. But really, I do like it. I love being so close to people.'

Nia noticed Jade had finished her glass of wine and poured her another one. 'So, who else lives here?' she asked.

'The longest residents are your neighbours, Lucy and Ian next door. They're our island health gurus! Ian started out as an accountant but moved on to being an advisor on the odd radio programme. He retired early but now he's dead excited as he and Lucy are making their name in health and fitness for the over sixties. They're on for a book deal and TV spot. I have to say they both look amazing for their age. Next to them is Wight's, a brasserie place, owned by Joe. He's Ruby's age; his parents set him up there. Then at the top of the close is the vet's, run by Ethan and Elvira, who are a couple now. Coming down the other side, Richie, Ruby's husband, works in the gallery, and they live above it. Next to them is a second home that is empty most of the time, and then the salon with my flat above. That's it. It's a small community.' Jade put her head to one side. 'Are you planning to stay for the whole of Gwen's time away? She's going to be over there for a few months, isn't she?'

'Oh no, I told her I could do a few weeks. She'll either leave it empty or find someone else when I go.'

'So did you fancy a holiday?' Nia could see the curiosity in Jade's face. She'd prepared an explanation.

'I needed a break.' Nia paused, could see Jade was waiting for more.

'I shall try and get fit,' she added, 'read some worthy books, stop drinking.' She smiled at the glass. 'After this one maybe! I'll go back a whole new me.'

'That's ambitious!'

'As my daughter would say, I need to get my shit together.'

'By completely changing who you are?'

Despite trying to keep it light, Nia suddenly felt close to tears. It was embarrassing. 'We'd all like to do that, wouldn't we?' she replied.

'Sounds exhausting,' said Jade, but then her tone changed. 'You don't always have to be changing yourself, you know. You can learn to like yourself for who you are. I know that sounds a bit heavy but, well, when you've been brought up in some scary religion, never feeling you could do anything right, you either go along with the idea you will never be good enough or you fight it and try to like yourself for who you are.'

Nia frowned. 'What religion was that?'

'They are simply called "The Righteous" and they get together at

The Hall. It's very strict and isolated, the teachings are extremely dogmatic.'

'That sounds the opposite of what a faith should be. I'm not religious but Gwen is. She finds going to church a great comfort.'

'I know, I think normal churches are, but that's not what our place was like. Anyway, I left, thank God, and so did Ruby's husband, Richie – he was brought up there as well. Ruby has kept going, unfortunately.'

Nia bit her lip. 'Gwen mentioned Ruby to me, I think she was a bit worried about her.'

'Yes, she talked to me about it, but I probably knew less than her. Gwen was one of the few people to get close to Ruby.'

'Gwen told me she spent a lot of time with your mum, and I got the impression she became very close to Ruby during that time. She told me Ruby would have made a wonderful nurse.'

Jade grimaced. 'You're right. I'm afraid I was pretty useless in the last few months of Mum's life. She was bed-bound and every time I went in, I just started crying. Ruby was brilliant, she moved in with her, sat up all night. I don't know quite how she did it. We had nurses come in sometimes, and then of course Gwen stepped in. Between them they took such good care of Mum. I am really grateful.'

'I'm sure Gwen was only glad to help. She's one of those natural caregivers.'

'She is, she's quietly helped a lot of people in the close. She's a kind of mother hen to us all and, as I say, even Ruby turned to her.'

'But Ruby hasn't confided in her lately?'

'Since Mum died Ruby has gone even more into herself. Losing a mum affects us all in different ways, doesn't it?'

'Yes, I agree. I lost my mum a few years ago. It's very hard.'

'It is.'

They looked at each other, but neither spoke, choosing to keep their pain to themselves. They both knew that grief for someone so loved was precious, and not something to be spoken of lightly.

Jade, in an apparent complete change of subject, asked, 'Do you like swimming in the sea?'

'The sea? I've not been in the sea for years, and then it was only paddling with my daughter.'

'You must come with me one morning. I go when I can.'

'I don't know – I'll think about it.'

Jade stood up. 'I'll let you settle in.' She looked closely at Nia. 'It's good to have you here. Take care.' She paused and laughed self-consciously. 'Sorry, I don't know why I said that. Things have been a bit weird lately – a kind of sinister undercurrent, if you know what I mean.'

She laughed, but it was forced and overloud. 'Sorry, too much wine. Now, come along to Wight's tomorrow evening. We all go about half past six, and it will give you a chance to meet everyone. Of course, Gwen always brought along some cakes – no pressure though.'

Nia went with Jade to the door, glanced out at the close. Jade's words had been unsettling. She didn't believe it was just the wine speaking. Could it really be true that things weren't quite as idyllic here as first appeared?

Later that evening, Nia took Romeo out for a final walk. The streets were quiet now, with light from the pubs, but few people wandering around. In the distance she could see the lights of the mainland, a vast dark sea stretching between them.

On either side of the entrance to the pier were small shingle beaches and Nia took Romeo down. Back in Cardiff, she realised, she'd stopped walking anywhere alone at night; her final words to her daughter whenever she'd gone out at night had been to ring her or get a taxi home. And yet standing here, she felt no fear.

She'd forgotten how much she loved being by the sea.

Slowly, she found her breathing syncing with the waves, coming and going as if they were healing her in a way all the mindfulness CDs and videos never had. She was confused about so many things, but one thing was certain: at that moment she was glad to be here, and glad to be here alone.

Before she left she took a photo, which she sent to Safi and Chris with the message:

I'm on the island!

Later that night, she went up to her room. She decided Romeo could sleep on a cushion next to her. She had a quick chat with Chris to say goodnight, and then went to shut the curtains.

To her surprise, she saw Jade opposite, waving at her.

Nia smiled and waved back. What could have felt intrusive was actually a comfort. Her window was open and she could smell the remnants of chips from the pubs, sense the cold sea air, the sky now black, the stars bright. She heard the heartbeat of the waves, quietly lapping in the distance. The hint of a warning earlier from Jade made no sense now.

3

The sun shone through the thin curtains and Nia sat up. It was seven o'clock, but she couldn't stay in bed later than that, even on a Sunday. Back home she'd have allowed herself a leisurely breakfast, read the papers, walked around the park and lake opposite her house. Chris had always worked through the weekend, always been ambitious. It was how he'd ended up as head teacher, but Nia had never been like that. When her daughter, Safi, had been younger it had been their day. They'd go to a museum or art gallery in the town centre or drive to Barry Island and paddle if it was sunny.

Nia saw a text on her phone, another from Chris, and sent a quick answer. After this she showered and sat at the dressing table to do her make-up. It took time, as she always liked to face the day fully made up; she had been doing her heavy smoky eye make-up in the same way for years. Chris liked her eyes this way: a lot of mascara, eye shadow and thick eyebrows. She combed her hair back into a tight bun, gave herself a quick smile, slipped on her old trainers, went downstairs, and took her coffee and toast out into the garden where there was a small metal table and matching chairs. It was a dry crisp spring morning: blue sky dotted with wispy clouds, just enough warmth to sit outside.

The garden was a bit wild but there were spring flowers peeking through the borders. Sparrows shot in and out of the hedges.

'Morning.' The voice startled her. Looking towards the fence, she saw an older man with the sparkling white smile, thick, well-cut grey hair and bright eyes of an afternoon quiz show host.

'Oh, um, hiya.'

'You must be Nia. How charming to meet you.' He gave a deprecating shrug. 'I'm Ian, Ian Robson.' He paused, awaiting a response.

'Of course, Jade told me you were on the radio. You have a book and TV deal on the cards?'

The smile broadened; he was clearly flattered. 'It's nothing, really. Now, my mission here is to extend a warm invitation to lunch with Lucy and me. We are of course vegetarian, but I can promise you a great meal.'

'Thank you very much. Can I bring a bottle?'

He gave a mock look of horror. 'Please don't worry, just bring yourself. We'll see you about half twelve?'

At that moment Romeo came running out of the house. Ian was ecstatic.

'A cocker spaniel, my favourite breed. Hello, you.'

'This is Romeo; my daughter named him.'

'Fabulous. What a handsome fellow. Now, that colouring is orange roan. Am I right?'

'Dead right.'

'He is, of course, invited to lunch.'

'You're sure?'

'Of course.'

Nia thought it best to take Romeo for a long walk before the lunch.

As she left the house, she saw Ruby walking past. She was in similar clothes to those she'd been wearing at the salon, but today she wore a headscarf.

'Hiya,' Nia said.

Ruby gave the fixed smile. 'Good morning, Nia. I hope you are settling into your new home.'

'Thank you, yes. It's a lovely morning. Are you off somewhere?'

'To The Hall. It's where my religious group, The Righteous, meet.'

'Of course, Jade told me about it.'

Ruby sniffed. 'It's not as awful as she makes out.' She then seemed to relax her shoulders; her voice softened. 'Have you heard from Gwen? I hope everything is going OK for her daughter. She was such a wonderful help with Mum.'

'I can imagine, and I know you spent a lot of time caring for your mum as well. Gwen said you would have made a very good nurse.'

Their eyes met, and Nia saw a kind of desperation in her eyes. 'Gwen said that? I never felt I was doing enough, you know. I kept feeling I should give up work altogether. I kept thinking if only I'd prayed harder, lived better, then maybe Mum would have been healed...' She paused, and Nia felt a wave of pity for her.

'You must never blame yourself; you did everything you could.'

Ruby shrugged. 'I wish I believed that. I disappointed Mum in some ways and that can only have added to her heartache.' She looked down the road, shook her head. 'Anyway, I must be off. I assume someone has invited you to Wight's this evening?'

'They have. I'll see you there.'

Ruby walked off down the road and Nia followed behind her with Romeo and then turned left towards the harbour. She kept well away from the edge of the harbour, glancing occasionally at the white yachts jostling side by side. It was quiet and, so far, she'd only passed the occasional dog walker. However, she did see a good-looking young man walking along the pontoon, clearly having left a yacht. He had a large carrier bag in each hand. On seeing Nia, he smiled, and greeted her with a polite, 'Good morning.'

Nia eventually turned back, took a short walk through the town, and arrived at the entrance to the pier. Nia had never been along a pier that was so quiet. No attractions, just a long row of planks of wood joined by nuts and bolts with a high metal rail either side. At the end she could see a small shelter, some fishermen, and she began to walk along with Romeo, his nose twitching, taking in the smell of sea, fish, and seaweed. The sea was calm, and to her left she could see a ferry approaching. People were out on deck; some waved excitedly as they approached the dock.

As she strolled along, it struck Nia that piers were a strange idea, long walks that took you nowhere. She wondered if anyone had thought of carrying on laying plank after plank until they reached the other side.

Before going back to the house, she went into the grocer's. There were the basics, but also fresh loaves of soda bread, local honey, jars of olives and a large variety of cheeses. The range of wine was impressive, and Nia realised it was a shop that catered as much for the yacht owners as the locals. Apart from a few things for herself, she decided that, despite what Ian said, she wanted to take a gift.

She walked up and down the aisles. Her usual standbys of wine and chocolate she guessed wouldn't be what they would like. However, she found a gift set of locally made condiments, hoped they were acceptable and took them to pay.

'Good day,' said the woman behind the till, then, screwing up her eyes. 'Now, I'm guessing you might be Gwen's niece who has come to stay.'

Nia smiled. It reminded her of going into the village shop at home. 'I am.'

'Welcome to the island. Gwen asked us to have a loaf put by for you. Do say if you need anything. So how are you settling into the close?'

'I only arrived yesterday.'

'It's a very tight-knit group there.' She held up the condiments. 'A gift?'

Nia smiled again. 'I've been invited to Sunday lunch with my neighbours, Lucy and Ian.'

'They'll like these – expensive taste. Lucy and Ian only buy organic, spend a fortune on a few carrots. Don't go expecting a nice bit of beef and Yorkshire round there, though.'

'That's all right, I eat anything.'

'Just as well. They have a book coming out soon, you know, and apparently there is talk of a spot on one of these morning programmes. Keeping fit when you're older, that kind of thing. Ian is loving it, always likes to be in the limelight.'

Nia headed back, changed into a pencil skirt, tights and heels, and set off to meet her neighbours.

The door was opened by a petite, attractive woman, expensively made up, with beautifully styled, shoulder-length glossy brown hair. She wore skinny jeans and a white T-shirt, Burberry silk scarf and high heels, and Nia guessed she must be a few years younger than her husband.

Lucy smiled shyly, held out her arms, but not wide enough to embrace. 'I'm Lucy, welcome to the close.' She placed her hands on Nia's shoulders and air-kissed her on each cheek. As she did an expensive fragrance wafted over Nia.

'I recognise your perfume,' said Nia. 'Is it Romance?'

'Well done, yes. I love Ralph Lauren perfumes.'

Nia handed Lucy the condiments. 'A little something.'

'Perfect. Thank you so much,' Lucy replied with a measured smile. She had the charming phrases of her husband but there was a feeling of her holding back. She glanced down at Romeo. 'Ah, a dog.'

'I can take him back—'

'No, no, Ian will love him – come in.'

Nia followed Lucy into the house. It was frighteningly white and clean, with framed collages on the wall, crystals scattered around on surfaces. Nia was glad to walk quickly through the living room to the kitchen and let Romeo loose in the garden.

Lucy came out and offered her a glass of chilled sparkling elderflower cordial. 'I saw you arrive yesterday. You don't have a car?'

Nia explained what had happened.

'What a nuisance for you. When you collect it, at least you have a garage. Like you, we only have one car, our garage is perfect for us. Ethan and Elvira have a space beside the vet's for their cars, but Joe, Richie and Jade have to use the public car park over the road.'

Nia felt unreasonably smug, as if she'd joined an exclusive club.

'Gwen told me you've come for a rest. Life sounded as if it had become rather complicated?'

Nia pressed her lips firmly together and Lucy quickly added, 'Of course, all of that is your business. Gwen is no gossip. I've not heard anything from Gwen, have you?'

'Not since I've arrived.'

'I do hope all is well with her daughter. We are all very fond of Gwen.'

Ian appeared. He put his arm around Lucy's shoulder, and it emphasised the difference in their height.

'Nia, I thought I heard your voice. Glad you brought Romeo with you. Lucy is a bit scared of dogs, but I'm hoping she'll get used to them. I'd love a Labrador one day. I could take him out running with me.' He kissed his wife gently on her head.

'I'd better get on with lunch,' said Lucy. 'You take Nia through to the garden.'

The garden was very tidy, with raised beds for vegetables and herbs. 'We like to grow some of our own produce – you can be sure then of the provenance,' said Ian. 'It's one of the things we promote in our new books.' Nia felt she was being either preached to or being sold the book and was grateful when she heard the ring of the front doorbell.

'Ah, there's our other guest,' said Ian. They sat and waited while Lucy answered the door.

Nia heard exclamations, greetings. The man's voice was low and rich. She wondered who it was.

4

Lucy came into the garden with the guest. 'Nia, this is Ethan,' she said, gesturing to Nia as if she were some kind of exhibit. 'We asked him along as Elvira, his fiancée, is off seeing a friend and we thought he could do with a decent lunch; he is always working.'

Ethan, with his messy light brown hair and stubble on his chin, despite obviously never looking in a mirror or giving any thought to his appearance, was very good-looking.

'Ethan, Nia's home is in Cardiff. Didn't you go to university there?'

'I did,' said Ethan. 'How is Caerdydd?'

'Let me get you a drink, Ethan,' interrupted Ian.

'Something soft would be great, I'm on call.' Ethan sat down and his face lit up at the sight of Romeo, who had come running to him. He knelt down and made a fuss of him. 'You can smell all the other dogs, cat, rabbits, horses and everything else in my life,' said Ethan in a calm voice that somehow summoned up a look of complete adoration from Romeo.

'Ethan is our vet in the practice up the end of the close,' explained Ian, coming out with a glass of lemonade. 'I'll leave this with you, go and see if I can help Lucy.'

Romeo flopped down beside Ethan. 'What do you do in Cardiff?'

Nia shrugged. 'I was a hairdresser, but I'm, um, having a break at the moment.'

Ethan sat back. 'How interesting. So, where in Cardiff do you live?'

'A village, well, more like a suburb of Cardiff now, called Whitchurch.'

'No way! I know it well.'

'No! Are you Welsh, then?'

'No, I'm island born and bred, but I moved over there for a few years with my wife to attend university and then moved on to Bristol where I studied to become a vet. I had a friend when I was in Cardiff who had family living in Whitchurch.'

'That's amazing. So, what degree did you do?'

'Chemistry.'

'My husband read Chemistry in Cardiff, as well, and then he went into teaching. He's a head teacher at a large comprehensive school now.'

'Wow, that's impressive. It must be stressful. Give me animals any day. So, do you have children?'

'One girl, Safi. And you?'

'I have a son, but don't see much of him unfortunately. My wife and I are divorced and she's miles away now, moved up north.'

'I'm sorry—' she began just as Ian appeared and called them in for lunch.

In the kitchen-diner a banquet was laid in front of them. The large oak table was covered in a beautiful white lace cloth, crystal glasses caught the light, the dinner service was light blue Wedgwood, vintage silver cutlery was arranged next to their plates. Candles matched the green foliage of the expert flower arrangement in the centre of the table.

'I'm sorry we're eating in here,' said Lucy. 'Ian wanted to be in the town here, so we had to settle for this little cottage. We do have a place in Surrey as well but now Ian has retired, we are tending to spend more time here.'

Nia looked around nervously for Romeo, but he had slipped in beside Ethan and settled next to his chair.

'Now, we have a locally made apple juice to go with a wonderful vegan wellington, the pastry made with milled flour from Calbourne over here, and the filling all from our garden or the farm shops.'

Lucy tutted. 'That's enough, Ian. Now, I do hope you all enjoy it.'

Ian poured red wine into three of the glasses. Lucy brought a bottle of sparkling water to the table, went to pour some into Ethan's glass, but missed the edge and spilt some onto the table.

Ian jumped up. 'It's OK, Lucy.' He found a cloth, wiped it up, joking, 'No point crying over spilt water.'

Nia could see Lucy was close to tears, and so she followed Ethan's example and started to serve herself from the dishes on the table. Soon Lucy turned to Ethan and asked, 'How are the wedding plans going? Getting engaged in January, the wedding is in June, isn't it? You've not given yourselves much time.'

Ethan scratched his chin. 'I'm just starting to realise that.'

'You could look more excited,' said Lucy. 'You're not having second thoughts, are you?'

Ethan smiled. 'Of course not. It's nothing like that – just the cost. Doing things so quickly, we didn't have time to save, and everything has to be paid for upfront. What has surprised me is how many people are asking Elvira for cash. I didn't think anyone handled cash now.'

'It sounds very odd to me,' said Ian. 'Also, you need to be frank with Elvira. I know how the costs of these things can run away from you. Put the word wedding in front of anything and it seems to treble the price.'

Ethan shrugged. 'I know, but I want Elvira to have the wedding she's always dreamed of.'

'You are such a softie, Ethan,' Ian teased, then turned to Nia. 'Gwen told us you were a hairdresser, but I understand your husband is a headteacher.'

Nia gritted her teeth – even absent her husband had managed to upstage her. 'Yes, he has a very stressful job.'

'And you have children?' asked Lucy.

'One daughter, Safi. She's over in Spain at the moment with her boyfriend but planning to go to university in September.'

'How wonderful,' said Lucy. 'I saw our local hairdresser, Jade, tottering out from your house yesterday. I'm sure she has been filling you in on all of us.'

Ian laughed. 'You'll soon learn there is no private life here. We're so physically close you can't help but see everyone's coming and goings. Jade and Ruby do all our haircuts, and we all have a good natter.'

'I think it must be lovely to be part of a close community like this.'

'Yes, we are very fortunate,' said Ian.

Lucy laid her hand on Ian's. 'And they are very fortunate to have you.' She turned to Nia. 'Ian is always helping people out with their money problems. Ian has probably seen over everyone's books at some time or other, and, of course, he never charges.'

'Of course not,' said Ian. 'It's a hard time to be running any kind of business, and I'm only too glad to help. I was only up at Joe's the other night. Oh, Ethan, Elvira seemed a bit concerned about some of the bookkeeping. She wanted me to check the vet's credit card usage was being correctly accounted for.'

Ethan scowled. 'I know about this, and I agree our present accountant is not addressing this. However, I also told her that I was taking on an accountant that specialises in veterinary work and that it would all be sorted out soon. There was no need to be bothering you about it.'

'I really don't mind—'

'No, really, Ian, it is all in hand.'

Ian lifted up his hand. 'Of course, sorry, I was only trying to help.'

Lucy patted his hand. 'Of course you were.' She looked around at Nia. 'Ian is very generous with his time helping people around here. He's spent hours lately teaching Jade about the basics of bookkeeping for the salon and things.'

'She's a good pupil. I admire her. What with renting out a property as well as running the salon with Ruby, it's impressive for a young woman of her age. She and Ruby work hard. They deserve to succeed.'

'I'll give you that. Jade is doing well, and Ruby has to be the best hairdresser I have ever had. However, you have to be careful what you say to her. She interferes in things that are none of her business. I've seen a different side to her in the last few months, first after the accident and then again lately.'

Nia caught the sharp edge in Lucy's voice – animosity.

'What accident was that?' Nia asked.

'Ruby and I had a little bump, that's all,' said Ian. 'It was nothing. I like Ruby. She means well.'

Nia caught Ian sending Lucy an anxious look and, in an effort to lighten the atmosphere, she said, 'You two have so many plans, it sounds very exciting.'

'It is,' said Ian. 'We have a lot to share. Lucy and I are fitter now than we were twenty years ago.'

'That's impressive,' said Nia.

'This book and particularly the TV spot could be fantastic opportunities,' said Ian.

Nia glanced at Lucy, whose lips trembled as she smiled. 'Ian will be very good. Of course, he is used to being on camera and talking on the radio.'

'And you will be great,' said Ian. 'If we get this, the possibilities are endless. My agent was saying that we could consider clothing, food, franchise. This could be huge.' His eyes were bright with passion and excitement.

Ethan grinned over at Nia. 'I daren't tell these two that yesterday I had two sausage rolls heated up in the microwave for my lunch and takeaway burger and chips last night.'

Nia laughed, and even Ian had the grace to smile, but he said, 'It's about time you started coming out running with me. You're not getting any younger now. Elvira will thank you for it.'

'I'm on my feet all day. I don't need to be running around the downs to keep fit.'

'Well, come swimming with Richie and me on a Sunday evening.' He turned to Nia. 'You're very welcome to come any Sunday. A friend of mine in the TV business has a house over here, close to Fort Victoria.

It's a massive place and out the back he has this huge pool and a gym. Richie and I go there most Sundays. My friend is hardly ever there.'

'It sounds amazing.'

'Any time you fancy it. We go about ten. I know it sounds late, but I love swimming at night, and it's a good time for Richie as Ruby goes off to her night work for a charity then. Just come along. You can't miss the house. Turn off down to the fort, it's on the right. It's called "Mare Visum", Latin, you know.'

'Thank you, although I usually spend my Sunday evenings with my feet up watching TV.'

'Sounds my kind of evening,' said Ethan, but then his phone rang, and he got up from the table to answer it. He returned quickly. 'I'm afraid I'm going to have to go. I've an emergency coming in.' He kissed Lucy on the cheek. 'Lovely to meet you, Nia. Try and come to Wight's this evening about half six. Everyone from the close should be there.' Turning to Lucy, he said, 'See you later at Wight's and thanks for a wonderful lunch.'

As they were clearing up Nia looked more closely at one of the collages on the kitchen wall. It was a seascape of blue silks, and the frame was made of driftwood.

'This is lovely,' she remarked.

'They're Lucy's work,' said Ian. He turned to Lucy. 'Why don't you leave this to me and take Nia upstairs and show her your craft room?'

Upstairs, Lucy took Nia into a room dominated by a long table with neat piles of materials in different shades of blue and, in one corner, a heap of driftwood. Lucy rushed over, picked up a pair of glasses, a bottle of her perfume and some rough paper and as she shoved them into a drawer she mumbled, 'Sorry about the mess.'

'It all looks very organised.'

Lucy swung around. 'Sorry... what?'

'I was saying it all looks very organised to me. You're so clever. You make the frames as well?'

'I try to. I enjoy working with the wood I find on the beach. Richie helps me sometimes. It's lovely to work with someone. It's quite lonely working all the time on your own. I used to belong to a craft group and one of the women there showed me how to do it. It was great. We'd meet in Newport every Saturday evening and would all swap ideas.'

'But you don't go now?'

'No, I left the group in February. We have everything taking off now with the fitness work, so I felt something had to go. Mind you, I did lead a few sessions with the women in the close in February. The weather was miserable, and Elvira had asked me if I could teach her to make little favour bags for her wedding. I decided it would be fun to ask Ruby and Jade around as well, and we had a lot of fun making things. Elvira naturally concentrated on the bags, but Jade made some lovely little frames from driftwood, while Ruby made some beautiful little mobiles, hanging shells from them. I think she sold a few at a sale for the charity she works for.'

'It was lovely to share your skill like that, and what about your pictures? Do you ever sell them?'

'Yes. Richie kindly allows me to sell some of the pictures at the gallery. It's a wonderful space – you must visit. His paintings are stunning. He's very gifted. He's building up a very good business there.'

'He's fortunate to have such an amazing location.'

'That's because his dad supports him; he's very lucky. I'm very fond of him. As I say, he comes round sometimes to help me with things like framing, I try to cook him a nice meal occasionally to say thank you.'

'Jade was telling me Joe's parents set him up at the brasserie here. Wight's, I think it's called.'

'That's right, but how else are these young people meant to get a business off the ground nowadays? Joe's parents are nothing like as well off as Richie's dad, but they're lovely people and adore their boy.'

Nia glanced around the room again. 'You are so talented. I'm not at all creative.'

'Don't underestimate yourself. Being a hairdresser has to be one of the most creative professions and it's important. My weekly visits to the hairdresser are a real treat. To sit and be fussed over, chat about your problems. Well, it's a bit like therapy except you also come out with your hair looking good.'

Nia grinned. 'That's a great way of describing my job.' She picked up a large piece of rose quartz. 'I noticed these around the house. Do you have them as ornaments, or do you believe in their powers and that sort of thing?'

'They definitely make a difference to my life. That one brings me unconditional love. If I've been feeling down it really helps.' Lucy picked up a pretty yellow-orange stone. 'I keep this up here. It's sunstone, helps with my creativity.'

Nia picked up a smooth black stone. 'This is onyx, isn't it?'

'It is. I have one in every room. It's for protection, you see, as many of the darker crystals are. This crystal can wake up your inner confidence. It's good for self-esteem.' Lucy replaced it carefully on the table. 'Ian thinks it's nonsense but, well, we all need to find help where we can, don't we?'

They returned downstairs, where Ian was waiting with Romeo. It was clearly time to go.

'Thank you so much again,' said Nia.

'Any time you need anything, you know where we are,' said Ian.

As they all walked towards the front door Lucy appeared to stumble and Nia grabbed Romeo, worried he'd got under her feet.

'I'm so sorry, he gets too excited when he's leaving the house. I should have put his lead on sooner,' she said and quickly attached it to his collar.

'Don't worry,' said Ian. 'We're not used to having a dog around.'

Nia thanked them again for the meal and returned home. She let Romeo out into the garden and started to inspect the borders. Maybe she could do something like plant a small herb garden for Gwen, a way of thanking Gwen for letting her stay there. However, she'd need advice. At that moment she thought she heard voices the other side of the fence and went over to see if Ian would be able to help her.

As she approached the fence, she could hear Ian. 'All I'm saying is that you need to be careful what you say.'

'I had to prepare Nia; we have no idea what Ruby could say to her.'

'That's just paranoia. She won't be talking to a stranger about all that stuff. Everyone has forgotten about it. Don't go dragging it up.'

Nia frowned. What a strange thing to say. What were they so worried about Ruby telling her?

5

After her walk with Romeo, Nia started thinking about the evening ahead. She'd imagined a largely solitary visit here, although of course she planned to have a few chats with Ruby and pass on impressions of the close to Gwen. However, despite it only being her second day on the island, she felt herself drawn to the people here and intrigued by their lives. In a way it was refreshing to have a distraction from her own problems, and to be among people who knew nothing about her.

Nia remembered Jade's comments about Gwen's baking and wondered about taking cake that evening. However, although it had been acceptable for Gwen to take food into Wight's, she wasn't sure if the owners would mind her doing the same. She decided to take some in her bag and see how it went.

As anticipated, the kitchen cupboards were well stocked, and she found the heavy iron griddle on which Gwen had taught her to bake Welsh cakes and crempog. She decided to make the crempog, small Welsh thick pancakes, for that evening.

There was something comforting about standing in the kitchen, mixing up the batter, with Romeo now curled up on a blanket on the floor. After leaving it to rest, she dropped the batter, a tablespoon at a time, onto the heated griddle, turning each over as it turned golden brown.

As a reward for her labours, she made herself a cup of tea and allowed herself one of the warm pancakes, thickly spread with butter. After this she had the courage to find her phone and turn it back on. There were more messages from Chris, which she replied to, as she had before, that she needed time to think, and that she would talk to him soon. Safi had also messaged but seemed to accept at face value her mother's need for a break.

Later, with the pancakes neatly packed in a tin, Nia left the house to walk up the road to Wight's that evening. It was still light, a dry, chilly spring evening. She changed into jeans but kept her heels.

Wight's was in the left-hand corner of the close and stood at right angles to the veterinary practice.

The front of the brasserie featured enormous windows, the wooden frames painted a stylish grey. Nia hesitated at the door. Usually Chris would walk in front, make the entrance. Taking a deep breath, she pushed open the door and went in.

The room was tastefully decorated, with sofas as well as dining chairs and tables with chic green star-shaped candles. Nia could imagine them serving good coffee and wraps in the daytime, and then tapas and light plates of food with a glass of wine in the evening.

Nia spotted Lucy and Ian sitting with others at a large low table covered in small bowls of nibbles. Ian waved her in enthusiastically. There was no turning back. She approached the bar, situated at the far end of the room, and found the young man she'd seen at the harbour. He gave Nia a wide, confident smile.

'You must be Nia. I'm Joe.'

'Oh, you've heard about me?'

'We're very close here, look after each other. I promised Gwen I'd keep an eye on you.'

Nia laughed. 'She said the same to Jade.'

'Good, right, now, what can I get you?'

Nia gave a slight cough. 'I'll have a glass of red, a Merlot?'

Joe poured her a glass and handed it to her. 'It's good to have you here, Nia.' To Nia, he had the air of a younger person acting the part of a host. However, Nia realised that even at the age of forty she was starting to find people looked young for their position, be it a doctor, dentist, or teacher.

'Thank you very much, Joe. I saw you coming off a yacht this morning. Is it yours?'

'I wish. No, it's owned by a friend of mine. I'm not in that league.'

'This place is great.'

'Thanks, yes. It's starting to take off now. It takes a year or two to start bringing in the returns. Is it Cardiff you're from?'

Again, Nia felt everyone here knew a lot more about her than she did about them.

'That's right. There are certainly a lot of places to eat and drink down there now. The student population is huge. It's changed a lot.'

She could see someone waiting to be served. Joe tactfully said, 'I see Ian's been holding a seat for you. I'll come and join you all in a minute.'

Nervously Nia leant forward. 'Um, I heard Gwen used to bring cakes on a Sunday evening. I brought some, but of course if you'd rather I didn't...'

Joe laughed. 'Of course I don't mind. We don't serve food on a Sunday evening, and it cheers us all up. I shall look forward to them.'

Nia went and took her seat between Ian and Ethan but as she did the others stopped talking, which was rather disconcerting. She was suddenly aware of feeling too formally dressed.

Opposite her sat Jade in her casual clothes and Ruby, wearing the same skirt as the day before, with a chunky knit cardigan with wooden buttons slung on the chair behind her, a hemp shopping bag hung over the arm of the chair. She sat with her legs crossed, her body turned slightly towards the young man she sat next to. Although she had a fixed smile on her face, Nia noticed her hands were tightly clasped, one hand squeezing the fingers of the other, the knuckles on her hands white.

The young man who Nia assumed was Ruby's husband, Richie, looked of similar age, but was far more fashionable, with thick-framed black glasses, carefully trimmed stubble, his head shaved at the side with a thick wedge of black hair lying flat on the top of his head. He sat with his legs pushed together, arms tightly crossed, and he stared down at his knees.

Joe came over to join them. He leant over Jade, kissed her on the cheek, then jumped over the back of the seat to sit between her and Ruby.

'Everyone, this is Nia, Gwen's niece,' said Ian. He was back to his normal, charming persona. 'I think most of us in the close have had a chance to say hello by now. There are of course Lucy and me, your neighbours.' He waved his hand at Lucy, who was sitting the other side of him. Nia leant forward to send her a smile. Lucy was wearing the same white jeans and high heels as before but had added a blue cashmere jumper and large sunglasses.

'Now,' continued Ian, 'this is the proprietor of this wonderful establishment, Joe, then Ethan and Elvira. Of course, you met Ethan at lunch, and now you have the opportunity to meet his fiancée and fellow vet, Elvira.'

Nia took the tin out of her bag. 'I thought I'd carry on Gwen's tradition.' She removed the lid and put the box on the low table in front of them.

'They look fantastic,' said Joe, diving in. 'Gwen makes these, doesn't she?'

'She does. In fact she taught me how to make them,' said Nia, smiling.

'Brilliant,' said Joe, laughing. 'You really are ever so like her.'

'That's what I said,' interrupted Jade. 'We all have a new shoulder to cry on,' she added, laughing.

'And now, Elvira,' said Ian, 'maybe you would like to introduce yourself.'

Elvira was sitting back, twisting a strand of long rich chestnut-brown hair around her fingers. She was clearly quite a bit younger than Ethan, maybe early thirties, her eyes a sparkling blue. She had a kind of Kate Middleton look: classy jeans, white shirt, and Converse trainers.

'Hi, Nia, it's brilliant to meet you.' The inflection of her voice rose at the end of the statement. 'I'm Elvira. I know you had lunch with Ethan today and so you'll know something about me, I'm sure. The exciting thing I have to show this evening to everyone is this.' Elvira held out her left arm, dangled her hand in front of them all with a flourish. 'I finally have the ring.'

She thrust her hand out. The enormous sapphire and diamond ring was the kind of thing that would look tacky if the cut and shine had not spoken of it being the real thing.

'Good God, Elvira. It's huge,' said Jade. 'I'm impressed, Ethan.'

He shrugged, blushing.

'I designed it. It's unique,' said Elvira. She gazed lovingly at the ring.

Ruby's attention, though, seemed to be drawn to the black macramé bracelet, with a charm of a blue glass eye, and her face crumpled in concern as she said, 'You know, you shouldn't wear that bracelet, Elvira. You shouldn't be messing about with things like that.'

Elvira tutted. 'Rubbish. All the celebrities are wearing them now.'

'They're not a joke, you know,' said Ruby quietly.

Elvira shot her a short, fierce glare, so quick that Nia guessed most people missed it, but it was laser-like in its directness and ferocity.

However, she quickly softened her expression. 'Don't take any notice. Nia, I've known Ruby for years. She came over to sixth form on the mainland and we met there. She started putting me right then and hasn't stopped since.' Her face grew sterner, no edge of humour now. 'By the way, I understand you went to visit my mum last week. I wish you'd asked me first. You know how she is.'

'I hadn't seen her for months. I wanted to chat to her,' said Ruby.

'You know I didn't want you to go. Ethan is very good, respects my decision to keep meetings with people other than myself to a minimum.'

'I thought she'd enjoy talking to someone else about the wedding. How are the dress fittings going?'

'Very well, thank you,' said Elvira stiffly.

Listening to the conversation, Nia was very aware there was some kind of underlying tension, but she wasn't sure what was causing it.

Ethan spoke, his tone bright. 'The big day is only eight weeks away and, now Elvira has the ring, we would both like you to come here next Sunday to finally celebrate our engagement. There will be champagne and, of course, there will be nibbles and a buffet, that kind of thing.' He looked at Elvira for confirmation.

'Of course. It's going to be a very intimate party, but a real celebration,' said Elvira enthusiastically. 'Make sure you come, Nia. You are part of the close now and we want everyone there.'

'We'll all be here for our free champagne,' said Jade. Nia looked over at her. Her voice was flat, her face pale. She looked very different from the woman who had bounced into her house the day before. Nia wondered what had happened.

'That's great,' said Ian and he looked around the table. 'Now, Ruby, maybe you and Richie could tell Nia about yourselves.'

Ruby spoke quietly but firmly. 'I'm a hairdresser with my sister, Jade, as you know. I've been married to Richie for six years now. We live over the art gallery. You must come and see Richie's paintings soon. They're beautiful seascapes. The kind of thing you don't mind hanging on your wall, if you know what I mean.'

Nia saw Richie cringe at the description of his work, which she understood, it wasn't exactly how an ambitious young painter would want his work described. Joe interrupted. 'You were meant to talk about yourself, Ruby.' He turned to Nia. 'Ruby also does lots of work for charity, working on Saturday and Sunday nights.'

The warmth of Joe's obvious affection for Ruby surprised Nia. They seemed so different. Ruby blushed slightly, her eyes fixed in her lap.

'That sounds exhausting. What exactly do you do all night?' Nia asked.

Ruby looked up, the fixed smile dropped, and it was as if she had closed the shutters.

'I'm afraid it's not something I can talk about,' replied Ruby, her voice tighter now, 'but Jade and I close the salon on Mondays. Richie also tends to shut the gallery and go off painting, it's nice and quiet, and I catch up then.' She turned to Richie, the fixed smile returned. 'Now, you should tell Nia properly what you do.'

Richie sat back, his feet resting on the low coffee table in front of him. 'I paint, I sell my paintings, that's it really.'

'And we have our swimming,' said Ian. 'So, are you going to tell everyone a bit about yourself?' Ian asked Nia. 'We know you used to be a hairdresser and now you do proofreading, is that right? What will you be doing with your time over here?'

'I'm not too sure. I've come for a break really.'

Ian leant forward. 'Well, on behalf of everyone I'd like to extend a very warm welcome to the close. We shall look forward to many more cakes.' He looked at his watch, more of a gesture than to check the time. 'We tend to keep our get-together quite short as most of us go on to various Sunday activities. Elvira pops to see her mum, Ethan and Jade go to help at a local animal rescue. Richie and I have a swim and, of course, Ruby is off to her charity. Lucy and I will do our meditation together before I go swimming and then I leave her to watch TV.'

'And don't forget some of us are still working,' said Joe.

'You won't be staying open much longer, will you?' said Ian, glancing around at the empty room.

'No, nine is late enough round here on a Sunday. I'll be off fishing later.'

Nia expected everyone to leave, but actually nobody moved. Elvira surprised her by asking her if she was interested in walking.

'I enjoy walking in woods and downland,' replied Nia. 'I was reading you have red squirrels over here. That must be exciting.'

Elvira grinned. 'It is for some.' She shot a glance at Ethan. 'I'm afraid I'm not that grabbed by it all. I prefer to ride when I'm out and about. Ethan, though, is a proper nature addict. You'll have to get him to take you for a walk. He knows where to see them.'

Ethan gave her a half-smile. 'Of course, I'd be glad of the company – I tend to go very early though.'

'I wouldn't mind that,' said Nia.

'If you're serious, I'm going this Tuesday.' He turned to Elvira. 'You could come as well, of course.'

'No way. It's way too early for me. You take Nia.'

'I go about half five,' Ethan said to Nia.

'Gosh, that is early, but still, yes, I'd love to come. Can I bring Romeo?'

'Of course.'

'Oh, no, I don't have a car at the moment. Mine's in a garage over in Southampton.'

'Don't worry, I'll give you a lift. It's greener anyway if we travel together.'

They were still working out the logistics of meeting up when Elvira broke off her conversation with Jade.

Jade stood up suddenly and pushed past them all, running to the back of the brasserie. Everyone stopped talking. Ruby glanced at Richie and rushed after Jade.

'Still hung-over from last night,' joked Joe. 'We had too many shots, I think.'

Everyone gave knowing smiles and went back to chatting.

Nia remembered seeing a back door leading to the garden and she suddenly felt desperate for some fresh air.

It was darker outside now, although there was subtle lighting around the long garden, most of which was paved over, with hedges and borders at the side. She discovered a rather abandoned patch of grass and a tall wooden gate leading, she guessed, into the vet's garden next door.

As she was starting to feel chilly, Nia headed back inside to the ladies but as she was opening the door she paused, realising she had caught Ruby and Jade in the middle of some kind of crisis.

6

Nia saw that Ruby had her arms around Jade, comforting her while she sobbed. 'You can't do this; you know you have to do the right thing.'

Jade stood back, shook her head. 'I have to decide this myself. The main thing is, Ruby, you're not to tell anyone.'

'But it doesn't only concern you.'

At that moment Ruby seemed to notice Nia.

'Sorry to interrupt,' Nia said.

Jade wiped her face. 'It's all right, I'm leaving.' She pushed past Nia.

'Can I help?' Nia asked Ruby.

'No, Jade and I will sort this out,' said Ruby, but she looked very pale and worried. 'I'd better get back out there,' and with that she left.

When Nia returned to the main room, she saw Ruby pick up her cardigan and bag, say something to Richie, and depart.

Richie turned to Ian. 'I'd better go and see what's up, but I'll be fine for our swim later. I'll text you.'

Elvira was leaving, presumably off to see her mother. Ethan and Jade were arranging to meet at the rescue centre, but Ian went back and sat with Lucy to have a drink with Joe. Looking at Lucy now, Nia thought she seemed completely at ease, laughing and smiling, far more relaxed than earlier.

Nia decided it was also time for her to leave and, after saying her goodbyes to Ian, Joe and Lucy, she left. Back at the house she received an enthusiastic greeting from Romeo.

'Well, that was a bit weird,' she told him. 'Honestly, Romeo, I'm not sure where we have landed. I reckon we could do with a good walk.'

She ran upstairs and found her old trainers. She quickly put them on and went down to find Romeo waiting.

'Sensible dog,' she said, stroking his head. 'All you are thinking about now is your walk. Brilliant.'

They left the house and headed on down the road and climbed down onto the beach. It was deserted and only her footsteps could be heard crunching on the shingle, mingling with the waves softly lapping the shore. The moon shimmered on the black oil-slick sea.

Nia walked down to the water, took her trainers, and socks off, and paddled. The icy cold waves lapped her feet, but it was gentle, cleansing. She took a deep breath. Gwen was right, she could breathe here. For the first time in what felt like a long time she felt well, almost happy. 'Thank you,' she whispered and then looked around, embarrassed. Of course, she was alone, and she looked at the sea, which seemed to glint in reply.

Carrying her trainers, she walked back up the beach. Her phone rang and without thinking she answered. It was Chris, just 'checking in'. As pleased as she was to hear from him, it broke the spell. She tried to tell him about the people in the close, her evening at Wight's, but he sounded bemused.

'You went there to rest, not to go socialising.'

'I know but it's nice to meet some new people. How is school? I guess you've been in today?'

As she said the words, she felt herself holding back. She had to trust him and part of that was not making him account for every moment.

He told her briefly about some paper he was preparing for the governors' meeting the following evening and eventually the call ended.

For some reason her heart was thumping against her chest. She got up and went back to the sea, where she stood, matching her breathing again to the motion of the waves, and slowly the trembling subsided.

Eventually she turned and went back up the beach and sat down. As always after an attack like that she felt exhausted. She put her head in her hands, closed her eyes.

'Are you OK?'

Startled, Nia opened her eyes and saw Ruby, who came and sat down next to her.

'Um yes, I'm fine,' said Nia, trying to steady her voice, and then added, 'I thought you were off to your charity work this evening.'

'Not yet. I like to come here, calm my mind, talk to the sea before I go.'

'You talk to the sea as well?'

'I do. To me it's like family. When you grow up on an island it's never far, it surrounds you. It has watched me since I was a baby, it knows me.' Ruby shrugged. 'I expect that sounds stupid to you.'

'No, I don't think so. I find a lot of comfort being close to the sea. I wish we'd had more holidays by the sea but my husband doesn't like it. I think he gets bored. He walks up and down the beach like a caged animal, which is strange when you see such expanses of emptiness. He's a city person, I guess. Still, I'm glad I'm here now.'

Ruby glanced down at Nia's naked feet. 'Good. It must be strange being here alone, without your husband, but of course you said he's very busy. He must miss you.'

Nia shrugged. 'I'm not sure. He says he does.'

'Why do you say that?'

'It's complicated. I came to sort myself out, but things just go round and round in my head and I don't resolve anything.'

'You could talk to me if you want – I'll not tell anyone else.'

Nia picked up some pebbles, rubbed them between her fingers. 'I don't think I can. You'll think I'm mad.'

'I doubt it. In my work with this charity, I sometimes listen to people share their problems – sometimes it's not that you need someone to give you advice, but saying things out loud can help you sort them out for yourself.'

Nia let out a long breath. 'Well, maybe if I tell you briefly, but please don't say too much to Gwen. She only knows the bare bones of this. She has no idea how bad it's been.'

'Of course not.'

'OK. A few weeks into the new term last September one of the teachers at Chris's school, who is also a client of mine, told me she had seen Chris kissing the drama teacher, Sian Grey. I'd met her a few times at social things, in fact she had taught my daughter the year before. I liked her, she was young, very pretty, she'd really turned the drama department around. I know Chris thought highly of her, and he helped out a lot with the productions they did. It had never entered my mind that there was anything between them. I was very upset, talked to Chris, who was very sorry, it had been after a few drinks after school, it meant nothing and would never happen again. The problem was I couldn't let it go. In October I went to a school social and saw her with him and it seemed to me they were very flirtatious.'

'You believed that your husband might be having an affair?'

The words seemed so stark, shocking even, said out loud.

'Well, yes, I think I did. I became obsessed with it, checking his phone, even going up to the school when he said he was working late to check his car was there. It was usually there, and I'd feel really stupid, but sometimes it wasn't. Of course, it was hard to ask Chris about it as I didn't want him to know I'd been checking up on him. I had to make up stupid stories like I'd gone up to see someone else at the school or something. It was madness.'

'And what did Chris say?'

'He always had a good explanation, said he'd forgotten that he'd gone out for an hour to see someone. I felt very foolish, but couldn't stop. There were other things, like a new watch he started wearing. He told me it was a present from the drama department to thank him for his help, but it seemed a very expensive present for kids to give a teacher.

'Chris knew how anxious I was, he kept trying to reassure me, bought me presents and the like. But I'd read online that was something men did if they felt guilty, so, you see, he couldn't win. Things came to a head one weekend in January. At Chris's suggestion, Safi and I went away for the weekend, a final time together before she went off on her travels. It was fun, we went to London, saw a play, but when I got back, I was sure the duvet had been changed. Chris said it hadn't, but I felt sure Sian, this teacher, had been in the house. I had no proof, only a feeling. I felt I was going mad.

'I became so tired, exhausted with it all, that I went to the doctor, and he suggested I take some time off work. That is when I left my job at the salon.'

'That was a bit drastic.'

'I know, but I didn't know how long I was going to need, and to be honest I knew they would always take me back; I had a very good reputation. My regular clients were upset, but they moved on to other people at the salon.'

'And did it help?'

'No, not really. If anything, I had too much time to think then because of course Safi then went away. Everything came to a head a few weeks ago. There was another school social and I got drunk, there was a terrible scene.' She paused, cringing. 'I can't go into it all. I was chatting to Gwen, just saying how tired I was and she suggested coming here.'

'It sounds to me like you have been under a lot of stress. For what it's worth, I don't think you sound crazy at all.' Ruby gave her a gentle smile. 'Maybe try not to think about it all for a few days, go for walks, enjoy the island, give yourself some time to rest. I understand what you mean about something going round and round in your head. Sometimes you need to leave something be and then suddenly you realise what you have to do.'

Nia turned to her. 'You sound like you have been through something as well.'

Ruby nodded. 'A lot, yes.' And she pressed her lips together.

'Do you want to talk about it? I hear it helps,' said Nia. 'Look, I'm a stranger here. I'll be gone soon – and don't forget I was a hairdresser like you. If I didn't know how to be discreet, I'd have lost most of my clients years ago.'

'Well, OK, it would be interesting to see what you think about something. I've not shown anyone, not even Gwen, so don't tell her about it.'

Ruby leant over and from her hemp shopping bag she removed a small, twiggy doll and handed it to Nia.

'What on earth is this?' asked Nia.

'It's a voodoo doll. It's used to curse people.'

'Good grief. Who on earth sent you that?'

'I have no idea.'

'I didn't realise people still did things like this.'

'Oh, yes, I've seen pictures of them on social media. You can buy them online. They're very popular again. People use them to try and help them lose weight, pass exams.'

'So, they're being used for good things?'

'That's the nice side of them. Others, like this one, are much darker. You can see there's no kind intent in this.'

Using the torch on her phone, Nia looked more closely at the doll. She could see the wizened face was carved onto a piece of driftwood, the eyes narrow, cruel, the mouth a thin, tight line. It was skilfully made, the main body from twigs, the dress of blue silk. Most disturbing were the pins thrust into its eyes, mouth and heart.

'I don't like it. It's nasty,' Nia whispered. However, seeing the fear in Ruby's face, she added, 'You do know it's all nonsense, don't you? A doll, voodoo doll, or whatever you call it, with a few pins in it can't really harm you.'

Ruby nodded. 'I know this voodoo doll itself can't harm me, but if you were sent one of these you'd not just laugh it off, would you?'

Nia shook her head. 'No, I wouldn't. When did you get this?'

'Last February. I found it on our doormat wrapped up in paper, when I got up early one Monday morning.'

'You've held on to it all this time? Have you any idea who sent it or why?'

'The problem is I know it has to be someone from the close. You see this wooden button? That was taken from my cardigan on Sunday night the week before. I'd thought I'd lost it in Wight's, but Joe never found it and when I looked again at my cardigan, I saw it had been cut off.'

'Someone cut it off your cardigan to sew onto this voodoo doll?'

'Apparently if you add things that belong to the person you are cursing, such as hair, clothing, that kind of thing, the curse works a lot better.'

'But that's awful. Still, if it's someone in the close, you must know who did this.'

'Well, I have ideas. The driftwood and silk are materials I've seen in Lucy's workroom. We had these craft sessions.'

'Yes, Lucy told me, you, Elvira and Jade?'

'Yes, we made different things and I remember someone saying you could make little dolls, but no one did.'

'Who said it?'

'I can't remember.'

'But you think it was one of them?'

'Not Jade, she'd never do something like this, but maybe Lucy or Elvira – but do either of them really hate me?' Ruby shook her head. 'No, I'm not being fair. They wouldn't do something like this to me. But who would? I know I upset people, people get fed up with me, but I always thought people realised I meant well, but this means someone has far darker feelings towards me. It's the intent. There's hate behind this. Someone sat, making this thing, all the time with hate in their heart. Someone who had been harbouring hate and anger against me for some time.'

'Oh, no, no one hates you.'

'Oh, they do.' Her hand started to shake. 'It scares me, Nia. Not just to think of someone hating me like this, but also hiding those feelings from me. It's so calculating, sinister somehow – what else have they been planning?'

Nia looked down at the voodoo doll. 'You shouldn't take this too seriously. It's probably someone messing about.'

Ruby shook her head. 'No, there is more to it than that. This voodoo doll is just a sign of the hate I know is hiding out there. It isn't a game. I've been thinking about what to do with this for a while now. Tonight I have decided.' Ruby stood up. 'Do you want to come for a walk along the pier?'

Nia called Romeo and left the beach with Ruby. The beach was partially lit by the light at the end, an old-fashioned street lamp.

When they reached the end of the pier, they found only one fisherman that night. He was busy sorting out rods and didn't look up as they went past. They walked right to the end, and then Ruby lifted up the doll and threw it out as far as she could. For a few seconds it floated in an area lit by moonlight, but a wave quickly swallowed it whole, and it disappeared.

'It's gone now,' said Nia.

'The voodoo doll has, but the hate is still out there. The hate remains.'

'People get angry. It blows over,' said Nia.

Ruby grabbed her arm. 'Exactly, but hatred stays, it festers.' Ruby shivered.

They walked back down the pier quietly; neither spoke until they reached the close.

'Good luck with work this evening,' said Nia.

'And thank you for coming along the pier with me,' replied Ruby and walked back up the close.

Nia entered the house, went into the kitchen. As hard as she tried to resist them, Ruby's words kept echoing in her head: 'The hate remains.' Ruby had been talking about someone here; someone in this close had sent her that horrible doll. The idea seemed incredible to Nia. She pictured everyone at Wight's. So normal, conventional, so, well, 'nice'. And yet one of them had made that thing, one of them was hiding hate so deep, so well disguised that even people who knew them well had no idea what was going on in their heart.

Jade had been right, there was something sinister going on here. And this was the place she'd come to sort herself out, somewhere she'd thought would be so safe.

Her mind went back to Chris. That initial feeling of relief at talking about her problems with Chris was wearing off. A feeling of hopelessness started to set in. She still had no idea if she'd been right or wrong. She still had that terrible feeling of shame.

Nia went to the fridge, and, as she frequently did recently, she poured herself a glass of wine, threw it back quickly. That first hit, that sense of the world stepping back, the memories becoming opaquer, crept over her. She poured another glass... people drank to forget, wasn't that what they said?

Nia opened the back door and let Romeo out and took the bottle and glass out with her.

It was as she was pouring her third glass that she heard someone say, 'Good evening.'

Lucy was peering over the fence, but Nia realised she was having problems focusing, she'd drunk too much, too quickly.

'Evening, Lucy,' she attempted to say, but she knew she was stumbling over her words. She was aware of Lucy looking at her, judging her, and leant forward, picked up the bottle, and staggered back into the house.

7

Nia walked up to the vet's early on Tuesday morning. Despite the early start she had made sure she'd had time to do her make-up and hair. Ethan was waiting beside his estate car, which was parked next to the surgery.

'Morning,' he welcomed her with the easy alertness of a morning person. 'Romeo can jump in the back. He'll be safe there. We're off to the woods.'

The car was untidy, and it smelt of wet boots and straw. Rubbish was strewn on the floor.

'Sorry about all this,' he said but the apology was perfunctory; he didn't even look around.

They drove along the main road between Yarmouth and Newport and pulled into the main car park in Parkhurst woods. They were the only ones there.

As Nia opened the car door, the sound of birdsong echoed around the trees. She breathed in the fresh air.

'Spring has certainly arrived,' said Ethan.

They were about to leave the car park when Ethan grabbed her arm and pointed to a tree. Nia gazed in wonder as three red squirrels scampered up the trunk and flew between branches. As they ran, they made a soft chucking sound.

'How come they don't fall?' she asked.

'They use their tails to balance. You know, they have a very flexible joint between their ankle and heel which enables them to run so easily down trees.'

'That's amazing. They look tiny. Are they babies?'

'They could be. It's a miracle they have any young at all. The females are only in season one day, twice a year. The poor females do all the work, building multiple nests, moving the babies around.'

'They're beautiful,' Nia whispered.

Ethan continued to stand very still, his mouth open but not daring even to breathe. He must have seen this sight hundreds of times and yet he was completely spellbound.

Eventually, the squirrels moved out of sight, and they started on their walk. Once away from the car park, Nia let Romeo off his lead and he disappeared into the bushes.

As they walked Ethan identified birdsong for her: jays, long-tailed tits, blackcaps, bramblings, a song thrush, as well as the more familiar blackbirds and robins.

At the top of a long path, they sat on a wooden bench. Ethan picked up a thick stick, took out his penknife and started whittling.

'You're right,' said Nia. 'This is worth getting up early for.'

'Good. I hope you enjoyed meeting everyone on Sunday.'

'I did. Everyone has been so friendly. I had a really good chat with Ruby on the beach after. She's a good listener.'

'She is,' said Ethan, but Nia noticed a hesitance in his tone.

Nia paused to watch a robin singing on a branch and then said, 'You obviously know her a lot better than me, but I was thinking a bit about Ruby. She's a complicated person, isn't she? When I shared things with her, she was kind, sympathetic, and yet it sounds like the religion she follows is very strict and ungiving. I wonder how she can bear to go there. Jade and Richie have both left.'

Ethan nodded. 'You are right, there is a mismatch there. Somehow it has a hold on Ruby that the others escaped.'

'Jade doesn't think it does her any good.'

'No, I agree. I think she gets very torn. On the one hand she seems to be understanding and shows empathy when you tell her something, but on the other, she has this strict moral code, where everything is black and white. Deep down there is like a voice telling her she must try harder, do the right thing.'

'You seem to know her very well. I overheard her saying something like that on Sunday evening to Jade.'

Ethan grinned. 'That would have wound Jade up. She's well and truly put all that behind her. She always says that leaving The Righteous was the best thing she and her parents ever did.'

'Oh, her mum and dad were in it as well? So, Ruby stayed when they left... What made them all decide to turn their backs on it, then?'

'Oh, it's a great story. It wasn't so much they decided to leave, as her parents were thrown out!'

'But why?'

'You'll never believe this. Their mum won the lottery.'

'You're kidding!'

'Oh, no, and of course gambling is strictly forbidden by The Righteous.'

'Did she win a lot?'

'Coming up to a million pounds. Apparently, the leaders said the only way she could be forgiven was to give the money away to charity. Her mum and dad refused and left with Jade.'

'That's a huge amount of money.'

'It was. Their parents never spent it, put it away for the girls. Last year Ruby's mum split it between Ruby and Jade. Jade bought a place over in Cowes outright, which she rents out as an Airbnb. She's got it well set up, with a local person doing cleaning between visits. It's clever, isn't it? All done with a key safe, no need to be doing handovers.'

'And what about Ruby?'

'Ruby gave all hers away to charity.'

'Good grief! All of it?'

'Yup. She believed it was tainted because in her mind it came from gambling. She split it between several charities she supports, including the one she volunteers for.'

'But she and Richie could have put down the deposit for a home, or even bought one outright?'

'Ruby could never have spent the money on herself. In any case, she and Richie are financially very well provided for by his dad.'

'I must go to the gallery sometime and see Richie's paintings.'

'Yes, do. They're very good. Elvira loves them. We have some on the walls in the vet's.'

'Didn't Elvira say she was at school with Ruby?'

'Yes, only for their sixth form. They stayed in touch. Elvira came over to Ruby and Richie's wedding with her ex. I think the four of them got on quite well for a while, but Ruby didn't like Elvira's ex, felt he was a bad influence on Richie, which at the time didn't go down too well.'

'But it must have helped Elvira settle over here having a school friend living so close by?'

Ethan picked a leaf from a bush and scrunched it in his hand. 'In some ways, but in others I think it's made things harder for Elvira. She came here wanting to make a fresh start. Ruby has a bit of a habit of trawling through the past.'

'I see. Elvira didn't seem very happy about Ruby going to visit her mother.'

'No, she was pretty annoyed. She couldn't see any reason for it. It's not like Ruby had known Elvira's mother well. We both had a feeling she was digging around, trying to find out something about Elvira, which is ridiculous.' He paused and then his face creased into a smile. 'I'm sorry, that's enough of all of us.'

Nia sat back listening to the birdsong. Although she knew the song was for a reason, attracting a mate or defending territory, it seemed to her this morning they sang for pure joy. Beside her, Ethan continued whittling away at the thick twig with his penknife. She saw that, rather than simply randomly slicing the wood, he was carving a face in profile.

'Wow, that's clever.'

'It's very basic. Elvira and I have been learning how to do it... It's very satisfying.'

'I would never be able to make that.'

'Of course, you could. I'll show you sometime.' He handed her the stick. 'There you are: a souvenir from your first early walk. Now, let's head back to the car – patients to see.'

* * *

It wasn't until the next morning that Nia realised how lucky they had been with the weather the day before. She woke to the sound of rain on the window, which was particularly annoying as she was going over to Southampton later to pick up her car. She was determined to spend the day reading the improving books she'd brought over, to start her new exercise regime using YouTube yoga classes and finally to start preparing wholesome vegetarian meals for herself.

There was, of course, Romeo to walk, and she left the house in her waterproof jacket and trousers. The difficult part was getting Romeo's waterproof coat on him. As soon as he heard the rustle of it being taken out of the bag, he ran to hide. Fortunately, he was very poor at hiding and just stood in a corner. Once it was on, however, he seemed to forget all about the coat and wagged his tail ready for his walk.

The town had the busy air she now knew signalled a ferry arriving. She weaved her way through the traffic and took Romeo down onto the beach. The sea was grey and churning up the pebbles today and when Romeo started to wade a bit too far out, she put his lead back on and they walked along the pier.

Nia was glad to return to dry them both off and have her morning coffee. It was half past five when she left the house again with Romeo. The garage had asked her to go over in the evening, which surprised her, but apparently about half past seven was a good time for them.

Nia had checked the buses and realised she would have to get a bus into Newport and then back out to Cowes. She was planning to get the fast Red Jet over and then the vehicle ferry back.

She was standing under an umbrella, stepping back as cars whooshed past and starting to regret not getting a taxi, when a car pulled up. Ruby called out of the window, 'Can I give you a lift? Where are you off to?'

'I'm off to Cowes, and then Southampton to pick up my car. I'm heading for the Red Jet.'

'Are you sure you don't mean East Cowes and the vehicle ferry?'

'No, I'm just coming back by that.'

'Well, OK. I can give you a lift, then. Hop in.'

'You don't mind Romeo?'

'No, he can go in the back of the car, it's an estate.'

Once Romeo was settled, Nia went around the side of the car to the front passenger door. She was surprised to see Richie in the back of the car and Ruby indicating to sit in the front passenger seat. Richie was practically hidden in a duvet-type, puffy coat.

'Richie goes over to Southampton on a Wednesday for a course. He usually cycles, but he had a new tattoo on his leg yesterday, so I insisted on giving him a lift.' She looked at Nia. 'I need the car in order to pop round and do the hair of an elderly customer, bless her. It's too much for her to get over here now.'

Nia put her dripping umbrella on the floor next to Ruby's red one.

'So what course are you doing over in Southampton?' Nia asked Richie.

'Richie has a still life class. He enjoys meeting up with other artists. It can be a bit solitary painting on your own and running the gallery. Oh.' She sniffed. 'Could you pass me a tissue from the glove compartment, please?'

Nia leant forward and opened the compartment, but it was crammed with stuff. A torch and a phone fell out. She found the tissues and handed one to Ruby and then held up the phone. 'Do you need this now?'

'Oh, no, it's a spare one I keep in the car. A friend who is a policeman once told me to do that. He said that way if I take pictures when there is an accident, like when Ian and I had a bit of a collision —' She stopped abruptly, gripped the steering wheel.

'Ian mentioned you had an accident. He said it was very minor.'

'Yes, no one was hurt. I was going to my charity on a Saturday night back in January when we collided. There was minimal damage, but it shook me up. I was going to carry on working, but Donna said to go home. I'm glad I did.'

They continued along the main road, past Parkhurst woods where Nia had seen the squirrels, until they reached the roundabout and turned left.

'I always drive this way. I prefer to use main roads. I also like to pop into the garage at Northwood to get petrol. There are so few places over by us, I top up when I can. Here it is.'

Nia sat listening to the rain drumming on the roof of the car. Richie was staring out of his window, clearly not in a mood to chat. It was a relief when Ruby returned.

Fortunately, by the time they arrived at the Red Jet terminal the rain had eased.

Ruby got out of the car with them and kissed Richie on the cheek. 'Text me when you are on the Red Jet coming back. Are you sure you don't want to borrow my umbrella?'

'You know I can't stand them, but thanks,' he said begrudgingly, and then turned to Nia. 'I have to go to the newsagent. You go on ahead and get your ticket. I'll see you in the queue or on board.'

As he walked away Nia thanked Ruby for the lift and then went with Romeo to buy her ticket.

Romeo was very excited, greeting other dogs, sniffing the ground and the posts. Nia was standing in the tunnel waiting to board the Red Jet when she heard someone call her name. It was Ruby. 'You left your umbrella,' she shouted.

After she'd handed Nia the umbrella she looked around. 'Where's Richie?'

'The newsagent?'

'No, I drove around and then had to park by there to bring this to you. He has to be here.' Ruby walked to the front of the queue and returned. 'He's not here.' She stood, staring at Nia as if she should have an answer.

'I'm sorry, I don't know where he is,' said Nia. Suddenly, Ruby's face filled with panic: she looked so young and confused. 'I don't under-stand, he told me he was coming over to his class. Where is he?' Her voice was frantic.

Nia, shocked at Ruby's reaction, tried to calm her down. 'Hey, he's probably gone to get something to eat. He'll be here in a minute.'

Ruby shook her head. 'No, something's not right.' She looked down the tunnel and froze. 'What is *he* doing here?'

Nia followed Ruby's gaze and saw a good-looking man, very fair. He reminded Nia of some of the celebrities on programmes Safi watched.

Nia wondered if Ruby would go to speak to the man, but she turned away and rushed back out of the tunnel. Feeling rather helpless, Nia suddenly realised the queue was starting to move forward. She had no option but to board, and so she made her way onto the Red Jet.

As Nia took her seat, she looked around but couldn't see Richie, and she wondered what was going on. However, she suddenly felt the boat bumping over the waves and closed her eyes. Never the best trav-eller, she tried to relax. Romeo lay close to her feet.

When they reached Southampton and left the Red Jet, Nia glanced over at the opposite queue of people visiting or returning to the island. Some were laden with shopping; there were excited children returning from a school trip, chattering like sparrows, and quiet, weary adults returning from work. And she, Nia, was returning, after what seemed weeks rather than days, to the mainland.

Instantly it seemed busier, messier, than the island. She turned left from the terminal and caught a taxi to the garage.

It was about nine when Nia boarded the car ferry back to the island in her car. She'd been quite nervous about driving onto the ferry and was aware of not wanting to stall or roll backwards. As they were on the upper deck they had to wait to be allowed out of the car, but she felt relieved when they were told they could go onto the ferry.

It was dark now, but she took Romeo out onto the deck. The lights of the mainland behind her slowly became pinpricks on the horizon, ahead the island. But between them both was the endless black wilderness of the sea. Nia took Romeo to the front of the ferry. The harbour, floodlit, was gradually coming into view. She remembered that feeling of the arms reaching out to welcome her. Had she been naive, indulging in some fanciful notion of escaping to an island? Was she returning to light and safety or something far darker?

8

On Sunday, the party for Ethan and Elvira at Wight's was set for half past twelve, and so Nia took Romeo for a long walk in the morning along the seafront.

It was a beautiful morning, and Nia was quickly coming to the conclusion this was her favourite time of day here, a real feeling each day of a fresh start. She saw a ferry had arrived and went to watch the cars unloading, people arriving on their holidays, or returning home. From the side of the ship, she saw a long stream of passengers walking, and was surprised to recognise the man who Ruby had been so horrified to see in the tunnel, and wondered who he was.

Nia returned home to get ready for the party at lunchtime. She decided on her red shirt dress and heels and made her way up the road. As always, she felt a flutter of nerves going in on her own.

Everyone was already gathered down the end of the brasserie. She discovered that curtains had covered a wall of patio doors, which now stood open, and in the garden a few couples sat at tables enjoying early drinks.

Elvira was glowing, in a short white dress and flat sandals, her hair loose down her back. Ethan was wearing his usual cords and shirt.

Guests were mingling, drinking glasses of Prosecco and orange juice, and chatting, but the atmosphere seemed tense, with the laughter too hard, the smiles too tight.

Ethan made a short speech, thanking them for coming, then pointed out a buffet and the table where they would all sit. Wine and soft drinks were offered by the waiter and then the bottles left on the table for people to help themselves. It was a quiet meal. Joe and Elvira did most of the talking.

Ruby was particularly quiet, the same knitted cardigan and hemp bag on the back of her chair. Nia noticed she was hardly eating, and was sitting with her back to Richie, who glared at his food. It was clear they had rowed.

After they had finished the meal, a waiter brought over a beautiful cake, decorated with buttercream icing, and country roses. The cake was sliced and served and once everyone had their piece Lucy spoke. She was wearing a smart blue shift dress with one of her signature silk scarves and large sunglasses.

'I brought a little gift for the happy couple – many congratulations, Elvira and Ethan.' She picked up a small bag that had been hidden by her feet and handed it to Ethan.

From this he pulled a glass jar full of shiny green stones.

'I was going to give you rose quartz,' explained Lucy, 'but I thought maybe these were more appropriate. They are Aventurine. They encourage trust and honesty. They are good crystals for setting out on new ventures, like getting married.'

Ethan smiled. 'Thank you so much, Lucy. I know how much thought you will have put into this gift.'

Elvira's smile was tighter. 'Yes, thank you, although I hope we don't need crystals to make us be honest with each other though.'

A rather strained laugh followed.

Jade handed them a card; the envelope sealed with a wax stamp. 'Ah, your signature,' said Elvira, carefully breaking the seal.

Jade held out her hand towards Nia. 'This is my sealing or signet ring,' she explained. Nia saw a gold band, engraved with a bird, similar to a delicate signet ring.

'That is very pretty,' said Nia. 'I see you wear it on your ring finger. Some people wear them on their little finger, don't they?'

'Think they used to, particularly men, but nowadays you can wear them on whatever finger you like. Ruby has two now. Richie gave her a small one as an engagement ring – that's what got us both interested in them. As I make candles, we started using them for seals on letters and presents. And then of course Richie's father gave Ruby a very expensive one on their wedding – show Nia your rings.'

Ruby held out her hands. On her left hand with her wedding ring, she wore a delicate signet ring with a rose engraved on it. On her right hand she wore a much larger thick gold ring. The carving was intricate and very skilful, a woman's face in profile with an R wrapped around it.

'They are both lovely, but I can see this one is very special,' Nia said.

'It's eighteen carat gold. Richie's father had it engraved. It was my wedding present from him. I only use it to seal very special letters. I'd hate to damage it.' Ruby looked more carefully at the ring. 'It's getting a bit loose actually, I should see to that, and it needs a clean. I must do that when I get home.'

Elvira raised her voice, speaking to Jade. 'Thank you. I guess you made this,' she said, standing up a handmade card of blue silk forget-me-not flowers.

'You are all so creative,' said Nia. 'That's lovely, Jade.'

Silently, Ruby got up, and returned with a bag, which she placed without speaking in front of Elvira.

The present was wrapped in red tissue, sealed with wax and Ruby's rose ring.

Elvira opened it and held up a small painting of the sea signed by Richie.

'Thank you so much,' she said. Although the subject matter was pretty conventional, Nia found herself staring at a painting that seemed to draw her in. There was no doubt Richie was a very talented artist and was capable of far more than 'something to hang on the wall', as Ruby had described it.

Joe leaped up and returned with a bottle of champagne and then invited everyone out in the garden for coffee.

Nia carefully carried a mug of steaming coffee to a seat outside and sat next to Lucy, who asked Nia about her daughter. Nia filled her in on Safi's travels.

'You must miss her.'

'I do. She's not been gone long but I miss her. Still, it's good for her and she's loving it.'

'That's all you can hope for, that she is happy, blooming.'

Lucy clasped her hands together. Even through the sunglasses, Nia saw pain in her eyes. 'I expect you've realised by now, Ian and I have never been blessed with children. I would have loved to, but it wasn't to be. I would have adopted or fostered even, but Ian didn't want to, so we never had the privilege of bringing up children.'

Lucy took off her sunglasses briefly and dabbed under her eye with the crook of her finger. It was a tiny gesture but, in it, Nia sensed years of private suffering.

Before they could talk more, they were distracted by raised voices from Jade and Ruby further down the garden. Although it was impossible to make out exactly what Jade was saying, she was clearly upset. She ran inside, while Ruby went to the bottom of the garden and retreated to the spot behind the shed.

Excusing herself from Lucy, Nia went down to find Ruby and was shocked to find her sitting on the ground, her arms wrapped tightly around her.

Nia sat next to her and laid her hand gently on her shoulder. 'Ruby, what is it? Hey, shush now.'

Ruby sniffed and wiped her face with the back of her hand. 'It's all falling apart. I try so hard but it's never enough.' She started to cry again. 'I'm only trying to do the right thing. No one understands me, not even my sister. I only want what is best for her. Lying and secrets are so destructive. Why can't anyone see it? I tell you, Nia, finding out someone you trusted with your soul has betrayed you just kills you.'

'What's happened?'

Ruby stepped back and thumped her heart with her fist. 'He's broken my heart.' The colour drained from her face, the tears poured down her cheeks, and again she was that child Nia saw at the Red Jet terminal: scared, abandoned, fragile.

'Has this anything to do with Wednesday night and the Red Jet?'

Ruby nodded; her face crumpled in pain. 'When I couldn't see him with you, I started to drive away. Then I saw Richie walking into town. I had to follow him and find out what was happening. I parked and then followed him up the hill towards Northwood House. I don't suppose you have ever been up there, but it's really steep and it was hard to keep up with him. At the top of the hill is a large car park and I followed Richie past and then turned into the main road off that. Opposite is a small sprawl of houses and he headed to them. It was so nerve-wracking, and I was wondering if I should turn back, all he had to do was turn around and he would see me. However, just as I was starting to think about that he walked up someone's drive—' Her voice broke.

'He went into someone's house?'

Ruby nodded. 'He did, he had a key, he let himself in.'

Nia held her breath but didn't dare speak. Did it mean Richie was having an affair?

Ruby continued. 'It seemed to confirm my worst fears. I knew something was not right.' She paused. 'You know what I mean, you told me you've had the same feelings. I'd had this sense of Richie keeping things from me, but I'd dreaded saying anything. Sometimes anything is easier than the truth.'

'And have you talked to Richie now?'

Ruby looked away. 'Yes, we talked. It's complicated, we've a lot to sort out now, but it's a relief in some ways to have things in the open. I hope we can work on this now, but it will take a long time for me to trust him again.' She looked intently towards the rest of the people in the close, clustered at the top of the garden. 'It's made me realise the importance of facing the truth for us all. My experiences and then a phone call last night brought home to me that there are other people here who need to do the same. It's time everyone here stopped hiding behind lies.'

Nia picked up on the phone call – what was that about? she wondered, and asked Ruby.

'It came while I was working at the charity last night...' Ruby hesitated. 'I'm going to talk to the group about it in a minute. It concerns everyone.' She squeezed Nia's arm. 'Thank you, look after yourself. You need to watch yourself here.'

Nia blinked. 'What do you mean? When I arrived, Jade told me to be careful – why the warnings?'

Ruby's face creased in concern. 'Jade said that? I'm surprised, but she's right. As I said when I showed you that horrible doll thing, someone here is hiding some very dark thoughts. But it's not just that – no one here is quite what you think.'

Nia noticed people were gravitating back to the tables and places they'd sat at for lunch and so she and Ruby walked over to join them. Elvira was sharing her 'wedding planner' album, which was divided into sections for flowers, dresses, and the like, and Elvira had cut and pasted various pictures and ideas for each.

Nia picked up her glass, which still had some wine in, and sipped it. Lucy appeared to be the only person showing any interest, but Elvira was clearly enjoying showing someone her album.

'I'm not going to tell you all the details of the dress I'm having made, but it does have a simple square neckline like this and is very fitting, like this one.'

Eventually Elvira seemed to sense the lack of interest and closed the album.

'I won't bore you all any more,' she said. 'Lucy asked to see it, that's all.'

'I'm glad we're all here,' said Ruby. She spoke firmly, her voice a bit too loud. She took a long swig from her glass. 'Look, I'm sorry if this breaks up the party, but I have to say something.' She paused, took a deep breath. 'I've been through a lot lately and I've learned a few things. One of the most important is that you can't live a lie, you have to be honest with yourself and people you are close to. Since Mum died, my life has been a bit of a mess, to be honest, but I am trying to put that right now. There are personal issues, but also things that relate to people in this group. I am ashamed to say I have lied but I intend to sort that out.' She glanced at Ian then, looking down, fiddled with a glass on the table. 'The reason I am saying all this is because I think it's something we all have to face. Something happened last night that brought this home to me.' She paused again; her fingers shook now. She coughed, paused to steady herself. 'You all know I work for a charity on Saturday and Sunday nights, but none of you know exactly what I do.' Ruby continued, 'I work for an island-based helpline, similar to the Samaritans. Obviously, I have had to keep it confidential. It would be terrible if someone was put off seeking help because they knew who would answer.'

Ian looked at his watch. Lucy was picking up her bag ready to go. Joe had started to collect glasses from the table. No one was taking much notice of Ruby. But that was about to change.

'Last night I received a call, and it was someone whose voice I immediately recognised. It was one of you.' Ruby appeared to be consciously avoiding eye contact and stared down at the table.

Joe slowly put the glasses down. Lucy clutched her bag. Ruby had everyone's attention now.

'I felt the right thing to do was to pass this person on to a colleague but before I could stop them, this person started to pour out their problems. They were hysterical, clearly very distressed. Finally, I managed to speak, and I then suggested they might be better talking to someone else. At that point this person recognised my voice and, well, they were very angry and rang off. The point is that this is serious, and I'm very concerned. You need help. The thing is I can't simply forget what I heard. I have to do something; a number of people are affected. Please come and talk to me. I would much rather we worked this out together.'

'Now hang on, Ruby,' said Jade. 'That call was made to you in confidence. You shouldn't be telling us any of this. If you're that worried, you should speak to the person individually.'

'I don't think that would work. Putting this problem to the whole group I hope will convince this person, show I am prepared to bring it out into the open.' Ruby looked around the table. 'It's time we all stopped playing games, isn't it? I want to help everyone here sort things out.' She glanced at Richie. 'Things have to change.'

Nia dragged her gaze away from Ruby and scanned the faces of everyone at the table. They all looked stunned, shocked at Ruby's outburst, but there was something deeper than that: in every face Nia saw fear.

Ian thumped his fist on the table. 'That's enough, Ruby. We're all adults, capable of sorting out our own lives.'

'He's right, you know,' said Jade. 'We have a right to choose how we live.'

'But we shouldn't all be living with lies and deceit, it's not right,' said Ruby. Her colour was high now, her voice more hysterical, her eyes bright with tears.

'But how we live is actually nothing to do with you,' snapped Elvira. 'You've always been the same: interfering, thinking you know better than everyone else. It's plain dangerous.'

'Dangerous?' Ruby repeated.

'I agree.' This time it was Lucy, her voice full of emotion. 'You have to stop interfering in other people's lives.'

'To put it bluntly, Ruby, you need to butt out,' said Ian.

'You'd prefer to cover things up, wouldn't you?' Ruby replied to him. 'You've even got me to lie – to enable you to have your five minutes of fame? Well, not any more. I have to be able to move on from the accident.' Ruby turned to the others. 'Tonight, I won't be going to the helpline. In fact, I may have to give up my work there after this. But it will be worth it. I need to talk to the person who phoned last night. Please come and see me this evening. I'll be in the flat. The door of the gallery is always open; just come on up. Later, I'm doing the books at the salon, and then I'll be down on the beach by the pier. Please, I know you're frightened, but we can work this out. It's the same for everyone here. I can help you face up to what you have done. This can be a fresh start.'

She was breathing fast, her face shining with a kind of missionary zeal. However, her words were met with cold, hard stares. It was then Nia remembered the voodoo doll. Ruby had said one of the people here had sent it, but who? She could see annoyance and, yes, fear on their faces, but one of them must have something deeper. If Ruby was right, someone here hated her. She should be able to see it, but she couldn't. But then someone had been hiding this feeling for some time now.

Nia shivered. A cloud had covered the sun, the air turned cold. It reminded her of when she'd stood by a lakeside during a partial eclipse. The world had fallen silent, but it hadn't brought with it a sense of peace, rather one of unease and foreboding.

Ruby grabbed her cardigan and hemp shopping bag and left.

'Good God. What's got into her?' asked Elvira.

Ian leant over, picked up Ruby's glass and took a sip. 'This isn't lemonade. There's vodka in this.'

An uneasy silence fell. Slowly, everyone's eyes came to rest on Richie. He stood up. 'I'm sorry. Ruby's not herself at the moment.'

As it was approaching half past four, Ethan suggested it might be a good time to wrap things up, and everyone seemed relieved to be given permission to leave.

As they gathered their things together, the guests quietly made plans for the rest of the evening. Ethan told Jade he'd see her at the rescue centre. Ian and Richie arranged to meet much later for their swim. Elvira wrapped up the remaining cake, which she said she would take later to the nursing home for her mum and staff to enjoy.

Nia was pleased to return to Romeo at home. He, of course, was ready for a walk and so she changed into jeans and trainers and went out. There was no one about, she kept the walk short and was glad to return and cuddle up with Romeo on the sofa.

The events of the day had left Nia feeling on edge; the uneasy atmosphere at the party was difficult to shake off. Ruby had upset everyone; everyone had looked shocked and fearful. Nia wasn't sure why they had reacted so badly to this, but she did agree with them that Ruby was in the wrong sharing about the phone call to the helpline. That call had been made in confidence and now everyone in the close would be wondering who made the call. What was so serious that Ruby had felt the need to break her promise of confidentiality and risk losing her job at the charity?

* * *

At about half seven Nia went upstairs to find her book and looked out onto the close. She saw Ruby walk up the street, go into the salon, turn on the lights and sit in front of the laptop at Reception.

Somehow Nia doubted that the person who had made the call had been to see Ruby. The problem was Nia had a feeling Ruby's speech, rather than making everyone more open, had simply frightened them, and might make them even more secretive. Who had used the word dangerous? That was it, it was Elvira. The word had shocked her, but Nia felt she was right. There had been a sense of danger, threat in the air after Ruby spoke. Nia looked down at Ruby working alone in the salon. She suddenly looked very vulnerable and alone and Nia was scared for her.

9

It was ten o'clock when Nia took Romeo for his final evening walk. She'd received a text from Safi asking if they could video call at about eleven and she knew she'd easily be back by then. It would be good to talk to Safi properly, see how she was getting on.

It was a quiet, still night. The only light she could see shone from Lucy and Ian's next door and Nia guessed Lucy was home while Ian and Richie would be swimming. Joe had shut up shop and must be off fishing. There were no lights on in the vet's, no cars parked next to the surgery and Nia wondered where Ethan and Elvira might be this late. Surely the nursing home Elvira visited would want visitors out well before ten, and would Ethan really be this late at the rescue centre?

Nia walked towards the town square and followed the now familiar route to the beach.

It was very dark, and Nia hesitated, wondering if they'd be better walking along the pier. However, Romeo was pulling her, and so she took out her phone to use as a torch to guide them down the steps. She let him off the lead, knowing he'd not venture into the sea. Suddenly she became aware of someone huddled up on the pebbles, their back to the harbour wall. They had lit a candle that was propped up among a circle of stones, flickering in the wind.

Nia was nervous, wondering what they were doing there, and was about to call Romeo when the person called out her name and she realised who it was.

Walking over to her, she said, 'My God, Ruby, you scared me. What are you doing sitting down here on your own?'

'I do this sometimes, come down with a candle, sit and think. In any case, I said earlier I'd be down here, not that I really expect the person who made the phone call to come now.'

Nia sat down, the stones cold, noticing the strong smell of the dry seaweed strewn here above the tideline. 'I have to admit most people looked pretty frightened by what you said. I guess we all have secrets we'd rather not share.'

Nia was aware of Ruby pouring whisky from a bottle into a small sturdy glass. It disturbed Nia to see her drinking like this and she remembered Ian saying there had been vodka in Ruby's glass at the party. It surprised Nia; she'd not thought of Ruby as someone who would be drinking spirits.

As if reading her mind, Ruby said, 'It's OK. I don't do this often and, see, I measure it out. I allow myself some alcohol for solace occasionally.' She held the glass out to Nia. 'Join me.'

Nia took the glass and knocked back the drink. It burnt the back of her throat, but as Ruby refilled the glass Nia drank another before handing it back.

'How are things with Richie?' Nia asked gently. 'Have you managed to talk to him again since the party?'

Ruby started to pile little pebbles one on top of the other. 'I couldn't face any more today.' Her face crumpled in sadness. 'I don't understand how he could do it. Richie has always talked about integrity. I don't understand how he could betray, not just me, but everything he believes in.'

'But you want to try and save your marriage?'

'Of course. I want to forgive him but, of course, he has to be prepared to make changes as well. If we can do that it's possible our marriage will be even stronger.' At that moment the pile of stones collapsed. Ruby turned back to Nia.

'I won't give up on us, in the same way as I won't give up on the person who rang the helpline. I did think about what people said. Maybe there is a better way to approach this person. I had an idea.'

'And that is?'

'I've written the person a letter.'

'Wow, a letter?'

'Yes, I know it seems a bit old-fashioned, but I think there is something special about letters. Texts and social media are so impersonal.'

Ruby pulled out a piece of A4 paper from her bag and read it to Nia.

'Hi, I'm sorry if I made a mistake talking to everyone today. I know you're angry that you accidentally told me about your problems on the helpline but maybe it was meant to be. I really want to help you. I can't act like nothing has happened. Please talk to me before it is too late. Love Ruby.'

'You're very worried about this person, aren't you?' said Nia.

'I am.' Ruby took the letter back and folded it, then carefully picked up the candle, rested it between some rocks and, in a very ritualistic way, poured some of the red wax to seal the letter. Nia noticed Ruby slip off the ring Richie's father had given her.

'I think this person deserves my best ring,' she said.

She pressed it carefully into the molten wax and, even in the dim light, Nia could make out the imprint of a woman's face and the letter R.

Before putting the ring back on her finger, Ruby took a cloth and wiped it. 'I forgot to clean this earlier. I must do it later,' she added, and then she slid the ring back on.

But she didn't appear to have finished. She ran her hands over the pebbles, occasionally picking one up, examining it by the light of the candle. Each time she shook her head until finally she kept one. 'That's the one I want.'

She showed it to Nia. 'See this, it's a fossil, part of an ammonite. This could be four hundred and fifty million years old. It came from the sea and the creature fossilised in this has survived and all this time the island has held on to it, preserved it. I find that very comforting.'

Ruby picked up the candle and poured the remaining wax onto a large stone in the shape of a heart. She did it carefully, filling in the shape.

'There, my love letter to the sea,' she said, and placed the stone carefully down beside her. 'What would I do without it? Sometimes it feels like the sea is the only one who understands me.' She turned to Nia, tears now weaving their way down her face. 'I am confused. I try so hard to do what is right, but it's never enough, is it? I am never enough. I still can't forget that voodoo doll I was sent.'

'You still don't know who sent it?'

'No, today when I was talking at the party, I looked around trying to figure out which one of them could have sent it, who there hated me. I could see anger on their faces, but who hates me? I could feel it, but I didn't know where it was coming from. As I said when I threw the doll in the sea, the hate is still here, the hate remains. I read somewhere that hate hurts the hater more than the person they hate – maybe it's true, but I tell you, Nia, knowing someone out there hates me hurts like hell. I hate myself enough as it is, I don't need anyone else doing it.'

The words echoed into the darkness like the noise of a lost, injured animal, howling into the night.

'I am so sorry,' said Nia, close to tears herself. 'I wish there was something I could do to help.'

'You are here, thank you.'

The wind was gathering. The glass that was resting on a stone as Ruby refilled it started to topple. They both went to grab it at the same time and Ruby accidentally spilt whisky on Nia's sleeve.

Nia shook her arm, but Ruby seemed oblivious. Aware she was

getting cold, Nia wrapped her arms around herself. Romeo had also cuddled up next to her.

'It looks like it's time for you to go,' said Ruby.

'I don't want to leave you.'

'Please. I'll be OK and I need some time on my own.'

'Well, Safi will be phoning in a minute. Come with me. You can even stay overnight with me if you want.'

'No, I'll go back to talk again to Richie. I'll just get my head sorted out first.' Ruby poured herself some more whisky. 'Don't worry. I won't be finishing the bottle.'

'Promise me you'll go home soon.'

Ruby looked away.

'Please, Ruby, go home. Look, after this call with Safi, I shall come back to check up on you, but it would be much better if you go home now. We can talk again tomorrow.'

Ruby wiped her tears and gave a sad smile. 'You are a good woman, Nia, thank you.'

Reluctantly, Nia stood up and made her way up the steps. As she did, she stumbled on one of them, and fell into a fisherman who was making his way down the pier. She muttered apologies and carried on home. Just as she turned the corner, she thought she heard the crunch of shingle on the beach. She staggered home, exhausted, but anxious. She went inside, turned on her laptop. Hopefully this wouldn't take long and then she could get back to Ruby and check up on her.

10

Safi looked pale and tired on the call. She was clearly far more anxious about Nia's move to the island than she'd let on in texts because after a few preliminary words about herself, she asked, 'Are you all right, Mum? What are you doing there?'

'I needed a break, that is all, and it was handy for Gwen to have someone to keep an eye on the house.'

'It's not like you to go away without Dad.'

'He obviously couldn't come, and I needed a change of scene. We text and talk – he's very busy at school.'

She saw Safi's eyes wander around the room. 'Where's Romeo? Dad said you'd taken him with you.'

'He's asleep on his bed. He's getting loads of exercise here. He loves the beach.'

'The house looks very small. What's it like there on an island? Are you getting lonely?'

'Surprisingly not. The people in the close have included me in everything. I think Gwen had instructed them all to look after me. I feel I've got involved here very quickly. It's quite nice getting to know new people although it can be a bit intense here. Anyway, enough of me, tell me about you. Are you eating? You look tired – where are you staying now?'

Safi settled into telling Nia properly about everything that had been going on. It sounded as if things had become strained between her and her boyfriend.

He wanted to stay up late partying a lot more than her. The couple had been travelling now for a few months; it was inevitable that they would have a few problems. Safi needed to talk, and they were on the call for at least an hour. However, at the end of it Safi seemed a lot happier and Nia was about to end the call when Safi suddenly blurted out, 'Are you and Dad having problems? Has something awful happened?'

'Why do you ask?'

'I know you were arguing a lot. You never used to and then you are giving up work. I've been worried about you; you mustn't think you're going mad or anything—'

'I've been very tired, love; I just needed a rest.'

'You're not splitting up, are you? Please, Mum, I couldn't bear it if you two divorced. It's happening to all my friends, and I couldn't bear it.'

'That's not what is going on.'

'But, Mum – I know...' Safi paused and started to scratch the back of her hand hard, something she always did when she was very stressed. Usually, Nia could gently take her hand, stop her hurting herself, but obviously this evening she was unable to do that.

'What's wrong, love? Tell me,' said Nia.

'It's nothing, but you know whatever Dad did, you'd always forgive him, wouldn't you?'

Nia frowned. 'What do you know?'

'Nothing, nothing at all. I just can't stand the thought of you two not being together.'

'Safi,' Nia said firmly, 'this is not your problem. Dad and I are quite capable of sorting things out between us. Meanwhile I am enjoying a change of scenery.'

'Well, don't get too settled. Remember you have to go home soon.'

She saw Safi had calmed down, her hands resting one on the other, and they exchanged a few more words about the weather and plans before ending the call.

Despite reassuring her daughter, Nia felt very stressed by the call. She poured herself a large glass of wine, drank it quickly. She'd tried so hard to keep everything from her, but Safi wasn't a child any more, she should have expected her to have picked up on things. It was awful being far away from Safi – at times like this video calling was a poor replacement for actually talking in person. She was sure Safi was keeping something from her, something about Chris. What did she mean about forgiving Chris? What did Safi know?

She poured another glass of wine, sat back. The call had made her realise this wasn't just between her and Chris; it affected Safi as well. She had to work hard at getting better, sort things out.

Nursing her glass, she closed her eyes, and fell into a deep, uneasy sleep. She was jolted awake by Romeo, pushing against her hand, mystified as to why she'd never made it to her bed.

She crawled off the sofa, picked up her phone; it was five in the morning, still dark outside. Slowly her mind started to put together the night before. There had been the phone call with Safi, but of course before that it had been Ruby on the beach. It all felt like a dream now – Ruby drinking and so unhappy. God, Nia had promised to go back down, make sure she got home. She glared at the empty wine glass. 'This is your fault,' she mumbled.

Of course, Ruby would have gone by now, but Romeo had the look of a dog ready to go out, and, somehow, she had to clear her head that was thumping.

Slowly she made her way upstairs, changed her top, threw some water over her face. No point in make-up, no one was going to see her at this time in the morning.

Romeo was waiting by his lead hanging up by the door. 'I don't know how you can look so lively,' she grumbled at him, and they left the house.

There were no lights on in the houses; the flat above the gallery was in darkness. She was pleased to imagine Ruby tucked up in her bed. She hoped things would seem less hopeless to her when she awoke.

They walked along the harbour and then finally made their way towards the pier. Lighter shades of blue were starting to push their way through the darkness of the sky; the street lights would turn off soon. There was a gentleness about the light that morning. The town looked at peace with itself. Through the windows of the post office, she saw two young boys being given their papers to deliver.

She approached the entrance to the pier, planning to walk along, but, as always, Romeo pulled her towards the beach.

They went down the steps and Nia leant down to let Romeo off his lead. However, as she did, she glanced over to where they'd sat the night before and her heart began to race. Ruby was lying where she'd left her the night before. Nia dashed over, horrified that Ruby had been down there all night.

'Wake up!' she shouted. Ruby didn't respond. Nia leant down and gently squeezed her arm, but as she did she took in Ruby's open but unseeing eyes staring at the sky, her beautiful hair tangled and splayed across the pebbles. Beside her lay an empty whisky bottle and her hemp bag, with a letter poking out, and a candle propped up in a circle of stones.

Nia grabbed her chest, then she covered her mouth, scared she was going to be sick. She kept Romeo close to her and knelt down beside her, touching Ruby's hand lightly. Like the pebbles on the beach, it was stone cold.

'Oh, God, Ruby, I am so sorry. I should never have left you,' she whispered.

With shaking hands, her eyes blurred with fear and tears, she fumbled for her phone, and rang for an ambulance. The operator spoke gently but firmly, and somehow Nia managed to give details of what had happened.

'Are you alone?' the operator asked. 'Do you feel safe?'

For the first time since finding Ruby, Nia looked around. It was early, and, yes, she was alone and, no, she didn't feel safe, but nothing would induce her to leave Ruby.

'Come back, Ruby, please come back,' she begged. 'You can't have died here, not on your own, alone in the dark. What happened?'

Slowly, she started to take in the rest of the scene. Ruby's body was above the tideline. The sea hadn't touched her. The empty bottle disturbed Nia. Would Ruby really have drunk all that? Would that have caused her death?

The operator had gone now. Nia sat next to Ruby, Romeo close to her. She could hear Ruby's words: 'the hate is still here'. Looking at Ruby now – no breath, no life – Nia knew that, despite saying she was going nowhere, Ruby had gone. Ruby was no longer here.

All Nia could hear was the sea crashing onto the shingle and she turned. 'You know, don't you? You saw what happened to Ruby. Why didn't you look after her? She loved you, trusted you.'

Her gaze strayed to Ruby's hands. She was wearing the small signet ring on her left hand, but the expensive one from Richie's father, which she wore on her right hand, was missing. Nia frowned as she desperately tried to piece the evening before together. Ruby had read out that letter to the caller and then used the candle and her ring to seal it. Nia shook her head; she could have sworn Ruby used her best ring to do that, but if she had where was it now?

Nia looked around but couldn't see it among the pebbles. Where had it gone?

She looked back at the candle. Of course, that was wrong as well – this one was green. Surely Ruby had used a red one. Where was it?

Nia searched around, trying not to touch or disturb anything, but couldn't find either. She looked again at the letter sticking out from the bag and, despite knowing she shouldn't, she eased open the bag. It was the only letter, and it had the green seal of a rose. Surely it should have been a red seal? She looked again in the bag – maybe the red candle was in there. But no, there was no other candle.

Nia sighed. Maybe she was wrong. Chris had said she was ill. Maybe she was mistaken. Her eyes went back to Ruby. None of these other things mattered, did they? Poor Ruby, what had happened to her? She shook in shock and anger. This wasn't right, it wasn't fair. Ruby should never have died here alone, she should not have been down here feeling so unloved, even hated.

She became aware of voices on the pier, people taking an early morning stroll. Ruby's body suddenly looked so vulnerable and exposed. Nia didn't want strangers staring at her. Fortunately, at that moment she heard sirens, as ambulance and police vehicles arrived.

A police officer took Nia aside and talked to her gently. He checked she was the person who had found Ruby, and Nia mentioned she'd also seen Ruby the night before. She was aware of people starting to gather, and then saw Richie arrive. He was pushing past people, talking to the police officer now guarding the steps that led down to the beach.

'That's her husband,' Nia told the police officer.

'Thank you,' he said, and went quickly to find someone to talk to Richie.

'We need to take a statement; do you feel able to talk now?' he asked her when he came back.

Nia turned to him, stared without speaking. She felt almost as if she were floating, watching herself on the beach. The voice of the police officer was muffled. What had he said?

'Nia.' He spoke louder. 'I know you have had a terrible shock, but would I be able to have a few words with you? Do you live close by?'

She nodded slowly. 'Yes, in the close.'

Nia gave her address, looked down at Romeo. 'I need to get home. Romeo hasn't had his breakfast yet.'

'Of course. Is there someone who could walk with you?'

'No, but it's OK,' she said quietly.

'Make yourself a cup of tea, then. I'll be along shortly.'

Nia walked away, hardly feeling the ground under her feet.

As she turned into the close, Elvira came running towards her. 'Is it true? Is it true about Ruby?'

Nia nodded. 'I'm sorry, yes – I found her.' She started to shake.

'Oh, God,' said Elvira, 'let me help you.'

She took Nia's key and opened the front door.

'Let me get you a cup of tea or something.'

'No, please, I'd rather be on my own.' It was only then she noticed how white Elvira was, all colour gone, not just from her face, but from her lips, her neck. 'You need to sit down.'

'No, I need to find Ethan. Where's Ethan? I need Ethan.' She turned and left the house.

Nia went into the kitchen, fed Romeo, and opened the back door. On the work surface she saw an opened bottle of brandy and poured herself a drink. Her hands shook and they wouldn't stop. Her teeth knocked against the glass as she tried to pour the liquid into her mouth.

She wrapped one of the dog's blankets around herself, shuffled to the sofa and sat down, stunned. Romeo jumped up next to her, pushed his nose under her arm. 'Poor Ruby, to die all on her own like that. Oh, Romeo, I promised to go back, didn't I? If I had, maybe this wouldn't have happened...'

There was a knock on the door. Nia put down the glass, and let the police officer in.

11

Taking one look at Nia, the police officer said, 'We can do this another time. You're in shock. Is there someone I can get to come and look after you?'

'No, please. I'd rather do it now.'

He was very tall and broad, and he seemed to fill the small room. Nia was glad when he sat down. Romeo decided to lie at his feet.

'I'm Ben. First, let's check we have all your details.'

'Before that, can you tell yet how she died?'

He shook his head. 'Oh, no, it's far too soon to be speculating about that. Now, let's get through some of the basic questions, shall we?'

They talked briefly about her coming to the island, getting to know Ruby.

'Right, now, you mentioned you saw Ruby last night. Maybe you could tell me about that.'

'Um, I went down to the beach, I was taking Romeo for his final walk, when I got there, I saw Ruby sat at the top—'

'What time did you go down to the beach?'

'Um. Time? About ten, I think.'

'Was there anyone else about?'

'No. I let Romeo off the lead and went to sit with her.'

'It was a bit odd, wasn't it, to be sitting alone on the beach at that time of night?'

'I thought that. I asked her what she was doing down there, but she'd told me before she went down there to talk to the sea – she found it comforting, I think...' Nia's voice broke.

'I'm so sorry, take your time,' said the police officer. 'How did Ruby seem to you?'

Nia crossed her arms, holding herself. It was important she tried to concentrate, remember every detail she could. 'Um, she was upset. She'd had a few arguments with people, and felt people were angry with her.'

'Did she say who she'd argued with?'

'There had been a difficult time at a party yesterday afternoon.' Nia told him about the call Ruby had received on the helpline, how she'd been sure it was someone from the close. 'No one owned up at the time, most people felt she shouldn't be sharing about it, but Ruby was worried about this person, wanted to help. Ruby talked more about it on the beach, in fact she'd written a letter to them. She read it out to me and then she sealed it.' Nia paused. 'But I could have sworn she sealed that using red wax and an expensive ring on her right hand.' She looked over at Ben. 'That had gone as well.' She shook her head. 'I don't understand any of this. Nothing makes sense.'

'Let me make sure I've got this right. Are you saying the candle was red not green, and that Ruby used a different sealing ring, one that appeared missing when you found her this morning?'

'I am... well, I think so.' Nia frowned. 'It's hard to remember things, isn't it? I'm sorry, I've not been too well recently. My husband says I misremember things.'

'Don't worry, just tell me what you can. In any case, you are still in shock. Things will come back to you. How would you say Ruby's mood was when you left her?'

'She was very unhappy. It wasn't only the scene at the party. I think things with her husband were complicated.'

'In what way?'

'I think she was worried he might be seeing someone else, but I don't know anything more than that.'

'I see, well, we can talk to her husband about that. Was there anything else?'

'She was still upset by this doll thing she'd been sent.' Seeing the police officer's confused expression, she explained what had happened.

'This voodoo doll had been sent to her back in February, you say. But she didn't know who had sent it to her?'

'No, she mentioned about being in a craft group with Lucy, Elvira and Jade when I think they used those materials. She hinted maybe one of them might have sent it, but she wasn't sure.'

The police officer, who had been writing down everything she said, looked up.

'Thank you, that's helpful. We certainly have plenty to be looking into. I expect you saw the empty bottle of whisky on the beach – did you see Ruby drinking?'

'I did, and it surprised me. She didn't usually drink like that and when I left her, she'd told me she wasn't going to drink much more.'

'Did you drink as well?'

'A few glasses, not a lot.'

'And drugs? Did you see Ruby take anything?'

'Oh, no, no drugs. I can't see Ruby ever taking drugs.'

'And you?'

'God, no, never—'

'Do you know what time you left her?'

'It was about quarter to eleven – I had a video-call with my daughter, but I wish now I'd stayed.'

'And did you see anyone as you were leaving?'

'No. We were on our own. If only I'd gone back, but I forgot, that's terrible, isn't it? If I'd gone back, she might still be alive.'

'You mustn't blame yourself. Was there a reason you forgot to go back?'

Nia felt herself blushing. 'I had a difficult call with my daughter,

Safi. She is abroad, travelling. After that, I drank some wine and fell asleep on the sofa here. I feel very guilty about that.'

'Try not to worry too much. I am sure we will have a much clearer idea soon what happened.' He closed his notebook.

'Thank you so much. You've been very helpful. Now, how long will you be staying here?'

'A few more weeks, I guess.'

'So, you're not planning to go anywhere soon. Good. We may have a few more questions.'

He stood up. 'Thank you again, Nia. I'm sure you are exhausted. If you think of anything else, don't hesitate to call. Someone will pop out to see you next week, check how you are getting on. It can be a terrible shock, something like this. Take care. I know you are here alone. Can I contact someone to sit with you?'

'No, it's all right. I'd rather be on my own, to be honest.'

He glanced down at the glass. 'Maybe have some coffee?'

She gritted her teeth and nodded. She didn't reply but opened the front door and he left.

Nia slumped down on the sofa, exhausted. It all seemed like some horrible nightmare. Was Ruby actually dead?

She looked out of the window; it was so quiet out there. The salon, the gallery and Wight's would be closed today, although she guessed Ethan and Elvira would still be working. Nia looked across the close, thought of Jade and, further up the road, Richie. Should she see if she could help?

She knew the answer to that was no. This was a time for close family and friends. The truth was she was a relative stranger, it would be intrusive to call on anyone. What if they blamed her in some way? Was there something she could have said or done to have stopped this?

Nia's thoughts returned to the beach, the sight of Ruby lying there. It was odd about the ring, but the police would probably find it. As for the colour of the wax, maybe she had been wrong. How could she be sure?

Nia knew she would have to leave the police to investigate now. She had told them all she knew. They'd find the ring, explain the seal on the letter, find out who had been down on the beach after her. The police officer had said he would be back. Maybe she would learn more then.

Nia spent the rest of that day and the following one alone, peeping through her curtains, watching comings and goings. She took Romeo for short walks, slipping out when no one was about.

One thing she realised she had to do was contact Gwen. She would want to know what had happened to Ruby. She was dreading telling her, not only because she knew how shocked she'd be at what had happened, but also because she was aware that Gwen had asked her to watch out for Ruby, something she'd failed to do. However, she forced herself to sit and email Gwen, tell her what had happened.

She waited until the evening to ring Chris, who was still at school. He was sympathetic, worried about the effect it had had on her and she confessed to her nerves about giving a statement to the police. She told him about the business with the candles, how confused she was. Chris advised her not to commit to anything, to allow for the fact she might have made a mistake and allow the police to find out what had happened. It was quite comforting in a way not to feel responsible, but for Nia it wasn't quite that simple. She was involved, she'd been with Ruby, and she'd broken her promise to return.

* * *

On Wednesday, she woke to sunshine and knew she couldn't bear another day hiding in the house. She needed to get away and clear her head. On a bookshelf she found the file Gwen had left of walks and decided to head for somewhere called Mottistone Down and maybe go on to the beach after. The directions were straightforward and she found the car park, and then went through the wooden gate that led to a chalky path up to the downs. It was steep but the view from the top was stunning. The view along the island coastline was breathtaking, taking in long stretches of beaches and the chalky cliffs of Tennyson

Down and, on a clear day like today, the monument. The wind washed her face, and then she heard it. Far over in the woods, the distinctive sound of a male cuckoo, the call of spring. He had made a treacherous journey from Africa, over deserts and seas, at the dead of night, to come back here. Nia blinked. Nature continued: the circle of life, death, new life. It was here, and it comforted her.

From the downs, she drove down to a new beach she'd found, Compton Bay. Nia read the notice at the top of the steep metal steps, and after she'd climbed down turned left to the area of beach where dogs were allowed. Here she let Romeo off his lead, took her old trainers off and walked along the sand. She loved the way every day the sand was a fresh canvas, that in places hers were the first footsteps to make their prints that day. Romeo's confidence had grown on the beach and today he splashed among the pools, rolled on the seaweed, jumping over the waves as they hit the shore.

When she returned, she saw she'd received an email in reply from Gwen. It was short, but it was clear she wanted to talk properly.

They arranged a phone call that evening, and Gwen rang promptly at seven.

'Hiya,' she said, and the familiar voice warmed Nia. 'I should say good evening to you, although it's only eleven in the morning here.'

'How are you? How is Ceri?'

Nia learned that the midwife was pleased with the way things were progressing, it shouldn't be too long now until the baby arrived. After a cursory chat about Nia's time in the house they moved quickly on to the subject of Ruby.

Gwen was naturally very shocked. 'I can't quite believe it; how could such a tragedy occur?'

'I am sorry. I feel so guilty. You'd said you were worried about Ruby and asked me to befriend her, I feel I have let you down.'

'There is no way you could have foreseen this happening. Tell me everything.'

Nia went through the night before and the morning she'd found Ruby's body on the beach.

'It sounds like she was very unhappy. I wish she'd told me about the voodoo doll. It sounds horrible. No wonder she was upset.'

'Have you any idea who could have sent it?'

The line went quiet. 'I don't know. But if Ruby says it was someone in the close, I should, shouldn't I? I know things had been difficult between her and Ian after the accident, and she seemed to have a rather strained relationship with Elvira, but I can't think of any major falling out. Poor Ruby, she was so sensitive, it's the kind of thing that would have really upset her.'

'I know, I wish now I'd stayed down with her, not left her alone on the beach.'

'You weren't to know.'

'But I promised to go back to her, and I forgot. I failed her, Gwen.'

'I am sure Ruby's death was not your fault, and anyway, you hardly knew her and at least you sat with her. She told you things she didn't tell anyone else.'

'Whatever you say, I do feel partly responsible. Although I'd only just started to get to know her, I feel we connected. I was able to talk to her, and she shared things with me. It doesn't seem right that someone who was, after all, only trying to help people and do the right thing should have spent her last hours so unhappy.'

'I agree. I think her religion had messed her up, she could be too dogmatic and black and white, but she was a good person. The way she cared for her mum was wonderful. Now, did you say some things seemed different the next morning when you found her? Did you say something about a candle?'

'Yes, I could have sworn the candle she had was red, also I thought she'd had an expensive signature ring on, in fact had used it, but it was gone.'

'I know the ring you mean. It was beautiful; she always wore it. Oh, Nia, I am so sorry all this has happened,' said Gwen. 'You poor thing. I wonder when the police will work out how Ruby died.'

'I've no idea. She was drinking whisky but that was all.'

'A few glasses of whisky aren't going to kill her, are they? I guess we'll have to wait for the police to look into things. Of course, if you are right and things had been changed, then that would mean someone else went down to Ruby after you.'

'I suppose so, but, Gwen, I could have been mistaken. It's hard to tell colours in the dark... but I could have sworn it was red and that she used the expensive ring...'

'You could be right.'

'But we both know I've not been well; I could be wrong.'

'I don't see why being exhausted should mean you can't trust your memory. Tell me, do you think the break is helping you?' Gwen asked gently.

'Sometimes it seems to. On the beach, up on Tennyson Down, I feel almost normal, like my old self.'

'That's good. You must keep going out. I'm sure Romeo is loving it. How are Richie and Jade, by the way?'

'I've not seen much of them. It must be awful.'

'Of course. Look, I have to go, but can you email me if you find out anything else? Maybe we could arrange a call again.'

'Of course, give my love to Ceri.'

When the call finished Nia felt at a loss and so she went to the kitchen. She made a pot of tea, but left the lid off for it to cool, then she found a large mixing bowl, added in a mountain of mixed fruit, breathing in the rich smell of the sultanas, currants and mixed peel. Finally, after testing the temperature of the tea, she poured it over the fruit.

'There we are,' she said to Romeo. 'We'll leave this to rest until tomorrow and then we shall make some scrummy Bara brith. You never know, someone might call.'

However, the next day no one called. Instead, Nia sliced up the cake and took it out with her as she explored the woods. She did the same the following days.

On Sunday evening Nia guessed no one would be going to Wight's and was settled with a glass of wine and reading when she heard a sharp knock at the door.

Opening the front door, Nia saw Ben, the police officer who had taken her statement the day she had discovered Ruby's body.

'Good evening. I thought I'd come and see how you are doing.'

He followed her into the house, and they sat down.

'I'm much better now, thank you. Do you have any news about what happened to Ruby?'

'I'm afraid there is very little I can share at this point.'

'Oh, I see. Did you find out anything about the candles or the ring? Remember I thought it had been a red candle and a ring was missing on her right hand.'

'I do remember. We did take note of everything you said. I'm afraid we have yet to find any evidence of the red candle you mentioned or the ring. We understand Ruby had said the ring was rather loose and also it needed cleaning. It could be that she had taken it into a jeweller or put it somewhere for safekeeping.'

'And so, I was mistaken in what I saw?'

'It's possible, but of course we are still looking into everything. We have carried out a very thorough search of the beach and Ruby's home.'

'I see. I'm so confused – you know, I could have sworn that candle I saw was red.'

'It would have been difficult to distinguish colours in the dark.'

'I realise that. Did you get any further in finding who sent the voodoo doll?'

'That is ongoing.' His lips were firmly pressed together; he wasn't going to say any more than that.

'And the caller – did you find who rang the helpline?'

'Again...' He shrugged.

'You can't tell me... but surely you can at least tell me if you know how Ruby died.'

'We are starting to put a few things together, but I can't share that with you yet either. There is, however, one thing I need to discuss with you.'

The officer rubbed his lips together and Nia knew he was preparing himself to ask something difficult. 'I need to ask you, Nia, if you have any recollection of exactly how much you drank on the beach with Ruby.'

'I accepted a few glasses of whisky, no more.'

'I see. The problem is we have a witness, a fisherman who you apparently bumped into as you left the beach. He said, in his words, that you reeked of booze. The point is your memory must be sketchy.'

'You're making me feel like some kind of alcoholic... but I wasn't drunk when I was with Ruby.'

The police officer coughed. 'Of course, you will think that, but it's difficult for us to be sure.'

'You don't believe anything I have told you?'

'I am not saying that. In fact, we have taken everything you have said very seriously. As possibly the last person to see Ruby alive and then find her body the next day, we are looking very closely at your statements and movements during that time.'

Nia stared in alarm as the implications of what he'd said sank in.

'I didn't have anything to do with Ruby's death,' she said quickly.

He gave a glimmer of a smile. 'We have been able to reassure ourselves about that. We know Ruby was alive when you left her because the fisherman spoke to her, checking she was OK. We know also you made the call to your daughter as we were able to check your phone records.'

'You checked my phone?'

'We did – you see, we don't physically need your phone to trace your calls. Also, assuming you were in the same location as your phone, we can be pretty sure you were in this house all night.'

Nia was shocked. 'It never crossed my mind that you would be checking up on me.'

'We are very thorough in a case as serious as this.' Ben stood up. 'I'll leave you now. Thank you for all the help you have given us. Do get in touch if you remember anything else.'

With this he left. Nia felt she'd learned very little apart from the fact she'd clearly been checked up on, and the police seemed to think she'd been pretty drunk that night on the beach with Ruby.

Nia was in the kitchen making a cup of tea when she heard the clatter of a note coming through the letter box. Romeo was barking at the intrusion. She picked up the note and read it.

We will be holding a vigil tomorrow evening at nine on the beach where Ruby died. We will light white candles, read some poems, and have a time of quiet to remember our lovely Ruby. Everyone is very welcome to join us. With love, Jade and Richie.

12

Nia left the house at nine the following evening, in the hope that everyone else would have gone ahead to the vigil. She was right, the close was empty, and she walked to the beach alone.

She could see a small group of people huddled on the beach, while others stood up on the harbour wall or on the pier. Jade gestured to Nia to come down to the beach. Nia climbed down the few steps and walked towards Jade, who was standing with the others in the place she had found Ruby's body. To her surprise Jade reached out, put her arm around her shoulder. They were standing in a circle, and at the centre Nia saw there were rings of white candles. The breeze was gentle, and the candles flickered.

Nia noticed an older man standing next to Richie, and, despite the age and fashion differences, they were unmistakably father and son. Both had their arms crossed and avoided eye contact with each other or anyone else. There was a look of sadness, even anger on their faces, but all other feelings and thoughts were tightly locked inside.

It was very still now, and the time had come for Jade to lead the vigil.

'All life came from the sea, and somehow it feels fitting that we are here to remember Ruby, who loved this more than any other place. There is salt in our tears, salt in the sea, we are one. My Ruby, she took her last breath here. It is both shocking and a comfort. She would have wanted to be here.' Jade sniffed, paused. 'I loved my sister so much. We were very different. I always said she was the saint to my devil. Now she is an angel. No one can hurt her any more.'

Jade looked towards Ian, who read a poem. Nia hadn't noticed how rich and full his voice was before. Filled with emotion, and yet clear, his voice echoed off the stones as he read. Even the sea seemed to still and listen as phrases resonated with her '... dancing with waves... whisper with the waves... you are here...'

They stood quietly, remembering, grieving. Nia felt Jade's body shake and understood what it meant to cry inside.

Slowly, other islanders came, added their white candles to those in the circle and then they melted away into the night, back to their homes.

Eventually only the people from the close remained and Jade blew out the candles. The air was suddenly dark and cold. She picked up the remains of the candles and placed them in a bag. Nia looked down; the beach had returned to being itself.

Only then did Nia turn and look at the place where she had found Ruby, but there was nothing but a dark, empty space.

'This is your fault.' The words cut through the night air. Joe was standing in front of Richie, his face so close Richie had to feel the heat of his words on his cheek.

'You never loved her, never looked after her.'

Joe stepped even closer and, in a flash, raised his fist, hit Richie with such force that he staggered back. The blood streaming from his nose shone in the darkness.

'I did love her,' said Richie, his voice shaking. 'She was the only good thing in my life. You're the one I saw rowing with her that Sunday morning, the day she died. What was that all about, then?'

'We never argued—'

'You did. I saw you. It was early in the morning. I was watching

Ruby walking down the close, and she met you coming up with bags in your hands.'

'We were just saying hi.'

'Oh, no, I heard some of what you said and I saw your face. You were so angry, and she was shaking her finger at you. So, what was it you need to own up to your parents about, then?'

'You're mad. It was nothing. That's guilt talking.' Joe lifted his hand again, but Ian stepped forward and grabbed it.

'Enough. Ruby's death is a tragedy, none of us know yet why she died, but no one here is to blame.'

'Then why did the police ask me all those questions? I can understand why they needed my impressions about how Ruby was, but why were they asking me where I was, how I got on with her? They even asked me about that blasted call Ruby talked about, and some really weird stuff,' said Joe.

'I think we were all asked a lot of things. It's only natural – we in the close probably knew Ruby better than anyone else. I was surprised by some of the questions, I'll admit, but they explained it was just part of their normal enquiries after an event like this. No one is seriously considering any of us had anything to do with Ruby's death. In fact, no one apart from Lucy was even here, were they? Richie was up swimming with me. Joe, I guess you were fishing, Jade and Ethan were at the rescue centre and Elvira with her mother. Only Lucy was close by, but she was watching TV as usual. You see, that is how it was. All we can do now is support each other, just as we always have,' said Ian.

Nia found herself lulled by his words; they washed over her, like a warm shower, but then she remembered the voodoo doll.

A symbol of hate, Ruby had called it, and it had been made and sent to her by someone standing on this beach. So, no, they hadn't all loved Ruby; someone here was acting a part.

Ian left Joe and went back to Lucy, but Nia noticed a tiny shrug from Lucy as he tried to put his arm around her. Lucy was breathing fast, her eyes wide, and Nia was surprised that in them she saw fear, not sadness. Maybe it was natural. Sudden death made everyone realise how vulnerable they were – their life could be snuffed out as easily as one of those candles in an instant. But Lucy seemed to have more on her mind. Her eyes darted from face to face.

Richie's father had handed his son the kind of old-fashioned cloth handkerchief men of that generation carried, but Nia noticed that was the only comfort he offered. It was Elvira who went to Richie and asked him if he was all right. She gently eased the hanky away from his face, felt the bridge of his nose. 'It's not broken,' she said gently. 'Just pinch it here, keep the hanky there until it stops bleeding.' Her gesture was tender, maternal, and helped defuse the anger hanging in the air.

'I think it might help us all if you could tell us, Nia, about that last evening you spent with Ruby,' said Jade. 'Would you be able to do that? Or is it too painful?'

They were all waiting for her answer. 'The police say my memories of that evening might be muddled.'

'Hmm, maybe so, but I think we'd still all find it a comfort to hear what you remember.'

She nodded. 'I'd like to tell you all. The burden of knowing I might have been the last person Ruby spoke to has been huge. I'm worried I should have said or done something to help her.'

'No one has been thinking that,' said Ian.

Nia was grateful for his words. 'Thank you,' she replied.

She heard a crunch on the pebbles and saw Richie's father quietly leave them. She swallowed hard and began. 'I came down with Romeo, about ten o'clock. Ruby was sitting just here.'

Nia paused and they listened to the waves quietly breaking on the beach, and it took her back to her evening with Ruby. Suddenly it was as if she were there.

'I'm afraid Ruby was very unhappy.' She glanced at Richie.

'It's OK. You can tell us what you remember,' he said.

'I don't want to embarrass you, but she did tell me that you and she had rowed. She said she was hoping to sort things out.'

'That's right. We'd talked that morning. It was just a misunder-standing, nothing important. We loved each other—' his voice broke.

'Did she say any more about the person who made the phone call to the helpline? It obviously had upset her,' asked Ian.

'Ruby was very concerned about them.' Nia glanced around, but no one was giving anything away. 'Because they'd not been to see her, she decided to write them a letter. She had it with her, she showed it to me.'

'And what did the letter say?' Ian asked.

'Just that she wanted to help this person. Then I think I remember her sealing the letter with red wax, using the larger of her sealing rings.'

'What do you mean, you think you remember? Aren't you sure?' asked Ian.

'The problem is the colour of the wax and the seal. The letter I saw when I went down the next morning, and the one the police found, had a green seal and the small ring had been used. In fact, the larger ring wasn't even on her finger. The police noted what I said, and they think I must have been mistaken.'

'I suppose it was very dark. It must have been very difficult to see or make out specific colours,' said Ian.

'But you don't think that?' Jade asked Nia.

Nia shrugged. 'I don't know any more.'

'I am concerned about the ring,' said Richie. 'I have been looking everywhere for it. I hate the idea of something so precious to Ruby going missing.' His voice cracked with emotion. He wiped away a tear.

Elvira put her arm around him. 'Hey, it's all right. It will turn up. You wait and see.'

'But what if it's got lost down here?' he said.

'I think the police would have found it. They did a thorough search,' said Nia and then added, 'One other thing, a week before she died, Ruby showed me this doll thing she'd been sent back in February. A kind of voodoo doll. It had pins sticking in it. Ruby was sure the voodoo doll had been made and sent to her by someone in the close.'

'So that is why they asked me about it,' said Joe. 'I thought they'd gone mad. Ruby never mentioned it to me.'

'They asked me about it as well,' said Lucy. 'It was made with the kinds of materials I use, blue silk, driftwood, but of course I had never made anything like they described. I also told him none of us in our little craft sessions had made such a thing.'

'Of course not, it sounds horrible,' said Elvira. 'Why did she think someone in the close would do such a thing?'

Nia explained about the wooden button.

'Did Ruby really feel she'd been cursed or something?' Elvira asked.

'Well, she wasn't exactly frightened of it, but she was upset about the hate she felt was behind it.'

Joe frowned. 'It's a horrible thing to do. Poor Ruby.'

'I think she might have been overreacting,' said Elvira. 'Those dolls are all over the place now. It's nothing, but certainly no one in the close would do anything so childish.'

'It doesn't sound like Ruby saw it like that,' said Jade.

'I heard Ruby was drinking a lot,' said Ethan. 'Is that true?'

'She was drinking whisky, but I wouldn't say she was really drunk. Of course, the bottle was empty when I saw it the next day, so maybe she drank a lot more after I left.'

'How come you didn't notice she hadn't come home that night?' Joe demanded of Richie.

'We had separate rooms for when Ruby was on shifts. I got back from swimming, went to bed. I thought maybe she'd gone into the helpline after all. Our car is over in the car park, so I wouldn't have seen if it was still there or not.'

Jade sighed. 'I think that's enough for one evening, don't you? Thank you for coming, but let's go home.'

Nia bent down and scooped a pile of pebbles from where Ruby had lain. Maybe she would make a small memorial for her in the garden.

Ian, using the torch on his phone, led Lucy off the beach. Nia walked behind them. As they approached the steps she saw Ian lean down, kiss the top of Lucy's head, and speak in words barely louder than a whisper. 'It's over now, it's finished.' The two of them went up the steps; from behind Nia felt someone grab her elbow.

She turned and saw Jade; they smiled and walked home together.

Once home Nia let Romeo out into the garden. No long walk this evening. She looked up at the black sky. What a strange evening it had been. The vigil had been very moving and she was sure it had given many people in the town a sense of communal grief and support. But it didn't mean there was closure.

Nia was confused. When she'd been talking at the vigil, her mind had been clear. And yet the officer had been so convincing.

Back in the kitchen she emptied her pockets of the stones before she hung up her coat. Returning to the stones, she started to sort through them. Then she saw it.

On one stone, a fossil, was the shape of a heart made of red wax. It had to be the heart Ruby made: the ammonite fossil. It had been her 'love letter to the sea'. And the sea had kept it safe to pass it to her. It was telling her she was right.

Nia burst into sobs. 'Oh, Ruby, it's red wax. This must mean I really saw that red candle.'

She hugged the fossil. This was important: if she was right, then someone must have been down on the beach after her. She had to tell the police; she would ask Jade for a number to contact them. She paused. Hang on, could this have come from one of the candles at the vigil? She shook her head. No, they had all been white, she was sure of that. Anyway, this was the fossil, the shape Ruby had made.

If she was right, of course, it meant someone else had taken down the green candle. And, of course, they must have changed the seal on the letter. It was all very odd.

After making a cup of camomile tea, Nia went upstairs with Romeo. She went over to the window and looked down on the close. She remembered her first impressions the day she'd arrived, smug, content, a cat curled up in the sunshine. It wasn't what she saw tonight.

Now she saw darkness and shadows, that smug smile had morphed into something less friendly, something threatening. She knew that one of the people at least was hiding a dark secret that they'd unintentionally confided to Ruby, someone had created that horrible doll, stuck the pins in its eyes and heart, someone out there had hated Ruby. Ruby had said, 'No one here is quite what you think.' Nia shivered. Those words had been spoken the day she died, almost as if Ruby had had some kind of premonition of danger ahead. But surely her death on the beach couldn't be to do with anyone here, could it? One thing Nia was sure of, however, was that there was a lot hidden out there in the shadows.

'It's over,' Ian had said. 'It's finished'. Nia didn't agree; she felt very much that things had only just begun.

13

It was pouring with rain the next day. Nia decided to catch up on emails and set up her laptop on a small table facing the window. There were signs of normality returning to the close. The vets were as busy as ever, but Joe had also reopened Wight's and Nia noticed a few people pass her window on their way to find shelter and an early coffee.

Opposite she saw the lights on in the salon. Jade was clearly preparing it to restart business. Nia felt for her, it must be very hard with so many poignant reminders of Ruby.

Nia was just going through her emails when she noticed two police officers walking up the close. She recognised Ben, but not the woman with him. Suddenly alert, she wondered if they were coming to her, but they walked past, and she saw them enter the gallery. Sometime later, they went to the salon and eventually left again and then she saw Jade leave the salon and walk up to the gallery.

The visits had seemed significant, and Nia was longing to know what news they had imparted. However, she also knew that frustratingly she would have to wait for the news to come to her.

At lunchtime the rain eased off and she took Romeo out for a walk. On her return she glanced over at the salon and saw Jade at the reception desk close to the window. Their eyes met and Jade gestured to her to go in. In a complex mime exchange, Nia explained she would take Romeo in, dry him off and then come over.

The rain had started again by the time she left, and even in that short distance Nia could feel the rain penetrating her 'showerproof hood' and bouncing off the cobbles soaking her feet. She entered the salon bearing a tin full of Welsh cakes, and quickly peeled off her wet coat.

Jade was sitting at the far end of the salon nursing a cup of coffee. She was very pale, very still, her eyes staring at the floor. The rain was attacking the windows now, and despite the lights the salon felt dark and gloomy.

Nia approached her quietly, as if visiting a sick person in a nursing home. She placed the tin on a table and sat down close to Jade.

'I noticed the police came to see you.'

Jade nodded, slowly raised her head. 'Sorry, do you want coffee?' Her eyes drifted to the kettle and mugs standing close by.

Without asking, Nia went and made herself a cup and then opened the tin. Jade picked out a Welsh cake but put it down untouched.

Jade raised her mug to her lips, sipped slowly, and then looked at Nia.

'They have done the post-mortem and are starting to put together what they think happened to Ruby.' Jade took another sip of her coffee. 'They think—' Jade sniffed; tears started to fall down her face. 'Oh, Nia, they think Ruby killed herself.' She burst into sobs. Nia leant forward and took her mug away.

Jade grabbed a handful of tissues and wiped her face. 'I'm sorry, I suppose this was always going to be a possibility, it's just such a shock when they say it. They are not sure if it was accidental or if she did it on purpose, but apparently they found a letter. She said life had become impossible, she couldn't go on.'

Nia shook her head. 'Oh, no. I knew she was unhappy and very upset about the voodoo doll, but she was talking about making things better. There had been some row with Richie, but she felt that could be resolved, and then she'd written to the caller, suggesting they meet. I'm shocked, Jade. It never entered my head she might be thinking of doing anything like that. If I'd known, I'd never have left her down there.'

'At least you listened to her. If this is what happened, then Richie or I should have seen it coming.'

'So, had Ruby been drinking more than we thought?'

'No, it wasn't only alcohol, she'd taken drugs as well. Ketamine.'

Nia gasped. 'Drugs? But I never saw anything – and anyway, Ruby never took drugs, did she?'

Jade's shoulders relaxed, her expression calmer but deadly serious. 'Ruby was a complicated person. She had these high moral standards, but there were times when even she lapsed. She drank sometimes, not very often, but I knew she went to the beach on her own to drink when she got very down. It was her only way of escape.'

'But drugs?'

'As far as I know it was only the once and that was recently. It had been a very rough few months for us all after losing Mum last year. It was Ruby's birthday at the beginning of February and everyone in the close decided to go out for the night. We went to a large pub in town. It was quite late, and I realised Ruby had disappeared. I went to look for her, found her in the toilet in a right state, crying hysterically. She'd bought some pills off a girl in there, taken them. I was shocked. Ruby never did things like that. Anyway, Gwen suggested we take her to A & E. They said it was ketamine, but she was OK, came home that night. She promised me she would never do it again.'

'But why did she do it?'

'Ruby talked about her grief over losing Mum, how she felt she'd disappointed her, and then about some lie she felt guilty about. The trouble with Ruby was she gave herself impossible standards to live up to.'

Nia was stunned.

'I thought that night that maybe she'd turned a corner,' continued Jade. 'She seemed to see it as a fresh start, and she was happier for a while, but I guess nothing was really resolved. I should have seen it at her outburst at the party. We all got so cross with her, when really it was a cry for help. I had my own problems, I guess, but I should have seen beyond them. She was my sister, for God's sake.'

They sat quietly with only the rain battering the windows breaking the silence. Nia slowly tried to take things in.

'Where was the letter saying she couldn't go on?'

'It was in her bag; it had a green seal.'

Nia frowned. 'But there was only one letter and that was to the caller on the helpline. Ruby read it to me.'

Jade shook her head. 'The police never mentioned that one.'

'That doesn't make sense – even if I got the colours and seal wrong, I know what she read to me. I looked in her bag the morning I found her – there was only one letter. That must be the one the police found, so where is the one Ruby read to me? By the way, I'm pretty sure I was right about the red candle and the wax – I am sure she used that to seal the letter.'

'How come you are so sure now?'

Nia told Jade about the fossil. 'I was excited when I found it, but now I don't know what to think.'

Jade shook her head. 'I'm sorry, Nia, I don't understand it either. Maybe you should talk to the police, tell them about the fossil.'

'I don't want to mislead them or waste their time.'

'It's their job to decide what is right. Your responsibility is to tell them what you know.'

'I guess you're right. OK, I'll ring them, maybe you could give me the number. By the way, did they say if they've found who sent the voodoo doll? From what people said at the vigil, it sounds like they have been asking everyone.'

Jade explained that the police hadn't been able to trace the doll back to anyone. In fact, it had been suggested to them by someone that Ruby could have sent it to herself.

'But that's ridiculous... who said that?'

'They wouldn't say, but they certainly appear to have been given the message from the others in the close that Ruby had serious problems.

This suggestion apparently was that Ruby gave herself this doll thing because she hated herself. It was like she was cursing herself.'

'And do you think that?'

Jade shook her head. 'No, I don't. I think she was unhappy, and I think she had been badly affected by her upbringing that made her believe that she and others should live to some impossible standard, but she wasn't going round doing things like that. Actually, after you mentioned the voodoo doll at the vigil, I was trying to remember back to the time it must have happened. Ruby didn't say anything to me, but I do remember her telling me about losing a button off her cardigan. She was annoyed – she didn't have that many clothes. She was going to ask Joe if he'd found it. If the police are right, then Ruby would have had to remove that button herself and therefore been making up some story to me. I honestly don't think that is what happened.'

'It all seemed very genuine to me as well. She was very upset.'

Jade screwed up her eyes in concentration. 'I think we are right; I think the doll was sent to her and that is awful. Who on earth did such a thing?'

'You should have a better idea than me – you know the people here.'

'My first thought, to be honest, was Elvira. There's been tension between her and Ruby for a long time now, but even so...'

'Ruby herself suggested Elvira or Lucy, but she dismissed them.'

Jade sighed. 'It's all so horrible, isn't it? I always thought of our close as somewhere safe, cosy. Boring even. What has happened?' Jade sipped her coffee, started to nibble on a Welsh cake. 'You know, what with the candle, the ring and now the letter, it's a lot of things to be mistaken about – what if you're right?'

'But the police have explained them all away, and they did look into them. It's not as if they just dismissed them.'

'No, true, but I have to be honest, Nia, the more we talk, the more I realise that in my heart I can't believe she killed herself, intentionally or by accident.'

Nia was surprised but Jade spoke with a steady conviction.

'But if that was true, then someone else had to be involved in her death.'

Jade nodded. 'I know, and who would do that? Who slipped drugs into her drink? It would have to be someone she knew, someone she trusted. If a stranger had approached her down there, she'd have left, wouldn't she? Maybe someone had gone down there and taken drugs with her and then, because she died, they've been too scared to own up.'

'It could have happened but why change the candle? And what about the letter? Surely that proves Ruby intended to take her own life.'

'It's so confusing.'

'I saw you walking up to the gallery. I assumed you went to see Richie. How is he?'

Jade told Ruby about her conversation that morning with Richie. He was, of course, still in shock. As regards the letter, he was very distressed at the thought of Ruby being so desperate, but he seemed to think it was possible. The police discovered Ruby had actually typed the letter on her office laptop the afternoon she died. In fact, they were able to tell the time; it had been about five o'clock. Richie hadn't even realised she was in her office, he'd been working, but he told Jade how upsetting it was to think he'd been totally oblivious to the nightmare Ruby had been going through.

'He's in pieces. He really loved her, you know. I can remember their wedding day. It was at The Hall, so a bit odd, but in the middle of it all I saw them look at each other when they said their vows and I knew it was the real thing. I know he's young and he has his art, but Richie is going to be so lost now.'

Nia nodded. 'You know, it's good for me to hear that. All I know of Ruby and Richie's relationship is the conflict I've seen since I arrived. It's easy for me to forget how long they've been together and how deep their love has been for each other.'

Jade looked at her questioningly. 'When you say conflict, what do you mean?'

Nia told Jade about the incident at the Red Jet terminal, and how upset Ruby was about what happened when she followed Richie and then how distraught she'd been at the party.

'Right, Richie actually mentioned that when I was speaking to him this morning. He asked me to keep this to myself. He feels guilty about lying to Ruby. However, you're not going to tell anyone, are you? What happened was he'd been visiting a friend – it was someone Ruby wasn't too keen on, too "arty" for her. He'd found it easier to pretend he was going over to his class than telling her what he was actually doing. He was shocked when he saw Ruby coming up the drive and had run out to explain. She'd left and he thought it was over, but she was upset, felt he'd lied to her. They'd talked about it, but he knew they hadn't totally resolved it, and he regrets that.'

'But it wasn't that big a lie, it doesn't account for how devastated Ruby seemed when I talked to her at the party. I was sure she thought he'd been having an affair.'

'No, it wasn't that. The trouble is, like I said, things got way out of perspective with Ruby. A little lie was as much a sin as a terrible one. It comes from the religion, it's what they taught, and Ruby believed it.'

'That doesn't make sense. You can't live like that.'

'Ruby tried to, and it was tearing her apart because it's an impossible standard to live by. But she was still in The Righteous and that is what they taught. Poor Ruby, if only she had got away.'

'I agree. Now, do you think the police are sure that Ruby took her own life?'

'They told me that they would still be open to any new information. They would like to find the ring and they would like to be certain about where Ruby obtained the ketamine. I wondered if she'd bought more than she let on that night, maybe she'd been hiding it away. They said they'd thought about that. They are trying to track down the woman Ruby bought it from, but that could be hard. They are being pretty thorough, you know. That's why I think you should tell them about the fossil and remind them of the letter she read to you. These things matter.'

Nia nodded. 'I'll do that.' She looked around the salon.

'I saw you sorting things out in here this morning. Do you think you will reopen?'

'I have to, and people are already asking about it, tactfully, of course, but, well, I can't really afford to let the business stagnate. People need their hair done and if I don't do it, they will go somewhere else, but it's so hard. Everything here is about me and Ruby. This is our place. I feel her everywhere, hear her voice...'

'I'm so sorry,' Nia repeated. 'If there is anything I can do...'

Jade sat forward, her eyes focused very firmly now on Nia.

'Gwen told me you worked as a hairdresser for nearly twenty years down in Cardiff. She also told me you had won awards for your cutting – the salon you were in was highly thought of.'

'All that is true, but I've been out of it for a while now.'

Jade smiled and sat up. 'Look, I know you came here for a holiday, but I'm stuck. I need someone to take on Ruby's appointments. I can't find anyone who could start immediately and then I realised I had the answer on my doorstep, so to speak. What do you think?'

Nia felt a wave of panic. 'But I won't be here for that much longer.'

'That's OK. We'll take it on a day-by-day basis, but it would be a real help.'

Nia bit her lip. 'I don't know, Jade; I've lost my confidence. What if I can't do it any more?'

'That's not very likely, is it?'

'I don't know, it's a huge risk. I can't mess up someone's hair. I'm frightened, Jade. I know it sounds stupid, but the thought of cutting someone's hair is terrifying.'

Jade pressed her lips together in thought. 'I know, how about you come over tomorrow evening and do mine? It's in a terrible state and you know how it is for hairdressers, we are always the last to be fitted in. Ruby always cut mine, I trusted her... So what do you think?'

Nia grimaced. 'I don't know.'

'Please, I'm desperate. And who knows? You may enjoy it.'

Nia reluctantly agreed and said she would be round about seven. 'You won't believe this, but I packed my scissors. Crazy, isn't it?'

'Not at all. I don't know a decent hairdresser who wouldn't be the same. Some may save a photo or money in a burning building; a hairdresser will always have their scissors.'

Nia smiled. 'OK, I'll come, but don't blame me if you are wearing a hat for a few weeks.'

'That's fantastic. Thank you.' Jade paused. 'And you will ring the police, won't you?'

Nia nodded. 'I promise. I will go back now and ring them. Do you have a contact?'

Jade gave her the number.

'Right. I'll see you tomorrow.'

* * *

Nia returned to the house. Before ringing the police, however, she gave herself a moment to digest what she'd learned. The thing she guessed that had shocked her the most was that Ruby had taken drugs in the past. It was so at odds with everything she knew, or thought she knew, about Ruby. It reminded her that she had only been here a few weeks and she still had a lot to learn about this small group of people.

Nia picked up her phone and rang the number Jade had given her.

14

When Nia rang the police station, she spoke to an officer who took down her details and the information and promised someone would get back to her soon. The call came much quicker than she expected and, to her surprise, it was Ben the police officer she'd met, late that afternoon. Her heart sank when she heard his voice, convinced he wasn't going to take anything she said seriously. However, he was very courteous. He had followed up on the message, checked the files and he asked her for more details of the letter Ruby had read out to her.

Nia began nervously, 'I can't remember it exactly, but, like I told you, the gist of it was that she would like to speak to this person and help them.'

'That is interesting. You see, I had taken note of the letter you said she read out to you, and we noted it was very different from the letter we actually found on the beach.'

'Jade told me that you found a letter saying Ruby wanted to end her life.'

'Um, I can't really discuss that with you, but it was very different from the one you are describing. However, we did find a copy of a letter with very similar wording to the one you described on Ruby's laptop in the salon. She'd printed it off at about half nine.'

'I saw her in there at that time,' said Nia, excited. 'So you have a copy, but why wasn't it on the beach?'

'We don't have the physical copy she printed off, only a record on the printer's history that she did. We can only assume she discarded it somewhere. We have checked the bins in the salon but can't find it. Maybe she threw it away on her way to the beach. The bins had been emptied before we could check.'

'But surely it could be that she took it down to the beach – it is what she read out to me.'

'It's possible but, of course, that would have a number of implications. By the way, did she actually show you the letter? Did you read it yourself?'

'No, she read it out but—'

'I see, so it could be possible that she used the wording of the letter to the caller but was holding a different one.'

'I suppose so, but not very likely, is it?'

'The contents of the letter we found could have been, um, disturbing. She might not have wanted to upset you.'

'It all seems odd. She didn't need to show me the letter at all.'

'That is true, but she was in a very stressed and highly emotional state of mind.'

'I suppose she was,' conceded Nia, and then she remembered about the voodoo doll and the wooden button, and she told Ben the things Jade and she had discussed.

'So, this, you feel, suggests she didn't make the doll herself?'

'Yes. If you'd heard her, she was convinced it had been sent to her by someone in the close. She was very upset.'

'We did question everyone in the close. No one appeared to know anything about it, or to have any motive to have sent it. They all seemed totally mystified by it.'

'But Lucy had the materials to make one. Elvira and Jade had been using those things.'

'Of course, but we can't see any reason why they should have created anything like that. We did do a quick search of their homes and flats, you see, we did take this seriously, but we found nothing to suggest they had been making voodoo dolls or involved in that kind of thing. It wasn't as if anyone before or after had received such a thing, no, the explanation about Ruby making the doll was the only logical thing we could come up with.'

'Ruby would never have done anything like that. It was against her religion.'

'But drinking and drugs presumably were as well.'

'Well, yes, but why would she cut off the button from her own cardigan? It seems so calculating.'

'I agree, it is a very strange thing to do. We haven't written off the chance that it was sent to her, but, even if it was, it doesn't necessarily have an impact on how she died.'

'But Ruby was certain it meant someone in the close hated her. That has to be important, doesn't it?'

'We have no evidence for that. Ruby appears to have been held in very high esteem. People spoke very kindly of her.'

Nia sighed. 'You seem to have an answer to everything. But I told you about the fossil, at least that is evidence.'

'But you found it the night of the vigil when a number of people had been lighting candles,' he added gently. 'Listen, Nia, everything you told me has been noted and investigated. We have limited resources, but this is a very serious case, which is being given a lot of time and attention. I will feed back to the investigating team this conversation. The case is not closed, it is ongoing.'

With this, Nia had to be content, and the conversation ended.

She sat down feeling very dispirited. Ben had been so convincing, maybe she had got it all wrong. But the ring, the candle – could she really have misremembered so much? Had Ruby really been reading from a different letter on the beach?

The police had to go on the evidence before them and the testimony of people in the close who knew Ruby far better than she had. Who was she to dispute all that?

The one thing Nia still felt sure of was that the voodoo doll had been sent by someone in the close. She couldn't believe that Ruby had sent that to herself. It was a relief to know Jade agreed with her, and if anyone knew Ruby it would be her sister.

Nia's thoughts were interrupted by a text from Ethan inviting her on an early walk the next day. He added a warning that wellington boots would be needed, but Nia readily agreed. A brisk early morning walk could be just what she needed. Also it occurred to her this was a chance to find out more about people in the close, dig a little deeper into their feelings about Ruby and if anyone had a motive to send that doll.

Nia left the house with Romeo very early the next morning. The sky was streaked with pinks and yellows, elements of the sun greeting the day. On a morning like this it was easy to push away the fears of the day before.

Ethan was already standing by his car and his enthusiasm for a new day reminded her of Romeo.

'I'm so glad you wanted to come again. It was Elvira's idea, actually. She said you probably haven't visited the place I'm going to today.'

'That sounds intriguing.'

'It's really special. I think we both deserve this after everything that's happened.'

They didn't have far to drive. Soon they arrived at a small parking area and Nia got out of the car.

The air was full of the sound of birdsong, the sky light blue through the tall trees. Nia felt that woodland was the place, more than anywhere else, that shouted the arrival of spring, everything waking up after the long winter.

'This is Newtown Creek, the only national nature reserve on the island. This part, Walter's Copse, is my favourite part. Further along you can see the mudflats and salt marshes, but I love going through the woodland and when you reach the estuary it's like stepping out of a Tardis. Oh, keep Romeo on the lead; there are a lot of ground-nesting birds at this time of year.'

Nia walked over to the wooden gate, next to which stood a board, with a packed list of the birds and wildlife people had seen over the past few weeks. 'Wow, do people actually see all these? The list goes on and on... black-tailed godwit, lapwing, buzzard, oystercatcher, kestrel, redshank and spotted redshank, goldeneye, merlin, cormorant, golden plover. I have no idea what half of those birds even look like.'

Ethan laughed. 'Good, it means I can bluff my way round. I'm not very good at identifying birds at all.'

Once they'd entered the woods, Nia felt her senses attacked by the sights and sounds. The riotous birdsong, the blue of the swathes of bluebells, grabbing the light before the buds on the trees burst into leaf, the rich aroma of the woodland, the fingers of breeze through her hair – it was magical.

They walked quietly, taking in the show nature was putting on. However, Ethan pointed out squirrels and woodpeckers, and then a hare moving among the bluebells.

'It's huge,' said Nia. 'I'm not sure I've ever seen one before.'

'I love them. You see so much here,' Ethan replied. 'Apparently if you come at dusk, you can even see glow-worms in the hedges.'

Soon they reached a path that led them out of the woods and on to the flats in front of the estuary. Ethan had been right; it was like entering a whole new world.

Having spent so much time on the beach, Nia was struck by the stillness here. Seabirds soared above the water, oystercatchers with their long orange beaks dug for food. The water itself was completely still. At one end she saw white yachts and a bird hide, but to the right was endless water weaving between the banks. They were the only people on this new planet. The birdsong here, with such an expanse to fill, carried in an eerie echoing way.

They walked along to a bird hide, prominent at the end of a harbour wall.

Inside was dark; they peered through the slats. Nia recognised the oystercatchers, the egret standing proud, white feathers shining.

Ethan's phone buzzed. She saw him typing a reply, then rub his eyes, and suddenly the confidence and enthusiasm seemed to melt from his face.

'It's been a very hard week,' Nia said gently.

'Nightmare. You know, I'm meant to go and buy a suit for the wedding at the weekend. It seems so trivial now.'

'Life has to go on, I guess.'

'But it doesn't feel right, and it's hit Elvira badly. I mean, she never seemed to like Ruby that much, but she has gone to pieces over this.'

'Do you think she needs some time off? You two didn't even close the day we found out about Ruby.'

'Elvira insists on coming in and, in any case, I've no one to replace her. We are actually a satellite branch from the main vets in Newport. That's where we carry out most of the surgery, but they're short-staffed as well. It's not easy getting people to come and work on the island. It's the same in medicine, the schools, everywhere. Anyway, I'm relieved Elvira is at least able to function.'

'I guess Ruby and she had known each other for a long time. Have you spoken to Jade or Richie since the police visited them yesterday morning?'

'Yes, Richie came to see us. They are saying Ruby took ketamine. It sounds like she took her own life. Richie was obviously very upset; it leaves us all wondering what more we could have done. I know Elvira is concerned that she was too hard on Ruby for visiting her mother, but, well, hindsight is a wonderful thing, as they say.'

'I find it shocking enough and I knew very little of Ruby. By the way, what is this ketamine? I don't really know anything about it.'

'We use it at the surgery as an anaesthetic, sometimes a painkiller. We have it in liquid form and inject it. Unfortunately, it's being abused now, youngsters taking it in clubs and the like, more often in powder form. I understand it is usually snorted.'

'But Ruby didn't do that. The police said it was in her glass.'

'It can be dissolved or added to a drink. Apparently, it tastes bitter, but it is fast-acting, and you could be unconscious very quickly.'

'I'm surprised Ruby got hold of it so easily.'

'I agree. It should be a lot harder than it appears to be. After all, it's a class B drug, which means it's illegal to have it on you or give it away. I was reading about it in a veterinary magazine recently. Apparently you can get up to five years in prison for possession, fourteen for supplying. I was shocked – why would anyone take that kind of risk?'

'There must be a lot of money to be made, then.'

'Yes, the demand is there, and the dealers are desperate to supply it. It's everywhere. Look how easily someone like Ruby, who was totally unused to the world of illegal drug use, got hold of it. It means we have to have very tight security. One vet surgery I know on the mainland has been broken into three times now.'

Nia looked through the slats of the bird hide again at the idyllic scene of sparkling water and seabirds swooping across the sky. It seemed wrong to be talking about these things on such a day in such a place, and yet she might not get the opportunity to talk like this to Ethan again.

'I was shocked Ruby had taken it.'

'It was very out of character. The night she died they said she also combined it with a lot of alcohol, which was so dangerous. It's terrible to think she was that unhappy and I never knew.'

Ethan sighed and looked out at the day. 'Anyway, let's get out of here and enjoy the morning.'

Nia decided to let the subject drop and instead allowed herself to take in the beauty of the place. They walked beside a meadow; he explained that some of the fields hadn't been ploughed for centuries or treated with fertilisers or pesticides. This meant that some of the rarer wildflowers could still be found there. It reminded Nia of the fossil she'd found on the beach: the past somehow held lightly but never forgotten here on the island.

Changing the subject, Ethan said, 'I wonder what Jade will do in the salon now. I imagine it won't be easy finding someone at such short notice.'

Nia was still very unsure about whether she would help out or not.

She said, 'I hope she gets some help. She seems very hardworking, and she has been very friendly since I arrived.'

'I can imagine. I worry about her. She always looks a bit of a lost soul to me. That upbringing of theirs has left its mark. I know she looks so much stronger than Ruby, but she's vulnerable in her own way. She does have a remarkable way with the animals at the rescue centre, a real empathy for them.'

'That's special. She's great with Romeo. Animals know, don't they, who they can trust?'

'They have better instincts than people at times. Yes, I have a lot of time for Jade. She has worked very hard at building a life for herself, what with the salon business and the flat she lets out. It's a lot for a young person to be doing on their own. I've often wondered why she chooses to remain single.'

'Maybe she's just too busy to meet anyone.'

'I wondered about her and Joe at one point. I think they went out on a few dates, but nothing seemed to come of it.'

'Joe's busy as well, I guess. He has Wight's to run, and didn't he mention he goes fishing on Sundays? I don't know how much of his spare time that takes up.'

'He talks a lot about fishing, but it's funny how he is never on the end of the pier when I go down there.'

Nia wasn't sure what Ethan was implying by this; she looked at him quizzically.

'I'm sorry, I've never really known what to make of Joe, and I am convinced it's a mistake for any lad that age to have the responsibility of taking on a business. It's so easy to get into a mess with a business, and I'm talking thousands, not a few hundred. You get desperate, try anything...' He paused.

Nia heard the anxiety in his voice, remembered Ian's offer of going over the books with Ethan and guessed he felt the pressure of that side of his business.

'Maybe Ian will lend him a hand. He's very willing, isn't he? They seem a nice couple. They must be upset about what happened to Ruby.'

'I'm sure they are.' Ethan held back an overhanging branch to allow Nia to walk through. 'I know Lucy expressed a few reservations about Ruby, but they have been friends a long time. If it hadn't been for the accident...'

'Yes, what was that about? Lucy said it changed how she felt about Ruby, and then Ruby mentioned it the day of the party... It was as if she'd had to tell some lie about it.'

'I know, and it wasn't a big thing. That is why I don't quite understand why it's caused this rift. It was back in January, a Saturday night, about ten. Ruby was on her way to her charity job; Ian was driving back after a run. He swerved. They had a minor bump, no one was racing along. That was all there was to it.'

'It doesn't sound much at all.'

'It wasn't. My impression is that Ruby got in a state about it. It's not like anyone was blaming her. Ian paid for all the damage. No, all I can think of is that one of them might have been speeding a bit and Ruby failed to mention it to the police.'

'Could one of them have been drinking?'

'No, both were breathalysed.'

'Hang on, what were the police doing there if it was such a minor incident?'

'Ruby called them. Ian wasn't too happy, what with him being a minor celebrity and all that, but it was nothing. No one was going to think any the worse of him because of that. I guess it was a case of Ruby's overactive conscience again, bless her. It was no way to live. Ah, look, we are back at the car.'

As they drove back to Yarmouth Ethan remembered an invitation he was meant to extend to Nia.

'I nearly forgot. Elvira is having a girls' get-together on Saturday evening and wanted me to invite you. It's an early hen night. She's inviting some friends from the mainland as well. It's difficult with all that happened to Ruby, so she'll be keeping it low-key.'

Nia was surprised. 'Oh, thanks, yes. I'd like to go.'

'Great. They'll start off at Wight's at seven. I don't think she's planning to go into town. As I said, it's very low-key.'

Nia thought about their conversation. She had learned a lot about ketamine, particularly about its connection to work with animals and the vet's. She didn't feel she had learned anything new about the accident, but there had to be more to it. She remembered that it was Lucy and Elvira who had been mentioned by Ruby as possible sources of that voodoo doll; she needed to keep digging, see what more she could find out about them.

When they arrived back in Yarmouth, Nia, after such an early start, felt she and Romeo deserved a rest in preparation for her visit to the salon that evening.

However, she did email Gwen to tell her the latest news about the police investigation into Ruby's death. Gwen replied quickly. Her first piece of news was about her new grandchild, who had been born two days before, a little girl, Megan; both mum and baby were thriving. However, Gwen did also write about her shock over the news about Ruby. One part of her email struck Nia:

I find it very hard to accept Ruby took her own life. When her mother was so ill, we had a long talk about euthanasia, and end-of-life care. Ruby made it very clear she believed only God had the right to end someone's life. I know she sounds very distressed that night, but the letter means it was premeditated and that doesn't sound right. Something is wrong here. If you are able, keep asking questions, keep talking to the people in the close. Also, I don't believe Ruby would have sent that doll thing to herself. I think this is one of the things she had been so upset about and I only wish she'd talked to me about it. I'd really like to know who sent it to her. X

Nia felt she'd been sent a commission and it was one she was willing to undertake.

15

The evening's trial run at the salon went well and Nia was relieved to find her confidence flooding back. Jade seemed delighted with her hair, and Nia felt more appreciated and flattered than she had for a long time.

They didn't discuss Nia's call with the police officer until they were sharing a glass of wine after the haircut was finished, and this was as a result of something Jade needed to show her.

'Come and see this,' she said to Nia, and took her over to the reception desk. 'I knew you were going to be great...' she threw Nia a huge smile '... and so I started to go through Ruby's appointments. Now, what I found was, that night before she went down to the beach, I know she came in here.'

'She did, I saw her and actually the police told me it was in here she typed the letter to the caller on the helpline.'

'I see. I'd not realised that. Well, as I say, I was looking through the book and found she'd gone through her appointments for the following week, making notes by some of her clients, suggestions for things they might like to try.'

'Gosh, that's very conscientious. Did she do that regularly?'

'I know she came in here some Sunday nights before she went off to her charity work. I had a theory she felt guilty for having a day off on the Monday and this was her way of doing some work. The point is, she did this the night she died, and if she was planning to kill herself, why on earth would she do such a thing?'

Nia pursed her lips. 'You have a point, it is strange. Did the police tell you that this was the laptop Ruby wrote the letter I was talking about on, the one to the caller?'

'No, they didn't mention it.'

'I suppose because it wasn't the one they found on the beach, they didn't think it was important.'

Nia told Jade about the explanation the police had given her.

'Granted she wasn't actually holding the letter to the caller, it still leaves the question of what happened to it – you say it was printed off?'

'Oh, yes, but the police think she must have thrown it away.'

They returned to their seats. 'Nothing adds up, does it?' said Jade.

Nia told Jade about her email from Gwen.

'So, she has her doubts as well?'

'It sounds like it, yes. She wanted me to keep asking questions, at least see if I could find out who sent the voodoo doll to Ruby.'

'But the police didn't find anything, and they are able to make searches and things.'

'I know, but I think my advantage is that Ruby had shown me the voodoo doll and I saw how upset she was. I know in my heart that there is no way she sent that to herself, and I am determined to find who sent it. In fact, I made a start this morning. I went for a walk with Ethan and asked him about that car accident between Ruby and Ian. That seems to have caused a lot more ill will than it needed and why did Ruby talk about having to lie?'

'She didn't say much to me. I have no idea. Did you get any answers?'

'Not really, it's a bit of a mystery.'

'But you are checking on them because you think Ian may have sent that doll?'

'I don't know. It was actually Lucy that Ruby had suggested.'

'That seems more likely, but why? That's the problem – why on earth should Lucy or Ian hate Ruby that much?'

Nia shook her head.

'By the way, I was thinking more about that candle, the red one,' said Jade.

'Oh, yes?'

'As you have probably noticed, Ruby and I had separate colours for our seals. She used red, and I used green. To everyone else it was just a cute thing we did – the colours matched our names. What no one knows is that it was actually very important to Ruby and me that we never used each other's colours. We promised we would never do that. It was like a pact we had, and I know that sounds daft but the whole seal thing was almost like a ritual to us.'

'I remember watching Ruby and thinking that she took it very seriously.'

'Yes, we did. When I first heard about the candles and the seals, I was too upset to think clearly about it. But now I realise the idea of Ruby using a green candle is just absurd. She would never have done that.'

Nia was struck by the passion in Jade's voice. 'I can understand that, but I guess the police would think that in the state of mind she was in, maybe she overlooked that, took the wrong candle down with her.'

'I can see they might say that, and the evidence would point to that, but in my heart, I don't believe it.' Nia saw tears of frustration in her eyes.

'I'm so sorry, Jade. This is a nightmare for you.'

'It is. I don't see how I am meant to mourn my sister until I am sure of how and why she died.'

'I can understand that. Getting answers really matters.'

Jade put her head to one side. 'It does, you're right. But tell me, Nia, why do you care about it so much? It's not like you knew Ruby well. I mean, you could get on the next ferry home and forget any of this ever happened.'

'No, I couldn't do that. I feel too involved now. How can I forget that last conversation I had with Ruby, or the fact I failed to return to her? And it's not simply about guilt or making amends. I need to find out if I really have imagined things or if they are true. I want to know the truth of what occurred the night Ruby died. And it's not just you and me that have questions. Gwen asked me to keep digging and I think a lot of her. I want to help. I'm not just walking away from this.'

'I'm glad and I shall talk to the police about the importance of the colour of the candle. I should have said that to them before. I shall also share my problems with the idea of Ruby taking her own life. I am her sister. I have to stand up for her.' Jade took a sip of wine; Nia could see the ends of her fingers trembling. She allowed Jade time to sit quietly. Finally, Jade, after taking another sip of wine, spoke again, this time in a far more measured and matter-of-fact voice. 'Anyway, back to the salon – how do you feel about coming to work tomorrow? Honestly, I'd trust my most valued customer with you. It would be great if you'd come.'

Nia nodded and it was agreed that she would start the next day.

As she returned to the house Nia thought about what she'd said about needing to know what had happened to Ruby. Jade was right, she'd hardly known Ruby. However, the time she had spent with Ruby had been so intense, and the events following that so extraordinary that they seemed to eclipse even her own problems. She had to know the truth; she had to know what had happened to Ruby.

* * *

The next morning Nia woke with a sickening, deep sense of dread. She was going back to work in a salon today. The confidence of the night before seemed to have evaporated overnight, but she had promised Jade; there was no way out.

It would have been easier to have an early appointment. As it was, she had a whole morning to sit around and worry.

She took Romeo out for a long walk, and, while she was out,

received a call from Chris. He had a few moments free at work and had rung for a chat.

Nia found herself reluctant to tell him about going to the salon; maybe she'd wait and see how it went first. He did tell her he'd mentioned about her finding a body on the beach to Safi and asked if she'd heard any more about it. Nia passed on that the police appeared to think Ruby had taken her own life but said no more. When she'd given her reasons to Jade about feeling a commitment to asking questions about Ruby's death, she'd known Jade would understand. However, she didn't think Chris would see it like that at all and would expect her to leave such work to the police. It was better not to say anything.

When the call finished she realised it would soon be time to walk over to the salon, and went to get changed.

Nia checked herself over in the mirror. Back home, she had clothes she saved for work. Few people realised how messed up your clothes got in her job. The hair itself managed to get everywhere, then there were all the products you sprayed and massaged into hair. There was always the danger of getting dyes on your clothes and Nia had discovered that buying cheaper clothes for work was the answer. However, despite how sore her feet and back got, she had always worn heels.

Today she had to rethink. Jade wore far more casual clothes to work and, as there were only the two of them, she didn't want to look over-dressed. Also, she seemed to be living in her old trainers here – maybe she could get some smarter shoes that might do for work? Today, however, it would have to be heels and tight jeans.

After giving Romeo a good walk, she settled him down. In the past he'd got used to being left for about three hours at a time; she'd always managed to get home for lunch, to let him out for a walk and food. But since she'd left work they'd hardly been apart and so today she gave him an extra hug and biscuit. 'I'm only in the salon opposite,' she reassured him. 'I'll come back as often as I can.'

With this, she left and walked across the close.

Jade greeted her with a relieved smile.

'You've come. Thank God. I wasn't sure if you'd chickened out.'

'You don't know how close I came to that.'

'Quick, I'm getting you coffee and locking the door – you are going nowhere,' said Jade, laughing. 'Now, I explained a lot of stuff last night, but you were so nervous I'm not sure how much you took in. Let me recap quickly.'

They went to the reception desk. 'As I said, we will need to be careful making appointments for the future, as obviously I don't know how long I have you. However, I will start asking up at the college and looking around – I'd rather find someone through word of mouth. I think the best thing to do is for you to use Ruby's appointment book but make sure you take a note of everyone's phone numbers in case, when it comes to it, I am on my own and have to fit them in a different time.' She swallowed, took a breath. 'The laptop and printer we use for accounts, emails and the like – none of that needs to bother you.'

Jade went through payments and then took Nia around the rest of the salon. It was all pretty much what she was used to, and Nia quickly felt at home. Finally, Jade took Nia to where she would be working – something they'd avoided the night before. This had been Ruby's area but everything of Ruby's had been cleared away.

Nia caught Jade's eye in the mirror, could see her eyes screwed up with hurt, gave her an understanding smile. Jade nodded back. 'I've cleared everything out,' she said and then checked her watch.

It was two o'clock. First a customer for Jade arrived and she was quickly followed by Lucy, who had obviously been told Nia would be doing her hair and walked over to her. With such a short distance to come, she had none of the paraphernalia that clients often brought, not even a coat, although she was, as always, smartly dressed in high-heeled shoes and wearing her large sunglasses.

Nia helped Lucy with her gown, smelt the familiar perfume. Lucy sat down, took off her sunglasses, tucked her silk scarf neatly into the neck of the gown.

'Right,' said Nia, 'tell me what you would like done today.' As she spoke, she touched Lucy's hair lightly, studied it. 'Your hair is in beautiful condition; it has been very well cut.'

'Thank you. Ruby was very good. I wouldn't usually go to a local place like this, but I spotted immediately Ruby knew what she was doing.' She looked at Nia via the mirror. 'It feels very odd being here without her.'

'I'm sure it does,' said Nia gently.

'I suppose life has to go on. So today, can I just have a tidy up?'

Nia smiled, recognising she was on trial. 'That's fine. Let's wash first, then.'

Lucy stood up, but she seemed slightly unsteady as she walked over to the sink.

Nia hadn't washed a client's hair for some time, but she enjoyed it. She could tell a lot about her clients and how they were feeling from the tension in their scalps.

Lucy held herself very tightly, was reluctant even to bend her neck backwards. Nia helped her ease her head back and tested the water. Slowly she felt Lucy relax.

Once Lucy's hair had been washed and combed away from her face, Nia felt that, despite all her make-up, Lucy looked much closer to her real age. Nia was sure she'd had some kind of cosmetic procedures: Botox, fillers, she would guess. Nia had no objection to them, but she was aware that Lucy was a woman very much fighting her age.

Nia started cutting and as she did she realised she ought to try and use the occasion to see if there was any way she could tactfully ask Lucy about Ruby, but decided that being direct was the best way.

'Um, I was thinking about Ruby,' she said. 'You said she interfered. You said that after the accident you'd changed your opinion of her. You sounded angry with her.'

Nia sensed Lucy freeze and look up. She saw a look of horror on Lucy's face. She waited, felt Lucy's shoulders relax.

'Goodness, no. I was never angry with Ruby.'

'I see, sorry, I got that wrong. I'd been wondering why, you see.

After all, it sounds as if the car crash Ian and Ruby had was all settled very amicably.'

Lucy shot her an anxious look in the mirror. 'That was a very minor accident – to even call it a car crash is an exaggeration.'

'But it sounded like it worried Ruby quite a lot.'

'She overreacted, that's all. It was completely unnecessary to call the police and take photos in the way she did.'

'Ruby took photos?'

Lucy's eyes grew even wider. 'No, erm, perhaps not, but she did call the police, which upset Ian. With him being so well known on the island he didn't want it in the local paper.'

'If it was only a small bump, why did Ruby call the police?'

'Ian said she was hysterical. Apparently, she got straight out of the car and rang them. There was no stopping her.'

'I see, and was the accident in the paper?'

'Oh, yes. It was on the second page, picture of where it had happened, and a picture of Ian. He was very upset, and I can't blame him. Anyway, that's all in the past, isn't it?'

'Of course. I think we all want to move on after everything that's happened. Although it's hard, isn't it? Memories of that last evening with Ruby keep flashing through my head. I keep going over and over it.'

'I can understand that it must have been very traumatic for you. I think about it, you know, how I was just sat there watching TV, Ian was up there swimming with Richie, all completely unaware of what was happening.'

'It's late for Ian and Richie to be swimming, isn't it? I'd not thought about it before, but why do they go so late?'

'Ian loved night swimming and I think Richie liked to go once Ruby had gone off to her charity work. Ian is usually back about twelve. They swim for about two hours. Do you fancy joining them? I'm sure Ian wouldn't mind.'

Nia laughed. 'It crossed my mind, but that's a bit late for me.'

Lucy smiled. 'Well, you just need to ask. I'm sorry you've had such a difficult time here. It's normally such a quiet, friendly place.'

'I can see that; I think it's lovely you all get together on a Sunday at Wight's. Joe has got a great business there, hasn't he?'

'He has, but you must try out other places to eat and drink. The island has really come on gastronomically in the last few years. We even have Michelin-starred restaurants now.'

Nia felt Lucy relax, and soon they were chatting easily about the kind of food they enjoyed. It was while Lucy was describing a particularly lavish meal at an Indian restaurant that the salon phone rang. Jade, who was in the middle of applying tints, looked up and went to remove her gloves.

'I can take it,' said Nia, and excused herself from Lucy.

The call was an electrician checking he had the correct address for work he would be carrying out the following day on Jade's property.

'Is it thirteen or thirty Haven Way in Cowes?' he asked, and Nia went to ask Jade.

'Oh, sorry, that's my place in Cowes. It's thirteen, one three.'

Nia told the electrician, hung up the phone and returned to Lucy.

When she had finished Lucy's hair Nia was rewarded with a beaming smile.

'That's very good. Yes, perfect,' said Lucy. She put her sunglasses back on, removed the gown, straightened her scarf, made an appointment for full colour the next time and left clearly happy with her hair. Nia was pleased: she'd obviously passed the test.

As she watched Lucy leave she wondered if she'd learned anything new from her. Lucy had certainly been very defensive about Ian's accident, but it was interesting to hear there had been an account in the paper; she would have to see if she could find it. Also, she'd learned Ruby had taken photos; it would be good to try and track them down. There had to be more to learn about the accident, but she couldn't imagine what.

At the end of the afternoon Jade and Nia were clearing up and chatting.

'How did you find it, then?'

'You know, I really enjoyed it. It made me feel... I don't know. Normal.'

Jade laughed. 'What a weird thing to say. You seem the most normal person I know.'

'Thank you.'

'I was aware of throwing you in the deep end with her. If anyone was going to complain it would be Lucy. You did a brilliant job; you cut very well.'

'Cutting is my favourite thing. My strength, I think.'

'So, have you been invited to Elvira's hen party on Saturday?'

'Yes, I was thinking about going. Do you know any details, though? I wouldn't want to be going into town clubbing. I think I'm past all that.'

'As far as I know it's just drinks at Wight's and then back to the flat, very low-key. She has some friends coming over from the mainland.'

'That sounds tame enough. I can always go home if I need to escape.'

'I'm glad you'll be there; it'll be good to see a fellow islander. By the way, I've not forgotten I said I'd ring the police. I shall do it later, after we've finished here.'

Nia was pleased at the idea of being called an islander. Although far from accurate, it did make her feel accepted.

After promising to work the following afternoon, Nia returned home, where Romeo was ready to greet her. She took off her shoes and flopped down onto the sofa. 'Gosh, I'm out of practice,' she said to him. 'I'm completely done in after half a day.' She picked a stray hair off her top. 'First I need to change. I'd forgotten about all the hair.'

After she'd showered, she decided she should ring Safi. Knowing Chris had told her about Ruby, she was expecting a lot of questions. However, there was no possible way she could have anticipated the conversation she was about to have, or the revelations Safi was to make.

16

The conversation with Safi had started much as Nia expected and it wasn't long before Safi was asking her about Ruby.

'Dad tells me you found a dead body on the beach. I can't believe you've gone to some tiny little island cut off from everything and this has happened to you.'

'It was all very sad actually.'

'Yes, Dad said you'd spoken to her, knew her a bit.'

'The night before she died, we had a long talk, I may have been the last person to speak to her.'

'Oh, Mum, that is sad, Dad didn't say. What happened?'

Safi seemed to have an endless list of questions. In fact, Nia started to wonder about the level of her concern.

'You are not to worry about this,' she said. 'It's tragic, but, you know, these things happen. The police are being very thorough.'

'I know, but I do worry. You shouldn't be going down there on your own.'

'I am careful, love. It's a very small beach and easy to get off if I see anyone I don't like the look of. It's very quiet here at night.'

'Good. Dad said you'd been worried about some kind of muddle with the candles, that the one the next day was a different colour from the one the night before?'

'Yes, I'm just not sure. You know how tired I've been.' She gave a hard laugh. 'I felt I was going mad at times, getting things wrong, making mistakes.'

Safi didn't smile. 'Did you really think that? Is it the reason you gave up your job? I never understood – you loved it so much.'

'It is. I didn't want to worry you. It's not like there was anything physically wrong with me. I thought maybe I was just tired.'

'Do you feel better now?'

'A bit, yes, thank you, but I'm still confused, I have to admit. It's made it difficult for me to trust myself...' she paused '... but, I'm sorry, you don't need to worry about any of this.'

'But I do, Mum, and I've been wondering if there was something I should have told you. I've been trying to hold back but, I don't know, it might be better if you knew. At least you'd know you'd not been imagining everything.'

Nia frowned. 'What are you talking about? You know you can tell me anything.'

'Well, I remember how upset you were when we came back from our weekend in London.'

Nia glanced at Safi; she'd not realised she'd picked up on any of that.

'I could hear things, Mum. I heard what you both said. You were convinced, weren't you, that someone had been there while we were away – you said the duvet had been changed and things moved in the kitchen. Dad said you were imagining things and you got very upset.'

Nia went cold. Safi had heard everything.

'The thing is,' said Safi, clearly picking her words carefully, 'I know Dad was lying.'

Nia could feel her heart miss a beat, her chest felt on fire. 'How could you know that?'

'Because I asked Colin down the road if he'd seen Miss Grey's car at ours and he had. It had been left opposite our house overnight.

Everyone knows her car, it's a stupid bright red thing with a butterfly on the side. The thing is, Mum, I'd already been told by people in school Dad and Miss Grey were having an affair. When I heard you two arguing, I guessed he was lying, and I hated hearing you so confused.'

'How long had you known about Dad and Miss Grey?'

'Back at Christmas time, remember he had that new watch? I was shocked that the kids had given Dad something as posh as that and I asked someone who was still doing drama at school if they'd given the present to Dad. She said no way and then told me the story that was going around...'

'And that was?'

'Well, this girl saw Dad and Miss Grey in the room at the back of the hall after school, just before they broke up for Christmas. They'd gone in to look for a jumper they'd lost, everyone else had gone home. They saw Dad and Miss Grey open a posh red box together and there were two watches, they had one each, and then, well, then they kissed.'

Nia was shaking. 'Are you sure? How could they have seen all this without being noticed?'

'You know how it is in the hall. If you stand on the stage, you can look through a window at the back and into the room. This person heard voices and peeked in. And, well – kept watching. Apparently, rumours had been going around about Dad and Miss Grey for weeks.'

Nia clutched her stomach. So she'd been right, and Safi had known all this time.

'Why on earth didn't you say something, love?'

'I didn't want to. I kept waiting for it to blow over. I didn't want you to split up.' To Nia's horror Safi began to cry. 'You won't tell Dad I told you, will you?' she pleaded. 'I've not said anything to him but I'm sure it was nothing, just a fling.'

Nia was stunned. Chris had been lying all this time.

Nia took a deep breath. 'Lovely, this is not your problem, and I won't tell Dad you told me anything. Thank you for being honest with me. I really needed to know this.'

'What are you going to do? Please don't leave him, Mum.'

'I need time to think, but you are not to worry, and I will not mention you when I do get around to talking to him about it.'

They finished the call; Nia sat there, shocked, and then the tears began to fall. She hugged a cushion, rocked herself as she felt her heart slowly break, shards of glass tearing it apart. She'd been right but there was no comfort in that. Chris had been and was still having an affair. There was 'another woman' who he shared his life with, slept with, loved maybe even more than Nia. He certainly was more honest with her because for months now he had been lying to Nia. And more than that, he'd let her think she was going mad, he'd encouraged her to go to the doctor, give up a job she loved – how could he have treated her like that? Nia remembered Ruby's words: 'finding out someone you trusted with your soul has betrayed you just kills you'. She was right – at that moment Nia's world collapsed and all sense of who she was shattered into a million pieces.

Nia eventually forced herself to get up from the sofa and let Romeo out into the garden. She stood numbly watching him sniffing around, but as she breathed in it was as if she'd lost all her senses. There was no smell, no touch, no light, only darkness.

Eventually they went back inside and went upstairs. Nia closed the curtains tight and climbed onto her bed, too exhausted to get undressed. Instead she curled up tight in a ball and cuddled her pillow. Romeo, despite never before having been allowed on her bed, curled up next to her and, exhausted, she fell asleep.

* * *

Nia woke bleary-eyed, her head thumping, the next morning. She was surprised to find she'd slept at all, but it had helped, and she sat up and saw the light creeping around the edges of the curtains, trying to make its way in.

Despite the shattering events of the night before, the sun had risen on a new day. Romeo looked up at her and she stroked his head. 'We've another day before us,' she said to him, 'but it's not the same now, is it? Nothing is going to ever be the same again.'

She got up, showered, and dressed. A text came from Chris hoping she had a good day. There were so many things she wanted to say back, but she also wanted to keep her promise to Safi. In the end she simply replied in a similar manner and left it at that. After she sent it, she was quite relieved. If she spoke to Chris, she knew he would simply try to deny everything, even find a way of explaining things away. She was too vulnerable for that; she wanted it to be true too much. No, it was better to wait.

She had a few friends back in Cardiff who she could talk to, but she didn't really feel like talking to anyone yet. The hurt, the betrayal, were so deep that she didn't quite have the words to talk about it. Sadly, the only person she could have imagined talking to was Ruby, and of course that was not possible any more.

Realising she had the morning to herself, Nia decided to take Romeo over to Compton. As she climbed down the steps she noticed a few more dog walkers in the direction she was heading. 'It's getting busier here,' she said to Romeo, but at the same time realised that, compared to many beaches, it was practically deserted.

Romeo was very confident now and they both headed down the beach to the sea. The vista before her seemed endless and stunningly beautiful with the sun shining on the white cliffs to her right. The sea glinted invitingly, although she assumed it would be really cold once in. However, she thought of Jade swimming and was tempted to ask her about joining her.

Nia looked out to sea, felt the fingers of the breeze on her cheeks as nature reached out to her as if recognising her pain and wanting to soothe her. Slowly she started to whisper to the sea questions she dare not say out loud; once she started the list of agonising questions seemed endless. How did he feel when he was kissing her? Does he love her more than me? Does he ever feel guilty? Why hasn't he left me yet? Why is he pretending? Why let me think I was going mad? Who else knows? Why didn't anyone tell me?

She walked along the shore with Romeo, and slowly the questions ebbed away. Soon she would ask Chris some of those things, soon the whole thing would have to be faced. However, the one thing she did have was time. Time to think, time to adjust, and in a way being in a position where Chris had no idea what she knew made her feel stronger. For the first time in this whole mess, she was in control.

Nia returned to the close, calmer, resolved to get on with her life here for now. She changed for work and went to the salon, and actually enjoyed the distraction the clients provided. At the end of the afternoon, she was close to telling Jade about what had happened, but somehow she wanted to leave it outside her world in here.

The next day was Saturday, that evening would be Elvira's hen party. Part of Nia felt she should be cancelling everything, but, on the other hand, sitting in the house would do her no good either.

She decided to go into town and buy some work clothes. However, before she left a postcard arrive from Safi. The card had clearly been posted before their phone call. As they both loved paintings, Safi had been sending her beautiful postcards from all the museums she visited, but this was the first card to come here.

The picture was of two women in Victorian white dresses standing by the shore. The painter had captured the warmth of the sun shining on the women. It was magical.

Nia turned the card and read her daughter's message.

I love this – hint for my birthday! All fine, still have enough money!
Eating loads of pasta – put on loads of weight! Loads of Love, Safi xx

It was the work of a Spanish painter, Joaquín Sorolla. A few years ago, they had managed to buy an original work of an up-and-coming Welsh painter for Safi online. Nia looked again at the postcard. If only she could afford this kind of work for Safi, but she'd have to settle for a print. Nia showed the picture to Romeo. 'I don't think you and I look quite that serene on Yarmouth beach, do you?' she said, laughing. The card reminded her that she still hadn't visited Richie's gallery, and she decided that she must visit soon.

She propped the card up on the shelf, left the house and drove into Newport. There was a fair range of shops still, although, like many town centres, there was a large number of mobile phone and charity shops. However, she did manage to find the casual shoes, and even bought some slightly comfier trousers – 'mom jeans', as Safi called them. They were the kind of clothes Chris would hate but she certainly didn't care about that today. She also remembered to buy a swimming costume. She had no idea if she would use it but maybe she'd go one morning with Jade.

Nia enjoyed walking around the town. She went into the art centre for coffee, walked along the river a short way, saw the court buildings and the town hall. It was as she was exploring a side street that she spotted Elvira.

Nia would have called out but there was something in Elvira's manner that stopped her. Without looking around, Elvira dived into a small shop. Curious, Nia walked towards the shop and saw it was a kind of pawn shop. Nia walked quickly away. It was getting late and so she decided to head back to Yarmouth.

Before going into the house, however, she decided this might be as good a time as any to visit Richie's gallery. She walked up the road, imagining walking around looking at a few pictures, maybe chatting to Richie to find out a bit more about him. What she'd not anticipated was that the discovery she was about to make would be pivotal to her investigation into Ruby's death.

17

Nia pushed open the door and there was a white wall facing her. She turned a sharp left to walk along a fairly narrow, short corridor between the wall and the shop window and, before entering the main gallery, she passed a door with a wooden sign that said, 'Ruby's Office'. The gallery was a large, airy room; the light flooded in from the large shop window. Towards the back of the room a long high counter divided the gallery from where Richie was working. He had positioned his easel next to a large window at the back of the room looking over the garden. She was the only one in there, and as Richie was working with his back to the room, headset on, he didn't notice her.

She glanced back at the office door. Ruby had sat in there writing that letter, saying she couldn't go on. Nia wondered what it was like in there now. Had Richie cleared it out, or had he felt unable to go in? She imagined it would be very painful. She was curious however about that room, wondered if some clue might be left behind about Ruby's state of mind the day she died.

Walking quietly across the room, she returned to the office door and pushed down the handle. The door opened easily.

It was very dark, and Nia felt around for the light switch; there were no windows in the room. It was larger than she expected and very tidy;

she guessed Richie had not been in here yet. On the desk were a laptop and printer. The police must have worked on them in situ as they were still set up. There were photos on the wall of Richie and Ruby, as well as information and magazines from various charities Ruby supported, a wall calendar showing Ruby's plans for the year, mainly highlighting scheduled volunteering times at the helpline but also fundraising events. At the end of the desk stood a rather sad plant badly in need of watering.

Nia suddenly realised how easy it had been to come in completely unnoticed. It dawned on her that if she had done it, so could anyone else who knew about this room.

Checking nervously over her shoulder, even though no one could see her, Nia switched on the laptop and printer. No password was needed, and she was able to open a blank Word document easily. She quickly typed a few random words and pressed print. A piece of A4 paper slid from the printer. She picked it up, folded it, shoved it in her pocket. Without planning, she realised, she had made an important discovery. If the office had been vacant, anyone could have come in here that Sunday afternoon, typed and printed off the letter the police had found on the beach. Of course, at five on a Sunday the gallery would have officially been closed, but anyone who knew the set-up, anyone in the close, knew the front door was open and that the office was never locked.

But what did that really mean? Jade didn't believe Ruby had taken her own life and if someone else had written the letter, it would mean she was right. However, why would someone want to do that? Nia shook her head; she needed to speak to Jade.

She left the office and went back into the gallery. Her heart was racing, but Richie was still painting, completely oblivious to her.

Nia walked around the gallery in a daze as she thought about her discovery. She needed to tell the police, or maybe they already realised this; maybe she would check with Jade. As she looked around she spotted a small collection of Lucy's collages displayed with some of Richie's wood carvings, on a stand covered in blue silk.

The bulk of the wall space was, of course, occupied by Richie's seascapes, which she soon realised were all of beaches on the island. Nia found them fascinating, each one very different. Richie captured the sea in all weathers, all times of day and night. Nia, who knew little about art, sensed they were very skilfully painted. In a rack at the side were small prints of some of them and she decided to buy one.

Nia picked out one of stormy seas in which Richie had caught the enormous waves the second before they broke, the jaws of a monster waiting to consume its prey. The colour of the waves graduated from the white foamy peaks to the deep, threatening undercurrent and behind them the sea stretched in dark blues and blacks. It wasn't pretty; it was unsettling, but there was something about it that made it difficult to put down.

Nia went to pay at the counter where there was a small notice that said, 'Ring the bell hard or shout to get my attention.' She rang the bell and eventually Richie answered. He looked pale and tired; a weak smile greeted her.

'Could I buy a print?'

He blinked. 'Of course.'

'Your paintings are wonderful.'

'Thank you.' His voice was flat and his eyes dull as they scanned the walls.

'It must be hard being back at work,' she said gently.

'It's not too demanding churning these out.' He waved at the paintings.

'They don't look churned out. They're lovely. I know Ruby was very proud of your work.'

'Yes, she was. Her taste was similar to my father's, as you heard – she liked a picture you could hang on your wall.'

'You sound frustrated. Don't you enjoy painting these pictures?'

'It's OK. I'm know how fortunate I am. Because of my father's help I have this beautiful gallery and I am making a tidy business here. Not many artists can do that, and I don't despise all the work I do here. The print you are holding is of the beach here. I remember taking loads of photographs on a stormy evening and coming back, working hard while it was all still there in my head... yes, that one is one of the better ones. You have good taste. Ruby liked the quiet ones painted on sunny days, the ones I can paint in my sleep.'

'I shall treasure it, thank you.'

Nia left the gallery and walked down the street. She could see Jade in the salon, sweeping the floor. There was no client in there at that moment and she went in.

'Can I talk to you, just quickly?' she asked Jade. Nia told her what had happened in the gallery.

Jade's eyes widened. 'That was very daring. I can't imagine you doing that.'

'I know, it's not like me at all. I was just curious to see if it could be done. That letter is so important, it has taken precedence over everything. Any idea of anyone else going down the beach has been cancelled out by it, and all the facts made to fit around this one thing. Ruby must have taken her own life because she wrote the letter.'

Jade nodded. 'You're right, but if she didn't write the letter, I'm right in my belief she didn't kill herself...' she looked up, her mouth open '... but if she didn't kill herself, and someone else faked this letter, well, surely that means...' She paused, and Nia held her breath. They looked at each other, neither daring to say the words they had been skirting around for days.

'The obvious reason for someone to fake a suicide letter is to cover up the fact they killed Ruby,' said Nia.

Jade slumped into a chair. 'I know I've never believed that Ruby took her own life but I'd always thought it was an accident. I realised someone had probably been down with Ruby after you, but I'd not seriously thought they'd wanted to hurt her. I'd assumed they'd simply sat with Ruby, maybe not even realised she'd overdosed and left her with no idea that she was in danger. When Ruby was found dead I guessed they'd been too scared or cowardly to admit to being down there. However, like you say, if they took down a fake letter, then surely there has to be more to it than that. Did someone really plan to kill my sister?'

Nia sat down. She felt sick; it was too much to take in.

Jade seemed to read her mind, tapped her knee comfortingly. 'I know, it's scary, isn't it? I never got around to ringing the police last night. I keep putting it off. I don't like to look like I am fussing but they should know this. I'll phone them before the party tonight, OK?'

Nia stood up; her lips were trembling. If she tried to speak, she knew she would cry.

'Hey, are you OK? You looked very pale yesterday afternoon at work – is this all too much for you?'

Nia shook her head. 'It's not just the shock of what happened to Ruby. Something happened with my husband. It's complicated. I don't want to talk about it, but I will have to sort it out.'

'That's OK. Listen, I'd sussed out something must be wrong. Any time you want to talk...'

'Thank you.'

Nia left Jade; it was a relief to have told her about the letter.

Maybe it would be good to get out that evening, let her hair down and forget everything.

* * *

Nia spoke to a police officer; he took note of what she told him and told her someone would get back.

She spent a lot of time on her make-up and wore one of her body-con dresses, high heels, her hair of course tied back, and large hooped earrings. As she was checking how she looked in the mirror she received a visit from Jade.

She was dressed in her usual clothes, the only concession to the party being lash extensions and a slightly tighter cropped top. However, she looked serious and not in any other way ready to party.

They went and sat down.

'Tell me what happened,' said Nia.

'I rang the police, talked to that officer, Ben.'

'Oh, right, what did he say?'

'I started by telling him that I was finding it very difficult to accept that Ruby had taken her own life. I told him I knew my sister and it was just not something she would have done. He was very conciliatory and said he could understand why this was so difficult for me. He suggested I talked to a therapist explaining what a traumatic experience this was being for me.' Jade paused. 'I tried to tell him that it was more than just a gut reaction. There were other things that needed to be considered. I then told him Ruby always used red wax and he interrupted me then and asked me if I've been talking to you about the candle.'

'Oh dear.'

'I was getting fed up with him by this point and said actually I'd come to my own conclusion about this and what you told me made perfect sense. He went on again about not being able to see colours clearly in the dark on the beach, but I reminded him about the ring, and he had to admit they still haven't found that. Then we moved on to the letter. I told him about your experiment at the gallery and this is when his mood changed a bit.' Jade cringed. 'He didn't like that and said we should not be interfering, that we should be leaving the investigation to the police.'

'I suppose he was bound to say that. But tell me, had they realised that anybody could have been in that office and faked the letter?'

Jade sighed. 'Ben told me they had been through every eventuality, but they had to concern themselves with facts and he went through it all again about Ruby having taken drugs before and that she'd been very unhappy. He pointed out there was no evidence of anyone else going down on the beach. They had interviewed people, and no one had seen or heard anything. Also, they had extensively interviewed everyone in the close and no one had an apparent motive to want to hurt Ruby. Indeed most people weren't even in the close when it happened.'

'And the voodoo doll? Did you say you didn't think Ruby had sent that to herself?'

'I did, but again he said there was no evidence of anybody sending it to her. He basically told me the case they would be putting forward to the coroner was that it was an accidental or deliberate overdose. He calmed down a bit then and told me it was very natural to be looking for answers, but the best thing I could do for myself, and Richie, was to try and accept what had happened.'

Nia saw the despair and exhaustion on Jade's face and for the first time she wondered if it would be better for Jade if they accepted what the police were saying. After all, they could dig around, upset a lot of people and still not prove anyone else had been involved in Ruby's death. Indeed they might discover the police had been right all along.

'I am wondering, Jade, if this might be a good time for us to drop this. Nothing is going to bring Ruby back; we could be wrong—'

'No, no way,' said Jade.

'Jade, this is your home, you could lose friends, it could even threaten your business.'

'But if we stop now, I will still have all these questions in my head. I can understand if you've had enough and want to go, but I have to carry on.'

Nia saw the determination on Jade's face. 'Then I shall stay and help you. I told you before why I wanted to keep digging, I just didn't want to force you into something you might come to regret.'

Jade smiled and reached across, holding out her hand. 'It's agreed, then, we fight on. Everyone in the close is a suspect and, I guess we are saying, one of them faked the letter and went to the beach after you left. What we are really saying is that it is possible that someone in the close killed Ruby.'

Nia took a deep breath. 'I agree. As to means, well, it seems to me that there could be a way for anyone to get hold of this ketamine if they were determined to do it. If nothing else, they know they could find someone on the island selling it. We need to keep digging around for motive and also check if everyone was where they say they were the night Ruby died. If we are right, someone from the close has to be lying.'

She looked over at Jade. 'But one thing, Jade. I am still worried about you and your place here. I think I should be questioning people more than you. Let them think of me as some interfering woman, but you have to be careful. In any case, I have a bit more time on my hands than you to go running around.'

Jade smiled. 'Fair enough.' She stood up. 'Right, then. Maybe we can make a start tonight. Let's go to this damn hen party.'

18

Nia and Jade arrived at the hen party to find a small group of women sitting at a table. Nia was surprised to see Lucy had joined the group and was sitting next to Elvira. There were only two other women, who looked like fair-haired versions of Elvira in expensive preppy clothes. This really was a very small affair and Nia immediately felt over-dressed. Spotting her, Elvira called her over and poured her a drink.

Elvira broke the ice by announcing, 'Thank you so much for all coming to my hen party.'

One of the friends, called Petunia, raised her glass. 'I have to say this is rather different from when we drank champagne in Florence for your engagement to Hugo.' She glanced at Nia. 'Hugo was Elvira's ex.' And then over at Jade. 'No offence, but the island is hardly the place for a proper night out.'

Jade raised her glass and smiled thinly. 'Offence taken,' and she gave a cold laugh.

Elvira coughed. 'Anyway, with everything being done so quickly, and weddings to pay for, you will have to make the most of this evening. It's all I had the time and budget to arrange.'

Petunia grabbed her hand. 'Where's the ring? I demand to see it!'

'I took it to a jeweller this morning. He's very good, has done work for the royals, you know. He's going to make it smaller for me,' Elvira said, blushing. Nia frowned. The place she'd seen Elvira going in that morning certainly didn't fit that description. Maybe Elvira had been to more than one place.

Petunia's voice threatened to drown the others as she gave a detailed account of the last hen night she'd been to, in Barcelona. Nia was sitting next to the other friend, a quieter woman called Millie.

'So, Elvira has been engaged before?'

Millie flicked back her fair hair. 'Rather. All very intense.'

'And who was that to?'

'Really nice chap called Hugo. We all love him, such a laugh, we were all so jealous when she nabbed him. Tragic it didn't work out.'

'What happened?'

Millie moved closer, lowering her voice. 'Elvira suddenly broke it off, no explanation. They'd named the date and everything. Still, he bounced back in the way Hugo always does – still on the market actually. Anyway, Elvira moved over here, which shocked us all. I know her mother is here, but, really, fancy burying herself over here. I usually come over once a year for Cowes week but that's my limit.'

'I've not been here long but I think it's lovely. The beaches are gorgeous. I went to Newtown Creek the other day, which was stunning, and we were the only ones there.'

Nia began describing her visit but soon realised Millie's eyes had glazed over. She paused and a gap in conversation seemed to alert Millie that a response was called for. 'Oh, yeah, sounds great, super. I have to admit Elvira seems to have found herself a decent man here. That's quite something.'

'Ethan?'

'Exactly, only seen pics of him so far but he's good-looking, although a bit rough. A kind of Heathcliff look, I guess. Elvira will get his clothes sorted out.'

Nia sipped her drink. 'This ex of Elvira's – Hugo – was he a vet?'

Millie laughed hard. 'God, no, you'd never find him putting his arm up a cow's arse. Hugo likes the finer things, though no one knows quite how he pays for them. Not like he has rich parents or anything. He's worked a few auction houses, dabbled in bitcoins. He's a survivor, is Hugo, not always keeping this side of the law, but gets away with it.' She took out her phone. 'Here's a picture of us all together two years ago, sailing.'

Nia scanned the photo, and then she saw him, Hugo: tall, fair, with sunglasses, sky-blue shirt and white trousers. She gasped; she instantly knew where she'd seen him before.

Hugo was the man Nia had seen arriving at the Red Jet terminal and on the morning of Ethan and Elvira's Sunday drinks at Wight's.

'Oh, goodness, I recognise him. So that's Elvira's ex?' she exclaimed. 'I've seen him over here a few times. Does he work here?'

Millie shook her head. 'Not that I know of, but he has friends who sail. Maybe he was meeting up with them. So, tell me, what is this Ethan like? Elvira tells us next to nothing.'

'He's quite a lot older than Elvira's ex, Hugo. He's very kind, clever. He seems a nice person, loves Elvira—'

'Sounds a bit lame – still, if he's got money...'

Nia was starting to get fed up with her companion. 'You don't marry someone just for money. Ethan is a good man, caring and very good at his job. As an intelligent woman herself, I am sure Elvira appreciates that.'

Millie raised an eyebrow. 'I'll take your word for it. She's changed a fair bit if you're right, though.'

Petunia raised her voice even more and called them all to attention.

'I have to say a few words about my gorgeous friend, Elvira Johnson. A month today Elvira will be getting married. I can't wait and I want to wish Elvira all the best. We go way back.' Petunia embarked on a string of long rambling stories of various drunken nights out in London and Nia switched off. Finally, she sensed the speech coming to an end. 'And so, we all want to say good luck and make sure we're all invited to the baby shower.'

As they were such a small group, the applause was muted, but Elvira then invited them back to hers to celebrate more. Having not been inside the building, Nia was intrigued to see the flat. Everything was in darkness, and Elvira quickly turned off the alarm before the rest of them entered. Once they were inside, she pressed a few more buttons. 'Sorry. This is so much more complicated than the other one.'

'Ethan said you'd tightened security.'

'Yes, I insisted when I came here. There are so many break-ins on the mainland.'

'There was one in your last place, wasn't there?' said Petunia. Before she could answer Jade dashed over to look at a stand with pet toys. 'Oh, these are new. I may come in and get some of these for the animals at the centre.'

Jade enthused about the toys and started pressing the squeaky ones, the sound echoing around the empty reception area.

'It's as well Ethan has decamped to the other surgery this evening,' said Elvira to the others. 'They've a few patients in and so he offered to be on call there. He doesn't mind doing the occasional Saturday night. It's only Sunday he insists on keeping free. That's his night at the rescue centre. He stays there till the early hours if necessary.'

'I bet he's avoiding meeting me, doesn't want the interrogation,' said Petunia. Nia wouldn't have been surprised if she was right.

Elvira still had her own flat and it was clear Ethan and she hadn't yet merged their living quarters.

'With us working different shifts and things it seemed sensible to keep open the option of separate bedrooms,' explained Elvira.

Her flat consisted of a small living area and bedroom. There was a shared kitchen.

Elvira had prepared snacks and drinks, and after a few more drinks Elvira handed over to Petunia, who had prepared suitable hen-night games, including Bridal Bingo, and Never Have I Ever. Nia had to admit Petunia did a good job of getting everyone to join in, and they all started to relax.

Finally, Elvira suggested they go on a gambling site she'd heard of called Lady's Night, and gave each of her guests a small pot of money to get them started.

'Ethan's tips are to avoid alcohol,' Elvira said, laughing as she filled up her glass, 'and never chase your losses.'

Nia was nervous, frightened the others were going to start placing high stakes. One of the things that surprised Nia was the content: a lot of the games featured Barbie, pink fairies, and cute cartoon animals.

Nia started to relax; it was just a bit of fun. She placed her bets, not caring really which way things went. However, she soon realised she was the one pushing for another game, placing more money than she intended.

The person who surprised her was Lucy. She'd not had any more idea of the rules of these games than Nia, but she quickly picked them up and played skilfully. It was a side of Lucy Nia hadn't seen before. Behind that nervous, vulnerable exterior was a bright, determined woman.

It was Elvira who decided when she was going to shut down. Nia would have liked to have carried on, play one more game to win her money back.

'You have to know when to stop,' Elvira said to her firmly and closed down the site. It was as if a spell had been broken and Nia was shocked at how easily she'd been hypnotised by the games. Maybe she'd better not rush into that again.

'How are you getting on with those party favours? Did you have enough silk?' asked Lucy.

'Thanks, there's more than enough, although I've bought some other colours as well. They're all cut out now, spread on a table in my bedroom,' said Elvira. They followed her in and saw a production line of cut-out pieces of silk ribbon and net.

'What will you put in them?' asked Lucy.

'Richie has been helping me collect things off the beach, shells and fossils. I'll put some in each bag. It's greener than a load of plastic.'

'That's really tasteful,' said Petunia, surprise in her voice. 'You've changed since you came here.'

Nia stepped back to let Jade have a look at the bags and pushed against a wardrobe door. She felt the door open and turned to close it again. To her surprise she saw the edge of a long white dress, but what really shocked her was the label.

'Shut the door,' shouted Elvira. 'Sorry, it's just you mustn't see my dress.' She shut the door firmly.

'I thought that was still being made,' said Jade.

'The seamstress finished earlier than expected,' said Elvira. 'Now, let's get out of here. Too many secrets in my bedroom,' she added, laughing.

Everyone, apart from Lucy, who Nia noted stuck to soft drinks, continued drinking. Elvira lit white candles and they sat in the flickering light talking.

'How is your mum doing, Elvira? She's still at that nursing home?'

'Yes, she likes The Pines. They're kind, and the food is good, which matters to her.'

'I must go and have a look at it sometime. Dad is going to need somewhere soon, and he loved the island. Is it out over Brook way?'

'That's right, not far from the pub we went to last time you came over.'

Petunia turned to Jade. 'I'm so sorry to hear about your sister Ruby. I met her a few times, such a sweet person. Can you believe she died on my birthday?'

Nia was horrified by her tactlessness, but Petunia carried on regardless. 'We were all staying over in the New Forest, gorgeous little place, brilliant chef. Anyway, Hugo had been over here that day but, thank God, he made it back in time for drinks at six. I'd have been furious if he'd bailed on us. I'm glad we didn't hear about it until the next day. Hugo knew Ruby better than the rest of us. It would have ruined the evening.' Petunia then caught the look in Jade's eyes and even she seemed to realise she'd crossed a line. 'That, of course, was not important in the scheme of things. We were all mortified when Elvira rang the next day. I am so sorry she took an overdose. How terrible to feel that desperate.'

Jade glared. 'My sister didn't take her own life.'

'Petunia didn't mean that,' interrupted Elvira.

'Yes, she did. To her it's a bit of gossip to pass around, something that nearly messed up her birthday,' said Jade, her face red, her eyes bright with anger. 'In any case, I'm not convinced Ruby was alone on the beach. Nia might not have been the last person to see Ruby alive. In fact, we both think someone went down to the beach after Nia left her.'

Nia gasped; why had Jade said that? She could feel all eyes on her, all waiting for an explanation. 'I'm just worried about a few things.'

'So, you think some random stranger went down on the beach after you?' asked Petunia, making no effort to disguise the excitement in her voice.

'I could be wrong,' replied Nia.

Elvira flipped her hand dismissively. 'Of course you are, the police know what they are doing. And anyway, Ruby left a note, didn't she? She said she couldn't go on. As terrible as that is, the sad fact is Ruby took her own life. The police know it, and you need to accept it as well, Jade.'

Nia saw Jade bristle at this and throw back another drink before, glaring at Elvira, she said, 'But how can we be sure Ruby wrote that letter? Everyone in the close knew you could walk into the gallery and Ruby's office unseen. Anyone in the close could have written that.'

'In theory I guess you could be right,' said Elvira coldly. 'I do hope you are including yourself in that.'

Nia glanced over at Jade. She was sitting with her eyes wide with panic, her mouth open, but she seemed too stunned to speak.

Lucy sat up. 'That's enough. Jade, why are you suddenly throwing accusations around about people in the close? Firstly, it's ridiculous to suggest someone else wrote that letter, and secondly, you know how much we all loved Ruby. It's a terrible thing to insinuate.'

'This is all a bit heavy,' said Millie, who Nia guessed was more conciliatory than her friend. 'How about a drinking game...? How about some shots?'

Nia decided that this was her cue to get away and as she stood up she saw Lucy and Jade taking her lead.

'We'll see you at the wedding, I'm sure. Don't know if I'll get over for Old Gaffers,' shouted Petunia.

Elvira accompanied them to the front door of the surgery to let them out. They thanked her for the evening, but it was clear everyone was glad to get away.

'Bloody hell, that was some evening. Sorry to land you in it, Nia,' said Jade.

'You need to be more careful about what you say,' said Lucy.

Jade shrugged. 'I realise that, Lucy, and, look, I'm sorry if I offended you.'

They had reached their homes. 'Either of you fancy a quick swim in the morning?' asked Jade.

Nia laughed and then saw Jade's face. 'You're serious?'

'I am. Seven in the morning. I'll give you a lift.'

'Much too early for me. Goodnight, you two,' said Lucy. She'd taken her keys out of her bag but tripped up the step to the door.

Jade grabbed her arm. 'Careful, don't want Ian to think you're plastered. He won't let you out on your own again.'

Lucy looked at her, offended. 'Some of us have stuck to soft drinks all evening,' she replied, opening the door and slamming it behind her.

'Oh dear,' said Nia. 'I think she's upset.'

'Lucy is pretty thick-skinned; it'll be forgotten by tomorrow.'

'I hope so. By the way, what was this Old Gaffers that Petunia mentioned?'

'I can tell you're not a sailor,' Jade said, smiling. 'There are posters popping up all over town for it. The bunting will be up soon.'

'But what is it?'

'It's a regatta and for the people here it marks the start of summer. It's on the first weekend of June and is great fun. There wasn't one last year, so it makes this one even more exciting. They have races for a traditional type of sailing boats and there's lots happening in the town, street markets, food, juggling, marching bands, all kinds of things.'

'It sounds quite something.'

'You'll enjoy it. So, what about the swim?'

'I'll think about it,' said Nia.

'I'll look for you when I come out... if your curtains are closed, I'll know you've chickened out.'

'By the way, I saw Elvira's wedding dress in the wardrobe. The thing was... it had a label on it – it was from Oxfam.'

'You're kidding, she said she was going to some posh dressmaker. I've nothing against Oxfam, always thought it was a good idea to get your dress second-hand, but why pretend it's designer?'

'I know, I don't get it. Also, you know Elvira said she'd taken her ring into a jewellers? I saw her go into a pawn shop this morning.'

'My God. What's going on? I bet Ethan doesn't know.'

Nia was starting to feel guilty. 'Look, don't say anything to anyone. I probably shouldn't have told you. Maybe they are having money problems or something.'

'I guess they are. Whatever is up, I wouldn't mind betting Ruby knew something about it.'

'You think so?'

'It's possible. I was wondering, you know, why she went to see Elvira's mother. That was odd. It's not like she knew her well. Elvira was very angry about it, wasn't she?' Jade looked around. 'Anyway, need to get to bed. Early start tomorrow... don't forget. I expect you to be here at the crack of dawn, raring to go.'

Forcing a smile, Nia went in the house, let Romeo out in the garden, and poured herself a long cold glass of water. She'd actually been careful drinking and had quietly done her usual when out of alternating her glasses of wine with water. Now she was home she was relieved she shouldn't be too hung-over in the morning.

She let Romeo in and within minutes he was snoring quietly on his bed. 'Sensible dog,' she said and turned off the light. However, she lay with her eyes open, unable to stop her mind racing. She'd successfully put Chris to the back of her mind for the evening, but didn't want to get drawn back into the darkness of thinking about that now.

To prevent that, she decided to try and plan what she was going to do about looking into Ruby's death. The hand-grenade approach that

Jade used of throwing out accusations might get reaction, but it hadn't taught them much. No, she needed a more methodical approach than that. A good place to start might be to check out if people were where they actually said they were. The police would have asked everyone, but, sensing no motive, they might not have dug too deep. Where to start?

She went through what had become her list of suspects, going round the houses in the close in her head. Lucy, Ian, Joe, Ethan, Elvira and Richie. She stopped at the gallery but, of course, there was one more person and that was Jade.

Nia pulled away from the idea. Why would Jade be pushing her to investigate Ruby's death if she had anything to do with it? The answer might be that Jade had sensed Nia's concerns and known she would keep asking questions and wanted to check up on what she was doing. Nia remembered that look of panic in Jade's eyes when Elvira had turned things on her; she also remembered that Jade and Ruby had been arguing at the party and she'd never got to the bottom of that.

Nia hated the idea of suspecting Jade and decided that the first thing she would do was go to the rescue centre and check if she had been there the night Ruby died. Thinking about it, would she really have been there so late? In fact, Nia realised she could also check up on Ethan. Yes, tomorrow after drinks she would arrange to go to the rescue centre.

19

Nia was up early the next day and met Jade outside the house.

'You made it, well done. We have to walk round to the car park. Some of us don't have private parking,' Jade said, smiling.

They walked out of the close, through the deserted town and over to the car park, opposite the bus station.

'I park at this end. Ruby and I liked our cars to be under a street light.' She looked over at a small red car. 'I don't suppose that will be driven much now; Richie cycles everywhere.'

Glancing over at Richie's car, Nia remembered the phone, possibly with pictures of the accident in the glove compartment. She had no idea how to break into a car so how was she going to get to look inside?

It was a dry, still morning as they drove along the Military Road. The sea was sparkling and, from the comfort of the heated car, appeared as inviting as the Mediterranean. However, as she stepped out of the car at Compton Farm car park, Nia felt a chill that made her question why she'd come.

'I thought we'd tackle the climb down from here,' said Jade. 'It's even better swimming at this end of the beach than from Hanover Point. Just don't forget anything. I'm not popping back up here to get your towel.'

They crossed the road, walked through a field of cows until they reached the wooden steps that led down the cliff to the beach below.

'Every time I come more of the cliffs have been eroded. The National Trust work hard maintaining the steps but it's not an easy climb down. Still, it's worth it when you get to the bottom.'

Nia grabbed the wooden rail and carefully began to climb down, not made any easier by Romeo, who she kept on the lead. Occasionally she paused to take in the breathtaking views, and finally they reached the enormous expanse of empty sandy beach.

She was about to let Romeo off his lead, when Nia realised they were on part of the beach dogs were not allowed at that time of year.

'Oh no,' she exclaimed to Jade. 'I shouldn't have brought Romeo here.'

Jade looked down the empty beach. 'You're right, I'd forgotten. Look, it's very early and we're not upsetting anyone. I think we're OK for a quick visit today, but we'll make sure we go to the part dogs are allowed again next time.'

Nia let Romeo off his lead and his tail wagged frantically as he sniffed the seaweed and dug in the sand.

Jade grinned at Nia. 'Come on, you can't back out now.'

'How come you look so awake? You drank a lot more than me last night.'

'I was very restrained, I'll have you know. I watered down my drinks.' She sighed. 'Gosh, I'm getting far too sensible for my age. It's very worrying.'

They both had their swimming costumes on under their clothes and Nia was glad she didn't have too long to think about getting into the water. She quickly took off her jeans and top, put her things in a heap with Jade's and they ran down to meet the water.

Jade ran straight in, dived under and was swimming within seconds. 'You need to take the plaster approach: tear it off all in one go,' she shouted.

As the freezing water numbed her toes Nia hesitated. Romeo was close by her now and she knew he was nervous of this unfamiliar vast expanse of water.

'I'm not going far,' she reassured him, and waded in up to her waist. Fighting the desire to run back out of the sea, she leant down and managed to get her shoulders under. Slowly the sea began to work its magic and despite the cold there was comfort. Nia had read somewhere that people were hard-wired to love the sea, and for the first time she understood why. Out there was energy, life.

Jade surfed on the waves that took her closer to shore. Nia was standing but watching her constantly and she didn't stay in too long.

Despite there being no one about, Nia found herself attempting that impossible task of getting dressed while preserving her modesty on the beach. Jade eventually came out of the water and joined her and was dressed far more quickly and with less fuss.

Nia laughed. 'I don't know how it's possible but that managed to be agony and fabulous at the same time.'

'It's good for you! My mum always loved swimming in the sea. I used to come with her a lot.'

Once they were dressed, Jade produced a Thermos and they sat cuddling the small hot metal cups of steaming coffee. 'So do you think we learned anything last night?'

Nia looked at her sideways. 'You certainly stirred things up.'

Jade grinned. 'Elvira got ever so het up when I suggested someone went down to the beach after you, didn't she? She's always on edge and it seems more than just pre-wedding nerves. That business of the dress is odd, isn't it? I feel like I don't trust her any more. To be honest, I wish her and Ethan weren't getting married so quickly. I'm very fond of Ethan. I don't want him getting hurt. Ruby said she thought they were rushing things.'

'I get the feeling Ruby knew something about Elvira and was actively trying to find out more. Remember she went to see Elvira's mother – Elvira wasn't happy about that. Ethan said he thought Ruby was digging around for something.'

'Maybe she was.'

'I was learning all about her ex, Hugo, last night. It's funny, I saw him coming over to the island the day Ruby took me to the Red Jet. She didn't speak to him, but I saw she wasn't pleased to see him.'

'Ruby couldn't stand him. I think that was when her friendship with Elvira started to break up. Ruby made no secret she didn't approve of him and, to be fair, I think she was right. He's a leech, and all he cares about is making money.'

'Petunia seemed keen enough.'

'That's because she is as superficial as him. Elvira has done well to get away from that lot. She is much better off over here with Ethan.'

'I've been on a few early morning walks with him. He is a really nice man, isn't he?'

'He is, and amazing with animals. They seem to instinctively trust him.'

Nia sensed this was a good moment to ask. 'I was wondering if I could come to the rescue centre with you this evening? I'd love to see the work you do there.'

'Of course, they can always do with a hand.'

'I'll take my own car; I don't like to leave Romeo too long.'

'I was going to suggest we went separately. Ethan and I do – it means we can all leave when we want. I tend to stay very late, in fact all night sometimes if they need me.'

'Really?'

'Oh, yes.'

'Elvira said Ethan was home very late that night.'

Jade frowned. 'Yes, but he's not at the centre. He goes on to the other surgery.'

Nia frowned. 'That's odd. Elvira thinks he is at the centre with you all night.'

Jade shrugged. 'Maybe she'd not be happy with him doing more work at the surgery.'

Nia wasn't so sure but didn't comment. Instead, she said, 'What about you? How do you cope with Mondays after a late night at the centre?'

'Ruby and I agreed on shutting the salon on a Monday as she was also all night at the charity helpline.' She stood up. 'Right, I think it's time for home – bacon rolls on Sunday.'

Once they reached the steps Nia put Romeo on the lead; she didn't want him wandering onto the crumbling cliffs. The climb was steep, and she was glad to get to the top. Once there she paused and looked out at the view. It was stunning, with long stretches of the coast in front of her.

'It's fabulous here, isn't it?' she said.

'I know, we're so lucky. By the way, I've been thinking about Lucy. There is no delicate way to put this, but do you think Lucy could have a problem with drink?'

Nia blinked. 'I confess that has never crossed my mind. I've seen her stumble a few times, but I've not given it a lot of thought. Why? Do you think she has?'

'Ages ago Ian had mentioned that she'd had problems with drink in the past, but she has been dry for years now. It crossed my mind that maybe it was becoming a problem for her again.'

'But she told you herself that she'd not been drinking last night.'

'I know, but she went off to the bathroom quite a lot. I wondered if she was drinking on the sly. I noticed her stumble at her front door, and it's not the first time she's done that lately.'

'I suppose I saw her nearly fall when I went for lunch and she was a bit unsure on her feet a few times at the salon. I didn't give it a lot of thought though.'

'I could be wrong, but I have a feeling Ruby knew something. I tried to talk to her about it, but all she said was that she was very sorry for Lucy. She did hint, however, that Lucy should "come clean", as she put it, if she was going to be writing a book or going on TV to talk about healthy living in later years. It's not that she thought they shouldn't do it, but just that she should be honest – a typical Ruby stance.'

'That's interesting. I have been trying to understand Lucy's thinly veiled animosity towards Ruby, and assumed it was something to do with Ian's accident. However, it could be explained if she thought Ruby was going to expose some problem, upset her and Ian's plans. She is one of the people Ruby suggested may have sent her the voodoo doll.'

'And she has no alibi for the night Ruby died.'

Nia gasped. 'You don't think she really went down to the beach and killed Ruby just to keep her reputation?'

Jade shrugged. 'It's possible. Of course, the same motive goes for Ian.'

'But he says he was swimming with Richie.'

'That's true.'

They started to walk back to the car, and then drove back to Yarmouth, and Nia went home for a well-earned breakfast.

She was thinking about Lucy. Could Jade be right about her drinking? Her mind went back to overhearing Ian admonishing Lucy for her criticism of Ruby, and then those words as they left the beach: 'It's over.'

There was something to be uncovered there. It could be a drink problem with Lucy. However, it had been the accident Ruby talked about when she'd mentioned the lies that had so upset her. Nia knew she couldn't simply write the accident off; she had to find out more about it. Suddenly she had an idea – yes, that would be a very good place to start.

20

It took some time for Nia to find the article about the car accident, but eventually, by following references to Ian, she tracked down a brief article that had been in the local paper.

Local celebrity Ian Robson was involved in a minor accident on the main road out of Yarmouth on Saturday evening. No one was hurt, and parties involved were breathalysed and drink driving was ruled out. When asked about the incident Mr Robson said, 'I'm afraid I lost concentration for a brief moment and swerved to the other side of the road. Fortunately, no one was hurt, and there was very little damage to either vehicle. I apologised unreservedly and will pay for any repairs needed.'

The article was accompanied by a photograph of the stretch of road taken the following day.

Nia hadn't been sure what she expected to find, but this did feel a bit of an anti-climax. Maybe everyone was right, Ruby had overreacted.

That evening, Nia set off to Wight's with a sense of purpose, determined to learn anything she could about Jade's and Ethan's movements on Sunday evenings.

As Nia walked up the close, she noticed that bunting had appeared as if by magic, giving the place a festive air. The poster on the window of Wight's reminded her that this was part of the preparations for the Old Gaffers Festival the following weekend. Nia paused, looked around. All this seemed a million miles away from her life back in Cardiff. Sunday evening used to be one of the few evenings Chris, Safi and she would sit together for a family roast dinner. It had been her favourite moment of the week and they'd kept it up until Safi left on her travels. However, she now realised it had been a sham. For all his smiles, had Chris been secretly impatient for the meal to end so that he could go and speak to Sian under the pretext of working in his study? She remembered now the times he'd had to go and pick something up from school, had a phone call from a distraught teacher he'd had to go and see... Had all of those been lies to cover up a visit to Sian? Nia wiped away tears that had started to creep down her face. Chris had not just destroyed her plans for the future, he'd desecrated her most precious memories. Every precious jewel she now had to question – was it real, was it fake?

Nia took a deep breath. She wasn't strong enough to face this, not yet. If she allowed herself to think too much it would be like falling off a cliff and she had no idea if she would survive. No, for now she must lose herself in her life here.

She continued to walk to Wight's, but before she entered, she glanced at the group through the window. It was a sobering sight. They were sitting quietly, talking politely, like a family on their best behaviour. This was the first time they had met together since Ruby's death, and no one looked too sure what to do or say.

As Nia approached them Ian jumped up, clearly relieved to have something to do, and offered to buy her a drink.

Nia sat down, smiled nervously, not knowing the right thing to say. Everything she thought felt either too flippant or too poignant. Any sentence she considered seemed loaded with meaning.

Ian returned with her glass of wine and fell naturally into the role of leader, asking considered but inoffensive questions.

'I don't know how you ladies are after your night's drinking,' he started. Elvira was drinking orange juice, taking small sips and looking very pale, and gave a weak smile. Lucy, despite not drinking, gave a knowing laugh, which came out too loud and forced.

Ian now turned to Nia. 'How are you finding working at the salon, then?'

'I'm really enjoying it.' She shot a glance at Lucy. 'My first client was a delight.'

'Nia is coming with us to the rescue centre this evening,' said Jade. 'She's becoming one of us!'

'You didn't tell me about that,' said Ethan, frowning.

Jade's eyebrows shot up. 'I didn't realise I had to ask permission.'

'Of course not, it would have been good to have known, that's all.'

'OK for a swim this evening, Richie? Usual time, about ten?' Ian asked.

Richie nodded but didn't speak.

'How are you? I saw your dad visit, didn't I?' Jade asked him.

'He came but I didn't want him to stay. I'm back to painting; it keeps me sane. The police are hoping the coroner will release Ruby's body soon; we'll be able to have the funeral then.'

'That's good,' said Ian. 'A funeral will give you and all of us a sense of closure.'

'Where will the funeral be held?' Lucy asked.

'Dad wants it to be at The Hall.'

'Oh no! Not there,' interrupted Jade and added more gently, 'I know your dad is not an easy man to stand up to. Me and you will have a chat sometime, see if we can reach a compromise.'

An hour later Nia left the others in Wight's, walked Romeo before she left him again and started to follow Jade to the rescue centre.

Nia was used to turning left towards Newport when she left the town, but this evening they went right and crossed Yar Bridge, a swing bridge that opened when necessary to allow the taller yachts through.

They drove past the turning for Fort Victoria, towards Totland, and then turned down a country road that led to the rescue centre.

The place was smarter and larger than Nia expected, and she realised she was pretty nervous. She had bought Romeo from a breeder she knew and had never been inside a rescue centre in her life.

As it was late on a Sunday evening, there was no one on Reception, but Jade signed them both in. A young woman came to greet them and at that moment Ethan arrived, carrying his work bag ready to make a start on the list of animals needing his attention; he seemed familiar with a number of them.

'Come on, I'll show you around,' Jade said to Nia.

The shelter was well designed, with separate housing areas for different animals. It was clean and light, the animals obviously very well cared for.

'We have rooms down here where the visiting vets can see animals. I think Ethan is with one of the cats at the moment.'

Jade eased open a door, and she was right; Ethan was in there treating a tiny black cat, gently calming her, and Nia was struck by his patience and skill. He looked more at home here than anywhere else she'd seen. He saw them and nodded to Jade, who seemed to read his mind.

'Give me a second,' she said, and went to hold the cat while Ethan gave her an injection. They worked silently but in complete harmony.

As Jade settled the cat back down, Ethan thanked her, and a look flashed between them. Nia saw a closeness she'd not seen before. She remembered Jade's protests on the beach about Elvira not being good enough for Ethan and she wondered if jealousy played any part in this.

They walked past a few rabbits, guinea pigs and birds until they reached the dogs. As soon as they entered a few started barking for attention.

Nia's task was to walk individual dogs on a lead around an outside area that had lighting and she enjoyed it. She had to admit some walked a lot more politely than Romeo, but she felt very sorry for the nervous ones who'd clearly had little experience of walks and the outside world.

As she was walking, she met another volunteer and introduced herself.

'It's good to meet you,' said the older man. 'Jade is one of our best volunteers. She even sleeps here sometimes if a dog is particularly stressed out. She's amazing. She never misses a Sunday, even through the terrible loss of her sister, she's always here.'

'Maybe the animals are a kind of comfort.'

'You could be right; I've always said we get back double what we give the animals here and we are a close team. Jade was here when she heard the news about her sister. She'd been up most of the night with this poor dog who'd come in that day. She took him into our lounge and cuddled him all night.'

'When did she hear the news about Ruby?'

'The police called her on her mobile. The day shift was coming on, took over with the dog; he was so much better after a night with Jade. I'd kept popping in with a cuppa for her. She'd hardly slept.'

As Nia listened she realised that at least she could be sure Jade had an alibi for the night her sister died.

After walking the dogs who needed it, Nia was ready to leave. Jade thanked her, and Nia promised to come again.

As she left, she saw Ethan getting into his car. Nia was aware he'd given two different accounts of his Sunday evening. Elvira thought he was staying late at the rescue centre, Jade thought he went on to the other surgery.

Well, it appeared he didn't stay here that late – maybe she should just follow him and check he was going on to the surgery. Nia hesitated; she'd never followed someone covertly before. However, she reminded herself that Ethan did not know her car that well – in fact, she wasn't sure he'd ever seen it. If she kept her distance, hopefully he would not be able to make out her face.

She waited until Ethan had arrived at the exit to the car park, saw him indicate left and then started her engine. She followed him down to the junction, and then she saw him signal left. That was not the way to Yarmouth or to the other surgery, so where was he going? Nia was not used to driving at nights on country roads and she found the blackness that surrounded her, the total dependence on her headlights to show a few feet in front, unnerving. It did however make following Ethan easier as the road was long and pretty straight, and she could see his rear lights ahead.

They reached street lights on the outskirts of Totland, and Nia saw Ethan was slowing down as he approached a hotel called Cliffs. He indicated to enter, but Nia pulled in and parked on the street to avoid being seen. Once out of her car she walked quickly to the hotel and was just in time to catch sight of Ethan emerging from what she assumed was a car park to the rear. She hid in a secluded spot and watched Ethan enter the hotel.

What on earth was he doing here? She desperately wanted to follow him but what excuse could she give for going into the hotel?

21

Nia pulled her coat more tightly around her, walked quickly to the front door, thinking all the time, and finally took a deep breath and went in.

The interior of the hotel was smart although rather old-fashioned with flocked red and gold wallpaper and red velvet chairs. She caught sight of Ethan entering a room at the further end of the lobby and closing the door firmly behind him.

Nia was wondering what to do next when she heard a gentle cough behind her. She swung round to see a receptionist behind the desk.

'Can I help you?'

Nia's mind was racing; what was her excuse for being here? 'Um, I was wondering if you have a pamphlet with details about your hotel. I have elderly relatives coming over for a holiday.' The words tumbled out, but she was pretty pleased with her improvisation.

'Of course.' The receptionist took a pamphlet from a smart wooden stand on the desk, but she did look rather puzzled. 'Most people look us up online now. The website has a virtual tour of the hotel, everything you need to know.'

'Oh, they hate doing anything online.'

The receptionist smiled. 'Ah, like my aunt. Funny, isn't it? My grandparents show me new things, but my aunt won't even try.' She looked around. 'You know, I could give you a quick tour; things are very quiet this evening.'

As the woman seemed glad of something to do, and seeing an opportunity to learn something helpful, Nia accepted the offer.

Nia was shown an empty bedroom, which she had to admit looked extremely comfortable, admired the en suite, and then came down to be shown the lounge and dining area. This was empty, although she was assured it was busy on a Saturday night, open to non-residents and booking was advised.

They finished the tour back at Reception. Nia pointed to the door behind which Ethan had disappeared. 'And what is that room for?' she asked. It was a ridiculous question, she realised that, but it was worth a shot.

'People hire it for meetings.'

Nia sighed. That wasn't any help, but she couldn't see how she could ask any more. Also, rather alarmingly, she saw a man about Ethan's age coming out of the room and decided it was high time she left.

'Thank you so much. I'm sure my relatives will look forward to coming,' she said and was about to leave when she heard someone call her name.

'Nia?'

Her heart sank. She turned to face Ethan striding across the lobby towards her, scowling.

'What the hell are you doing here?' he barked.

Aware the hotel receptionist was watching them, probably enjoying a bit of drama on a Sunday evening, Nia said to Ethan, 'I was asking for details, that's all. I have relatives who may like to stay here.'

Her mouth was horribly dry; the words fell like a stone. Ethan took hold of her arm and steered her out through the front door and to a place in the shadows.

'Now, tell me why you are really here. Did you follow me?'

Nia was very aware she was alone, and she was scared. Ethan

loomed over her, his face red and angry. Unable to speak, she nodded, and he stepped back, throwing his hands in the air.

'Why the hell would you do that?'

His voice now held more bewilderment than anger, but she was still on her guard.

'You told Elvira you stayed at the rescue centre, but Jade said you left early to go to the other surgery.'

'And you needed to find out where I actually went... but why? What possible interest could it be to you?' He was scrutinising her face as if she were some strange insect he'd never seen before and then his face cleared. But it wasn't a look of relief she saw; his mouth was tight, his eyes narrow.

'I was wondering what you do on Sunday nights.' Even to Nia it sounded weak.

'Why Sunday?' He paused. 'My God, is this to do with Ruby? Are you checking on everyone, seeing if anyone could have gone down to the beach after you? All those things you said at the vigil about the letters and things, those questions about ketamine on our walk.' His face darkened. 'My God, you don't just suspect someone of going down to talk to Ruby or mess around with letters, you think one of us may have been responsible for her death.'

Nia felt like a child caught out doing something foolish.

'I'm sorry, I don't know,' she stammered.

His eyes were bright now. 'Good God.' A car drove past them heading to the car park.

'You do know this is absurd,' said Ethan.

'I'm confused.'

'Elvira told me what you and Jade said at the hen party. I assumed you were both drunk. You have to understand this: no one, and I mean not one person in the close, would hurt Ruby. Insinuating anything else is deeply offensive.' He nodded towards the hotel. 'As to what I'm doing in there, I don't see that is any of your business. And what you actually need to do is sort out your own life, go home, back to your husband, and stop using the tragic death of someone we all loved to avoid facing the problems in your own life.'

Without another word he left her and marched back into the hotel.

Her face burning with humiliation, Nia ran back to her car. Her hands trembled as she opened the door and as she slumped over the wheel she burst into tears. There was truth in what he said, and it hurt. What the hell was she doing?

Nia looked around, half expecting Romeo to be there to comfort her. But, of course, he was back at the house. She found a crumpled old tissue in the side pocket of the car, blew her nose, and turned to retrace her route home.

As she was driving, she calmed down and cleared her thoughts. He was wrong. Ruby's death wasn't a distraction: it mattered. The truth was that Ethan had been lying and he'd not explained what he'd been up to in that hotel. He'd humiliated her but actually he was the one who was deceiving his partner.

Nia realised she was on the road to Fort Victoria; she must look that up and see what it was. Glancing at the clock in her car, she saw it was just gone ten, the time Ian and Richie were meant to be swimming.

Maybe she should check they were there.

Well aware of the fool she'd felt after following Ethan, she hesitated at the idea of any further adventures that night. Nia slowed down as she saw the turning approach: was she really going to do this? What the hell? She had nothing to lose; her pride was already in pieces.

She began the twisty descent to the fort, passing smart houses and woodland. The house was on the right, wasn't it? A Latin name... Mare something.

And then she saw it. A huge, immaculate, modern house. Security lights shone brightly out the front, Ian's car parked on the run in, Richie's bike leant against double garage doors.

She could simply turn around, leave – after all, they were here – but she had to see for herself.

Nia parked next to Ian's car. Getting out, she was aware of being flooded with light, but neighbouring houses were far apart. The lights weren't going to bother anyone.

To the side of the house was a large metal gate. She pushed it and was surprised to open it easily. More lights lit her path until she reached the back garden. This was subtly lit so that she could see the perfectly manicured lawns, trimmed hedges and trees. To her left was a large wooden studio, but over to her right was an enormous swimming pool.

Nia walked along the tiled pathway to the pool, listening to the rhythmic splash of Ian and Richie swimming.

Ian looked up, waved, and swam towards her. With little effort he climbed out.

'What the hell are you doing here?' At least there was amusement rather than anger in his voice.

'I don't know. After you mentioned this place, I thought I'd come and have a look.'

'Have you brought your swimming gear?'

She shook her head. 'No, I was just passing.'

'At this time of night?'

'I've been to the rescue centre with Jade and Ethan and called in here on my way back.'

'Bit of a roundabout route.' His eyes were screwed up now. 'Lucy said you were asking if Richie and I swam the night Ruby died – you'd not be checking up on us, would you?'

The laugh she attempted was too loud and harsh, and she quickly sidestepped the subject and started to enthuse about the pool.

'We're so lucky.' He pointed over to the studio. 'That's the gym we have access to as well.'

Nia looked over at the black outline of what appeared to be a rather unglamorous solid brick building, although she guessed inside it would have all the latest gym equipment.

'I much prefer it out here,' said Ian. 'I love swimming at night under the stars. You can't beat it.'

'Is it heated?'

'Certainly is. I come all year round, apart from January. No one in their right mind does exercise outdoors then.'

Richie had reached her end. He didn't stop, though, and as he swam away from her she saw the dragon tattoo on his leg. Nia had often thought of having a small tattoo, a lotus flower or Safi's name, but knew she'd never have the nerve to have anything as large and impressive as that.

Ian shivered. 'I think I'd better get back in – are you on your way now, then?'

'Of course, I'll see you around.'

Nia left quickly, glad to get back to the car, and drove home. It was very late, and she was greeted enthusiastically by Romeo.

'I'm so sorry. I've been gone too long. Come on, let's get out.'

She started to walk him through the town until she reached the pier. Together they walked along the wooden planks, the bright light at the other end lighting her path. Each plank had the name of a sponsor on it in white paint and the words shone in the darkness. The sea below and surrounding them was a dark inky blue black but the waves were gentle and soothing.

At the end of the pier, she found a few fishermen. She recognised the one she'd bumped into the night Ruby died, but she couldn't see Joe.

The fisherman suddenly seemed to realise who she was. 'You're that girl, aren't you? The one that came off the beach the night that poor girl died.'

'Um. Yes.' She held her breath, waiting for him to shout at her, tell her off for drinking, deserting her friend.

But his reply took her by surprise. 'I'm sorry about dobbing you in to the police like that.'

'That's OK, you had to tell them if you saw someone.'

'Yeah, but I didn't expect them to go on about you drinking and all that. It's becoming a police state, that's what it is.'

'It's all right, I understand.'

'As long as you know I wasn't trying to get you into trouble.'

'You spoke to my friend Ruby on the beach after me?'

'I could make out the shape of a person, I just shouted down and she told me she was all right and I left her be.'

Nia looked out to sea. 'It must get very cold out here at night. Do many of you fish here?'

'You have to have permission like, there's only a few of us regulars.'

The wind was building up. Nia shivered. 'I'd better be getting back, nice to chat, good fishing.'

As she made her way home she glanced up at the vet's, saw the parking spaces next to it empty. Ethan and Elvira were still out. It struck her again that this was very late for Elvira to be visiting her mother. Maybe it suited Ethan for her to be out late, as it stopped her looking too carefully into what he was up to. Nia needed to know more about what they were both up to, and now it seemed she had to check up on Joe. He'd clearly been lying for some time about what he did on a Sunday evening – Ethan had not been convinced. So where did he go and, more importantly, where was he the night Ruby died?

22

The next morning Nia checked out of the window, saw it was dry and seemed to hold the promise of a sunny day. Finding Gwen's file of walks once more, she chose a different walk, this time to Headon Warren.

'Right, Romeo, let's get ready for a good long walk.'

Nia packed up food and drinks for them both and set out. They parked on the roadside and then walked together up an unmade road that led to a sandy path.

They were surrounded by the creamy yellow flowers on the gorse bushes. To her right, she'd read, was the narrowest stretch of Solent between the island and the mainland and she could see the Tudor fortress of Hurst Castle.

They kept climbing and when they reached the top the views were breathtaking. The sun shone down on blue, glistening water and ahead she could see what had to be one of the most iconic pictures of the island, Alum Bay with its famous-coloured sands, and the Needles lighthouse at the end of the stack of jagged white chalk rocks.

'Look at that, Romeo,' she said. 'Isn't it just fabulous?'

The wind was cool but gentle on her face as she sat sharing her lunch with Romeo, watching an array of birds. She recognised the gulls and wagtails but there were some that were new to her. The freshness of the air seemed to blow away the heaviness she'd been feeling the past few days. Not for the first time she felt the island reaching out to her, and she knew that, despite all the trauma around Ruby, something inside her was healing and she was getting stronger.

The next day Nia had a full day's work ahead, and so she slipped into her new work clothes and went to the salon.

Jade was very quiet and pale that morning, that Nia asked if she was unwell. Jade replied rather abruptly that she was fine and so Nia began her appointments for the day.

Most appointments were straightforward colours and cuts. She noticed that Joe had an appointment that afternoon and was looking forward to talking to him. It would be interesting to see if she could find out what he was up to on a Sunday night after he closed Wight's, and, of course, she still needed to find out what his argument with Ruby had been about.

Joe rushed in ten minutes late and dived into the chair. 'Sorry, nearly forgot,' he said. 'Now, I was thinking of trying something new, but trendier. What do you reckon?'

Nia was surprised but asked him what he had in mind.

'I've a few celebrations coming up as it's my thirtieth this year. Dad is planning some big do, and some friends on one of the yachts are throwing a party for me. Also, of course, there's Old Gaffers this weekend, although I'll be busy manning the bar then. It's always a good weekend for business. Anyway, I was thinking kind of short at the sides, long on top.'

'That kind of style is popular and looks good. Let me find some magazines to get a better idea of what you're thinking of.'

It soon became clear to Nia what Joe wanted; she'd done the kind of cut many times for students in Cardiff.

'Come on, then, let's wash your hair.'

As she washed Joe's hair she could feel him moving, his foot tapping on the floor, and his fingers drumming on his knees. He was not one to stay still for long.

Once he was back in the styling chair she tried gently to position him upright, keep his head still, but he was going to be like a child, she could see, and it would be a major achievement to give him a perfectly straight cut.

'Weird, I mean, even here it's odd. I keep expecting Ruby to show up.'

'I think everyone finds that. It's very hard. You and Ruby were close, weren't you?'

'We were, she had a good heart. I know she had all that religious stuff but despite that she meant well.'

'Yes, I think that as well. It was all so traumatic, wasn't it? I remember how shocked everyone was at the vigil. It was a very emotional night for everyone, particularly Richie. Does he often get violent like that?'

'He's never hit me before, if that's what you mean. I guess I was a bit hard on him – but Ruby meant a lot to me, and I never felt he took as much care of her as he should.'

'I am sure you have wonderful memories of your times with Ruby. You must cherish those.'

'I will,' said Joe. 'I only wish my last day with her hadn't been so fraught. It was so tense at the party, and I wish I'd been gentler with her, especially as we'd had a few words earlier in the day.' She felt him suddenly hold his breath, caught his eye in the mirror; she was sure he regretted saying that. He added quickly, 'That was nothing, of course. Ruby thought I'd had a late night drinking, that's all. She liked to keep me on the straight and narrow.'

Nia smiled but wasn't sure this was the real story. Surely it had to be something more significant than that if Ruby had told him he should be telling his parents about it.

However, she replied, 'I see. I'm sure she was looking out for you. So, tell me, how has the fishing been going?'

His eyes flitted sideways. 'Oh, you know, comes and goes.'

'I went down the pier the other evening. I didn't see you there.'

He blinked. 'I must have been busy at work. Are you enjoying working here, then?'

Nia could see she wasn't going to get any more out of Joe about the fishing and answered, 'Yes, and I like Yarmouth very much. You're so fortunate to have a business here.'

'That's my parents. They're incredible. They're not stinking rich or anything. Dad had put all his savings into this business for me.'

'A lot of pressure, then?'

'You bet. All my mates tell me how lucky I am, but they are out every night, drinking. I can't do any of that, I can't blow this.'

'But you enjoy it?'

'Yeah, I love it.' He paused as Jade came close to them to fetch some hair oil.

'You all right, then?' he asked.

She gave him a cursory smile.

'Dad was asking if you'd like to go out sailing sometime.' Joe caught sight of Nia in the mirror. 'Dad really likes Jade,' he explained.

Jade didn't reply but went back to her client.

'Has she come back too soon?' Joe asked quietly. 'She doesn't look right.'

'I don't know, maybe, but she wants to keep busy.'

'I get that.'

Nia dried and styled his hair and as he looked critically at his reflection she showed him which products to use so that he could keep the style going for himself. 'Wow! That's brilliant.' He called over to Jade. 'What do you think of the new me?'

She sent a half-smile but didn't say anything.

'It really suits you,' said Nia, grinning. This was one of the best bits of her job, seeing someone excited with their look.

He tore off his cape and stood up. 'That's great, thanks, Nia.' He paid and left.

Finally, the last client left after what had been a full day's work. They'd nearly finished when Jade suddenly put down the broom she was using and rushed to the toilets at the back of the salon. Nia could hear her being violently sick. Not wanting to intrude, she waited until Jade came back out before asking her if she was all right.

'Never better,' Jade said. She was as white as a sheet, her eyes red.

'Maybe you should take a few days off. I could try and cover some of your clients. You must still be in shock from losing Ruby. People will understand.'

Jade shook her head. 'This is nothing to do with shock.'

'Something you've eaten?'

Jade shook her head again, looked deep into Nia's eyes. Suddenly Nia remembered Ruby holding Jade in the toilets at Wight's, telling her everything would be all right. With a flash of insight Nia knew exactly what was happening.

23

'Are you pregnant?' Nia asked Jade gently.

Jade burst into tears and Nia put her arms around her.

'Hey, it'll be OK,' she said.

'I don't know what the hell to do,' said Jade, sniffing. She grabbed a tissue from the counter, blew her nose. 'Sorry, you're the only person apart from Ruby I've told.'

'You've not told the father?'

'No way. It's nothing to do with him.'

'But—'

'Don't. Ruby gave me the whole lecture. More than once. I was terrified she was going to go and tell him.'

'She knew who the father was?'

'She did, but I told her I wasn't telling him about this. It's my decision.' She grabbed Nia's arm. 'You are not to tell anyone, have you got that? This is nothing to do with anyone else.'

Nia saw the way Jade's eyes strayed to the window. 'Is it someone here in the close?' she asked.

Jade glared at her. 'Listen to me, this is nothing, I repeat nothing, to do with anyone in the close. None of them are the father, none of this is their business.'

'OK, I'm not going to say a word. Although you know if you have the baby the father should help out.'

'That's not an issue. I'm not having the baby. I'm in no state to look after a baby.'

'What will you do?'

'I've already spoken to my doctor. I need to go in for a day. I have problems with blood clotting. They want to keep an eye on me.'

'A termination? You're sure?'

'I am. I've had plenty of time to think about this.' Jade started to cry quietly.

Nia put her arm around her. 'Would you like me to come with you?'

Jade's eyes filled with tears. 'You'd do that? You don't hate me?'

'Of course not. And I will be with you if that is what you want.'

'Thank you.'

'Make sure you tell me when it is. We'll rearrange the appointments, close the salon. I'll be there, I promise.'

* * *

Nia was working in the salon the next day, but she didn't mind. The clouds were thick and grey. She wouldn't want to be out walking on a day like this.

As she looked over her appointments, she saw she had Ethan and Richie in that day. She was apprehensive at the thought of seeing Ethan again, even wondered if he might cancel. However, seeing Richie was coming in set her thinking.

It was Wednesday, the day he had maintained he went over to the classes on the mainland, but Ruby had discovered he went to meet a friend. Maybe it was time to check up on who Richie was meeting. She knew roughly from Ruby the direction he walked – could she follow him, see where he went? Another idea came to her. If she could get a lift to Cowes with Richie, maybe she would get an opportunity to check for that phone in the glove compartment. It was all a bit chancy, but she had to try.

Richie came in late morning. He looked pale and subdued, but calm, and Nia reminded herself this was a man who had only a few weeks ago lost his wife.

She spoke gently to him as he sat in the chair, the cape wrapped around his shoulders.

'Morning, how are you?'

He spoke softly. She had to lean forward to catch what he said. 'Still a bit numb, to be honest. People have been very kind. I've been sent flowers, and Lucy has brought me some cakes. I don't feel much like eating though.'

'I can imagine, but it's good to try and eat small meals, isn't it?' She looked down at his hair and he caught her eye.

'Ruby did the same thing each time. I just need it tidied up.'

'That's fine. I can see what I need to do. Let's wash it and then I'll style it for you.'

As she washed Richie's hair she could feel the tension in his neck, and the clench of his jaw.

Back in the chair she asked how he was managing at the gallery.

'I opened up again, it's not that busy but I need to be painting.'

'Elvira was telling me you've been collecting things off the beach with her for her wedding favours.'

A hint of a smile showed on his lips. 'It's amazing what you find on a beach: glass, shells, driftwood. It all tells a story, doesn't it? I can understand why Ruby loved it down there.'

'She told me she talked to the sea.'

'Yes, it's some comfort she was by the sea when she died. It's where she would have wanted to be. I just hate the thought of her being down there alone.'

Nia glanced up at the mirror, wanting to see his reaction as she said, 'You, of course, were swimming with Ian – it's an amazing pool.'

'Yes, we're lucky to be able to go there.'

'So, you go every Sunday. You must have been there the evening Ruby died – you and Ian stay so late.'

'We don't get there until about ten. Two hours' swimming isn't that much.' He looked at her curiously.

'No, of course.' Nia took a deep breath, held her scissors very still; she was about to try out her plan. 'I wonder if I could ask a favour. Wednesday is the night you drive over to Cowes, isn't it? Don't you go over to a class?'

She felt a flicker of inbreath, but he answered. 'Yes,' he replied and, as Jade had said, she saw he was still keeping up the pretence of going to a class.

That was the answer she was hoping for. 'The thing is, as it looks like rain, I was wondering if you were planning to drive?' She held her breath; he had no idea how much it mattered to her what he answered.

'Ruby never liked me cycling in the dark when it was raining. I'll be driving.'

Again, she looked up, caught his eye in the mirror. 'That's great.' She saw a weariness in his eyes but continued, 'Sorry, it could be great for me. I have a friend staying over in Cowes, a small B & B close to Northwood House. Me and her always have a few glasses of wine and so I'd rather not drive. I am guessing you would be parking around there?'

'Um, yes, probably.'

'That's brilliant. Could I come with you? Obviously, I'll be getting a taxi back, but it would be great to save the cost going over.'

His lips formed into a forced smile. 'Of course. I'll go about half five. I need to fill up with petrol.'

'That's great, thank you.'

She felt his shoulders relax and she let him sit quietly while she finished his hair. Richie gave a quick nod of appreciation when she had finished. As he was leaving, he said a cursory farewell to Jade.

Nia took a gap in appointments as an opportunity to pop over to see Romeo, let him out in the garden and have coffee. It was rather nice being close to work and to be able to leave the job for a short time.

At lunch she had a few minutes to catch up with Jade.

'How are you feeling, then?' she asked Jade.

'Not too bad. It helped to talk, thank you. Any news from you?'

Nia realised she'd not yet told Jade about following Ethan, Ian, and Richie.

'So, Ethan isn't going to the surgery? How odd. Why make up a story like that? I wonder what he's doing at the hotel. Maybe he's meeting another woman?'

Nia was aware of how sensitive this could be for Jade. 'I don't think so. He didn't go upstairs. He went to a room downstairs. I think it was more of a meeting room.'

'Maybe he's a Freemason or something?'

'I'd not thought of that. It's possible.'

'And what about Ian and Richie?'

'I went to the house, saw them swimming.'

Jade grinned. 'How on earth did you explain turning up there?'

Nia told her the story, adding, 'I only talked to Ian and I'm not sure he was convinced. Richie just kept on swimming.' Nia paused and frowned.

'What's the matter?' asked Jade.

'I don't know. I was picturing them swimming as I spoke and something wasn't right.' She closed her eyes but shook her head. 'No, I can't see it, hopefully it will come back to me soon. Anyway, I have Ethan coming in this afternoon. I'm a bit nervous, he could still be pretty angry with me after Sunday.'

'You'll be OK. Ethan doesn't hold a grudge.'

'I'm not sure, you didn't see him. I've no idea what he'll be like.'

Nia had another of Ruby's regular clients next, a chatty older woman who told her about her grandchildren and detailed the mistakes her daughter-in-law was making bringing them up. Nia, of course, didn't comment, but was glad she wouldn't be going to the family lunch they were all planning.

Eventually, Ethan arrived. He rushed in. 'Ruby usually sprayed my hair with water to save washing it,' he said as she handed him the cape.

Nia recognised that for Ethan having his hair cut was an evil necessity rather than a pleasure.

'I just need a quick tidy up. My clients, fortunately, don't care what I look like.'

'Of course, so the usual, then?'

He looked up, blinked as if seeing a stranger. Nia guessed he seldom looked in a mirror. 'Um, yes, that's great.'

Nia sprayed a liberal amount of water. Ethan had very thick hair and it would have been better to wash it properly.

As she combed through his hair, she saw he was scrolling through his phone. She found herself glancing at his reflection; he really was very good-looking. Nia remembered watching him with the cat who had been so frightened, the gentle way he had handled him, the adoring looks he got from Romeo and suddenly she could see how a young girl like Jade could have fallen for him. However, she reminded herself that Ethan may be guilty of turning his back on Jade and the warm feelings started to ebb away.

Making an effort to chat to him, she started to talk about the rescue centre, but Ethan's answers were perfunctory.

At first, Nia thought he must still be angry with her, but then she saw his attention was on his phone. She glanced over his shoulder, and saw he wasn't texting but was playing some kind of game. Frowning, she looked more carefully and then recognised one of the roulette games they'd played at Elvira's hen party.

Ethan suddenly looked up and their eyes locked. The stress, guilt, panic Nia saw told her everything.

At that moment Elvira came in. She spoke to Jade at the desk and then came over to Ethan.

'Hiya, Nia. I didn't know you worked here now – maybe I'll come and talk wedding hair with you sometime.' She talked to Ethan via the mirror. 'I thought I'd let you know Mrs Green would like you to see Rex again. She'll be about half an hour. She's so worried and she'll only see you with him.'

'Oh, God, poor Rex,' replied Ethan and then smiled up at Elvira. 'Thanks.'

'So, how are all the wedding plans going?' Nia asked.

'Oh, I leave all that to Elvira. I have my suit now.'

'Well, make sure I cut your hair again before the big day.'

He gave her a quick smile. It was clear he didn't feel like chatting and so she finished his hair quietly.

Before he left Jade stopped Ethan, wanting to talk about a dog at the rescue centre. They were still talking when Nia had finished brushing the floor and cleared up.

'I'm just popping home, be back in fifteen minutes,' she called to Jade.

Once home she let Romeo out into the garden and had a quick drink of squash. She was thinking about Ethan when there was a knock at the door.

Nia let Ethan in.

'I think I ought to explain a few things,' he said.

Romeo came bounding in at the sound of Ethan's voice and, despite obviously being very agitated, Ethan bent down to give him a fuss.

'You don't have to explain anything to me,' said Nia.

'No, I want to talk to you. Firstly, I'm sorry for the way I handled things on Sunday. I was very abrupt, sent you off looking pretty frightened. I didn't mean that.' He sat down on the edge of a chair. 'As you saw on my phone, I am gambling online.' His face went a deep red; he couldn't keep eye contact as he said, 'But I don't have a problem. It's something I have been doing to try and get in some extra money for the wedding, that's all.'

'Oh, I see.'

'I do also play poker sometimes on a Sunday evening, and that is why I was at the hotel. I am well aware of the problems; I can promise you I don't have any issue with it.'

'Had Ruby picked up on you gambling?'

'God, yes, she saw my phone when I was having my hair done, just like you did. She went mad. She was fiercely anti-gambling; she was so angry with me. I told her it wasn't an issue, but she didn't believe me, told me if I didn't tell Elvira she would. I was petrified she'd tell Elvira and blow it all out of proportion. I mean, I could have lost Elvira if she'd done that.' The lightness had left his voice. 'The thing is, you see, Elvira's father was addicted to gambling, they lost their home when she was little because of it, and that's the reason I keep it secret from her.'

'But why do it at all?'

'Just to get some easy extra money for the wedding. Elvira seems to always be asking for money and I never like to say no. I have won a fair bit, but, of course, I also lose money. I've not got in debt or anything though. I tried to explain all that to Ruby.'

Nia sipped her coffee, saw Romeo resting his head on Ethan's knee.

'I pleaded with Ruby. I just had to trust she'd not say anything.' He gently moved Romeo's head and stood up. 'I have to get back, and you have work. I simply wanted to apologise and to ask you please not to say anything to anyone about this.'

'I'm not going to say anything.'

'Thank you. I promise you it's nothing to worry about.'

And with that he was gone.

Before returning to work Nia gathered her thoughts. Ethan had many more layers to him than she'd imagined. Was Ethan telling her the whole story? Was he actually as in control of his gambling as he made out? He'd certainly looked very stressed when talking about Ruby. Was it possible he'd cracked, killed Ruby, desperate to silence her?

She stroked Romeo, who was sitting patiently next to her. 'I ought to get back to work. I'll see you soon.'

Nia saw two more clients and then helped Jade clearing up. Jade was naturally curious about why Ethan had gone over to see Nia, but Nia wasn't going to share that conversation. However, before she left, Jade did have a favour to ask of Nia.

'The appointment book is full for the next few days. It's always manic over Gaffers weekend. Could you face three full days?'

'I could, as long as I get over to Romeo.'

'Of course. Honestly, the clients love you, and I need you to show me some of those cutting techniques.'

'Of course, and yes, I'll be here. See you tomorrow. Oh, and can you bring me the address of that helpline? I ought to go there sometime.'

'Of course, I'll text it to you.'

Nia left the salon, nervous about the evening ahead.

24

As Nia waited outside the house with Romeo, she was aware of a growing buzz around the town in the build up to the Old Gaffers.

Richie arrived on time, and they walked over to the car park together. She settled Romeo in the back of the car and then sat herself in the passenger seat next to Richie.

Conversation was stilted, and Nia was glad of the rhythmic sound of the windscreen wipers, needed now the rain had started, filling the silence.

They approached the garage and while Richie was outside the car Nia suddenly realised this was her chance to look for the phone in the glove compartment. She glanced up, saw Richie was preoccupied filling the car with fuel and she quickly opened the glove compartment and took out the phone.

As Richie went into the station to pay Nia switched on the phone, and, to her relief, it came on and she was able to go straight to the photographs without a password. She quickly found the ones clearly of the accident. Some were of Ruby's car and some of Ian and Lucy's car. Nia sent a few to her own phone, realised Richie was coming back to the car and threw it into the glove compartment just as he was getting in the car.

'Are you looking for something?' he asked.

'No, thanks, I'm fine.'

It wasn't long before they arrived at the car park. Richie went to get a ticket while Nia helped Romeo out of the car and put on his lead.

'So, you're heading up the road,' said Richie. 'We're going in opposite directions.'

'We are,' said Nia. 'Thanks for the lift. Have a good evening.'

Nia left Richie and started walking up the road. She glanced back and saw Richie heading down the road and wondered for a moment if he was actually going to carry on and catch the Red Jet to his class. Maybe he had only met this friend a few times and really had gone back to his classes now. She turned into the main road leading to Northwood House. There was a small area of grass with some large trees. The only thing she could do was wait and see if Richie returned. If he didn't then she would have to get a taxi home and that would be that.

* * *

It wasn't pleasant waiting in the rain, and she could feel it dripping down the back of her neck. 'Sorry, Romeo. I should have put your coat on you.'

Just as she was starting to wonder if she should give up, she saw Richie come round the corner walking along the road in her direction. Nia dived back behind a tree, saw him cross the road and enter a side road. As soon as he was out of sight she also crossed and went into the road. Fortunately, he was walking purposefully, although she kept an eye open for convenient driveways to dive into. He turned into another road and finally into a road called Haven Place.

She reread the sign. Haven Place. Why was that familiar? And then she remembered: wasn't that the name of the road where Jade owned a house?

Suddenly she realised Richie had stopped and was walking up a driveway. She gave him a few seconds to allow time for him to enter the building and then walked down the road.

She was surprised to see a rather old-fashioned-looking chalet bungalow, number 13. This was it. This was Jade's house. It wasn't at all the kind of house she'd imagined Jade owning or letting out, but why would Richie be visiting it?

Nia took out her phone, took a photo of the house, and was still standing in a daze, staring, when she realised she could see Richie closing the curtains.

Nia looked around. No one else seemed to be here.

The rain was getting heavier. There was no point in hanging about any longer and so she started to walk back to the town, but she was surprised to see Joe in the distance. She shouted his name, but he didn't answer and, as the rain was getting heavier, she walked quickly down to where she knew the buses stopped. However once there she felt exhausted and, spotting the taxi rank close by, she went over and spoke to one of the drivers.

'Are you OK to take me and the dog?'

'No problem. Where do you want to go?'

As she sat in the back of the taxi Nia tried to make sense of what she had just seen. That must be the house Ruby had followed Richie to. Ruby had been devastated. It had to be that Ruby suspected her sister and husband had been meeting in secret, having an affair. This was the betrayal Ruby had been talking about.

Nia placed a hand on Romeo's damp head. Jade was pregnant. Could Richie be the father of Jade's baby?

So many emotions filled her head. Anger on behalf of Ruby, shock that Jade could do this to her sister, fury at Richie, but most of all deep sadness for the pain Ruby had been through.

Nia was glad to get back home, shut the door on the close, take off her wet clothes, dry Romeo, and collapse on the sofa with a hot drink.

Did any of this have anything to do with Ruby's death? Had Richie and Jade decided the only way to be free of Ruby was to kill her?

Jade could have ensured a definite alibi at the rescue centre; it was

Richie who was to kill Ruby. Somehow, he'd persuaded Ian to say they were swimming together. He'd faked the letter, gone down to the beach, and put the ketamine in Ruby's drink.

Nia stroked Romeo's ears: was that it? Was that what had happened? If that was the case, why would Jade be planning a termination?

There were so many questions that needed answering. She leaned over and found her phone. She'd nearly forgotten about the photos of the car accident with all the excitement of the day's other revelations.

Obviously, they had been keen to get the cars off the main road and the photos Ruby took were when they were both parked in a lay-by on her side of the road.

Nia made the photos as large as she could and examined them carefully. Surely, she should be able to find some clue as to why this minor accident was so significant?

On initial inspection, though, there was little to see. Ruby's car was scratched with a slight bump. Ian's far smarter white BMW looked more tarnished, mainly because the remnants of red paint from Ruby's car shone out like bloody gashes on his white paintwork. His car had all the comforts of an expensive car, with padded headrests and the smart leather driver's seat that was pulled forwards. On the dashboard she could see designer sunglasses, ready for sunnier days ahead.

Nia sighed. The photos told her nothing. She had just put her phone down when it rang. Without thinking, she answered it, and for the first time in days she heard Chris's voice.

'Hiya, thought we ought to catch up. How are things going?'

He sounded so normal that for a moment she felt a rush of hope and wondered if, somehow, she'd got everything wrong.

'I'm doing well. How are things with you?' she replied, trying to steady her voice.

He told her some news about school, and then coughed as if to clear his throat and said, 'I understand you had a long chat with Safi.'

Her legs started to tremble, her voice to shake. 'I did.'

'She only told me today. The point is she got a lot of things wrong. I think I've reassured her. I am guessing you knew what she said couldn't possibly be true, but I just wanted to check everything was all right.'

Nia felt her stomach clench, her head thumping. 'Actually, I did believe her, but I'd also promised Safi not to tell you what she'd told me,' she said quietly.

'Honestly, Nia, her friends have been stirring things up. You know what kids at school are like. I can promise you nothing has happened between me and Sian.'

'How do you explain the watch, then? It was obviously an expensive present.'

'I thought I told you the watch was a present from the governors?'

'No, you said it was from children in the drama department.'

'No, I didn't say that. That would be ridiculous. It was far too expensive to be from them.'

'Oh, I thought you said it was not as posh as it looked.'

She heard him sigh. 'Love, you were in such a state, I don't think you were thinking or hearing straight.'

'But the child who saw you with Sian?'

'That is pure fabrication. I don't want to go raking it all up by doing some kind of witch hunt to find out who started all this, but it will be some little troublemaker looking for attention.'

'And what about Colin? He saw Sian's car. It's very distinctive.'

'It was parked outside on the road – actually she'd come round the night before just to give me some paperwork. When she went out it wouldn't start. It was late and so I gave her a lift home and returned home.' He paused and added, 'I am sure Colin can confirm my car was there the next morning. Apparently, she called out a rescue service the next day. I was in school, so I missed all of that. It's a shame Colin missed that.'

She could feel him grinding down everything that had happened; soon it would be a fine powder you could blow away. It was as if nothing had happened, it had all been in her mind.

'I don't know, Chris. I believed Safi when she told me, and I've been so upset.'

'You should have spoken to me instead of brooding on it. It's definitely time for you to come home and things can return to how they'd been. I know it wasn't working out for you being at home, but you know you can still walk back into your old job; they are really missing you.'

'I'm sure they are, I brought in the most money there. I am very good at my job, Chris.'

'Of course, you are,' he said, but she could hear that patronising tone he'd use with one of his staff who had just scraped through their assessment.

'Actually, I've been working in a salon here in Yarmouth.'

'You have a new hairdressing job? But how? No one knows you there.'

'It's a long story. But it's good to work somewhere new, meet new people.'

'If you need a change, I'm sure you could get a job somewhere else down here. You have a few years' experience under your belt.'

Nia gritted her teeth. She had more than a few years' experience. She'd been doing this job at a high level for a long time now. However, she knew none of this meant anything to Chris. It was his certificates that hung on the walls at home, not hers.

'Look, I can't just drop everything and come home,' Nia said. 'I have commitments here now.'

'You do believe me, don't you?'

She bit her lip. In her heart she wasn't sure, but she said, 'Of course, it's OK. I just need to help Jade out for a bit longer.'

The tone of his voice changed; it became sharper, more demanding. 'Look, if you don't come home by the end of the week then I am coming over there this weekend. We can have some time together. A few people needing their hair cut should not be taking priority over your marriage. You need to sort out your priorities. I mean it, Nia. If you aren't back here on Friday evening, I'm coming to get you.'

With this Chris ended the call. Nia knew this way he would feel he'd regained control. She could imagine him pouring himself a drink, satisfied with the way it had gone.

What was she to make of what he'd said? Was he lying to her again or was it possible that Safi had got everything wrong? She didn't have long to think – a text arrived from Safi asking if they could video call.

She rang Safi back immediately. 'Oh, God, Mum, I'm so sorry. I never meant to stir up trouble between you and Dad,' she stammered.

'It's OK, love, you were only doing what you thought was right.'

'I'm so confused, Mum. These were close friends who told me those things. I trusted them.'

'It's all right, you are not to worry. Once I've finished my stint here at the salon, I'm going home. You see – me and your dad will sort everything out.'

Nia finished the call. She'd assured Chris she believed him, Safi that she would make things work, but, in her heart, she didn't know what to believe any more.

She went out into the garden with Romeo, took a deep breath of the fresh salt air, everything clean and washed by the rain. One thing she was sure of: she had unfinished business here, and it wasn't simply the work in the salon. She had to find out what had happened to Ruby. And she meant what she said about keeping her word to Jade. It would be good to have a bit more time on her own as well. Of course, Chris had threatened to come over, but all she could do was hope he was bluffing.

25

Nia took Romeo out for a long walk before work. A ferry had just docked and cars were unloading, but it was a quiet business at this time of the morning, unlike the chaos when the later ones arrived. In the harbour she noticed some of the splendid Gaffers had arrived, decorated with bunting, their magnificent tall white sails reaching into the blue sky.

Nia and Romeo went down on the beach. Despite everything, Nia still loved it down there and this morning it felt so fresh after the sea had magically washed the shore.

She stood on the shoreline throwing pebbles in the sea, a game Romeo loved, barking and jumping, although never going in too deep.

From where she stood, she could see the supports under the pier. She'd read that a lot of them had been replaced a few years ago as the old ones had been eaten away by shipworm and gribble. It was rather scary to imagine most people had walked along the wooden pier in the years before totally unaware of the danger below, but then it was never easy to know what was happening below the surface.

As the tide was low Nia was able to get close at the supports, see the debris that was tangled around them. And then she saw it. It was tiny, a sliver of material, but she knew what it was.

Gingerly she picked it out and washed it in the sea. The salt had faded it slightly, but she knew the blue silk, slightly singed at the edges, was from the voodoo doll Ruby had shown her. The sea might wash the beach every day, but nothing was forgotten.

Seeing it made Nia think again about the curse and that voodoo doll, which she'd rather put to the back of her mind. Who had made it? Joe had suggested Lucy, hadn't he, and, yes, she'd seen all that blue silk in her workroom. Usually, she used it to make those lovely collages of the sea, but had she also used it to create the voodoo doll, to channel hate?

Lucy remained a bit of an enigma. Apparently so vulnerable, hiding behind Ian, and yet at the hen party Nia had seen a bright, determined side to her.

Nia picked up the piece of silk and took it home to place next to the fossil with the red wax. They didn't look much but they were proof of what she'd seen. Nia shook her head; she knew she wasn't imagining what she remembered of that night.

Nia had to work today so there was no time to dwell on everything. Somehow, she needed to put her worries to one side.

* * *

As she entered the salon, however, she found it difficult to say her usual friendly hello to Jade. Fortunately, Jade also seemed preoccupied and didn't notice.

Nia went to check her appointments for the day and closed her eyes: he was the last person she felt like seeing. She opened her eyes and there he was, striding across the close, and the look on his face did not bode well. Was this about Sunday?

'Good morning, Ian.' Her smile wasn't returned. 'I'll get the gown.'

Without speaking, he sat in the chair and glared at his reflection.

'So, what can I do for you?' she asked, desperately trying to keep things normal.

'You can make the idiots at the TV station see sense. They need to look at their demographic. Lucy and I are what they need, not more brainless B-rated celebrities talking about their latest boob job.'

'Has something happened?' The question was fatuous. It was clear something had.

'I've received a phone call from my agent. The station is thinking of ditching us for someone else. It's so disappointing and extremely frustrating.' He caught her eye in the mirror and his face melted into a smile. 'I'm sorry, this is nothing to do with you. My hair. Yes... well, I expect you can see what Ruby usually did. Same again, please.'

She washed his hair and could feel how angry he was.

Once she was cutting his hair, he returned to the subject of the TV programme. 'This would have been so great for Lucy. She has no idea how good she would be on camera. It would be a real boost for her confidence.'

'She seemed quite nervous about it all; she was quite shaky when she was last here.'

He glanced up; his eyes narrowed. 'Lucy is by nature a little on edge; it can make her clumsy. There's nothing wrong with her.'

'Sorry, I wasn't suggesting anything.'

'Weren't you? I was telling Lucy about you coming to the swimming pool and she told me about what Elvira said the night of the hen do. And you were probing Richie when he came in here. You were checking up on me, weren't you, seeing if Richie and I had been swimming together the night Ruby died?'

They met each other's eyes in the mirror. 'I was simply making conversation when Richie had his hair cut.'

'We both know that's not true, don't we? Richie knew you were digging, and he told me about it. We do talk to each other, you know; we are very close. We trust the police; we are good people, and you need to remember that. We may criticise each other, but when one of us is threatened we unite. So be careful.' There was no mistaking the threat in his voice.

Nia felt her hands shaking and put down the scissors.

'I need to go and fetch something,' she said quickly.

In the cloakroom she ran her hands under cold water until the shaking stopped, her breathing settled, and she returned.

As if the previous conversation had never happened, Ian began talking about the weekend ahead.

'We all meet up at Wight's on Saturday evening about eight – make sure you come.'

She smiled at him nervously. 'Of course, it sounds great fun.'

When she'd finished, he stood up, threw her a charming smile, thanking her for the haircut.

After he'd paid, he went over to Jade, who was with a client. He leant down, his face close to hers. 'Don't forget Saturday,' he said, and left.

* * *

As Jade had promised, it was a very busy day, with additional walk-ins, as people got ready for the regatta. It was six o'clock by the time the last client had left and they were clearing up. As Jade was putting the towels in to wash and Nia was wiping down her work trolley, a woman came into the salon. Nia recognised her from the grocer's.

'Hiya, can I help you?' she asked.

'It's all right. I don't need a haircut. I can see you are shutting up. I bet you are busy; everyone has their hair done for Old Gaffers.'

'It feels that way.'

'I brought these over for Jade.' She handed her some boxes of shortbread with a picture of a red squirrel and 'Present from the Isle of Wight' on the box.

Jade came out. 'Oh, I thought I heard your voice, Joan, thanks so much. I've been waiting for these to come in.'

'I know, I thought I'd make sure you got a few boxes before they sell out.'

Jade took the boxes and turned to Nia. 'I ask the cleaner to leave a box of these for each new visitor at the Airbnb. It's the kind of gesture that gets you pushed up to a super host.'

'You get a lot of bookings?'

'Yes, it's a good location and a lovely flat. Joe's friend who has a yacht here uses it quite a bit, but people come from all over the place.'

Nia caught the word. 'A flat? Not a bungalow?'

'No, a flat. It's in such a nice complex, feels very safe.'

'What's the address?'

Jade blinked. 'You looking for somewhere else to live? The address is 13 Haven Way.'

Nia closed her eyes; how could she have been so stupid?

'Something wrong?'

'No, nothing.'

After Joan had left, Nia found her phone and showed Jade the photograph of the bungalow.

'Have you any idea who lives here? It's 13 Haven Place.'

Jade grinned. 'You thought I owned that? No, I've never seen it. Why are you asking? In fact, why have you got a photograph of it on your phone?'

Nia explained how she had followed Richie and seen him go in there, avoiding mentioning her conclusions. Jade, however, was too quick for her.

'Hang on, you didn't think Richie was going into my place, did you? Oh, God, you didn't imagine me and him...?' The look of horror said it all.

'I'm sorry, I saw the road name and—'

'OK, but no, Richie doesn't come to my place... and we certainly have never had any kind of relationship. As if I would have done that to Ruby. And anyway, Richie? No way.' Jade's face settled any doubts in Nia's mind. Richie was definitely not the father of Jade's baby.

'What do you think Richie is up to, then?'

'I suppose he could be seeing another woman, but that bungalow looks like it's owned by an old lady, not some pretty young artist or whoever he'd be seeing.'

'It's all very odd,' said Nia. She sighed. 'Ian had a go at me earlier, accused me of sticking my nose in. I suppose he has a point.'

'I'm sure Ian didn't mean any harm. He'll be protecting Lucy. She's everything to him, you know. Don't let Ian put you off digging around. I heard him telling you about the TV thing. He was in a bad mood, that's all. Anyway, if everyone here is innocent, they don't have anything to hide.'

'Everyone has secrets, but it doesn't mean they're a killer, does it?'

Jade put her hand on her stomach. 'No, I suppose not. Still, I'd like you to keep looking. We've not got any answers yet. Oh, did you get the text about the helpline?'

'I did, thanks. I'm going this evening. At least no one will shout at me for following them there.'

Jade threw her a smile. Nia continued clearing up while Jade sorted out some admin on the laptop.

As she sat eating her tea, Nia felt a wave of despair. What if she'd got everything wrong? She went and found the fossil, touched the red wax.

'I can't give up, not yet,' she said to Romeo, who wagged his tail, more concerned that it must be time to go out.

As she walked, she tried to clear her head. She had said she would go to the helpline that evening, and, despite the fact it was nerve-wracking, she decided she would keep to her plans and go. This was going to be a long shot, she knew, but she had to try.

26

Nia pulled into the car park in front of a large building. To the right of the door was a list of the various businesses and she spotted the one she was looking for was on the third floor.

Inside were sterile, plain walls and concrete steps, which she climbed up quickly. Once at the door she knocked nervously, until a quiet voice called for her to come in.

Inside was much more inviting, with comfortable chairs, pleasant prints on the walls. In one corner a young woman was busy typing, but it was a man with a beard and easy smile who stood up to greet her.

'Hi, I'm Grant, how can I help you?'

Nia shuffled nervously. 'I hope you don't mind me coming, but I wanted to ask you something about Ruby who used to work here.'

The man's face creased in concern. 'Oh, I'm so sorry – I don't know if you have heard—'

'I know what happened,' she interrupted. 'I was wondering if you know who she'd been working with the night before she died. I had a question about one of the phone calls.'

He gestured towards a seat, and she sat down.

'All the calls that come in here are kept completely confidential. I can't divulge anything like that.'

'I understand but, well, let me explain.'

Nia told him about Ruby's conversations at the party and on the beach.

'The point I'm making is that this isn't just me being nosy. I am concerned about what happened to Ruby and it might be that person could help me understand.'

'I think that is a police matter, don't you?'

'The police have accepted that Ruby died either by an accidental overdose or she took her own life. I'm not so sure.'

'I'm sorry, I can't help you.'

'But it might be I could help this person. Ruby was very worried about them.'

'I can't give out any information. We are, of course, all distraught about what happened to Ruby. We miss her terribly and, of course, we owe her an enormous debt. Because of her generosity, we were able to move here, to new premises, and be financially secure for a few years. I am sorry I can't help you, but I'm sure you understand.'

Nia realised the conversation had come to an end and stood up. 'I do understand why you can't help me but, well, thank you for your time.'

She left frustrated, but she knew he wouldn't change his mind. She walked down the stairs. At least she could tell Jade she'd tried.

Nia was just opening her car door when she was aware of footsteps behind her, turned and saw the woman who'd been typing in the office.

She spoke breathlessly, fiddling with her hair. 'Um, I was listening to you talking to Grant. Sorry, I should introduce myself. I'm Donna. I was friends with Ruby.'

The name Donna seemed familiar to Nia, but she wasn't sure why.

Donna continued, 'I would usually agree with Grant, but I think this is different. I was on the phones with Ruby the night before she died.'

'You were?' Nia's heart was racing. 'Did she say anything about the call to you?'

Donna nodded. 'She came over to me after the call in tears. It was unlike her. I always envied the way she could be so sympathetic answering the phones but after a call she was able to put it to one side, move on to the next. This was different, though.'

'What did she say?'

Donna took a deep breath. 'Ruby told me that she recognised the caller's voice, it was someone living in her close. They were in a terrible mess, desperate and she had to speak to them again. I said all the usual things about it being confidential, but she said she had to do something. She told me the woman who'd phoned was getting married very soon but she'd got into some kind of trouble. Ruby seemed to think they shouldn't be getting married because of it.'

Nia gasped. 'It was Elvira?'

'Ruby didn't mention a name.' Donna looked over her shoulder nervously. 'I shouldn't be telling you this, but I was really fond of Ruby, and she was terribly worried.'

'Thank you so much. I promise I'll be tactful. If I see a way I can help, I will.'

'I appreciate that, and I wouldn't be telling you this if I hadn't seen the way Ruby had been.'

'Did Ruby tell you any more about the conversation?'

'No, nothing, although she did say the caller had been very angry at the end.' Donna sighed and then shook her head. 'I still can't believe what happened to Ruby. I wish she'd talked to me, but Ruby was always better at listening than talking about herself. You know, she would always come in early and say to me, "Now, Donna, tell me how you are." Bless her, she was a lovely friend.'

Nia paused. 'Hang on, Ruby mentioned you once. She was telling me about a car accident she had back in January on her way to work here. Was it you who told her to go home, not to try and come in?'

'That's right. Gosh, I remember that night. Ruby was in quite a state. She'd not been hurt, but she was clearly upset.'

'Did she tell you any more about the accident?'

'Not really. When I next saw her, she didn't want to talk about it.

She said she felt guilty, but I couldn't understand why. It hadn't been her fault, no one was blaming her, no one was hurt.'

Nia nodded. 'Well, thank you for talking to me, and, as I say, I will be very careful.'

Donna went back inside, and Nia got into the car, but before she drove she took time to catch her breath. Elvira had rung the helpline, desperate. Ruby had believed she shouldn't be marrying Ethan. What was going on with her? Ruby had been to see Elvira's mother not long before she died, and Elvira had been very upset.

Nia thought again about Elvira and her visits to her mother. She'd seen the other night how late Elvira was at the nursing home. That was a bit odd, wasn't it?

Nia tried to remember the name of the home; Petunia had talked about it at the hen party. What was it? Something to do with trees. Nia checked on her phone for nursing homes on the West Wight and there it was: The Pines. It didn't look that far, maybe she'd go and at least check out the location?

* * *

Following directions on her phone, she drove back past Calbourne and then turned up a narrow road that led to Mottistone Down, until, eventually, she reached the nursing home. As she sat in her car in the car park, she decided to go inside. She of course would need a reason for this, and she sat for a few moments working out what she considered to be a good explanation.

She got out of the car, walked confidently to the house and entered.

The home was very pleasant inside and they had clearly tried to make it appear as unclinical as possible. There was, however, a strong smell of disinfectant mingled with the waft of evening meal.

There was a desk with a registration book, with a polite notice asking people to make sure they signed in and out. One of the staff spotted Nia and came over. 'Have you come to visit someone?'

'Not today. Your home has been recommended to me and I've looked you up online. I saw you offered respite and thought, as I was passing, I would pop in and ask how I went about organising a visit with my mum.'

'I think there is a page on our website to book a visit, isn't there?'

Nia felt herself blushing. 'Oh, sorry, I must have missed that. I'll go back and check that out, thank you.'

'Any problems, just give us a ring and one of the managers will help you. Who was it recommended us to you?'

'My friend Elvira's mum is here – Mrs Johnson.'

'Of course. Elvira comes every Sunday; she is such a good daughter.'

'She is very happy with her mother's care here.'

'That's lovely to hear. Sorry, I didn't catch your name.'

'Oh, I'm Nia. Um, there was one more thing I wanted to check. The reason I am thinking about respite is that about once a month I have to go to the mainland to work and I get home very late. It's a long time to leave Mum. If I was to get back any time say by about nine in the evening, would that be too late to pop in just to say hello to Mum? It's just she sees me every day, and I know she'll miss me.'

'That is rather late. We ask visitors to leave by about half eight to give us time to quietly settle everyone down. It's much better, you see, to keep to a routine for everyone.'

'I quite understand. Well, I shall explain that to Mum if we get that far. Thank you so much for your help. I won't hold you up any longer.'

'That's quite all right. I look forward to meeting your mum soon.'

Nia left the home and returned to her car. So, as she thought, Elvira wouldn't be staying late when she visited her mother. What was she doing in the time between seeing her mother and returning to the close?

The only way she could think of finding out would be to follow Elvira after her visit, and that would have to wait until Sunday. One thing was clear: Elvira's life was a lot more complicated than it had first appeared.

27

As she left the house early the next day Nia was aware of the town feeling busier than usual. Activities were due to start at lunchtime and there was a buzz of expectation and excitement.

The salon had a packed day of appointments and Nia had no time to tell Jade what she'd discovered about Elvira the evening before. Instead, she worked through the day, only taking breaks to check on Romeo and take him for a walk at lunchtime. He was very excited by all the people, and she walked down the pier with him, enjoying the view of the ships.

Jade rushed off to meet friends after work so Nia took Romeo for another walk through the town and bought crêpes for her tea.

She was feeling very relaxed by the time she returned home and sent Safi a quick text to see how she was. She wasn't really expecting an immediate reply and was surprised when her phone rang, and it was Safi wanting to video call.

'Hiya, love, I wasn't expecting you to ring. I just wanted to check you were OK.'

'I was OK, but then someone sent me this video.'

Nia tutted, imagining some kind of offensive YouTube clip was doing the rounds. 'Oh, love, just delete it. People post all kinds of things, take no notice. Block the person if you can.'

'No, Mum, it's not like that. This is a video of you. Look, I'll hold my phone to my laptop – I've got it on there.'

Nia was completely mystified. What on earth could it be? However, she soon found out, and she stared at the images in horror.

Oh, God, who had taken that?

'I'm so sorry – I don't understand.'

'What's happening, Mum? Someone has put it on Dad's school's Facebook page and YouTube. It's everywhere. All my friends are sending it to me.'

The video was of Nia standing on a stage, holding a glass of wine, screaming and swearing. Safi paused it.

'When was this, Mum?' said Safi, who was crying now.

'It was a do at the school in April for the senior staff to celebrate the Ofsted report.'

'So why the heck did you behave like that? Were you pissed?'

Nia swallowed; tears escaped down her cheeks.

'It had been an awful week. There had been a night when Dad phoned me late and I could have sworn he was in a pub even though he told me he was at school. I'd not wanted to go to the school, but Dad said it would look odd if I wasn't there. So, I went. To my mind at least your dad and Miss Grey seemed to be openly flirting. I kept telling myself I was imagining it, but I found it all very hard to cope with. I knew I was drinking too much but I was so unhappy. Dad got up on stage and made this long speech telling everyone how proud he was of them all, how much they supported him and then he thanked me. "Always there to pick up the pieces after a long day," he said, and then he called for me to go up on stage. I tried to refuse, but he insisted, and you know what these things are like: everyone was calling my name. I had no option. I went up, and Dad handed me the mic and left the stage. I was shocked. I was expected to make some kind of speech. I stood there feeling such a fool. And then I looked down and saw Miss

Grey close to the stage looking up at me, her eyes full of contempt for me. I saw her whisper something to a friend, someone I'd known for a long time, and they both started sniggering. Suddenly it was as if I'd been right all along. She was having an affair with your father and in fact everyone there knew and approved. I imagined them all saying I'd never been good enough for him, he deserved someone better. The anger and frustration all boiled over and I started screaming at them all. I can't remember everything but once I started, I couldn't stop.'

'You only had to say a few words and get down,' said Safi quietly.

'I'm sorry, Safi, I was overwrought. I wasn't myself. I had no idea anyone had filmed this.'

But Safi hadn't finished. She held her phone again in front of the laptop, and it started playing again and Nia knew there was worse to come. She watched the rest of the video through her fingers. She watched herself jump off the stage, run over to Sian Grey and push her with such force that she staggered backwards and fell to the floor. Sian was crying now, the other teachers rushing to comfort her.

When it was finished, Nia lowered her hands, looking straight at her daughter. 'I know, it's terrible. I have never physically hurt anyone in my life. I promise you I was more shocked than her. After that the room started to spin, and I collapsed. Your father took me home.'

'He must have been so embarrassed.'

'He was, but I wasn't thinking straight. When Aunty Gwen suggested I come here, it seemed the right thing to do.'

'I can't believe it, Mum. Why didn't you tell me any of this?'

'I was ashamed of what had happened. I hoped you'd never know. I had no idea anyone was filming it.'

'You said Dad took you home after all that. He stood by you, Mum. He told me he'd forgiven you.'

'You've spoken to him?'

'I wanted to check he knew it had been put up on the school page. He told me he'd got it taken down from the school page. He's still trying to get it taken down from YouTube. He was so upset about it, for you more than him.' Safi spoke more quietly. 'I wish I hadn't seen it though.'

'So do I, love.'

'It doesn't feel like us, Mum. I've always been proud of the fact I have normal parents, that my home is stable.'

They tried to chat, but it was strained. Nia asked her if she'd been swimming but Safi replied defiantly that she couldn't as she'd had a tattoo on her ankle. Nia shuddered at the thought of Safi going into a random parlour to have her tattoo done abroad but was too exhausted to argue, and, in any case, it was too late for that now. Instead, she murmured a few cautionary warnings such as making sure it didn't get infected and keeping it covered until Safi changed the subject. In the end Safi said someone was calling her, and Nia was glad to finish the conversation.

She left the laptop, sat on the sofa, and curled up tight, feeling suffocated by the sense of guilt and shame. To be confronted by that evening that she'd successfully buried was awful and for Safi to have seen her acting in that way was humiliating.

Her instinct was to pack her bags and crawl back to Chris. Ethan had said she had been avoiding sorting her own life out all this time, and he'd been right.

Nia felt Romeo's nose push against her arm, and she reached out to cuddle him.

'What am I going to do?' she asked him. 'I can't hide here for ever.'

Nia went out into the garden and tried to clear her head. The way she felt now was exactly the way she'd felt when she'd come here, and she'd forgotten how desperately unhappy she had been. Her aim had been to return home stronger, and yet this had made her realise she was still very vulnerable. If she went back now nothing would change. Chris would persuade her she'd imagined all the hurt, maybe even that it was her fault.

Nia thought again of herself in that video. Yes, she'd been embarrassing but she'd been in so much pain. Chris should have looked after her, should have acknowledged his part in causing that pain, and he'd not done that yet. Before she returned, they needed to talk. She would keep her promise to Safi and talk to her father on the phone, but this was not the time to leave.

28

The next morning Nia discovered that the Old Gaffer's Festival had finally completely taken over the town. The noise, people, the smell of street food, everywhere was transformed. There was a fun fair, a huge marquee, but of course the real stars were the magnificent ships in the harbour.

Nia could tell that Jade loved the buzz; she even gave customers a glass of Prosecco as they arrived. Nia was nervous going into work, frightened that everyone would have seen the video but, of course, no one had, and there was a wonderful feeling of anonymity, being free from the life she'd had in Cardiff.

At the end of the day Jade reminded Nia about meeting up that evening.

'I think I'll give it a miss. I'm shattered. It's been such a hectic few days. I'm not young like you. I think I'll settle for a hot chocolate and box set on Netflix.'

'You can't miss all the fun. Honestly, this is the most excitement you are going to see here. Please, you have to come, I want to buy you a drink to thank you. I'd never have coped without you over the past few days.'

Nia reluctantly agreed before attempting to wake herself up by taking Romeo for a walk out of the town, along the harbour wall. It was a perfect evening, the sea glistening, people walking along laughing, eating candyfloss and ice cream. Strangers greeted her, and there was an innocence about it that warmed her.

After she'd settled Romeo at home, she went upstairs to get ready to go out but as she looked down at her 'mom' jeans and casual shoes, she couldn't face changing. It was only Wight's with the people from the close. She freshened up her make-up and checked her hair and left. Wight's was heaving and she had to push through the crowds in the bar to get out into the garden.

'Over here,' shouted Jade.

Nia joined Ian, Lucy, Jade, Richie, Ethan and Elvira at a table. Apart from Lucy, who was drinking fizzy water, they were sharing a couple of bottles of wine that were standing on the table.

Jade poured her a drink. 'Cheers.'

Nia was surprised to see Ian drinking wine. He seemed to have taken ownership of one of the bottles and was refilling his glass. Although superficially he appeared happy enough, Nia sensed he was simply putting on a show of bonhomie. His voice was louder, harsher; his laugh had a bitter edge.

'Any more news from the TV people?' Ethan asked.

'Bastards.' Ian spat the word followed by an unpleasant guffaw. 'Nothing yet. They know they can muck me about. I'm not exactly the next Graham Norton, am I?'

'It's not fair to offer you something and then change their minds like this,' said Elvira.

'I've no option but to wait.' There was no smile now. Ian slumped back into his seat and took a long slug of wine.

'Cheer up,' said Ethan. 'It's only a TV programme. There will be plenty of other offers.'

Ian sat up, his eyes burning. 'No, there won't, not at my age. This is a one-in-a-million opportunity for me. Don't you glibly tell me to cheer up.' He glanced at Ethan, who was scowling at him. 'It would be like me telling you to shrug off your money worries – it's not helpful, is it?'

Ethan didn't reply but sipped his drink. Ian sat back as if in retreat.

Elvira, however, seemed fired up now and slammed her glass on the table. 'That's pretty mean, Ian. God knows, life is hard for us all at the moment, we don't need to turn on each other.' She turned to Nia, glaring at her. 'Talking of which, maybe you could explain what you were doing at my mum's nursing home this week.'

Nia, seeing the fury on Elvira's face, didn't know what on earth to say.

Elvira continued, 'Apparently, you told them you were looking for information about the home. Is that right?'

Nia swallowed hard. 'Um, well...'

'Rose, the very kind nurse you spoke to, was grateful that I'd apparently recommended the home to you.'

'Who is this relative who needs respite at The Pines, then?'

Nia felt her face burning. Everyone was looking at her.

'There isn't anyone, is there?' sneered Elvira. 'You made up some stupid lie because you wanted to go and check up on me. You were digging around like Ruby.'

Before Nia could even stammer an answer, Elvira took out her phone, turned it on and then laid it on the table. As soon as she heard it, Nia knew what video Elvira was playing.

Ethan went to grab it, but Elvira pushed his hand away. 'No, why shouldn't everyone know what kind of person she is?'

'I'm sorry,' Ethan said to Nia. 'Elvira saw it online.'

'How on earth did you find it?'

'I decided to trawl around,' said Elvira, 'see what I could find out about you as you seem so intent on finding out about everyone's private business here. It was quite easy to find your daughter's Facebook page – she hasn't got any privacy settings, you know – and someone had sent her a link to the YouTube video of you. I guess she doesn't go on there often. Her age are all on Instagram, aren't they? She probably doesn't even know it's there; you should tell her.'

Ethan scowled. 'That's enough, Elvira.'

'I do think it would be nice if you supported me here. I wanted to show Nia what it felt like to have her private life exposed to everyone.'

The group leant forward; their eyes fixed on the video. Joe, who had been collecting glasses, came over and started to watch as well.

'Wow, Nia,' he joked, 'I didn't know you had it in you.'

For Nia the embarrassment was excruciating.

'So that's what you escaped from,' said Ian, his tone nasty. 'Lucy told me she'd seen you completely smashed in the garden the other night. You're so quick to judge everyone.' He looked around. 'It's not just Elvira she's been checking up on, it's all of us. She suspects one of us of killing Ruby.'

Jade reached out and turned the phone off. 'That's enough. If you're going to get mad with Nia, then you'd better get mad with me as well. I agree with her that things on the beach the evening Ruby died don't add up. I think one of us went down there and spoke to Ruby, tampered with the letters. Look, it might not be you who killed Ruby but, however bad it looks, you should own up. In the same way the person who sent Ruby the voodoo doll and the person who rang the helpline should.'

Nia glanced over at Elvira; their eyes locked, but neither said a word.

'Come on,' said Jade. 'Someone say something.'

Ian, who was sitting next to Jade, put his arm around her. 'That's enough. If anyone here had done any of these things, they'd have admitted it by now. Everyone here loved Ruby very much. I know how close you were. We all feel for you deeply, you know that.' He held his face very close to hers; their eyes met.

Jade shrugged his arm off and sat back. Elvira gave a cold laugh. 'I don't think anyone wants to play, Jade.' She picked up the phone and started the video again. 'I think you should watch to the end, see what kind of person Nia really is. She's not just a drunk, you see – she attacks people. Did you know that, Jade? And she was the last person to see Ruby alive.'

They all looked at Nia and suddenly it was as if she were back there that night, alone, everyone looking down on her.

'Stop it,' Nia pleaded, tears now streaming down her face. 'Turn that thing off.' But no one moved. Nia stood up to leave, but as she did she felt a hand on her shoulder.

'It's all right, love. I'm here now.'

She turned around and there was Chris.

Once she'd got over the shock of seeing her husband, Nia's first thought was how different Chris looked. He seemed taller somehow, his voice louder. Maybe it was seeing him away from home: it jarred for him to be here on the island, even though it did feel wonderful for a brief moment to have someone familiar to stand up for her.

He put his arms around her, and she found herself sobbing into his shoulder.

'It's all right, love. I've come to take you home.'

Nia wanted nothing more at that moment than to be scooped up and taken far away from this mess. Chris picked up her bag and, still holding her, guided her through the bar and out into the close. As she cuddled in, she breathed in the familiar smell, the feel of him. She'd missed this.

She wiped her eyes. 'You came over on a ferry?'

He laughed. 'I didn't swim.'

She smiled; it was a typical Chris reply, silly but charming.

'How did you know where to find me?'

'It was a guess. I'd have sat on the doorstep and waited otherwise, although Romeo saw me through the window and was going a bit mad.'

They went in; she immediately felt self-conscious. It was very strange to be inviting him into what she felt was almost her own home.

'It's a terrible mess,' she began.

'I'll help you tidy up before we leave.'

Nia blanched at the assumption she was about to drop everything to go with him but didn't comment.

Romeo went over for a fuss, and Chris leant over to stroke him, although the welcome wasn't the one he would have given Nia. Romeo had always been far more her dog than Chris's. 'Have you missed me, mate?' said Chris.

He looked around. 'It's very cosy.' Then he looked her up and down. 'Where did you get those trousers? Good God, you look like my mum... and no heels.'

She blushed. 'People are less fussy about things here.'

'You'll need to smarten up when you get back.'

Before she could comment he disappeared into the kitchen, put the kettle on and opened the back door. 'The garden is a bit wild but could be nice. We ought to think about getting somewhere like this as a holiday home, somewhere we can escape together. I'm looking for mugs, or do you have something more civilised?' She heard him open the fridge. 'That's more like it.'

In a matter of minutes Chris had made the place his own. It was always like this. He returned carrying two wine glasses and an opened bottle of wine. He poured her a drink and handed it to her as if she were his guest. 'It's quite nice here, bit pokey though. I'm sure you'll be glad to come home tomorrow.'

Slowly, she gathered her thoughts. 'We need to talk, Chris; a lot has happened.'

'But I thought you believed me. There's nothing to discuss and, admit it, you're pleased to see me.'

'Of course, but we still need to talk. Safi rang me, I saw the video...'

Nia felt herself getting red, tears filling her eyes again. 'I am so sorry, Chris, about that. Has it been very difficult?'

'Well, fortunately, I'd already spoken to the head of governors about it, and they knew Sian wasn't going to make a formal complaint. When the video went up, we decided the less said, the better.'

Nia bit her lip at the other woman's name mentioned so casually, but asked, 'Have you any idea who made that video in the first place? Did you see anyone holding up their phone?'

He shook his head. 'No, but after this I think maybe I should see if we can work it out. It has to be someone on the staff. I want to confront the bastard who did this to us.'

'I'm sorry, it was embarrassing for you.'

'It was—' he came closer to her '—but that is all in the past now. We'll go home tomorrow and make a fresh start.'

'But I told you I had obligations here. I can't just leave Jade in the lurch and it's not like I have a job waiting for me at home.'

At that moment there was a knock at the door.

'What the hell?' said Chris.

Nia went to answer it, found Ethan on the doorstep, and invited him in. He faltered.

'I'm sorry to interrupt you, but I just had to apologise for that business with the video. It's not like her to be so cruel, but she was upset about you going to the home. I know you mean well, but people don't like being checked up on, especially in connection to Ruby's death. You have to see why people would be upset by that.'

Chris had come over; he was used to being in charge of a conversation and hated not knowing what was going on. 'What's this, then? What's going on?' he demanded.

Ethan turned to Chris. 'I'm sure Nia can explain everything. I'll leave you to it. I just wanted to apologise, that was all. You'll have to come and join us all for a drink sometime.'

'Maybe we could do that another time, if we ever return, that is. Unfortunately, we'll be going first thing tomorrow,' said Chris confidently.

'Oh, right, well, if this is goodbye, Nia, it's been good to meet you. Jade is going to be lost in that salon without you, but do take care.'

As he let himself out Nia frowned at Chris. 'I'd not agreed to come back in the morning—'

'Of course, you will. Why did that chap mention a video?'

Nia explained about Elvira tracking it down.

'All the more reason to get away, I'd have thought. Also why was he talking about you and that girl who died? That's nothing to do with you.'

Reluctantly, Nia found herself telling him the whole story. He listened well, and at the end he put his arm around her. 'That's quite impressive.'

'You think so?'

'Of course.'

She smiled nervously. 'Thank you. I don't think it's made me too popular with some people. But you can see why I think I should stay here.'

He shook his head. 'No, I don't agree. You have to leave this to the police. You've done your bit now. This girl's sister and husband are here, leave it with them.'

'I suppose Jade might be able to follow things up—'

'Exactly. You must come back with me. You have to understand the only person I care about in all this is you. I've missed you so much, cariad.' He used his pet Welsh name for her, and she shivered. 'You and me, we've been together too long to let a little thing like this separate us.'

She stepped back. 'What's happening with Sian? She must be upset about the video.'

'Sian has handed in her notice. She's going to a big school in Bridgend as Deputy Head. She'll do well and I must say I am relieved. There was nothing going on, but I know it bothered you, and you are all that matters. You're the only person for me, always have been, always will be.'

He held her close, kissed her and slowly the world seemed to fade away.

29

Nia woke very early the next morning and crept out of bed so as not to wake Chris. She looked over at the bedside table where he'd put his watch, his clothes heaped next to the bed, and smiled. It was all so familiar and comforting. She gave Romeo his breakfast and opened the back door to let him out.

Chris's phone, sitting on the work surface, rang with the alarm and she grabbed it quickly to turn it off before it woke him up.

After she'd done that, she stared at his phone, suddenly desperate to check it. She hated the urge, just as she'd hated herself when she'd checked all those times at home. It was how she'd caught him out, seen the texts from Sian. Why he didn't have a second phone she'd never worked out, but that was Chris, always confident. It would never dawn on him he might get caught. And, of course, even if proved right, he'd convince Nia she'd lost the moral high ground by being someone who 'snooped on people's phones.'

The phone was still in her hand. This would be the last time. She quickly scrolled through emails: nothing. Now she felt even worse for looking, but it didn't stop her checking one more thing.

She went to Chris's gallery on WhatsApp, scrolled through the photos and videos. At first, apart from a few pictures from Safi she'd not seen, nothing surprised her, but then she saw it. And as soon as she saw the still of the first frame, she knew what it was.

Nia touched the still from the video and started to play it. Suddenly she saw one part that struck her as odd; she paused and enlarged it, yes, she was right. Her hand was shaking now as she carried on until the end. When it finished, she stared and asked herself what was this doing on Chris's phone?

She found the date and frowned: it was the date of the event. It must have been sent to him that evening. He must have known about it all along and been protecting her.

Surely there should be a way of tracing it? Yes, Safi had told her that despite all the encryption there was a pathway on WhatsApp videos, enabling you to track back to whoever filmed the video.

She kept digging, found again the date and the time it had been made and then finally she was able to trace it back to the person who'd recorded it. Her fingers started to shake as she slowly lowered herself into a chair, sipping her water to calm her.

'You're up early.'

Nia looked up to see Chris grinning at her. But as his eyes dropped to his phone in her hand his expression changed.

'What are you doing? Please say you're not checking my phone again. I promise you there are no texts from Sian. You're going to have to start trusting me.'

'Am I?' Nia's voice cracked as she spoke, and she turned the phone around to face him.

'Someone sent me the video. I'll delete it.'

He went to grab the phone, but she shook her head. 'No, Chris, no one sent this to you. The pathway shows you made this film. You stood next to the stage watching me falling apart and filmed me.'

He stood with his mouth open, clearly searching for words; it never took long.

'I guessed there may be comeback, and I also know how stories get embellished in schools. I thought it was as well to have an accurate record of what happened.'

'That was your first thought, not "let me go and get Nia down, she's miserable, she needs my help".'

'I expected someone else to, and I certainly didn't expect you to go on to attack Sian.'

It was meant to put her on the defensive, but she wasn't going to be distracted. 'Not only did you film this, but you must have been the one who put it on the school's Facebook page.'

'Other people had copies,' he stammered.

'How do you know? Who did you send this to?'

'Sian wanted one in case she had to give her side of the story.'

'You gave it to her?'

'She saw me filming, she nagged me. I knew she wouldn't use it. But, listen, the main thing to remember here is that I forgave you for what you did. You have no idea how embarrassing it was for me – for weeks after people were asking me about it, the pupils and parents sniggering behind my back. The chair of governors asking to have meetings with me. Can you imagine what it was like, the whole school knowing the headteacher's wife had been drunk and attacked someone? And yet despite all that I have been standing up for you.'

'But the video, surely it's reminded everyone about what happened? Why did you put it online?'

He grimaced. 'Firstly, let me make it clear I didn't think anyone would download it to their computer and put it on YouTube.'

'But why put it up at all?'

He sat down, put his head in his hands. 'I wanted Safi to see it, but I didn't want to send it to her. I knew if I put it up on the school site someone would send it to her. Everyone else knew what had happened, I didn't have much to lose, and I wasn't going to leave it up for long.'

Nia stared. 'Why would you want Safi to see this?'

'You don't understand. I don't think she believed me about you being ill. I could hear it in her voice – she thought I'd been unfaithful, let you down. I had to show her how unstable you had been.'

Nia shook her head. 'I can't believe you could be so cruel.'

'All I want is for us to be a family again.'

'But you lied to me, Chris. I was never ill. I know now you lied to me about the watch. I saw Sian's wrist in the video – she has an exact replica of the one you are wearing, only smaller. That child was right, they saw you, didn't they?'

He shrugged. 'It was nothing, it was a fling.'

'No, Chris, it was lies, and you let me think I was going mad. I don't know if I can live with someone who treats me like this.'

He stood up. 'So what are you going to do with yourself? You earn a pittance, no smarter house, no more living off my status. No, Nia, you need me.'

'I can live alone; I've proved that to myself. I've started a life here—'

He laughed. 'I've news for you. You're making a complete fool of yourself. I saw the way the people here were looking at you when I came to find you.'

'They were angry.'

'No, they pitied you like the staff on the night you gave your drunken speech. For God's sake, you're only a hairdresser, that's it. Don't get so het up. You need to get back to Cardiff now before you go completely nuts here.' He prodded the side of his head with his forefinger. 'You told me the police doubted what you said. I agree. I'm sure you were pissed. It's absurd to think you know better than them.'

Nia felt hot tears fall down her cheek and turned away, trying to hide them.

She felt Chris's hands on her shoulders, felt his breath on her neck. He spoke gently, seductively now. 'Nia, I don't mean to be harsh. I'm saying these things because I love you. Come home now. Come with me and I will look after you. I love you, Nia, you and me, we need each other.'

The words were like a strong magnet pulling her towards him, but she looked into his eyes. They were cold, unfeeling.

'Are you sorry for what has happened?' she asked quietly.

'Sorry for what?'

'For the affair.'

'I wouldn't call it an affair.'

'But it was an affair, Chris. You betrayed me.'

'Rubbish.'

She blinked. 'And until you can see that, I don't see how we can work things out.' She turned away. 'And there are people here who need me to stay. I want to find out what happened to Ruby. I wasn't drunk and I know what I saw. I want to help Jade at the salon.'

'So, strangers are more important to you than our marriage?' Chris threw his hands up in the air. 'There's no reasoning with you, is there? You'll come crawling back in a week or two; these people will have sent you packing by then. I'm going to get my stuff together and, while I do, think very carefully about what you are doing. There's still time to change your mind.'

Nia sat down. She was breathing hard. Her head was so hot it was as if she'd run a marathon. But she didn't move. She heard Chris thumping around, and then come down the stairs.

'Do you know when the next ferry is?' she asked.

'I think it's on the hour. Thank God. I can't wait to get away from this damn island. It gives me the creeps.'

He strode over to the door, slamming it behind him.

Nia sipped her water; her hands were shaking. She bent down and stroked Romeo, who was looking very confused.

'He never said goodbye to you, did he? Never mind, me and you are better off on our own for now.'

With a head full of rage, Nia went and got dressed. Opening the curtains, she saw her bedroom was a mess and no longer felt like hers. She stripped the bed, picked clothes up off the floor, straightened the things on her dressing table, tutting at the sight of her hairbrush. When she came back later, she would give it a good clean. From a drawer she took fresh bedding and made up the bed, and then stood back. She could almost pretend Chris had never been there. After putting the bedding in to wash, she took Romeo to the car and left the close. She needed to be up high, away from everyone. She drove up to the downs and walked to the top with Romeo.

Only when she could finally see the cliffs and the monument in the distance did she stop.

Breathless, she sank onto the grass. Yellow and white were the dominant colours today, with the white froth of cow parsley, contrasting with the cowslips and gorse. On one of the large prickly bushes sat a little brown bird with a black cap, singing like a nightingale, and far above a kestrel hovered.

In the distance the sea seemed scattered with diamonds, sparkling in the early morning sun. The breeze was fresh and sweetly stroked her face. This was where she needed to be. Romeo wandered close by, chasing scents of rabbits and pheasants, as content to be here as her.

What was she to do next? There was so much anger raging around inside her, combining with hurt, disappointment. She hugged her knees close to her.

When Chris had appeared last night, it had felt like her knight in shining armour arriving to save her from the battering she was receiving from Elvira and Ian, and from that humiliating video. How she'd wanted that to be true. As Ruby had said, sometimes anything was easier to believe than the truth.

Nia stood up, watched the kestrel dive arrow-like on its prey. She needed some of that determination, that clear thinking.

Slowly making her way back to the car, Nia arrived at the gate that led to the car park and waited for Romeo, who was busy sniffing at the grass. 'Come on, Romeo, I have things to do,' she shouted. He looked up and started to meander towards her. His recall had never been very good. The trainer always said he took the 'scenic route' back to her. Eventually he was back, she put on his lead, and they returned to the car.

Once home, she walked into the kitchen to give Romeo his breakfast. As she did, she spotted the back door was slightly ajar.

'Oops,' she mumbled, but opened it fully ready for Romeo to go out after he'd eaten.

Nia went upstairs to get changed, but then noticed her hairbrush was on the floor. That was odd.

She glanced around the room. Everything else was as neat as she'd left it, but why was this brush on the floor? As she picked it up, she saw the excess hair that had been tangled among the bristles had gone.

'Am I going mad?' she asked Romeo, who had come in to join her. 'It must have been cleaner than I thought.' Then she noticed the wastepaper basket. It had fallen over, and a few tissues were scattered on the carpet. She also noticed a few small clumps of hair were down there as well. That was odd. Then she remembered the open back door when she'd returned from the downs.

Was it possible someone had been in here?

But why go to all that bother to take a few clumps of hair?

She ran downstairs, checked the living room and kitchen. There was little of value here but nothing had gone. She must be imagining things; it was too ridiculous.

With that, she closed the back door and made herself breakfast, but even as she did a voice nagged at the back of her head. What if someone had been in the house while she'd been out? Someone had watched, seen her leave, and come in here, touched her things... It seemed ridiculous and yet deep down she had a horrible feeling it was true.

30

Nia found it difficult to settle for the rest of the day.

She was aware that the anger was still bubbling inside from Chris's visit. She kept churning over the things she wished she'd said, all the arguments she could have thrown at him. She even composed a text to send him but deleted it; it was pointless.

Her mind turned to Safi. Should she tell her what her father had done? Why shouldn't she know what kind of man he was? But then why should Safi be dragged into the mess of their marriage?

She was glad to get out of the house later that afternoon for a walk with Romeo.

Everywhere was still busy although there was the feeling of the end of an event as people were slowly packing up stalls and sweeping up the debris. It reminded Nia of taking down her Christmas decorations when there was part of her that was always glad to get the house straight and back to normal.

She walked through the town and down the pier.

When she reached the end, she recognised the fisherman she'd talked to the other evening.

'You're early,' she commented.

'My wife wants me to have this family meal tonight,' he said grumpily.

'That'll be nice, won't it?'

'I told her not to make a fuss – it's only my birthday. Don't see why I should celebrate being a year older.'

Nia smiled. 'I'll still wish you a happy birthday. At least you're getting in a bit of fishing first.'

'That's right. Doesn't feel like a Sunday if I don't.'

'I guess you would normally see Joe from Wight's. I know he likes to come fishing.'

'Oh, he's not been for a long time. I see him going on to the fancy yachts at all hours. That's more his style now, I think.'

Nia nodded. Ethan had been right, Joe didn't come here fishing. So where had he been the night Ruby died?

* * *

Nia returned home, settled Romeo down and then thought about going up to Wight's that evening. After the way things ended last time, she wasn't sure anyone would want to see her. However, if she was going to find out any more about Ruby's death she needed to keep in touch with people. Maybe she could find a way of making peace with them.

She went into the kitchen, quickly made a batch of Welsh cakes, which she took later with her as she headed up to Wight's.

They were sitting at their usual table, but the atmosphere was far more subdued than normal.

Nia put down the tin and opened it. She decided something needed to be said. 'Look, I'm sorry if you all think I've been interfering. I know I'm not one of you, but I believe something happened to Ruby and it's not right that we don't at least try to find out the truth.'

No one replied, not even Jade.

'You should all care about this.' Still no reply. No one even met her eye.

'Look, you've seen that damn video and with it you've seen the worst of me. I'm free now. But none of you are. It's normal to have secrets but not to hold on to them so tightly that you'd rather Ruby's killer got away with what they've done than let anyone know.'

Still, no one responded. Instead, Ian tried awkwardly to make conversation about Old Gaffer Festivals in the past while everyone else joined in. Nia knew they were purposely trying to remind her she was an outsider.

She clenched her fists and was thinking about leaving when she was distracted by the sight of Richie's dragon tattoo, the end of its tail sticking out from below the hem of his trousers. She thought of Safi, hoped she was still keeping hers covered. Richie's was quite new too. Ruby had mentioned him having just had it done the night she'd given Nia a lift to the Red Jet.

Nia frowned. If he'd had it done that week then, surely, he couldn't have been swimming the Sunday after. Apart from infection, he could have wrecked an expensive tattoo.

She leant down to look closer.

'Something wrong?' Richie asked, half grinning.

'Sorry, it's your tattoo. I was thinking that if you had that done the week before Ruby died, then you couldn't have been swimming with Ian on that Sunday.' The words spilled out before she could stop them.

Richie looked at her, blinking. 'What?'

Nia wished she'd kept her mouth shut, but it was too late now. 'You had a new tattoo; you can't have been swimming with Ian the night Ruby died.'

Richie narrowed his eyes, glanced over at Ian and then back at Nia. 'No, you're right. I went in the gym that night.'

'Of course,' said Ian in a bright voice. 'I'd forgotten that Richie was in there the whole time I was swimming.' Ian sighed. 'Now, Nia, I think we have all had more than enough of this.'

Her anger bubbled up. 'Don't patronise me. I've had enough of that from my husband. In fact, apart from Jade and Lucy, you've all lied about where you were the night Ruby died.'

'I have said Richie was in the gym—'

'But you didn't before. You wanted people to think you two were together the whole time in the pool, but you weren't. In the same way, Joe, you said you were fishing, but I know you weren't.'

Joe motioned to interrupt her, but she carried on. 'Ethan, you've given one story, but can I believe it? And, Elvira, you were only at the home for an hour – where were you the rest of the time?'

Nia saw Ethan flash a look of alarm at Elvira.

'You know something, I don't care what you think of me,' said Nia. 'I will find out what has happened, and, by the way, I know one of you went into my house today. If the aim of that was to frighten me off, well, it failed. I am going nowhere.'

Nia stormed out of Wight's, collected Romeo, and stomped down to the beach.

She let him off the lead, took off her shoes, rolled up her trousers and walked down into the sea. She was crying, sobbing, as she walked into the cold water. It numbed her legs. She scooped up sea water and threw it on her face, the salt sea mixing with her tears.

Slowly the storm calmed, and she started to wade out of the sea, most of her clothes quite wet now.

'Nia!' a voice shouted, and she saw Jade waiting on the shore.

She dragged herself over to Jade.

'Oh, God, are you all right? I should have stood up for you, I'm so sorry.'

'It's not just that, it's everything.'

'What happened with Chris?'

Nia told Jade that Chris had made the video.

'What a bastard,' said Jade. 'Sorry, I know he's your husband, but that's a horrible thing to do.'

Nia blinked, surprised at the strength of Jade's words. 'He says he did it to ensure there was a record of what happened. I suppose in a way he was protecting me, so, like he says, I shouldn't be upset, or angry with him. I'm just confused, Jade. I don't know what to think any more.'

Jade stared, open-mouthed. 'He's really messed with you, hasn't he?'

'I don't know. I don't know anything any more.'

'I'll tell you what I think. Chris has manufactured this whole thing to grind you down so that any self-respect you had left disappeared, and you'd be grateful to him for taking you back.'

'He did admit one of the reasons he put it up was to show Safi how ill I'd been. Maybe he's right.'

'God, he's so manipulative. Is that how he works, making you feel bad all the time so that you doubt your own mind, your own feelings?'

'I don't know.'

Jade shook her head. 'You don't, do you? You have no idea any more how you feel about anything. I'm really sorry, Nia.'

'Chris says he's trying to look after me. Look, I'm only a hairdresser and he's got such an important job. He's so bright—'

'I've told you before, you are bright, clever, and that makes you a great hairdresser and you should be proud of that because most people, Chris included, couldn't even start to do your job. Nia, he has totally crushed any self-confidence you have. It's so wrong. If he loved you, he would build you up, be proud of you and make you proud of yourself.'

'He says he loves me.'

Jade frowned. 'If he loved you, he wouldn't lie to you all the time and he would have got on that damn stage and looked after you. And then posting the video for everyone to see, that was so cruel.'

Jade grabbed Nia's arm. 'This is nothing to do with love. Nia, this man is messing with your head. Does he twist things like this a lot?'

'He tends to say things were nothing. He's done a lot of that over the fling with this teacher. I don't know, maybe I am overreacting – do you think so?'

'How many of these flings has he had?'

'Oh, a few. I forgive him, and then it happens again. He says it's nothing. I get confused because part of me is hurting so much and yet he's telling me it shouldn't.'

Nia picked up some pebbles, starting to pile them up.

'This is serious,' said Jade gently. 'This is emotionally abusive.'

'Oh, no, he's not like that. He's a good man. Honestly, if you saw the work he does—'

'That doesn't matter. What's important is how he's treating you, how he makes you feel about yourself. Does he make you feel loved, cared for? Does he love you for who you are?'

Nia shrugged.

'Why is it so hard to admit he's done something wrong?'

'I guess, he's always been my hero, the person I look up to. It made me feel good about myself that someone like him would choose someone like me.'

Romeo had come to sit with them and was leaning up against Nia's leg.

'So how did you feel about yourself before you met him?'

Nia shrugged. 'A bit rubbish. It wasn't anyone's fault. I was looking after family and so never even did my A levels. I loved hairdressing though. I met Chris when he came in as a client. He was still a student. We lived together, had Safi, got married. I liked looking after him and Safi and our home but when Safi left, I was lost. I think he was as well.'

'You've spent a long time looking after everyone else. Maybe it's time you started looking after yourself. Be your own best friend, that's what they say, isn't it?' Jade smiled. 'Maybe instead of becoming a whole new you, you should look after the one you already have.'

'I'm so tired.' Nia could feel tears burning her eyes.

Jade put her arm around her. 'You've been through so much. Thank God you got away. You have to take this seriously.'

'You used that word before.'

'That's because it is serious. Your husband has been repeatedly lying to you, telling you things that matter don't. He's someone who constantly minimises your feelings, makes you question yourself. I can see you never feel understood, you feel like you're going mad. The problem is then you can become more and more dependent on a person who does anything they can to avoid taking any responsibility for the things they do wrong.'

Nia stared at Jade. 'You understand, don't you? That's exactly how it has been. How do you know all that?'

'I was brought up in a strict religion, remember. I know all about control. About making people doubt themselves, stop trusting their own instincts – that's central to mind control. The Righteous made me feel so bad about myself I thought I couldn't do anything right on my own. I had to have validation from them for everything. It's what I think has happened with your husband. The fact that he claims he is doing this because he loves you makes it even more dangerous.'

Nia shook her head. 'I'd never thought about it like that before.'

'You need to, Nia; you need to think very seriously about getting out of this marriage.'

'Get a divorce, you mean? Oh, I don't think it's that bad.'

'Is that you speaking or him? Not that bad? How bad does it have to get, then?'

'I don't know, I can't think.'

'Then you must stay here until you can.'

Jade stood up and offered a hand to Nia. 'You're sopping wet; you'd better start the self-care with a shower, I think.'

Nia got up, put Romeo on his lead and they all started to walk back to the close.

'Everyone is very angry with me, aren't they?' Nia said. 'What am I going to do? I know I sounded confident before, but I don't want them to all hate me, and I don't want to make losing Ruby worse for people.'

When they arrived at Nia's front door, Jade said, 'I would love for you to find out the truth about Ruby. It's easy for me to say, but I would be very grateful if you could keep trying.'

'But the others—'

'They're going to have to learn to face up to some difficult stuff. For example, did you see Ethan's face when you said about Elvira only spending an hour with her mother?'

'I did, and Elvira is furious with me for going to the home.'

'What's up with her?'

'I don't know, but she's stressed out by something. You know, I should wait outside the home and then follow her, see what she does. There is something else I've been meaning to do as well.'

'What's that?'

'It's to do with Richie. I need to go back over to Cowes and find out who he is seeing at that bungalow.'

'I can see that, whatever anyone says, you're going to keep digging, aren't you? Just you stay safe. I need you in the salon. It's going to be another busy week with everyone getting their hair done for the Isle of Wight festival.'

'Oh, the big one in Newport. It's this weekend?'

'Yes. I usually go, but I sold my tickets this year. Shame, it's a good line-up. Kaiser Chiefs on Friday, Rod Stewart for the oldies on Sunday night.'

'Does Yarmouth get very crowded?'

'Nah, obviously the ferry is busy but most people camp and stay over in Newport. It's great for islanders, though. It's hard to go to live music evenings on the mainland as it means staying overnight, which gets expensive.'

'But you're not going this year?'

'I can't face it; it doesn't feel right to be going off partying somehow.'

'I can understand that,' replied Nia and they left together.

Nia went back into the house. The bedding she'd put in the washer-dryer that morning was dry now, and so she took it out and threw in her wet clothes.

Later that night she lay in bed, Romeo snoring beside her. Eventually she drifted off to sleep but was woken by the sound of a muffled thump downstairs, and footsteps outside. It took a few moments to orientate herself, but she glanced over at her clock. It was three in the morning. Romeo, oblivious, was still asleep and so she nervously got out of bed and peeped out of the curtains. Across from her Jade's room was in darkness, the street lights shone down on an empty road, silence. There was no one about.

She went to the top of the stairs, stood, and listened.

The house was in darkness, everything was still. She crept down a step, and then another, each time stopping to listen.

Finally, she reached the bottom and then she saw it, lying on her doormat.

Nia approached the envelope as if it were an unexploded bomb, taking slow, tentative steps, towards it.

31

Once she'd picked up the letter, she flung open the door, checking again outside. There was nobody to be seen. Whoever had posted the letter had been quick; maybe they were watching her now from behind their curtains. She shivered and went back inside.

Nia turned on the light. Romeo had come down to see what was going on. The wax seal shone brightly, the red like drips of blood on the white paper. She ran her fingers over the cold seal and held it to closer to the light. Was it Ruby's seal? Whoever had done this had lacked Ruby's expertise and it was impossible to make out the impression left by the seal.

Nia had never opened a letter with a wax seal before and it made a satisfying crack as she opened it. Ruby had been right; it did feel very special.

The excitement soon faded as she read the stark message inside.

Leave. Get out while you can.

The words had been typed. There was no signature. Nothing to tell her who had sent it.

Nia slumped down and Romeo came over to her.

'That's horrible. Childish, but nasty,' she said out loud to Romeo.

Someone had taken the time and trouble to type the letter, seal it and then creep down here in the dark. They had pushed it through her letter box, maybe even peeped inside; their breath was in her house.

Nia shook herself; she mustn't let this get to her. Grabbing the letter, she shoved it in a drawer, but the feeling refused to go. Hate mail, that was what they called it. Nia remembered Ruby using the word hate – and now someone in the close hated her.

Nia checked the locks and then went back to bed, but sleep eluded her, and she lay listening, waiting. As soon as light squeezed its way through the gap in her curtains she got up, dressed, and took Romeo out.

It was a grey morning and a light sea mist hung in the air. The remnants of the weekend had been cleared away. Some of the gaffers were still in the harbour but the bunting hung limp and lifeless, colours subdued in the damp morning light. The cries of the seagulls were muffled. It was as if the town were painted today in watercolours after the bright, thick oils of the weekend.

They walked along the harbour wall and it was then she recognised someone coming off one of the yachts.

'Morning,' she said.

Joe stepped back, startled. 'Oh, hi.'

He was holding loaded plastic bags in each hand, as he had the first time she had seen him, but this time it struck her as odd.

'You're up early,' she said, but as she spoke she realised he was wearing the same shirt as the night before.

'I had to go and see someone,' he replied and then peered at her more closely. 'Are you OK?'

Nia found the gentle concern touching and felt her lip tremble.

'Hey, come and have a coffee,' he said, and before she could hesitate she was walking up to Wight's with Joe.

Once inside he ran down to the cellar with the bags and then back up to make coffee.

It was strangely quiet, with no background music, no one else there. A slight stale smell hung in the air and Joe propped the door open before making them both strong cups of coffee and sitting down with her.

'Better?'

'Thank you.'

He sipped his drink. 'You look rough,' he said with a slight grin.

'I slept badly.'

'You really do believe something happened to Ruby, don't you?'

'Yes, I do. I want to get to the bottom of what happened, but it's hard when everyone is so secretive.'

'The thing is, Nia, when you live in a very small, tight community like this you have no idea how hard it is to keep things private. It feels like you are always being watched, everyone clocking when you leave the close and when you return.'

Nia was surprised at the vehemence of his words. 'I guess so.'

Joe's phone rang and he got up to answer it. He spoke quietly and then came back to Nia. 'I'm so sorry, I have to go out to see someone. I won't be long. Please finish your coffee. If you need to go before I come back, just pull the front door to. I'll put it on the latch.'

He hurried out, leaving Nia and Romeo alone.

It felt awkward being there now, but she sipped her coffee. Suddenly she heard a door banging. She tried to ignore it, but it kept on banging and it was coming from behind the bar. Maybe Joe had left a door open downstairs that was now banging in the wind.

She had another sip of coffee and, urging Romeo to stay, went to see what was happening. There was a flight of stairs up to what she assumed was Joe's flat, but the banging wasn't coming from there, it was a door further along.

Nia went to shut the door firmly but couldn't resist peeping in the room. It had specialist storage for wine but also for bottled beers and other drinks. Then she spotted the bags Joe had been carrying and couldn't resist walking over to them and opening one.

'What are you doing in here?'

She'd not heard Joe return.

'Nothing,' she said automatically, then added, 'I heard a door banging, and came to shut it.'

'Oh, thanks. This door is always like that – we get a draught through here.'

Nia realised she was still holding onto the top of the bag, somehow unable to let go.

'I store my personal spirits down here alongside the business stock,' Joe stammered.

'There's a lot of bottles,' she said, holding up one that appeared to have a label written in possibly an Eastern European language. 'I don't recognise these names.'

Joe grimaced. 'My friend brings them over for me.'

The pieces started to fall into place. 'Your friend from one of the yachts?'

He nodded. 'Look, I'll admit he suggested I decant these into bottles people recognise. No one would notice the difference, and these cost a quarter of the price. You have to realise, Nia, I am under enormous pressure to make this business work. My parents have sunk their life savings into the place. It can't fail.'

She saw the lines of stress in his face. He suddenly looked much older.

'I understand that, but you could lose your licence. This is illegal.'

He combed his fingers through his hair. 'I know, I know. Ruby was telling me not to do it, but it's hard. He keeps bringing them over. He means well. I don't want to offend him. So far, I've been secretly handing them on to other people.'

'But if you were caught, you would lose everything.'

Joe sat on a stool, putting his head in his hands. 'I know, it's the one thing that stops me, that and the fact my father would be absolutely mortified. Honesty means everything to him.'

'You should talk to your parents. You're young, they'll want to support you.'

He shook his head. 'I have to show them I can do this. I don't want to be a total disappointment to them.'

Joe leapt up. 'You have to promise me, Nia, you won't breathe a word of this to anyone. I promise you I won't try to use this. I have friends who would be glad of it, but don't say anything.'

Nia followed him out of the room. Romeo had actually stayed where she left him.

'I'll be off, then.'

'You'll not say anything?'

She gave him a reassuring smile and then leant to put Romeo's lead on him.

'Thanks for the coffee,' she said and then left.

* * *

In the afternoon she decided to try and tidy the garden. Romeo enjoyed having her outside and she enjoyed being out there.

She was having a cup of tea when Jade came to see her. Nia invited her into the garden and gave her a drink.

'I thought I'd let you know we have a date for Ruby's funeral. It's this Friday.'

'So soon?'

'We heard this morning that the coroner has released the body. When I rang the funeral directors and crematorium, we were told there was a space this Friday. The next would be in two weeks' time. I think we've all waited long enough.'

'Where will it be held?'

'Richie has agreed to compromise. We will hold a service at The Hall for Richie and his father, but it will be short, and then we go to the crematorium. That service will start at two in the afternoon, and we'll close the salon for the day. There will be people coming from the mainland. Joe is putting on a buffet in the afternoon.'

'And how are you keeping?' Nia glanced at Jade's stomach.

'I'm still planning a termination. I think part of me has been waiting for the funeral. I rang the hospital. I'm going in on Monday.'

'Then I will come with you.'

Jade squeezed her hand. 'Thank you. To be honest, I'm trying not to think about it too much. So have you found out anything new?'

Nia paused. She didn't want to betray confidences but there were some things she could share.

'I know that Joe isn't fishing on a Sunday night.'

Jade's eyes widened. She smiled. 'I'm not surprised. I never could imagine Joe enjoying handling bait, dead fish, gutting them, even standing out there in the cold. None of it seems like Joe.'

'Well, it's not. The fisherman I spoke to told me that Joe had stopped going and certainly hadn't been there the night Ruby died. It does leave the question of where he was that night.'

'I expect he was having a drink with friends or something. I can't see Joe ever harming Ruby. He loved her too much.'

'What are Joe's parents like?'

'Oh, they are gorgeous, really lovely. His mum worships Joe. He can do no wrong.'

'But how would they react if he ran into problems with the business?'

'Of course, they'd be upset to lose the money, but I was talking to his dad, and they have been sensible, not sunk everything into the bar. They have a nice home and enough to live on. I think Joe would find it harder than them. He so wants to do well for them.'

'He's an interesting person, Joe. I don't feel like I know him that well.'

'Joe's more complicated than most people realise and, to be honest, I don't fully get him. The only person who really did was Ruby – he loved her.' Her voice broke. 'We all did.'

'You two enjoying a cuppa?'

Nia saw Lucy smiling over the fence. 'Come and join us.'

'Oh, no, I've only just had one. How are you, Jade? Richie came over and told us about the funeral. We will be coming, of course.'

Jade got out of her chair; she had suddenly turned very pale. 'I need to go,' and rushed away.

'Is she all right?' Lucy asked.

'I think it's something she ate.'

Lucy seemed to accept the explanation. 'I saw you coming out of Wight's early this morning. Is everything all right with Joe?'

Nia was coming to realise that Lucy seldom missed much in the close.

'He's fine.'

Nia could feel a look from Lucy boring into her, but it wasn't until she spoke that she realised what was really going through Lucy's mind.

'He's such a good lad, isn't he? You'd love his mum. She can't be that much older than you.'

Before Nia could defend herself, Lucy moved on. 'I know, of course, Jade is grieving the loss of her sister, but she looks so pale, she doesn't seem herself.'

Nia looked away.

'I've been watching her,' continued Lucy. 'You two have got friendly very quickly. Has she mentioned anything to you? I'm not being nosy; I've known Jade a long time. I would want to help if I could. It's not easy when you're single, coping with everything.'

She gave Nia a very meaningful stare. She knows, thought Nia. I bet she knows.

'Jade hasn't said anything to me.'

'No? Well, if I've noticed, others in the close will have. I'm just saying. Right, I will see you tomorrow, at the salon.'

She disappeared behind the fence, leaving Nia feeling unsettled. Lucy's comments had contained an edge of threat. But Nia had no idea why.

Nia found it impossible to settle all evening, and realised she was continually listening for the sound of the letter box. What if someone this moment was about to post another of those letters?

'This is not good,' she said to Romeo. 'I know it's late but we need to get out or I'll drive myself mad and, anyway, there is something I need to do but I don't want to do it here. I need to get out of the town, away from our beach.' She grabbed her coat, and Romeo's lead, and finally went to the drawer, found that horrible letter and stuffed it in her pocket.

They went to the car, and she remembered the signpost to that fort further on down the road from the pool where Ian and Richie had been swimming. It was dark now, but she needed to go somewhere different, and she didn't have to get out of the car if it didn't feel safe.

It wasn't often that she turned right leaving the town, but tonight she drove over the bridge and carried on up the road. It wasn't long until she was once more at the signpost for Fort Victoria.

She turned off the main road and down a steep hill. Eventually she arrived at a large gravel car park. There were only a few cars there, looking very lost in the expanse. Two sides of the car park were surrounded by tall fort walls. To her left was woodland.

Nia found her emergency torch and got out of the car, and she heard an owl hoot from deep in the woods.

'Come on, Romeo,' she said, 'I think we'll be OK.' All the same she put on his lead, not sure of what she would find. He was wagging his tail, nose down, very excited to be exploring a new place at this time of night.

Nia looked up. The sky was enormous, with only a sliver of a moon, but thousands of tiny stars twinkled back at her. It was beautiful. Her own personal planetarium. There was enough light for her to make out arches in the wall and she could see beach beyond.

Carefully, she walked to an archway. Further along the sea wall she saw a few fishermen, and for the first time in her life she understood the attraction of coming out here alone for hours.

The tide was in; fortunately she didn't have far to walk to reach the sea. Taking the letter from her pocket, she tore it into tiny pieces. She moved Romeo's lead to her other hand and then walked carefully over the pebbles. Reaching up, she then threw the tiny snowflakes of paper into the sea. A gust of wind scattered them, and she was pretty sure they were all caught by the sea. The main thing was it was gone; the sea had the words now.

She went back to the safety of the arch and looked out into the darkness. It was time to go, but she was aware of a reluctance to return to the house. And then she realised why. The letter and those words might have been swept out to sea but, as Ruby had said, 'the hate remains'.

She guessed, like Ruby, this person would like her to also disappear. Nia took a deep breath. She had faced so much lately, but she was still standing; it had not broken her. She must now find the courage to face whatever lay ahead of her.

32

After a busy two days in the salon, Nia was reluctant to go out on the Wednesday evening. But she'd promised herself she would go again to the chalet bungalow, try and check what exactly was going on there.

She left the house about half past six and drove over to Cowes, where she parked where Richie had before. At least it was dry this evening and she arrived at the bungalow quickly on foot, immediately spotting Richie's car. He was here. She had to decide now if she was going to call at the house or go home. She'd made up an excuse, but it seemed even weaker now she was here. This one was no better than those at the hotel and the nursing home, but it was the best she could do.

Nia walked over to the bungalow. A man with his little Westie was on the other side of the road and Nia felt sure she was being watched. She smiled over, hoping the man would walk on, but he hung about, and Nia had a nasty feeling he was in some kind of neighbourhood watch.

Without thinking too much, she marched to the front door and rang the bell. Her heart was thumping. She could feel the man behind her watching still; there was no getting away.

Richie came to the door and had no time to hide the look of horror on seeing her.

'Is this Jade's place?' she asked desperately, trying to steady her voice.

'No.' The word was barely more than a whisper.

'Oh no, isn't this 13 Haven Way?'

'No, it's Haven Place.'

'Oh, God, I'm so sorry. I was only going to post some things for her.' She looked past him, trying to find a way to invite herself in. 'So, you have somewhere over here as well?'

Richie seemed to have calmed down and to be assessing her. 'Maybe you'd better come in, that is, if you have time.' He gave a knowing look, and Nia knew he had sussed out what she was doing.

'Of course, thank you.'

Nia followed him inside. It was clear the bungalow had not been decorated for years, with faded flowered wallpaper and carpets. In the hallway stood an ugly wooden coat stand with Richie's coat, umbrella, and bags. Nia was distracted by a large ornate mirror and glanced at her reflection. Her hair was a mess; she tried to push it back into style with her fingertips.

Richie took Nia into the lounge, which had an old-fashioned suite, and coffee table. There were no paintings or pictures anywhere.

She sat on the edge of a grubby sofa, but Richie remained standing.

'So, now you'd better tell me what is really going on.' Richie's voice was firm now and Nia suddenly felt very vulnerable and alone.

'Look, I didn't come over here to visit a friend. I followed you here.'

He sat down, waiting.

'Remember you and Ruby gave me a lift over here the Wednesday before she died? Ruby saw you didn't come on the Red Jet with me, and she followed you. She told me about it in the garden at the party on the Sunday. She was distraught.'

Richie leant forward. 'What exactly did she say to you? Please, I need to know.'

'All she told me was that she saw you come here. I assumed she thought you were seeing someone else. She talked about betrayal.'

Richie shook his head. 'No, she knew I wouldn't see someone else. I explained to her exactly what was going on.' He gave Nia a sideways look. 'I guess you'd like to know.' He waved a hand around the room. 'This place, this horrible old bungalow is my retreat. I was desperate for a place of my own where I could create, be myself, and this was all I could afford. The old woman who lived here was going into a home. Her son is renting it to me. They cleared it out completely apart from large items of furniture, curtains, carpets and kitchen appliances.'

'You come here to create?'

'Yes. Wait till I show you upstairs. I think you'll understand why I can work here.'

'But why keep it a secret from Ruby?'

'I guess I didn't want her or Dad to feel I was ungrateful. I am so lucky with that gallery. Most artists would sell their soul for that opportunity, and I do appreciate it. But over there I have to paint the kind of things that my father and Ruby approve of. I come here to be free.' His voice broke, and now he looked young and vulnerable.

'I would have thought Ruby would have understood that. She was such an empathetic person – her work on the helpline was about listening to people's problems.'

Richie stood up and looked out of the window at the darkening skies. 'I know, and that was a lovely side to Ruby. But she'd been brought up in a very controlled, black-and-white world. Right and wrong were obvious, no blurred edges. Creativity can feel dangerous to people like Ruby and my father. They just about cope with the work I do over in the gallery. It's safe, conventional. They didn't understand it's also suffocating.'

'I'd not thought about that side of Ruby. She was so sympathetic when I told her about my problems.'

'Yes, but don't let that fool you into thinking she was easy-going. You couldn't even say she had a strong moral compass. At least on a compass the needle moves. No, for Ruby there was only right or wrong.'

'I was surprised when Ethan told me that she gave away the money her mother left her because it had been associated with gambling. It seemed pretty extreme.'

She saw Richie clench his fist. 'It does to us, but to her it was perfectly logical. My father approved of her decision, and I wasn't surprised when she told me she had to give it all away. Gambling is wrong; therefore, the money was tainted, was the way she saw it. Black and white, right and wrong, love and hate. Nothing in between.'

'And so, you found this place to work.'

'Exactly. I was able to scrape together the rent without Ruby knowing by not putting some of the sales through the books. It was worth the risk and then, of course, there was that night on the Red Jet when she realised I wasn't going to the mainland and followed me.'

'And she came in, saw your painting?'

'No, she didn't. She stood on the doorstep and got very upset. All she could see was that I'd lied about where I'd been going. Lying is wrong. I lied to her. I lied by telling her I was going to the mainland when I was coming here. I lied when I hid a tiny amount of money to pay my rent. There was no coming back from that.'

'But couldn't she forgive you?'

'We spoke again on the Sunday she died, and she did offer to forgive me on one condition.'

'A condition?'

'Oh, yes, love and forgiveness were always conditional in the world we grew up in. They had to be earned.'

'And what did Ruby ask you to do?'

'She wanted me to give up the bungalow and confess to my father what I had done. I was heartbroken at the thought of leaving this place and I refused. I don't know why, but I'd imagined that we could find some kind of compromise. I guess it reflects how desperate I was. I was denying in my head everything I knew about Ruby. I should have known compromise wasn't in her vocabulary, and I should have realised how seriously she took it all. I'd have given up this place in a heartbeat if I'd known what she would go on to do that night.'

'You told the police your marriage was in a good place,' Nia said gently.

'I know, another lie, as Ruby would say. I said it when they first told me about Ruby, because I knew there had been a time when we had loved each other and, given time, we'd have sorted things out.'

Richie looked around the room. 'Let's get out of this room, it's so depressing. Maybe if you see the reason I come here you might understand – come.'

It was a command. Without thinking, Nia stood up and followed Richie out of the living room. He took her upstairs and to what must have been a bedroom but was completely cleared of furniture now. There were piles of blank canvasses, paints and a large, covered easel close to a long window. Even with the light fading Nia could tell that in the daytime it would be flooded with light.

'It's perfect, isn't it?' He spoke in awe, a child gazing at the lights on the Christmas tree.

As Nia walked around the room she was greeted by the same smells as she experienced in Richie's gallery, the oils combined with the hairs of the brushes, the solvent to clean them, the canvasses.

Richie seemed to relax, be at home as soon as they entered the room. It could have been a million miles away from the stuffy old room downstairs.

Nia wandered around. On the easel a painting was covered up. She lifted the cloth and saw part of an oil painting of a rather frightening old man whose eyes seemed to glint threateningly at her. She quickly covered him up and then saw two more finished paintings resting against the wall, alongside some old frames.

These were quite different from the portrait, and from each other. They both involved the sea but nothing like the seascapes back at the gallery. One was of a woman standing at the water's edge, the light flooding her face and white dress. The other was an abstract of the sea, using thick layers of blue and white paint, the changing forms of the sea and clouds captured beautifully.

'They are wonderful,' she said. 'They're very different from each other.'

'Thank you. I've been experimenting, trying out different styles,' said Richie, and she could see the excitement and passion in his eyes.

'If it's so frustrating back at the gallery, wouldn't it be best to break free? You're an adult. You don't belong to The Righteous any more; you don't need to stay tied to your father.'

'I need the gallery. It's somewhere I can make a name for myself, but I don't have the money to pay the rent. It's as basic as that, and so, yes, I need my father.' He paused.

They went back downstairs, and Nia headed to the front door.

'Thank you for explaining,' she said.

'Don't tell anyone, will you? I don't want anyone else coming over here.'

'I won't,' she said.

'Hang on, I'll leave with you. I have a wretched seascape to finish over at the studio. This is a commission, though, and pays well.'

Richie grabbed his coat and they left together. He locked the door and then put the key into a pretend rock key safe close to the door and grinned at her. 'I know, not such a good idea, but I am terrible at losing or forgetting keys. It's pretty safe around here. You might have seen the old man over the road with his dog. He doesn't miss much.'

Richie walked in one direction towards his car, Nia the other, to the car park.

As she drove back, she thought about what she'd seen. So, all this time Richie had been renting that rather grim little bungalow. However much Richie explained Ruby's reaction, Nia couldn't help feeling she'd overreacted, calling what he'd done a betrayal. It seemed so extreme. Maybe it was a side of Ruby she simply didn't understand. Richie sounded, though, as if he'd have been prepared to give it all up for her. Nia didn't see how he could have had any more reason for wanting Ruby out of the way.

Of course, her rationale for assuming Richie was the father of Jade's baby had been the address, and that had now been shattered. No, she didn't see any reason to think that any more. It did leave open the question as to who the father was. There were three other men in the close: Joe, Ethan, and Ian. Jade had been adamant it wasn't Joe, which left Ethan or Ian. Jade had been very protective of Ethan and yet at the same time Nia had witnessed the flirtation between Ian and Jade. And there had been those barbed remarks by Lucy. Did she realise her husband might have fathered a child with Jade? That would mean not only that he'd had an affair but also that he was fulfilling a long-held dream of hers with someone else. It was pretty clear Jade was keeping things secret, but, of course, Ruby had known. Was this at the root of Lucy's problems with Ruby? Was she scared Ruby would expose what Ian and Jade were content to keep secret? It had to be possible.

When Nia returned home, after greeting Romeo she went straight upstairs.

After the events of the evening, it wasn't surprising Richie was the person uppermost in her mind. It would be interesting to meet his father at the funeral, and also to get a taste of this religion that had been such a strong influence on, not only Richie, but Ruby and Jade as well. The other thing that struck her, looking at her notes, was how the list of questions against Ian's name was growing.

The thing with Ian, she realised, was that his reputation meant a huge amount to him. He was a man who needed to be liked, needed recognition. The way he was reacting to possibly losing his TV slot showed this. Someone like that might go a long way to hide secrets, and Ruby had possibly known more than most.

Nia put the list away and took Romeo out for his late evening walk. The town was quiet and the air cool. She walked along the pier, down on the beach; the crowds had been and gone. And yet down here it remained constant. The sea saw everything that happened, it never forgot. Nia remembered Safi showing her something she'd learned in Biology about the rings you saw in the trunk of a tree when it had been cut down. Safi said the gaps between each ring told you about the climate in that year. To think that a tree that was hundreds of years old held a memory of the weather from centuries ago. It was incredible. Down here on the beach, of course, there were fossils, holding memories of thousands of years before. And the sea out there? Well, it had seen what happened here the night Ruby died.

On Friday it would be Ruby's funeral. Traditionally a time to remember someone's life. All the close would be there, each with their own memories of Ruby, but one person there would have the last memory of her; one person sat down here watching Ruby take her last breath.

33

Nia arrived for Ruby's funeral, which was taking place at a plain brick building with small windows and a wooden door. There was a notice-board with the words in black: 'The Righteous. Phone this number for details of services.' The words 'All are welcome' were nowhere to be seen. Nia had never seen a religious building like it.

She ventured inside. The entrance room was as plain as the exterior, painted a sickly cream colour. There was a table with small black hymn books piled up, and next to this stood a steely-faced man in a black suit.

He handed hymn books out, but there was no funeral order of service and once inside the main hall Nia was directed to a seat at the back with other residents of the close. They all sat silent with the terrified air of pupils waiting to go in to see the headmaster.

The hall was painted the same horrible yellow-cream colour as the entrance hall; the seats were long brown wooden benches. On one wall were painted the words, 'All your righteousness is as filthy rags'.

Nia was fighting the urge to get out of the building as quickly as she could; the judgement in the air was stifling.

Richie was sitting at the front with his father. The coffin stood alone and bare. No flowers graced the top.

Nia looked around for Jade. She didn't recognise her at first. She was a few rows behind Richie, hunched over, wearing a black veil, the same as all the women close to her.

Nia was wondering what was missing, then realised there was no music; the place was silent.

Another man in a black suit stood up, spoke briefly about the sadness of death and grief. Ruby was described as someone who 'like us all, tried hard to live to the standard expected of us, but, of course, like us all, she failed'. A hymn was sung, unaccompanied, and Nia, who usually enjoyed singing, sang a note, before realising only her voice could be heard, and stopped.

The same man prayed, but not from a book, appearing to make it up as he went along, far more sermon than prayer. It felt to Nia like an endless, depressing list of everyone's shortcomings and mistakes, scattered throughout with pleading for love and forgiveness.

Nia remembered Jade talking about being made to feel so terrible here that she slowly became totally dependent on the religion for everything, and Nia tried to imagine how it had been for Richie, Jade, and Ruby to have had to listen to this kind of thing week after week. It must have slowly ground away at any self-esteem they had.

Finally, there was another hymn, then some of the men in suits carried the coffin out in silence. Richie walked with his father behind it, his hands crossed over in front of him, the knuckles white. The look in his eyes shocked Nia: dead, unseeing, his mouth tight. He didn't look their way but left the building with the coffin and his father.

It was a strange end to the service, and no one was sure what to do. Jade came over to them. Her eyes were red, her mouth pinched in a way Nia had never seen before.

'We can go to the crematorium now,' she said, and tore off the veil.

When they had left the building, Nia felt a sense of relief, as if they had all been holding their breath for the last half-hour.

'Bloody hell,' murmured Joe. 'That was weird. Those people freak me out.'

Nia agreed. 'It was a bit heavy. Come on, let's get to the crematorium. I've a feeling that will be very different. I'd like to come to Wight's, but, before I go, I'd like to go and speak to Richie's father.'

She looked over and saw he was talking to Ian, which surprised her, as she'd not known they knew each other. Ian had his arm around the other man's shoulder, and they were smiling. Once they had finished and as she saw Ian walk away, Nia went over.

'I came over to say how sorry I am for your loss,' Nia said to Richie's father.

Despite his stern expression she saw real sadness in his eyes.

'I was very fond of Ruby. She was a good wife for Richie. It was the one choice he made after leaving that I approved of. I regret he didn't come any longer, but at least Ruby did. I disapproved, obviously, of Richie choosing a career in the arts, but at least he had her.'

Nia saw the cold, granite-like eyes glaring at her. There was no compassion, no warmth there. Nia hoped Richie had received some love from this man, but she guessed it had been measured out in cold droplets, each one accounted for.

His gaze wandered over to Richie. 'I do hope he chooses his next wife with care. I couldn't support him if he shackles himself to an immoral woman, but he knows that.'

Nia was glad that at that point others came to speak to him and she was able to slip away from Richie's father.

Richie caught hold of her arm as she walked past him. 'I hope everything is OK, you know, about the bungalow.' He shot an anxious look at his father.

'I didn't mention it. I knew you wouldn't want me to,' she said gently.

'Thank you.'

'I could see your father was very fond of Ruby.'

'He approved of her.'

'I hadn't realised Ian knew your dad; I was surprised to see them talking.'

'Yes, Ian told me he'd met my father through some business a few years ago. They didn't get on then but, today, it was all smiles.'

Richie shot a look over at Ian that Nia couldn't quite make out, but the coldness in it unnerved her.

'I shan't come to the crematorium,' Richie continued. 'This next part should be for Jade. It was good of her to allow the service at The Hall. I'll go back to the gallery, maybe come over to Wight's later.'

'I understand. I hope to see you later.'

Nia drove herself to the crematorium and when she arrived, she saw people from the close but also another very different group of people. Some she recognised as clients of Ruby's; there were the people from the helpline, and a group of younger people who were like a breath of fresh air after the previous service. Elvira approached them, and they went in together.

As she entered the chapel Nia was handed an order of service, which had on its cover a beautiful and poignant photograph of Ruby on the beach. She was standing looking out at the sea, her face held high, smiling.

The music being played was from Ruby's favourite singer, Adele. The eulogy was by the vicar from the church in Yarmouth, who said wonderful things about Ruby's generosity, caring and her importance to the lives of everyone in the community. Jade read a poem, Joe the words of a song.

For all the solemnity of the previous service, Nia realised no one had cried. Here, people laughed but there were also many tears. At times she saw Jade shaking with sobs.

After the service Jade took her to one side. 'Thank you for being here for me.'

'It's been a hard day, hasn't it?'

'Going back to The Righteous was not a good way to start. I know I had to do it for Richie and his father, but I find everything about it oppressive. It triggers bad memories.'

'I was imagining what it must be like to go to such a place week after week, and as a child when you are so impressionable.'

'No one realises how damaging that stuff is. It never quite leaves you.' Jade sighed. 'Anyway, it's done, and I know one thing: I will never

ever set foot in that building again. At least here I felt I could grieve and remember Ruby. So, are you coming on to Wight's now?'

'Yes, but I'll go and check on Romeo first.'

'Of course. I'll see you there.'

* * *

Romeo greeted her, as always, as if she'd been gone for weeks, not hours.

'I'd take you with me, but I'm not sure how things will go,' Nia said to him. 'Let's go out in the garden and get some fresh air together before I leave.'

Feeling refreshed, Nia made her way to Wight's, where the mood was very different now. Nia reflected that there was often a release of energy after a funeral, and people were drinking and chatting animatedly.

Nia heard a loud laugh and saw Ian telling a story to a group of people.

'He's been told we can go ahead with the programme,' Lucy said to Nia.

'That's great, Lucy. You must both be so excited.'

'Yes. Yes, I think I must be.'

Nia noticed that the glass of orange juice in Lucy's hand was shaking.

'So, what did you make of that first service?'

'It was a pretty frightening place, wasn't it? Have you been there before?'

'Never, thank goodness. We did ask once about using their hall for one of our meetings when our own premises were being decorated, but there was no way they were going to allow us heathen women with our evil sewing in there.'

Nia smiled. 'That's crazy.'

'Yes. We thought it was very funny. Honestly, you couldn't wish to meet a less offensive, friendly group of women. I made some lovely friends there.'

'But you said you gave up going to the craft group?'

'Yes, I went every Saturday throughout January but then I realised night driving wasn't for me any more, and Ian and I have been getting very busy lately.' Lucy stood up. 'I'd better go and remind him of the time. He's due to speak to his agent soon.'

Lucy left and Nia saw her tactfully tap Ian on his arm. Ian had been in the middle of a story, and he stepped back, nearly bowling Lucy over. Ian turned apologetically and scooped her into the group and Lucy looked so tiny compared to him.

Was that how Nia herself looked next to Chris? She realised that before coming to the island she had been to so few social occasions without him, and yet here she was at the funeral of a woman he'd never met, with people who he'd had no contact with. Of course, there had been her friends at the salon, but she'd never socialised with them. Her life had centred around Chris and Safi.

Nia remembered when she'd arrived. It had felt so daring to have come here, leaving everyone behind, but now it felt almost normal. She had grown to rather like some of the aspects of living in the house on her own, liked being able to come and go as she pleased. Slowly, the volume on the constant commentary she heard in her head of Chris's endless remarks was being turned down. It was as if she was starting to be able to hear her own voice.

* * *

Later that evening she and Romeo headed down to the beach, and Nia was surprised to see Lucy there. She hardly recognised her wrapped up in a stylish waterproof, her headscarf on her head and sunglasses on.

'Hiya,' she said. 'I've not seen you down here before.'

'No. I should come down more often. You take things for granted when they are on your doorstep.'

Lucy looked around. 'It's hard to believe that Ruby died here. It's terrible that something like that should happen to someone in our close.'

'I can imagine. When I arrived, I remember thinking what a safe place it felt.'

'It appears none of us knew Ruby as well as we thought.'

Lucy bent down to pick up a shell but stumbled and was about to fall. Nia grabbed her arm, helped her to stand up.

'Are you OK?'

Lucy took her sunglasses off, wiped her eyes.

'What's wrong Lucy?'

'Nothing.'

'I don't believe you, something's not right. Look, I've noticed you stumbling, missing things.'

'It's none of your business.' Lucy spoke firmly, but Nia persevered.

She took a deep breath. 'I think I'm just going to have to come out and say this. Lucy, do you have a drinking problem?'

'How dare you?'

'I'm not the only one who has noticed things. Jade has as well. Lucy, you don't have to be ashamed. We can help.'

'I am not staying down here to listen to this,' said Lucy as she started to walk away.

Nia grabbed her arm. 'Stop, please – does Ian know?'

Lucy's eyes widened. 'Don't you dare go near him or—'

'Or what? Did Ruby know and threaten to tell him or even to scupper your TV and book deals?'

Lucy's eyes narrowed and she stepped closer to Nia. 'This is too much. Falsely accusing me of drinking is bad enough, but are you implying that I came here that night to hurt Ruby to protect myself?'

'And to save your five minutes of fame. And maybe your marriage.'

Lucy shook her head. 'You have no idea what you are talking about.'

Lucy stepped back, and Nia saw that the panic had disappeared from her eyes and a cold resolve replaced it. 'I have to go and talk to Ian. I'll come and see you later.'

With no further explanation Lucy left the beach.

'Well,' said Nia to Romeo, 'that's not got us much further, has it? Come on, let's go for a walk along the harbour front.'

The day had brightened up and it was a pleasant evening. Seagulls circled in the sky; the breeze was warmer. The harbour looked empty now without all the magnificent gaffers and their bunting. The more sedate yachts and dinghies bobbed quietly on the water. As she turned to go back to the town, Nia saw Joe walking towards her, but he didn't see her. Instead, he turned off to walk down a jetty towards a small yacht. Nia saw a young man with golden hair wave to him and she saw a look on Joe's face that startled her. Why hadn't it dawned on her before? She needed to think. Think about Joe, Lucy, about everything.

Back home she was making a drink, getting ready to settle to watch TV, when there was a knock at the door.

'I've come to explain.'

34

Nia invited Lucy in, and as they sat together Romeo snuggled up protectively to Nia.

'I told you I would explain things and I think the sooner I do, the better.'

Nia waited for Lucy to elaborate.

'You're right, I have been trying to hide something for too long.' Lucy started to twist her wedding ring around her finger. 'It's very difficult to explain to a young girl like you.'

'I'm forty, hardly a young girl!'

'And I'm seventy-three.'

'What?' The word shot out before she could stop it. 'I'm so sorry—' Nia stammered.

'No, it's all right. No one around here knows my true age. I'm ten years older than Ian. I was your age when we met and I'd been married before. My previous husband hadn't wanted children, but when Ian and I fell in love, we both wanted to start a family. Sadly, it wasn't to be. I kept waiting for Ian to leave me, find someone younger, prettier, but he never has.'

'He loves you; I can see that and, anyway, you look amazing.'

'Thank you, but age is catching up on me. In particular before

Christmas the doctor suspected I might have the onset of something called Ménière's disease.'

'I'm so sorry, I don't know exactly what that is.'

'It's a disorder of the inner ear which causes dizziness, vertigo, sickness, and hearing loss. Of course, the dizziness and vertigo can be mistaken for signs that I have been drinking.'

'I am very sorry, Lucy; I had no idea. It sounds awful. Can they treat it?'

'To a limited extent, the symptoms at least.'

'I shouldn't have leapt to conclusions in the way I did.'

'I only had the definite diagnosis at the start of February, but the symptoms have got worse since then.' Lucy's lips trembled; shaking fingers stroked her forehead. 'My hearing is getting so bad, I shall need hearing aids soon.' Her voice broke.

'Ian will stand by you, I'm sure.'

'He says that. In fact, he was just upset I'd not told him before today.'

'He didn't know?'

'No, I was dreading telling him. I keep all illness from him. I don't want to remind him how much older I am than him. I've already failed him by not giving him children.' Lucy burst into loud sobs.

Nia went and put her arm around her. 'Hey, you're a beautiful, intelligent woman with a husband who loves you very much. You must never think you've failed him.'

Lucy wiped her eyes. 'That's what he says. He noticed the slips and things; he'd even wondered about me drinking. I should have talked to him, but I was hoping it would magically disappear. Of course, it's not going to. And I was worried about all these books and TV programmes. I mean, how would it look if I'm ill?'

'But everyone gets ill. I would have thought it would help people to know how you were coping with it.'

'That's what Ian said. He doesn't see it as a problem at all. I don't know, talking to him now makes me realise how stupid I'd been.'

'Did Ruby know?'

Lucy nodded, speaking quietly. 'I told Ruby the week before she died. She'd known something was wrong, had been dropping more and more hints about me drinking. I went to have my hair done the day after I was given a definite diagnosis. I was vulnerable, and I told her. It was a mistake; she went on and on about telling Ian. She told me she'd asked him if I was drinking, and he'd said no but had seemed unsure. She said I owed it to him. But as far as I was concerned it was none of her business.'

Lucy sat forward. 'I can tell you this, however – I did not go to the beach and kill her in order to silence her. And as it happened, by then I'd come to understand that someday I was going to have to tell Ian, tell everyone, it was just a matter of time. Killing Ruby, apart from being wicked, would have been pointless.'

Lucy got up and walked towards the door. 'I'd appreciate you keeping this to yourself for now, although we'll tell friends and our agent very soon.'

Lucy left quickly, slamming the door behind her, and then Nia heard her opening her own front door.

Nia could understand her abruptness and she had a right to be very angry with Nia for the false accusations. Nia was fortunate that Lucy had been generous enough to explain anything.

But, for all that, Nia still had niggling doubts. Lucy had said she'd not trusted Ruby since the accident, and that was a few months before she'd told Ruby about her illness.

Nia shook her head. She was so confused and the more she tried to think, the more tangled her thoughts became. Maybe a good night's sleep would clear her mind.

* * *

The next morning Nia felt none the wiser. She was going for a swim with Jade before work and was looking forward to it as it promised to be a hot day. As they drove to the beach Jade said, 'I got a text late last night from Ian, asking me if I wanted to join him and Richie for a swim at the pool they go to. I turned down the offer, told him I was coming here with you.'

'I'm sorry, you could have gone with them—'

'No, it's fine. I'd much rather be here.'

It was a glorious morning to swim, with what looked like thousands of stars twinkling on the surface of a bright blue sea. Nia went straight in and relished the cold water on her face. Today, Romeo happily paddled and dug holes in the sand.

It was a day she'd have loved to linger but they both had work and reluctantly they got out and started to change.

Nia asked Jade how she was feeling, and she let out a long sigh. 'I'm doing OK. Still being sick but it's not as bad. Look, my tummy is starting to show now.' She laid her hand on a neat bump.

'You are so tiny. I was staggering around from about three months on.' Nia stopped. This wasn't helpful for Jade. 'So, I'm still coming with you on Monday. What time is the appointment?'

'At ten. Would you be all right to drive? I'll be in for the morning, all being well. Come out at lunchtime... could I phone you when I'm ready to come back?'

'Of course, I can hang about there, just in case. I can stay with you as long as they let me.'

Jade smiled. 'Thank you. I must admit to having a few wobbles, but I think I'm doing the right thing.'

'Think about it tomorrow. You know, if you have doubts there is adoption if you didn't want to raise the baby yourself, but I'm not putting any pressure on you. This is your decision.'

* * *

It had been a busy day at the salon, and Nia was in the garden about to take Romeo for a walk up on the downs when she saw Ian over the other side of the fence waiting to talk to her. She wondered if it was about Lucy but was surprised by the offer he made instead.

'I was wondering if you fancied a swim in the pool. I'm going again later, about ten.' He pointed over at her swimming costume hanging on the line. 'I know you and Jade went this morning, and I had a lovely swim with Richie. I can't resist going again – what do you say?'

Nia thanked him and agreed to go later.

Up on the downs with Romeo, it was a lovely evening, and as she walked up the path she could see the ancient Longstone standing proudly at the top of one of the fields in the distance. She'd read it was an ancient burial site and then a meeting place where important decisions for the villagers were made. That stone connected her to a past that was as vital and real as the present and she realised that the island didn't just remember its past, but the memories were a living, breathing part of it.

Her mind drifted to Ruby and her death, a pinprick in the scheme of things and yet the island would never forget. For Nia that brought some comfort. Whatever happened, whatever she did or didn't find out about what happened to Ruby, there was at least something that knew the truth and held it.

Nia walked slowly back to the car, thinking about her invitation from Ian. It had come so suddenly; she couldn't believe it wasn't anything to do with Lucy's revelations. Nia pictured the pool up there in the dark, and suddenly she felt nervous pangs in her stomach. She'd seen another side to Ian when he'd thought he'd been passed over for the TV work. The charm had disappeared, and as the desperation for that role had become more real, the lengths to which he might go to preserve it were far more apparent.

Nia thought of her conversation with Lucy, that feeling there was more, that the anger she felt towards Ruby was tied up with something deeper. This anger had to be connected to something Ruby knew about them that would jeopardise them getting the TV and book deals. But what was it? And, more worryingly, did Ian or Lucy suspect she knew about it? Had she become a threat to them in the same way Ruby had?

By the time she'd returned home, Nia had persuaded herself she was being ridiculous. Lucy and probably half the close would see her leaving with Ian. If he did have anything planned, surely he wasn't going to do anything this evening.

She went out about ten just as Ian was opening the garage door.

'Evening,' he called. 'Wait there and I'll get the car out.'

He backed the large car into the close, got out, closed the garage door, and motioned to the passenger door for Nia to get in.

Nia sank back into the soft leather seat. 'This is very smart.'

'Yes, I've had it a few years now. Lucy never liked driving it, complained it was too big. Still, she doesn't seem to be bothered about driving much any more.'

They drove out of the town, over the bridge and towards Fort Victoria. Nia was wondering if she should bring up the subject of Lucy's illness, but Ian mentioned it first.

'I understand Lucy talked to you.'

'Yes. I'm sorry she has this illness. It sounds terrible.'

'I wish she'd told me earlier; it would have made life so much easier. It's a relief to be honest, and, as I said to her, it's nothing to be ashamed of.'

'I think she feels the age difference between the two of you.'

'I know, which is ridiculous. It's never bothered me. I know she thinks she let me down about not having children, but, honestly, we've had such a full life together. I'm quite selfish, you know.' He threw her a quick grin. 'I like having Lucy to myself.'

'She seemed to be concerned it would affect you getting the TV or book work.'

'I realise that now, but, as I explained, what we're trying to share with people is how to live a healthy and full life in older age. That doesn't mean we won't have illness or disability. I think actually it will help people to identify with what we are saying if they see we too have our struggles.'

'Yes, I think you're right. And Ruby knew about all this?'

They pulled into the driveway; Ian turned off the engine and the lights. For a second, they were plunged into darkness but then the security lights flooded the driveway.

'I believe Lucy did tell Ruby; I think Ruby had been asking her all kinds of questions.' He gave Nia a sideways look. 'The symptoms could have been mistaken for drinking problems – I have a feeling Ruby might have had concerns about that. Anyway, the point is Lucy didn't and now I can look after her.'

Ian leant down, picked up his swimming bag and the goggles that had fallen out. Nia found her bag and they both got out of the car.

Ian unlocked the back gate to the side of the house. Immediately security lights shone down on them, and they made their way along the path. As before, Nia saw the large outbuilding in front of her. As they approached it more lights came on.

'That's the gym I told you about,' said Ian. He held up the keys. 'Come and have a quick look inside.'

He unlocked the door, and more lights came on automatically, illuminating a magnificent room full of equipment as well as an enormous flat-screen TV, bar, and seating area.

Ian put down his swimming bag and goggles. Nia had assumed the right wall that faced the pool was bricked, but she could see now that it had enormous patio doors.

'Goodness, it's so luxurious.'

'I know,' said Ian, grinning. 'Still, I'd rather swim. Come on.'

They left and Ian locked the gym up and the lights switched themselves off.

'Are all the lights here automatic? They don't seem to have heard of light switches.'

'My friend told me he was fed up with his kids leaving lights on all over the place. It also means it's much safer if you come out here after dark.'

As they walked along, Nia saw the outside light by the gym go out, but now more lights lit up the whole area including the pool.

Ian took her to a small building to the right of the pool. Again, lights came on and she let herself into a small changing room. Nia already had her bathing costume on and was ready quickly.

They both went to the shallow end of the pool. Nia sat down ready to lower herself into the water. Ian, however, seemed to change his mind and walked around the pool to the deep end. Nia had the impression he was strutting around for her benefit. There was no doubting he was in very good shape, but she thought he looked a bit foolish. He stood at the other end; his arms raised arrow-like above his head ready to dive. Nia had a feeling she was meant to watch this performance but instead she lowered herself into the pool and began to swim.

She had to admit it was a wonderful experience. The pool was a perfect temperature and to be out here under the stars was quite magical. Ian appeared to be determined to do as many lengths as he could, and noisily swam up and down while she swam breaststroke, then some backstroke, relaxing.

Suddenly there was a huge whoosh of water, and Nia saw Ian getting out of the shallow end.

'I need to get my goggles; they are in the gym. I thought I could manage without, but my eyes are really stinging.'

She waved in acknowledgement, watched him pick up the keys from the changing area, and then enter the gym, pick up the goggles, and return.

He was soon back in the pool, resuming his punishing routine of length swimming.

Nia continued swimming gently back and forth, and as she did something dawned on her. She had assumed that when Richie and Ian were up here the night Ruby died, neither could see the other as one was in the gym, the other in the pool. But, of course, with that wall of glass and all the automatic lights they must have been able to see each other exercising or leaving. If Richie had left the gym, the lights would have gone off. If Ian had left the pool, likewise the lights here would have gone off. They had to have both known where the other was.

Nia frowned; she was getting very confused. First, the two men had seemed to have the perfect alibi, swimming together, then she'd found out that Richie had been in the gym, which Nia had assumed meant they had been out of each other's sight. But now she saw that they would have been able to see each other, which meant they had an alibi after all. Why hadn't they pointed that out to her?

Nia noticed Ian was getting out, and so she finished her length and walked over to the changing area. She dried herself off and got dressed. Her mind was still churning. Why were they being so evasive? Surely right from the start they should have been shouting about this alibi. But they hadn't. She rejoined Ian and they started down the path.

'You're very quiet,' Ian commented. 'Thinking deep thoughts?'

'I was thinking about the gym and the pool here,' she blurted out. 'The thing is, Ian, I've realised, because of the windows and the lights, you and Richie had to know all evening what the other was doing.'

Ian shrugged. 'I guess you're right. Why does it matter? We were both here.'

'But why do you keep changing the story? Is one of you covering for the other?'

They had passed the pool and most of the lights were out as they entered the dingy pathway to the back gate. Nia was suddenly aware of being alone with Ian and realised this was a far from ideal place to be discussing alibis for murder.

Ian put his hand on the gate and paused. Nia's heart was racing. He was so much taller, stronger than her. There was no escape.

'You know, some days, like this one, have a way of changing perspective. The night Ruby died, I was here swimming. I know that, and it's all that matters to me. I wasn't watching the gym all the time I was swimming. In fact, for long periods I have no idea what was going on in there. I guess it might be the same for Richie. And that's all I think I want to say about that.'

35

The following evening Nia went to Wight's. Earlier in the day she'd seen Richie in the garden next door and guessed he'd been invited to Ian and Lucy's for lunch. She remembered her lunch with them the day after she arrived. It seemed such a long time ago now.

As Nia approached Wight's she thought how interesting it was that the tradition of the Sunday night meetings at Wight's had been maintained, despite everything that had happened. In fact, it was quite strange the way they went through the same ritual, buying drinks, chatting about the weather, the number of tourists and how business was going. Ian shared his news about the TV programme that he and Lucy would be going up to London to talk about the following week. He was very excited, but Nia noticed he was avoiding eye contact with her.

Elvira, however, patted her knee to get her attention. 'I'm sorry, but I haven't sent you an invitation to the wedding, and it's only three weeks away.' She made an excited grimace. 'God, three weeks left!'

'I hope it's all going brilliantly, and please don't worry about an invitation. I wasn't expecting one.'

'Oh, you must come. It's fine, actually. I had a cancellation for the sit-down, it would be lovely for you to come – that is, if you are still on the island, of course.'

'Thank you very much, then. I'd love to come.'

'I'll get you a proper invite. We start at the church at eleven, and then on to a hotel for the wedding breakfast. That will all be quite small. The big do will be here in the evening.'

'Thank you. I'll look forward to it.'

There was an air of things wrapping up when Joe clinked the side of his glass with a spoon.

'I should have mentioned this before, but next Saturday my parents are throwing a party for me at the house, if you're free, do pop in. It starts about seven. There'll be music and a buffet. Wear your posh gear.' He handed out invitations, which were gilt-edged, and clearly, however much Joe might be trying to downplay this, Nia could see this was a big event for his parents.

'Anyway, do come along if you can,' he said, and left.

'Right, all set for a swim later?' Ian asked Richie, who nodded in response. 'Nia came with me last night; we had a good time, didn't we?' He glanced at Nia.

'It was lovely,' she replied. 'So warm and a perfect evening.'

'I showed Nia the gym, and all those automatic lights. Nia pointed out that we would have been able to see each other when we were there the night poor Ruby died. I had to say I was rather taken up with my swimming, I obviously wasn't watching your way all the time, in the same way you wouldn't have been watching me. I guess it would be easy to miss one of us taking a break.'

Nia frowned; she had a feeling Ian was playing some kind of game with Richie, but wasn't sure what was going on. Richie looked equally confused but didn't reply.

'I need to get off,' said Ethan, completely oblivious to what was going on. 'I'll see you at the centre, Jade,' he said, and left.

It seemed to signal the end of the get-together.

Nia watched Elvira leave and go straight to her car. If she kept to her usual routine, she would be at the home for an hour and that meant Nia had time to walk Romeo and settle him down.

As she drove to the nursing home, she could see dark clouds starting to gather across the sky. She had planned things out this time. The nursing home was close to a church slightly up on a hill. Nia parked there and walked into the churchyard. Fortunately, all the services had finished, there was no one about. There was a seat, though, which had a perfect view of the car park at the nursing home and there was still enough light for her to look down and see Elvira's car. The seat also had a view of the clifftops and sea beyond, and Nia took time to take in the view as she waited.

Checking her watch, she saw the hour was coming to an end, and it was darker now, the cars silhouettes. She noticed a car arrive, drive in, but it parked at the far end, away from the entrance. She saw the headlights switch off, but no one left the car. Maybe someone had come to collect a visitor, although they were making the person walk a fair way across what was a pretty empty car park.

On the hour she saw the front door open, and the security light lit up Elvira, Nia went quickly to her car, and waited.

It wasn't long before she saw Elvira's car leaving the car park and Nia started her engine. As she followed Elvira, she was aware of a car coming out from the home behind her and driving her way. The road was the main route to Newport; it probably meant nothing.

The names of the villages flashed past: Limerstone, Shorwell, and then they were driving inland, past fields, some empty, some with sheep. They approached Bowcombe. Nia was aware of more houses now, and a bit further on they reached the village of Carisbrooke. There were street lights, and up on the hill she could see Carisbrooke Castle where Charles the First had been held prisoner.

They drove through the village to a roundabout, and she could see Elvira slowing down. Fortunately, a car had joined them and was between Nia's and Elvira's, which should ensure Elvira didn't see her if she looked in her mirror. However, as she slowed down and then came to a halt, Nia checked her own mirror. She noted that the same car that had followed her out of the nursing home was still behind her. She was about to put this down to coincidence until the street light settled on the face of the driver.

Their eyes met and she wasn't sure who was more shocked, her or Ethan. What was he doing here?

He attempted a casual wave, she gave a twisted smile back, and then noticed the traffic was moving. Elvira turned right and Nia followed, but she noticed that Ethan went straight ahead.

As she drove Nia was thinking about Ethan. He must have spent a short time at the rescue centre but not gone on to play poker at the hotel. Why follow Elvira, then? He must be as suspicious as she was about Elvira's movements on a Sunday evening. The obvious question was why didn't he just ask her? Why all the secrecy?

As Nia followed Elvira through the town centre, she could sense the Isle of Wight Festival was still in full swing.

At the roundabout there were large lit-up signs warning of road closures, diversions, and delays. Nia followed Elvira on the route sign-posted to Ryde.

They continued to drive through Wootton and Binstead. This was taking a lot longer than Nia had anticipated. Finally, they arrived at Ryde, and Nia could see the church spires reaching into the black sky.

Nia followed Elvira down the steep high street, past small clusters of smokers outside the pubs. Ahead of her was the sea. Nia had thought for a moment they were going to drive down the pier , thinking Elvira might be catching the Fast Catamaran to the mainland. However, Elvira continued along the esplanade until she reached the hovercraft terminal, when she drove into the car park, which the terminal shared with the ice skating and bowling rinks.

Elvira parked, and Nia parked some distance away in the spacious car park. Then she followed Elvira, keeping in the shadows. The car park didn't feel a safe place. On one side a large building loomed, and she could hear the sea crashing into the wall to her right.

Nia stayed as close as she could to Elvira. What was she going to do if Elvira boarded the hovercraft? But the hovercraft station was closed – what was Elvira doing here?

Elvira had remained outside the building until she saw a man walking down the road from the direction of the pier. Nia could easily make out his features; it was Elvira's ex, Hugo. She'd seen him that night at the Red Jet terminal and had been told who he was when shown his photograph at Elvira's hen party. He must have come over on the catamaran and walked along the pier.

Nia was horrified. What was Elvira doing having secret liaisons with her ex?

Nia had assumed they would go back to the car, but instead they began walking along the seafront, Nia followed. She had not been to Ryde before, and it felt much bigger and busier than Yarmouth. There were fish and chip shops, hotels and restaurants opposite a large funfair on the beach side. Past this was a large expanse of sand that seemed to stretch on for miles. The tide was out and she could make out groups of young people and dog walkers.

Nia suddenly noticed that Elvira and Hugo, who had remained on the concrete esplanade, had stopped, and were sitting down on a bench. She was very close to them now, but Elvira appeared engrossed in their conversation. Nia held back in time to see Elvira hand a small package to Hugo before they stood up. To Nia's horror they began walking towards her. Nia was trapped. She turned and started walking quickly away from them back in the direction of the terminal, but she was aware of their footsteps close behind. She pulled her coat around her and was nearly running now.

Back at the terminal she headed straight to her car and, without looking back, got in. She was breathing fast from nerves as much as the run. What a mess. She was hopeless at this detective game.

Nia saw Elvira heading to her own car alone. Presumably Hugo was going back to catch the catamaran off Ryde pier head. It seemed a lot of fuss for such a brief encounter. Maybe it had all been about that parcel, but what would Elvira be giving to Hugo?

Nia started to drive home and when she finally parked her car and got into the house, she saw it was gone eleven. She'd been out a long time.

Romeo was waiting and so she took him out for a quick walk down the pier. As they walked along, Nia thought about the evening. What had been in that parcel Elvira gave to Hugo? Could it have been cash? Was she helping Hugo because she was still in love with him? A terrible thought crossed Nia's mind – was it possible Elvira had been planning to marry Ethan simply for his money?

Nia paused as Romeo sniffed the bench on the pier and looked over at the beach. In the darkness she could make out patches of shingle, hear the waves crashing onto the shore, and she thought about Ruby. She'd been to talk to Elvira's mother, she'd listened to Elvira pour her heart out on the helpline. From Elvira's point of view, Ruby knew far too much. How far would Elvira go to ensure Ruby kept silent?

36

Nia was getting ready to take Romeo out early the next morning when she heard a knock on the door. She opened it, to find Jade had come over to visit her.

Nia undid the lead, Romeo gave a slight huff and lay down on the rug, resigned to his walk being delayed.

Before she had even sat down Jade said, 'I've made a decision. I'm not going to the hospital this morning; I'm not having a termination.' The words were blurted out, immediately followed by tears.

Nia put her arms around her. 'Hey, come and sit down.'

She held Jade close, and they sat together on the sofa.

'Now tell me, what you are thinking?'

'I've been up all night. I made myself think through everything. I knew there was a loud voice in my head saying I wanted to keep the baby, and suddenly knew in my heart it was true. More than anything now, Nia, I know I want this baby. I know I've been scared about the father. I've been worried he'd work out the baby was his but, you know, I don't think he will. If he so much as hinted at it to me, well, I could easily squash that. So, you see, I am free to do what I want.'

'I've no doubt you will be a great mum, but you have to be totally sure this is definitely the right decision for you.'

Jade nodded. 'I want this baby so much.' A smile spread across her face; a glimmer of excitement shone in her eyes.

Nia gave her a hug. 'Well, I'm really pleased for you, then. Having Safi was the best thing that ever happened to me.'

'We've had enough sadness around here. This is something positive, a new life.'

'But what will you tell everyone? Your pregnancy will show soon. Lucy has already hinted to me that you might be pregnant.'

'Typical. She'll be frantically trying to work out who the father is.'

'Everyone will.'

'It's a good job, then, it's not anyone in the close, isn't it?' Jade looked away.

'Look, if it's someone here – Richie, Joe, Ethan or Ian—'

'I certainly didn't have an affair with my sister's husband. Ethan or Ian? You must be joking. No, of course it's not them. I don't go out with married or engaged men.'

'My God, it's Joe, isn't it?'

Jade blushed deep red. 'Please, Nia, you are not to say anything. We had this one-night fling. It was nothing. I promise you Joe has no interest in me whatsoever. I realised it that night. It was a huge mistake.'

'You always said he loved Ruby.'

'He did, yes. I believe that. But not in the way you think.'

Nia paused, and slowly things started to knit together. The slinking off the yachts in the early hours, not wanting to upset the 'friend' who gave him the alcohol, and the vehemence of his words about the struggle to keep things private.

Nia screwed up her eyes. 'Tell me, is it possible that Joe is gay?'

A smile spread across Jade's face. 'So, you guessed. It's hard to believe that no one else in the close, as far as I know anyway, has sussed it out yet.'

'I saw him meeting someone down at a yacht, a good-looking chap with blond hair. And, oh, is he the friend who rents your flat sometimes?'

'That's him. Joe doesn't realise how obvious it is to me that his friend's rentals coincide with his occasional evenings off at Wight's.'

'I saw Joe over that way one Wednesday. He didn't answer when I called.'

'I'm sure he didn't.' Jade smiled gently. 'Poor Joe. This is all new to him. He's only acknowledged it to himself in the past few months.'

'Did Ruby know?'

'Yes. Joe told her after he and I had the dreadful date. It must have been only a week before she died that we both realised the other knew. She was worried that I'd fancied him and didn't want me to get hurt.'

'Did she disapprove? I should imagine your religion wouldn't have endorsed homosexuality.'

'It certainly didn't but Ruby had moved past that. However, she did think he should tell his parents. Joe was adamant that he was not ready for them to know. He was frantic for her not to say anything. When Richie said he heard them arguing that Sunday morning, I am guessing it was about that.'

'And Ruby knew he was the father of your baby?'

'She did. I think she would have told him eventually. When she had the row with him, I think she wanted him to first tell his parents he was gay and then another time tell them about the baby. You see, her reasoning was that by first letting them accept he was gay, when he told them about the baby, they would see it was pointless pressurising him to marry me.'

'I see – but you don't agree?'

'Firstly, I think Joe must only come out to his parents when he feels ready. He needs to have more confidence in himself before he can do that.'

'Do you think they'll accept it?'

'I think they love Joe so much they will always back him. But they're very traditional and I know they're longing for him to get married and provide grandchildren. It will take time to settle. As for the baby, that will have to wait. I think it would just confuse things.'

'But shouldn't Joe at least know he is a father?'

'This would blow his mind. No way should he be told yet.'

'Well, that's your decision.' Nia squeezed her hand. 'I'll support you whatever you want to do.'

Romeo had come over to her and was resting his head on her knee. 'I need to take him out. Fancy a walk?'

'Perfect. How about a swim? It's a lovely day.'

They packed up their things, Nia made a simple picnic of sandwiches and coffee, and they drove to Compton Bay.

The beach was practically deserted at the dog walking end. They had a short swim, got dressed and sat on the beach having their breakfast.

'This is perfect,' said Jade.

'The island will be such a lovely place to bring up your child.'

'I know. We were lucky as children having all this on our doorstep. Ruby loved it so much down here.' Jade sighed. 'She'd have loved being an auntie.' Jade turned to Nia. 'Have you any more idea about what happened to Ruby, or do you think it's going to be one of those things we never have the answer to?'

Nia shrugged. 'I've found out a lot of things, established some motives, but I don't know if any of them are strong enough to kill Ruby.'

'So, are there things you've not told me?'

'Well, some things I've learnt are private and it's hard to know what's relevant and what isn't.'

'Maybe you need to tell me everything. I promise you I'm very good at keeping secrets. I don't hold with Ruby's beliefs that everyone needs to know everything. It's very hard to keep things in perspective when you are keeping them in your head.'

Nia nodded. 'Well, OK, but you have to promise me to keep this to yourself.'

Jade agreed and slowly Nia went through all she'd discovered so far. She started with Lucy, explaining about Lucy's Ménière's disease, that she wasn't drinking.

'Poor Lucy, she should have told us. I hope Ian is being supportive.'

'I think so, yes.'

'Do you think Ruby knew?'

'Yes, she did. But Lucy did also say she had accepted it was something that was going to come out in time and therefore it certainly wasn't a motive to kill Ruby.'

'Which sounds reasonable, actually.'

'It does, but Lucy was definitely angry about it. The only reason I can think of is that Ruby was pressurising her to tell people about it before she was ready. She hadn't told Ian when Ruby found out.'

'Ian may have been worried it would ruin their chances with the TV programme.'

'But Lucy says that he doesn't think that. He thinks it's something they need to be open about, which sounds fair enough.'

'So,' said Jade, 'as Lucy hadn't told Ian before Ruby died, then Lucy would have a motive to stop Ruby telling Ian. Meanwhile, Ian might have been thinking, like us, that Lucy had a drink problem that Ruby knew about. And that would give him a motive.'

Nia grinned. 'Well done. You're thinking this through better than me. It is confusing, though. Ian is a strange one, isn't he? I saw a different side to him at the Old Gaffers. He was angry about possibly losing the TV programme. I hadn't realised how much it meant to him. If Ruby knew anything that would put a spanner in that would be a pretty strong motive.'

'I agree, but unless it's Lucy and drinking I can't think what it could be.'

'I know. But he is being very slippery about what he was doing on the Sunday night Ruby died.' Nia went on to explain the various versions of the night she'd been told.

'Hang on, now you're saying Ian had to know if Richie was there or not, and vice versa. Surely that clears them both?'

'It does if they're telling the truth. But I have a very strong feeling one of them is covering up for the other.'

Jade shrugged. 'Seems odd. Why would Ian lie for Richie? He's not going to put his reputation on the line for nothing.'

'Maybe it's Richie lying for Ian. Maybe Ian is paying him.'

'That sounds more likely. So, what else?'

Nia moved on to Elvira and told Jade about the phone call, wedding dress, the ring and Elvira meeting her ex.

'It's awful, Jade. How could she do this to Ethan?'

'You don't know that is definitely what is going on. Ruby had said she was pretty desperate when she rang the helpline. It could be more complicated than you think.'

'I'm sure I'm right, and if I am, and Ruby knew about this, well, Elvira definitely had a motive to kill Ruby. Out of everyone she had the easiest access to ketamine, and of course she may not have met her ex that night, and instead been on the beach with Ruby.'

'Goodness, you sound pretty sure it was her.'

'Not completely convinced but I definitely suspect her. I am also very worried about Ethan.'

Nia explained about his gambling and also about him following Elvira.

'I don't think he has a problem gambling, but I do think he is suspicious of Elvira. Poor man, he ought to be told what's going on.'

'Hang on, you're choosing to believe his explanation about the hotel and that he hasn't got a problem with gambling?'

'I am, he sounded very sincere.'

'Oh, God, I hope he's not getting himself into trouble. I also don't like to think of him stalking Elvira like that. It's creepy. Why doesn't he simply ask her what she's doing?'

Nia frowned. 'Maybe he doesn't want to upset her and, as for the gambling, I don't think he would get himself into too much debt or anything. He's such a nice, level-headed sort of person.'

Jade raised an eyebrow. 'You're very forgiving of him – you don't fancy him, do you?'

'Of course not.'

Nia could see Romeo chasing around with another dog and the owner waved over to her, happy to see his dog playing.

'Good, right, let's move on, tell me about Richie,' said Jade.

Nia told Jade about the bungalow, and in return Jade asked a number of questions. She shook her head at the end.

'I don't know. It seems a bit odd to me. Richie has a big studio. Surely, he could just experiment when no one is around? Why go to all that hassle of renting somewhere?'

'He said he needed his own space, and I can understand that. I think he has been pretty frustrated.'

Jade nodded. 'I agree with you there. Yes, it's interesting he should be doing that... So, well, that's everyone...'

'Well, of course, there's Joe,' said Nia gently. 'It sounds to me he was very anxious to keep being gay a secret from his parents and I know he wasn't fishing that night—'

'I can't see Joe committing murder. He's a softie and, anyway, he loved Ruby.'

'But there is something else.' Nia told Jade about the alcohol.

'The idiot. Why is he messing about like that? He'll lose his licence.'

'That's what I said. And Ruby said the same.'

'Ruby knew?'

'Yes.'

Jade suddenly went quiet, stroking her lip thoughtfully.

Romeo came running back, and Nia saw the man and his dog were leaving the beach.

'I think this one needs his breakfast,' she said, and they started to pack up their things. As they walked back along the beach Nia told Jade about the anonymous letter she'd received.

'Who would write that? And you say they'd used a seal. Do you think it's Ruby's ring, the one that's missing?'

Nia shrugged. 'They'd made a real mess of it. It's impossible to tell. I don't like them using her colour though.'

Jade looked up. 'It's not scaring you off, is it?'

'No, of course not, but it was a bit unnerving.'

'I can see that. Still, it's just nonsense. We've this party on Saturday. We'll see if we learn anything new there.'

Back at the house, as Nia gave Romeo his breakfast her thoughts turned to Jade and Joe. She felt it would be better for Joe to know about the baby, but that had to come from Jade.

She was still thinking about them when she received a text.

37

Nia went straight on a video call with Safi.

'Everything OK, love?'

'Actually, I bashed my toe on the beach. It's infected.'

'You should see a doctor, then.'

'I have. I've got antibiotics. Oh, and I lost my purse, but we've reported it, and we're OK for money for now. Anyway, that's not why I phoned.'

Nia tried to push away a hundred questions about the scatter bomb of problems Safi had casually tossed her way, and said, 'OK, so what's up?'

'Mum, someone sent me a video. You have to see it. I'm sending it to you now. I didn't want you to see this on your own.'

The video pinged onto her phone.

It showed Chris walking on a beach, his arm around Sian. They stopped, he kissed her passionately; they were walking along the beach at Penarth, arm in arm. They didn't simply look like lovers; they looked like a couple: relaxed, happy. And then the kiss. She saw the way Sian looked at Chris as he pulled her towards him, as if she never wanted him to let her go.

Nia gasped, clutched her stomach. Then another dagger plunged deep. She saw the date of the video, down in the corner: June tenth .Two days ago. Saturday afternoon.

'I'm really sorry, Mum.'

'How did you get this?' Nia asked quietly, her hand shaking.

'My friend, Jac, happened to be there with his girlfriend. Jac and I have been texting and chatting. He knew about the video of you at the school and he knew I was upset by it all, and I'd taken Dad's side, I suppose. He thought I should see the whole story.' Safi started to cry, and Nia felt her heart break.

'Darling, it's all right,' she said, but she couldn't stop her own tears now.

'But it's not. Last week when I spoke to him, he told me about coming to see you. He said you'd been difficult, but that he was trying everything to get you two back together. He lied to me, Mum. This is more than a fling, isn't it? It wasn't just a one-night stand, was it?'

'No, love. I'm so sorry.'

'You have to tell me now, Mum, everything. I don't want any more lies. Honestly, I can't be any crosser or more disappointed with Dad than I am now.'

Nia caught her breath, wiped her face and as gently as she could told Safi the story.

'I'm not surprised you went crazy at the school. God, Mum, how could he?'

'These things are never simple.'

Safi had stopped crying now; her face was stern. 'Don't make excuses for him. He's a bastard, Mum.'

'Hey, don't say that about your dad. I'll talk to him.'

'But don't let him get away with this. He can't go on lying like this, can he?'

'No, love. I know it's not right.'

'Should I come home? I don't want you to be on your own.'

'I can handle this. I'm stronger now. This is for me and your father to sort out. Of course, if you want to come home, you must, but don't do it because of us.'

Nia heard someone shout Safi's name. 'Sorry, Mum, we were meant to be going out but there's no rush.'

Nia was relieved. 'Don't worry, you go out now, it will do you good. We'll keep in touch, OK?'

Despite the smile she'd put on for Safi at the end of the call, Nia was shaking with anger. How much more could Chris put her and Safi through? She thought of sending a copy of the video to Chris but decided that, for once, she had the upper hand here and didn't want to give him time to prepare an argument.

She rang his phone and he answered straight away.

'Nia, hi.' He was surprised, off guard.

'I've been speaking to Safi.'

'Is she all right?'

'Not really. Her friend Jac sent her a video. It was of you and Sian last Saturday on the beach at Penarth.'

'That's impossible.'

'Oh, no. I'm sending it to you now.'

Nia sent him the video and waited. She heard the words in her head before he said them.

'It was nothing.'

Nia gasped. 'Don't do that. Not again. I can't bear it.'

'Do what?'

'Minimise things, trivialise things.'

'Oh, don't go all dramatic on me.'

'You're doing it again. God, how did I never notice?'

'What the hell are you talking about?'

'Are you actually saying that this video of you with Sian means nothing? That I have no right to be angry or hurt by it?'

'Yes. If you look at it sensibly, you'll see I'm right.'

'If I look at it like you want me to look at it, you mean. And if I do that it means you've done nothing wrong, and I have no right to react to it. God, Chris. It's like I'm seeing you properly for the first time.'

'This is ridiculous. I have no idea what you're talking about.'

'Maybe you don't, but I do. Don't belittle me. Don't tell me I'm talking nonsense. I've put up with your bullshit for too long.'

'I'm just trying to make you see things for how they are.'

'No, you are trying to manipulate me. No wonder I was such a bloody mess. It's like you had stabbed me in the chest and then said to me I was imagining the blood, the pain. You diminish my feelings, my thoughts, my work, everything, but I'm not going to put up with it any longer. All you do is lie. You lie to me, to your own daughter and I guess you do the same to Sian.'

'Don't go making out this is all my fault. I'm not the one who stood in front of the school screaming and went around attacking people. How do you think that made me feel? You humiliated me in front of everyone.'

'And you filmed it.'

'I told you why I did that. It was to protect you.'

'Rubbish. The only way you have used that video is to make me feel so awful about myself I'd come back to you. You should feel ashamed of what you did to me.' Nia was breathing fast; the words were tumbling out.

'Did you phone me to throw insults at me?'

'I phoned to talk about the video, to talk to you about Safi, but if you're not going to acknowledge you did anything wrong, I don't know how we are meant to talk.'

'Maybe you could start by leaving that damn island and coming home. You can't stay there. Your money will run out, and without my wage coming in you can say goodbye to your dream home and all the trappings of being married to a headteacher, a person respected by the community. Out there you will earn a pittance, be living in some student flat and all you will be—'

She interrupted him. 'All I will be is Nia, and that's great.'

'You're seriously telling me you want a life without me – you want a divorce?'

Nia paused, the enormity of the question sinking in, and then, very quietly but firmly, she answered, 'Yes. That is exactly what I want.'

'You won't last. You're nothing without me.'

And with that he ended the call. Nia lay back on the sofa with the overwhelming feeling of coming to the end of a very long battle.

She stared at the phone... the end of a battle but the start of what? She had no idea what she was going to do next in her life.

One thing she did know, though, was that the island, at least for now, was the right place for her.

* * *

Nia kept to her routine of work and walks for the rest of the week. She had a few chats with Safi, walking the tightrope of trying to explain the situation without making her daughter choose sides.

At least Nia had Joe's party to look forward to. On the Thursday she had a free morning and so decided to go into Newport and buy some new clothes. Everything she owned had been bought with Chris in mind, and she wanted to see if she could buy clothes just for herself.

She wandered from shop to shop not sure at all what she wanted to buy. She automatically went for the fitted body-con dresses Chris liked, but told herself she was looking for something different, something new.

Part of her was drawn to a more 'hippy'-type look but she couldn't see herself carrying that off. Eventually, she found a shop selling longer dresses. She found herself thinking about Elvira: she always looked good. Maybe she should aim for that. In the end she found a belted dress in light blue she felt suited her.

* * *

Saturday evening finally came around. Nia stood in front of the mirror wearing the blue dress; her long dark hair hung down. It was naturally straight and so she used curling tongs from the salon to add waves to it. The clothes combined with far less make-up made her look quite different, but she smiled at her reflection. The only thing that remained the same were the heels. She wasn't ready to forgo them.

She settled Romeo down and waited outside the house for Jade, so they could go to the party together. Jade wore her usual casual trousers, trainers but with a crop top and large earrings.

'Blimey, you look so different,' Jade said. Standing back, she scrutinised her. 'Very Kate Middleton.'

Nia felt herself blushing.

'God, I'm sorry,' said Jade. 'You look lovely, and you have gorgeous hair. You should wear it down more often.'

Joe's parents lived in a large, picturesque house on the edge of the village of Calbourne.

'Is it odd for you coming here, being with Joe's parents?' Nia asked.

Jade shook her head. 'Usually when I see them it confirms I'm making the right decision.'

There were fairy lights around the front door, and they went in together.

A large, red-faced man came to greet them. 'Jade, my beautiful girl,' he shouted, and then gave Jade a huge hug. 'You look gorgeous.' He winked at Nia. 'Nice to meet you...'

'This is Nia. She's staying in the close and working at the salon with me at the moment.'

'Of course. Joe told me about you. I hope everyone is making you welcome. So sorry about the terrible incident with poor Ruby though. How are you doing, Jade?'

'I'm getting there, thanks.'

'That's the way. You two were close, I know that. Poor Joe has been distraught. Just as well he has the business to keep him occupied.' Joe came over to them and his dad put his arm around him. 'Look at my boy: thirty. Can you believe that? Only seems yesterday I was taking him over the rec here to play football. Time he settled down, eh, Jade? You are still footloose and fancy free?' He gave her a knowing wink.

'For God's sake, Dad,' said Joe, but he laughed as he said it.

They were joined by a tall smart woman, and it was easy to see she was Joe's mother.

'Tony, are you keeping these poor girls hostage at the front door?' She gave Jade a huge smile.

'How lovely to see you. Goodness, you get prettier by the day.'

Jade grinned back.

'Now, come on in and I'll get you both a drink.'

There was a large living room that opened out into the garden, which was decorated with party lights, and there was a band playing.

Nia accepted a glass of wine, while Jade managed to talk Joe's mum down to an orange juice.

'Now, there's plenty of food. The caterers have set it all up in the kitchen diner. Please tuck in. I know what you girls are like, crunching on a stick of celery.'

Nia assumed this remark was aimed at Jade and smiled. Ethan was in the garden but came in to greet them.

'Hiya. Goodness, I feel old here tonight. Elvira is much more their age.' He was wearing, as always, his baggy cords but, Nia guessed at Elvira's bidding, a blue shirt that was actually ironed.

He frowned at Nia a second and blinked. 'You look different – your hair, it's long, and your face—' He scrutinised her as if she were some new kind of bug he'd stumbled over.

'For God's sake, Ethan, don't get too carried away with the compliments.' Jade laughed.

'Sorry, you look lovely,' he said, and gave her a warm smile. Nia could feel herself blushing and looked down. They went out into the garden and Ethan grinned.

'Fancy a dance, then? Elvira is off with some friends of hers. Come on.' He took her drink, placed it on a table and Nia found herself whisked away.

Neither of them were very skilful dancers, but it didn't matter. Chris hated dancing. Nia always felt he was embarrassed because he was so much taller than her. Ethan didn't seem to care; he took her hand, twirled her around. Nia felt quite heady on this feeling of being happy, of being with someone who seemed to feel she was pretty and fun.

She could have kept dancing all evening but eventually Elvira came over. With a slightly acidic tone she said, 'I think I'll pinch my fiancé back now,' and then glanced at Nia. 'You've had a makeover, haven't you? Copying my look?'

Nia felt her cheeks burning and she glared at Elvira. How dared this woman who was cheating on the man she was about to marry be so rude? Nia backed away but as she did she put on a sickly smile and said, 'It's much pleasanter here than in some creepy old car park in Ryde. You never know who you might bump into there.'

Elvira let out a tiny screech and covered her mouth. Ethan put his arm around her. 'What's wrong? Are you OK?'

'Of course, it's nothing. Let's dance.'

Elvira turned her back on Nia and headed off with Ethan. Nia was busy scolding herself for her lack of tact when Joe's father clinked a glass, the music stopped, and he stood ready with his wife to make a speech.

Joe looked suitably bashful but quietly pleased with the deluge of compliments paid by his dad. These were slightly modified by heckles from friends, but the mood was good-natured.

Towards the end of his speech, Joe's father became more emotional. 'Finally, can I just say how incredibly lucky Liz and I feel to have Joe as our son? I may be biased, but to me he's perfect.' He smiled over at Joe. 'So perfect that all we need now is for our Joe to meet a perfect, wonderful woman. They say you work for your children, and everything we've done has been for Joe and now, of course, for the generation after. Your mum has an empty photo frame waiting; you know that.'

Joe raised his eyes, but Nia was aware of the pressure hidden beneath the smiles.

The end of the speech seemed to mark the point for the partygoers to get stuck into the food and Nia was thinking of going inside when she felt a hand grab her elbow and sharp fingernails digging into her flesh.

'We need a word,' said Elvira, dragging her to a sheltered side of the garden.

'What's going on? Why were you following me?'

'Why were you meeting up with your ex?'

'That's none of your business.'

'Does Ethan know?'

'Look, keep out of this. You have no idea what's going on, but I'll tell you this: Hugo has some very unpleasant friends. You don't want to mess with them.'

'You're threatening me?'

'I am warning you, for your own sake, keep out of this.'

'Did Ruby find out about you and Hugo?'

Nia braced herself for an angry outburst from Elvira, but instead Elvira stood very still; her eyes were wide with fright. 'I had nothing to do with Ruby's death, leave me alone—'

As if out of nowhere Ethan appeared. Nia hadn't realised he was so close. He put his arm around his fiancée, glanced at Nia, but spoke to Elvira. 'Are you OK? Why don't we go and get something to eat?' Elvira didn't look at him, but Nia saw his hand tighten around her shoulder and gently lead her away.

Jade arrived a few seconds after. 'Have you seen the buffet? It's amazing.' She stopped, glanced at Nia. 'Are you OK? You look like you've seen a ghost.'

'Um, no. I'm fine. Let's get something to eat.'

Nia followed Jade into the house where she found an array of delectable dishes including lobster, oysters, roasts with all the trimmings, and colourful salads. There was also a dessert bar laden with profiteroles, pastries, puddings and cheeses to round off the feast.

Nia picked at the food but didn't want to linger inside and was glad to leave Jade and return to the garden.

She found a solitary bench where she could sit on her own.

Looking up, she could see a black sky full of stars and suddenly wished she could go home.

The party was well under way now. She saw Richie had arrived and was talking with friends. He looked younger and more carefree here. Ian and Lucy were also there now, and she saw Ian holding forth to a group of Joe's sailing friends, Lucy, as always, tucked behind her husband. As Nia watched she was startled to be joined by Ethan.

'What's going on with you and Elvira? What have you said to upset her so much?'

'I think she needs to tell you that.'

'She won't. You know how she is. I saw you on Sunday. Were you following her?'

Nia nodded.

'But why? Surely you don't suspect her of having something to do with Ruby's death. Please don't say that. Elvira is the sweetest, most innocent person I know.'

Nia pressed her lips together. What was she meant to say?

He moved closer to her. She could feel his breath on her cheek, and her heart was thumping. 'Nia, I like to think you and I have become close in quite a short time. Please talk to me.'

He was looking deep into her eyes now. Slowly she lifted her hand, laid it on his cheek, and leant towards him.

38

Ethan shot back, startled. 'Oh, God, I'm so sorry,' he stammered. 'I never meant, oh, God – I love Elvira. I just wanted you to tell me what was wrong. The only thing in the world that matters to me is making her happy. If I've given you the wrong impression, I'm sorry.'

Nia felt sick. Her eyes were burning. She covered her face, wanting to disappear. Take me away, she said to the universe, please, make me be anywhere else but here.

When she lowered her hands, Ethan had gone, and she flopped back on the bench and burst into tears. She was such a fool. Chris was right.

Nia was sitting sobbing quietly on her own when Jade found her.

'Whatever's the matter?'

'I'm such an idiot. God, I'm a forty-year-old woman acting like a teenager.'

'Hey, calm down. Tell me what happened.'

Slowly, gulping back tears, Nia told her the whole story.

'There are two things to sort out here,' said Jade. 'One is Elvira, and the other is Ethan. Tell me, do you really like him? I know I was teasing you about it, but is this serious?'

Nia sighed. 'I don't know; it was so nice to have someone take an interest in me. I love our walks, and tonight it was wonderful feeling happy, feeling pretty.' She covered her face. 'I'm pathetic, I'm sorry.'

Jade gently lowered her hands. 'There's nothing pathetic about wanting to be happy, to feel loved. We all do. Has something happened with Chris?'

Nia told Jade about the phone calls with Safi and Chris.

'He's back with her?'

'I'm not sure it was ever off, to be honest. I can see it now: it's like you said. He lies all the time. I told him the things we talked about. The more we spoke, the more I knew you were right. He twists and changes everything I say. He always tries to make everything my fault.'

'What did he say about the video?'

'Oh, that it was nothing.'

'Oh, no!'

'Exactly. And now Safi is upset. She feels her father has been lying to her.'

'Which he has.'

'Yes, I know, but what am I meant to do? I can't turn her against him. He's her dad.'

'And she's an adult. You have to be straight with her. So, what about you?'

'He asked me if I wanted a divorce, and I said yes.'

Jade sat open-mouthed. 'Good God, that's amazing. No wonder you're in bits.'

'You think I made a mistake?'

'I don't, but do you?'

Nia was calm now. 'No. I don't think so. But I don't know how I'm meant to live now. Chris said I'd be lost without him and he's right. Look at the way I flung myself at Ethan.'

'Chris has been controlling the way you live for years; no wonder you feel lost. But you can do this, Nia. You're stronger than you think. I've seen the way you've been battling for Ruby; you need to fight for yourself now.'

'But how do I face Ethan? I'm so embarrassed.'

Jade flapped her hand. 'As soon as the next emergency comes into the vet's it will all be behind him. He's not going to lose sleep over this.'

Nia smiled. 'I hope you're right.'

'So, tell me again about Elvira.'

Nia went through the story again.

'So, she threatened you? That's not good, is it?'

'No, I don't know what to make of her.'

'And she was saved by Ethan. I wonder what's going on with her ex, Hugo, then? By the way, he's turned up here.'

'You're joking – Hugo is here? Why?'

'Apparently Joe knows him through sailing. They all know each other. Ian as well. He sails but, as he said to me, seriously, mark you, "I'm between yachts at the moment".'

Nia smiled. 'It's another world, isn't it?'

'Quite. Living in Yarmouth, I should be used to it, but it's not me. I feel sick just walking on one of those pontoon things at the edge of the harbour.'

'So, this ex has turned up, then – that's awkward for Elvira, isn't it?'

'They seem to be successfully avoiding each other – he's over there now talking to Richie and Ian.'

'But Richie doesn't sail...'

'No, but he and Ruby used to be friendly with Hugo when he was with Elvira.'

'Of course. Ruby said something about that. Ruby didn't like him, did she?'

'No, couldn't stand him. Right. Look, I don't know about you, but I've pretty much had enough of this party. Fancy taking off soon?'

'I can't think of anything I'd like more.'

'Great. I have to go and see a few people, then we can go. Catch you in a minute.'

Jade left her and went over to a group of friends.

Nia saw that Elvira was now talking to Hugo. They were well apart from the rest of the group and Elvira didn't look happy.

'What are you doing sitting here all on your own?' Richie had come over to sit next to Nia.

'I don't know that many people here. Still, it was kind of Joe to invite me.'

'He has a lot of friends here, hasn't he? He spends a lot of time with the yachty lads.'

Nia caught an edge to his voice and looked at him. He gave her a knowing smile, and, in that moment, she was sure he knew. Glancing around, she wondered how many other people knew.

'I was surprised to see Elvira's ex, Hugo, turn up. I don't think it's fair on Ethan,' said Richie.

'I think Hugo knows Joe through sailing, doesn't he?'

'Hugo knows everyone – and everything about them.' Again, there was the knowing look. 'Have people been telling you about Hugo, then?'

'Friends of Elvira's were telling me about him at the hen party – one of them showed me a photograph of him. They all seem very keen on him.'

'He has a lot of charm. He's very popular.'

'But Ruby didn't like him?'

Richie grinned. 'No, she did not approve of him at all. She was probably right. He may have charm, but he's a crook. He'll make money any way he can, selling dodgy stuff, fraud, even drugs at times if you believe the rumours. But he seems to get away with it. Ruby was one of the few people not taken in by him. She was very upset when Elvira became engaged to him. She kept telling Elvira that he was using her, that he was no good, but Elvira was completely besotted with him. They came to our wedding. That's when I first met him, but Ruby told me to have nothing to do with him.'

'Who broke off the engagement?'

'They both claim to have done that.'

'Was Elvira very upset?'

'Yes, I think she came over here to get away from him.'

'Do you think there's any chance that she still loves him?'

'Why do you ask me that?'

Nia took a deep breath. 'Because last Sunday I followed Elvira and I saw the two of them meeting up over in Ryde.'

Richie's eyebrows shot up. 'You followed her? Why?'

'Because I knew she only spends an hour at the nursing home each week, and yet she returns to the close very late.'

Richie screwed up his eyes. 'You're checking up on everyone, aren't you?'

'Well, for Jade's sake, I'm trying to, but you don't make it easy! You and Ian seem to have a new story every time I talk to you.' She kept the tone light but held her breath waiting for the reply.

Richie moved so he was closer to her. He lowered his voice. 'I know it's not important, but the truth is I was at the bungalow the night Ruby died. Ian was frantic for me to cover for him, so I agreed. He paid well.' He cringed as if in apology.

'You mean you weren't together at all that night?' said Nia.

'Nope.' He shook his head. 'Look, it doesn't matter, does it? Ian is hardly the kind of person to be off killing anyone.'

'Why would he give you money if he wasn't guilty?'

'Because, as is always the case with Ian, he was worried about his reputation. He has a very inflated ego, thinks the world really cares what he is doing, and he is desperate for this TV job.'

'Yes. I can see that.'

'He simply wanted an easy explanation of where he was. I wasn't going to argue. It saved me having to go public about the bungalow, not an easy time to have shared that one with the world.'

Nia screwed her eyes up. 'And, of course, it gave you an alibi as well.'

'It did, but I'm not worried about that. If I need it, I'm sure someone in the street saw my car. I was there from the moment we left Wight's. In fact, just before I left the bungalow about midnight, I took a picture of one of my paintings and sent it to a friend to see what they thought.' He turned to her. 'Far more interesting, though, is this business with Elvira and Hugo. Did they look intimate?'

'I wouldn't say that, but it was strange that they should be meeting up. I saw her give him a parcel, well, a small package.'

'What do you think was in it?'

'I wondered about money. I know she pawned her engagement ring. She's pretending to have an expensive wedding dress made but I know it was bought in a charity shop.'

'Goodness, you have been digging around.'

'I have, but I'm not sure how far I've got.' Nia paused, then asked, 'So, how is your painting going?'

'Pretty well, thank you. I'm pleased with the work I'm doing over there.' Suddenly, Richie looked up. 'Where is Hugo off to now? That man is always wheeling and dealing.'

'He's going over to speak to Ethan, by the looks of it. I can't see that being anything to do with making him money,' said Nia, laughing.

'You never know with people like Ethan. What is it they say? Still waters run deep. I do wonder sometimes what goes on in his head. Ruby was worried about him, I know that. I saw her having a few deep discussions with him, but I don't know what they were about. I thought at first she was warning him off marrying Elvira, but I don't know. All she told me was that she was worried about him.' Richie stood up. 'I guess I ought to mingle. Good to speak to you, Nia, and I hope you know that, although I do believe Ruby took her own life, if there was any question of anyone else being involved then I would want the truth to come out. I appreciate what you're doing.'

Richie left her and Nia wandered about the perimeter of the garden. The bottom led to open fields, and she could make out the silhouettes of horses in the fields. She walked down and only then noticed a river the other side of the low fence. As she stood admiring the view, she realised she was not alone. She heard sobbing, walked towards a thick-barked old oak tree and behind it she found Joe. On seeing her, he wiped his face, forcing a smile.

'Oh, hi. Enjoying the party?'

'It's great, but you're clearly not. What's wrong?'

He turned away. 'Nothing. You couldn't possibly understand.'

She walked towards him. 'Um, listen. I might understand more than you realise.'

He turned and gave her a penetrating stare.

'I was talking to Jade,' she continued. 'I guessed. It's OK. I'm not going to tell anyone.'

He screwed up his eyes. 'What do you know?'

'I know you're gay.'

The growing apprehension in his eyes turned to terror. He stepped back, like a trapped animal looking for a way to escape.

'It's OK,' she said tenderly. 'I'm not going to say anything.'

'No one can know. It's my parents—'

'Why are you scared of telling them? They obviously love you so much. They'll understand.'

'You heard the speech my dad gave. All they want is for me to get married and have children.'

'You can still do all those things. You need to talk to them.'

'Not yet, I can't.'

Joe grabbed her arm with such force it hurt. 'And please don't you say anything. You can't.' The words came out hard like bullets.

Nia pulled away. 'Of course, I won't, but I should warn you that I've a feeling word is getting around. I was talking to Richie just now and I'm sure he was hinting he knew. Look, it's nothing to be ashamed of. You should be proud of who you are.'

'Out and proud, is it? That's easy for you to say.'

'I know and I'm sorry. I don't want this all to go horribly wrong for you.'

Joe glared at her. 'If that's some kind of threat, then think again. I'm no pushover. I won't let you get away with this.'

'Joe,' she shouted after him as he stormed off.

Nia looked up the garden and was relieved to see Jade had made it as far as the house and went to join her.

'Some of the others are planning to go over to Compton later. I don't fancy it, but I'll hang about and go if you want to.'

Nia shook her head. 'No, thanks. I've had enough.'

'Great, let's make a move, then.'

Nia was pleased to get home and took Romeo out along the pier. The darkness soothed her. She was still cringing with embarrassment about Ethan, but it was slowly being replaced by other thoughts from the evening. That threat from Elvira, and that very odd conversation between Ethan and Elvira's ex. What on earth had that been about?

She had learned so much and yet was she any closer to knowing the truth? The ring and the letter were still missing. She still had no idea who had made the voodoo doll.

She felt the weight of the evening sitting heavily on her. The humiliation with Ethan had not completely left her. She'd had a feeling of elation almost after deciding on the divorce but now the gloss had worn off. She wondered if she was going to be able to cope on her own. Maybe Chris was right: she was a fool who was lost without him. If she was bright and capable, why had she let him treat her badly for so long? He'd told her the people in the close pitied her; they didn't like her. The letter she'd received proved that. Who wanted her to disappear? Someone had made Ruby disappear, hadn't they? Would they do the same to her?

* * *

Later, as Nia lay unable to sleep, in a room very close to hers a person was sitting in a dark room, and with a cold, steady hand they lit a black candle.

On a piece of paper, they wrote a name, Nia, and pinned it onto a voodoo doll. They had worked hard creating this: every bit of wood carefully selected, the blue silk, cut and wrapped around its body. The face had taken the longest, skilful carving of the features. It was frightening how much it looked like her. The eyes were sneaky, watching, waiting for them to put a foot wrong, and the mouth was open, spitting out nasty accusations.

Picking up the voodoo doll, they said the words, loud and firm. 'The pain you gave me will come back to you a thousand times worse. You are cursed.' They didn't need to imagine or manufacture hate, it was there, waiting to be used. They smiled at their creation: it was perfect.

Each of the black pins was pushed in purposefully, and then the best bit of all. They took the hair they'd collected from Nia's brush and rubbed it so that it resembled string, and then slowly they wound it round the neck of the voodoo doll… tighter and tighter.

Finally, they stopped, lifted the voodoo doll, and placed it in a small black coffin, the one they'd used for Ruby. They put on the lid, blew out the candle and went to the window.

At that moment they knew someone out there was dying. They knew because they had caused it. No voodoo dolls or curses for that victim. That was different: no hate, no feelings at all. It was a job that unfortunately had to be done.

What a dark world it had become.

39

Nia woke very early the next morning. It was bright and sunny and, after the stress of the party, it was good to feel the warmth of a new day.

She pushed back her curtains and saw Jade opposite, looking out. They waved to each other, and Jade mimed swim and Nia gave her a thumbs up. Jade then held up five fingers, mouthed five minutes.

Nia felt Romeo next to her, all ready to go, wagging his tail.

'Come on, then, it's beach time. Hooray for Sunday, a day off.'

Nia left the house, glanced around the close. She paused. Something was different. No curtains were closed. There was an air of a close that hadn't slept. But no, she was letting her imagination get away from her. When Jade came running over, Nia shook off the feeling of unease, and they left together.

Jade had suggested they go to the Compton and they drove to the car park at Hanover Point and went down on to the dog walking end of the beach.

It wasn't until they were in the water that Jade pointed far along the beach.

'Look, there are police down there. I wonder what's up. Maybe it's kids getting into trouble, using drugs, that kind of thing. I can't see why they would have cordoned off the road for that, though.'

They swam for a while and sat drying themselves. 'So, have you got over the trauma of last night?' said Jade. 'You were quiet on the way back. It was all pretty exhausting, wasn't it?'

'It was. I didn't tell you, but I found Joe down the garden; he was in such a state.'

'Really?'

'Yes, it was so sad. I told him I knew about him being gay. I wanted to help him.'

'Oh, God. He must have been so angry. Does he think I told you?'

'No, I told him I'd guessed. I gently warned him that I think other people are starting to suspect. Richie seemed to have a good idea, that's for sure. It won't be long until someone says something to his parents. He should be the one to do that.'

'I agree, but he doesn't see it like that, and it's his prerogative.'

'We know that, but him putting his head in the sand won't stop people dropping hints to his parents. I fear I touched a nerve though, because when I said that to him, he went mad, seemed to assume I was threatening to tell them. He stormed off in the end.'

Jade sat back, resting her hands on the sand. 'What a mess, and it's all so unnecessary.'

'I said that. Look, but I was wondering – am I being naive? Is it harder to come out over here on the island?'

Jade shook her head. 'No. I have friends who are gay. They tend to go clubbing more on the mainland, but their families are fine. Everyone accepts it.'

'So why is Joe being like this?'

'I don't know. Maybe he needs to talk to someone. There are support groups over here. Maybe I should have been a bit more proactive with him. I'll talk to him, see if I can help.'

'I think that would be good.'

Jade looked again down the beach. 'The police are still there. What's going on, do you think?'

'No idea.' Nia looked at her phone. 'It's only six. For goodness' sake, what are we doing in the sea this time in the morning? I might even go back to bed. I'm too old for all the late nights and parties.'

She called Romeo and they made their way back to the car and drove home. To their surprise, when they returned to the close, they saw a police car parked by the vet's.

'What the heck is going on?' exclaimed Jade.

They instinctively walked up to Wight's together. Inside they saw Lucy, Ian and Richie huddled around a table with Joe.

Jade pushed open the door and, looking out at the police car, asked, 'What the hell?'

Joe gestured to come and sit down.

Nia took one look at the shock on their faces and knew that something terrible had happened.

'Hugo, Elvira's ex, had a terrible accident last night,' said Ian.

To Nia's eyes he had aged years since she last saw him: he was frighteningly pale, and his usually bright blue eyes were red with dark rings under them. His hands trembled as he played with his bottom lip. Lucy, next to him, sat very still, her hands clasped together, staring ahead.

'I'm afraid he's dead,' said Ian and sat up, clearly ready to explain. 'After you left the party last night a group of us decided to go up to the cliffs at Compton. There is such a beautiful view over the bay if you drive down and park at the farm. No one was too drunk. Actually, it was all very pleasant. Hugo walked away from us and as it started getting cold we began talking about leaving. It was only then we noticed Hugo was missing.' His voice broke. He looked down.

'We all put the torches on our phones, and we finally made out Hugo quite a way down the cliff side,' said Joe.

'We were all shouting,' said Ian. 'Ethan stayed the calmest. He rang for an ambulance. Of course, they had to send all sorts. The paramedics managed to get to him. The fire service came as well, but they were too late; he was dead. A helicopter came in the end to take him away.'

'Oh my God,' said Jade. 'We went for a swim earlier down the other end and saw the police. Obviously, we had no idea what had happened. So, who was there? All of you?'

'There was me and some of my sailing friends,' said Joe, 'and then Lucy, Ian, Ethan Elvira, Richie. I suppose it was about a dozen of us altogether. We all went to the police station and gave statements, but it was dark, so hard to tell where anyone was. None of us was anywhere near him though, were we?'

The group all shook their heads. Nia heard a car pulling away and saw the police car leaving and a moment later Ethan and Elvira came in.

'What did they say?' asked Ian.

'Not a lot. They wanted to talk to us because of Elvira's history with Hugo. They thought she might know more about him. As for the accident, we know no more than you. It was dark. Elvira knows even less, as she stayed in the car park. She was video-calling a friend. She only realised something was up when they saw the police and ambulance arrive.'

Elvira stood very still, her face frozen. Ethan put his arm around her, guided her to a seat. Joe gave her coffee.

'What happens now?' Jade asked.

'The police officer we spoke to said he'd come back at lunchtime to see us all. I hope it's all right, Joe – I suggested we meet here?'

'Of course, that's fine. I am closing the place today; Mum and Dad are upset. I'm going to see them soon but will come back at lunchtime.'

They continued going over the events of the evening, until Joe said he was going to have to shut things up and they all silently returned to their homes. Nia showered and made breakfast, but all the while all she could think about was Hugo's accident. Did he fall down the cliff or was he pushed?

She tried to think who in the close might have any reason to want Hugo dead. The obvious person was Elvira, but Ethan had said she was nowhere near him when he fell. Nia then thought of Ethan himself. Had he killed Hugo out of jealousy?

Lucy and Ian seemed to have little reason to hurt Hugo. Richie knew him better, but why would he want to hurt him? There was Joe, of course. Richie had hinted that Hugo knew about Joe. Was it possible that Hugo might even have tried to blackmail Joe? It would give Joe plenty of motive for killing Hugo. Still, maybe it was all just a horrible accident.

Nia was deep in thought that she nearly missed a quiet knock at the door.

When she opened it, she found Elvira standing there, her arms hanging limply by her sides. Suddenly, Nia felt desperately sorry for her.

'Come in, come in, sit down,' she said.

Elvira sat in an armchair, picked up a cushion and cuddled it.

'Everything has gone wrong.' She buried her head in her hands, then shook her head, wiped her eyes, and sniffed. 'Look, firstly I have to apologise,' she stammered. 'I shouldn't have spoken to you the way I did last night. I've been so stressed lately. Nothing is going right, and now this.' Her eyes filled with tears again.

'You must be in shock.'

'Why does death seem to follow me? First Ruby, and now Hugo. It's horrible. It's like I have some power, as if people I fall out with just die.'

'You'd had an argument with Hugo?'

'It's far more complicated than that. I know you got the wrong idea when you saw me meeting him. That was nothing to do with love. The truth was, Hugo was blackmailing me.'

Nia stared. Blackmail? Why would he be blackmailing Elvira? As if reading her mind, Elvira began to explain.

'As you know, Hugo and I were engaged. I was infatuated. I'd nabbed the man everyone else wanted. The only person who didn't think he was wonderful was Ruby and I assumed she was jealous. Anyway, I made a really stupid mistake. Hugo and I had gone out one evening. I'd had an exhausting day and I'd just settled down with a glass of wine in a cosy pub when I realised I'd left my phone at the surgery. Hugo offered to go back and get it for me. I know I shouldn't have done it, but I was so tired. I knew everything would be locked up by then, and so I gave him the security code for the alarm. He went and got my phone for me, and I thought no more about it. A few weeks after then there was a break-in at the surgery. It happened one afternoon when we had all gone to an emergency meeting at a neighbouring practice. We were only told about this the night before. I had seen Hugo that night and told him about it.

'When we returned from the meeting and realised there'd been a break-in, I had this horrible feeling that somehow Hugo may be behind it. I knew that he had sold drugs in the past. We'd talked about ketamine.

'The police arrived, and they talked to the senior partner. It was then I received a text message from Hugo threatening me to make sure I kept him out of it, or he would take me down with him. I realised, if he wanted to, he could implicate me in the break-in. I had given him all the information he needed. I was so stupid. I lied to the police; told them I had no idea who could have been involved. Once I'd lied, he had me. He could hold that against me as proof of my guilt. We spoke that evening, and he told me that as long as I continued to keep quiet that was the end of it. I broke up with him and moved. I thought everything was over between us.

'Not long after I came here, he started texting me. When he heard I was engaged he came over, demanded to see me, and said unless I gave him money he would tell Ethan that I had been involved in the break-in at the vets. Hugo asked me for a one-off payment of a thousand pounds. I'm not wealthy, but I gave him the money. That was a huge mistake, because then he could tell Ethan I was giving him money. It made me look guilty. He knew we had a wedding coming up and he told me to get as much money off Ethan as I could, so I ended up pawning my engagement ring.' Elvira had spoken surprisingly calmly up till now but at this point she burst into tears again. 'Hugo knew how much that ring meant to me, but he didn't care. All he wanted was money.'

Nia shook her head. She had got so much wrong about Elvira. 'And that is why you have a wedding dress from a charity shop?'

'Exactly. You saw the album I showed everyone at the drinks party. That would be my dream. Hugo stole it all.'

'Did Ethan have any idea about this? He must have suspected something, surely?'

Elvira nodded. 'He'd guessed something was up but had no idea what. Apparently, he'd even followed me some evenings – I'd not known any of this until he told me this morning. He was embarrassed and hadn't known what to do.'

'So, he'd seen you with Hugo?'

'Yes. He first followed me the night after Ruby's outburst at our engagement drinks at Wight's on that Sunday.'

'Ethan followed you the night Ruby died?'

'He did. He went to the rescue centre and then came to the nursing home and followed me. Of course, I didn't see Hugo that night – he was over at Petunia's party. I didn't want to just drive home. Ethan had always thought I should make shorter visits to Mum and said I should relax on a Sunday evening. I'd persuaded him she needed me there. I thought it was best not to disrupt the routine and so drove round to a pub in Freshwater instead. I did bump into some clients, actually, and sat with them playing board games until late. They asked me where Ethan was, and I explained about his work at the rescue centre. We were chucked out at midnight, and I came home. Unknown to me, of course, Ethan had been following me and sat somewhere in the pub I couldn't see him. I know he hung about because he was able to tell me the names of the people who joined us about eleven. He stayed until I left. I thought it was a bit of a coincidence him coming up the close just after I'd parked. Now it all makes sense.'

'But he didn't see you with Hugo that night.'

'No, he was still uneasy, and so he followed me the following Sunday and that's when he saw Hugo. He was shocked, but says he was worried more than suspicious. He saw me give Hugo money. He thought I was feeling sorry for him. He never even thought about blackmail.

'Anyway, a couple of weeks later he planned to follow me again but then he said he saw you and abandoned the idea and went home. He's been trying to summon up the nerve to ask me about everything but instead he asked Hugo what was going on at Joe's party, but of course Hugo didn't tell him.'

'How did he react when you told him everything?'

'He was so lovely; he'd not suspected me of still being in love with Hugo even for a minute. I should have spoken to him sooner. And he told me he'd been keeping secrets too.'

Nia looked up; their eyes met.

'Yes, Ethan told me you knew about the gambling. I was upset when he confessed it to me.'

'Do you think he has a problem with betting?'

'He's nothing like my father was. He showed me the books. We're not in terrible debt, he's not been using the work account or anything terrible like that, but he did say he could see how it could become a problem and he's promised he will stop the online stuff and the poker games now. We're going to do the accounts and our money together now, keep tabs on each other.'

Nia smiled. 'I'm glad you've sorted it out.'

'So am I. Ruby being right, we should have talked a lot more to each other. One thing we both agreed on was that I need to go and get my ring back. We can just about afford for me to do that. We'll have to be careful with the wedding plans, but we can manage it and I have cash that I was saving to give to Hugo.'

'What about your dream wedding, all those pictures in the album?'

'I've realised that none of that matters now. All that is important is that Ethan and I get married. No one can stop that now.' Elvira screwed up her eyes. 'And before you ask, I had nothing to do with Hugo's death. I may have had good reason to want him out of the way, but I have witnesses to say I was well away from him when he fell. Thank God I was on the phone. And if your mind turns to Ethan, I can tell you he was stood with another friend, all the time they were up on the cliffs. Neither of us would kill anyone, you have to believe that. And that of course goes for Ruby as well. I can give you the names of the people I was with at the pub. They can verify I was there.'

Elvira sat back. 'I think I should explain that I was the person who rang the helpline and spoke to Ruby. Before I realised it was her, I had told her I was being blackmailed by my ex, and I didn't know what to do. She recognised my voice, said my name. I panicked and I said to her, "If you tell anyone this, Ruby, I'll kill you."'

Nia gasped.

'I know,' said Elvira. 'It was a wicked thing to say, of course, then, when she died, I felt so guilty.'

'You must have been very frightened that she might tell someone. Tell me, did you make that voodoo doll to scare her?'

'God, no. I've no idea who did that. Didn't Joe suggest Lucy? She's a funny one. It could be her. But no, I didn't do that. I just said those horrible words and I will for ever wish I hadn't.'

Elvira stood up. 'Sorry. That was a long story, but I'm glad I've told you. I'm sorry I've threatened you, but I was frightened. I love Ethan very much. The one thing I am frantic to do is get my ring back. I'd drive in today if I wasn't so shattered. Also, I don't want Ethan asking me where I am going.'

Nia could see the desperation in her face. 'If you want, I could drive you?'

'No, I couldn't ask you to do that.'

'I don't mind at all, but are you sure it's open on a Sunday?'

'Yes, I've checked.'

'Come on then, it won't take long.'

And so, they left together and drove into town. Nia was excited to visit the shop – she'd never been in a pawn shop before. However nothing could have prepared her for what she would find that morning.

40

The pawn shop felt seedy. They were the only customers, Elvira went straight to the desk. Nia didn't want to intrude so started looking around. The stock was mainly jewellery, some coins, some phones. It was rather sad that things that had been so loved had been abandoned. Most customers would have been offered far less than the items were worth, but this was a place for desperate people.

She was looking through a tray of rings when suddenly she spotted one that looked very familiar. It was behind a locked glass door but the closer she looked, the more convinced she grew that she knew who had owned it. She took out her phone and photographed it.

When Elvira had finished her transaction, she came over to Nia grinning, her beautiful engagement ring sitting proudly on her finger. Nia congratulated her and then went to the counter and asked the man serving if she could have a look at one of the trays.

She pointed out the ring. He unlocked the glass cabinet and handed it to her. Elvira had come to see what she was doing.

'Fancy something for yourself?' she said, laughing, but she saw the ring in Nia's hand and frowned. 'That looks just like the one Ruby had,' she said quietly.

'It's not just similar – it's the actual ring,' said Nia. 'I'm positive.'

She looked to the shop assistant. 'Can you tell me when this was brought in?' she asked.

'Yeah. It was only a few days ago. Hang on, I'll have a look. It wasn't pawned, so if you want to buy it, we can negotiate a price.'

He looked in an old-fashioned white notebook and told Nia that it had been brought in on Thursday.

Nia's heart raced. 'What did they look like? Was it a man, woman, old, young?' She fired the questions.

'I can't remember much. Scruffy sort of person, I think, all wrapped up.'

'Weren't you worried it was stolen?'

The man stepped back and scowled. 'I don't ask too many questions, you know. People come here because they know I'm discreet.'

'Was it a man or a woman? You must have noticed something. This is an expensive piece of jewellery.'

'A man, I think. All wrapped up in a waterproof with the hood up, and those weird mirror glasses so you can't see their eyes, and gloves. I remember this stink of perfume. It's the one my mum wears, Romantic or something. I'd know it because she piles it on. Anyway, I was thinking it was odd for a man to be wearing that kind of thing. Then I realised the scent wasn't coming off the bloke, it was the box the ring was in. Look, what is this all about? Do you want to buy this or not?'

'I think the police have to be told about this. I'm sure this ring belonged to the woman who died over in Yarmouth last month. Her body was found on the beach there.'

'Bloody hell. How would you know that?'

'Because I was one of the last people to speak to her and I'm sure I saw this on her finger.'

The man looked scared now. 'Look, I don't want trouble. I'll phone the police; I don't get involved with messy stuff like this.'

'Good, I think you should. Do you have CCTV?'

'I don't think I should be discussing the security arrangements here, do you? I will talk to the police. I don't want stuff like that in here.'

The man practically pushed them out of the shop and locked the door behind them.

'Do you trust him?' Elvira asked.

'I think we have to, but tomorrow I'll phone that police officer who came to see me and check it's been reported.'

They headed back to Yarmouth.

Elvira was intrigued. 'That was weird, wasn't it? I suppose the person who went in could have found the ring on the beach and wanted to make some money.'

'It's possible.'

Elvira screwed her eyes up. 'You don't think that, do you? You think it was taken by the person who killed Ruby – but why on earth would they go to a shop with it?'

'The price tag was four hundred pounds, so, say he or she was given two hundred, well, that's something. Depends how desperate that person was for money.'

Elvira nodded but then looked down at her hand and smiled. 'I need to go back; I want to show this to Ethan. Good luck with the ring. I hope the police can track down who took it in.'

After Elvira had left, Nia went home. She took out her phone and looked again at the photo she'd taken and wondered if the police really would be able to tell who had taken the ring into the shop. It had been an incredibly risky thing to do.

* * *

She began to scroll through the photos on her phone, returned to the one of Ruby and Ian's car accident. She was sure she was missing something here. She stared at the photo, made it larger, and then, a flash, she saw it. How had she missed that before? Finally, she could see what Ruby had been made to cover up – that was the lie that had played on her conscience.

After she'd done this, with fresh determination, Nia prepared for the meeting at lunchtime. It was chancy, it was walking into the lions' enclosure, but it was time.

Nia first had a good walk with Romeo, then nervously set off for Wight's.

Everyone was sitting around a large table in the garden. They all looked up as she arrived but then past her: she wasn't who they were waiting for. She sat next to Jade, who gave her an anxious smile; no one was chatting; the atmosphere was tense.

Finally, the police officer arrived. Pulling up a chair, he sat slightly apart, holding himself with an air of a man not planning on staying long.

'Thank you for coming. I wanted to give you an opportunity to ask any questions you may have.'

'I guess what we all want to know is how this accident happened,' said Ian.

'Of course. It must have been such a shock for you all. I can tell you that we found drugs on Hugo, mainly ketamine. We also believe he had been taking cocaine. I wonder if any of you can remember seeing him taking drugs at the party or after?'

No one answered. 'We took statements from everyone about the trip to Compton and from them it's clear that, although you were pretty spread out and it was very dark, he took himself off on his own. Is that still how you all remember it?'

The response was vague smiles and nods.

'I see. Well, if anyone remembers anything different, do get in touch. To return to your question,' he said, looking at Ian, 'initial findings suggest Hugo had been taking drugs, stumbled or lost his footing, and fell accidentally.' He looked around the group. 'Now, is there anything else?'

Silence greeted this, and so he stood up to go. 'Thank you, and anyone who has anything to add, please don't hesitate to contact me.'

As he left, the group seemed to give a collective sigh of relief.

'At least that's over, then,' said Ian. 'Of course, it's terrible for a young man to lose his life like that, but it doesn't sound like the police are going to bother any of us again. I think we'd all agree we've been through quite enough.' He turned to Joe. 'I wonder, would it be OK for us to have a few drinks? I think we could all do with one.'

Joe stood up. 'Of course, I'll go and bring over a few bottles and some glasses.'

It was only then that Jade noticed Elvira's ring.

'You got your ring back from the jeweller's, then.'

Elvira shot a grin at Nia and held out her hand. Everyone was excited to see the ring again and started to chat about the wedding. It was such a change to see the group relaxed that Nia was hesitant about changing the mood, but she knew she had to say something.

She slipped her phone out of her bag, found the photograph she'd taken in the pawn shop and then held it out. 'I think you should all know, I took this today in a shop in Newport.'

Jade grabbed the phone off her. 'That looks like Ruby's ring. Where did you see it?'

Nia told them about going into the pawn shop, omitting for Elvira's sake details of why she was there.

'It was taken in last Thursday, sold to them. I told the man in the shop where I think the ring came from and he's reporting it to the police.'

'So, I guess someone must have found it on the beach and decided to get some money for it,' said Ian.

'Maybe,' said Nia. 'But what if it was taken in by a person who removed it from Ruby's finger on the beach, the person who killed her?'

'You've no proof at all of that. It's just speculation,' said Ethan.

'No, but the person was wearing a strange outfit that sounded like they were trying to disguise themselves.'

'Well, maybe they felt guilty for not handing it in,' insisted Ethan.

'Possibly, but it will be interesting if the CCTV shows any more. Also, I've remembered something the man said. The box containing the ring had a very distinct perfume – Romantic, I think he said, but I'm not sure he got the name quite right.'

She heard a gasp from Lucy, but by the time she'd turned towards her Lucy was staring impassively at the table.

'So, is the ring still in the shop?' asked Jade.

'Yes. I had to leave it with him. I'll call the police tomorrow and check he's reported it.' She looked around the table.

An ugly silence followed her words. She waited for someone to scream at her, threaten her, but instead, Ian, in a steady voice, said, 'That is that, then. This matter is best left to the police.'

Joe coughed and said, 'I'm afraid I'm going to have to close up now. I need to get back to Mum and Dad. It's all been a terrible shock for them. There is a lot to sort out. If anyone feels able to come and carry a few chairs, I'd be very grateful.'

Ian looked up. 'Of course, I can come over.'

Slowly others offered. It seemed to Nia they were glad of the opportunity to get away, but she guessed she wouldn't be welcome.

She stood up, saying, 'I have a few plans this afternoon so I'll catch up with you all another time.'

As Nia left via the main room of Wight's it felt darker than before, and she saw a woman light the green candle on her table. Nia paused. She watched the flame flickering and saw the wax melting down the sides. It disturbed her, and she couldn't think why. She looked at an unlit candle on the table beside her, cold, misshapen. She knew the answer. Nia picked up the candle, slipped it into her pocket.

However, before she left, she heard Jade call after her, 'Hold on, I'll walk down with you.'

She rushed over to Nia, and they left together. 'I can't face being with them all,' she said quietly, 'and anyway, me and you need a catch-up.'

They went back to Nia's. They sat in the kitchen and Nia placed a tin of biscuits down for them to share.

'So, you found the ring – that's amazing,' said Jade.

'I know, it was a stroke of luck really. I just hope the police can work out who took it in.'

'It has to be the killer, doesn't it? Good job you went with Elvira, she'd never have noticed it. How is she?'

Nia told Jade what she'd learned.

'Ruby was right about Hugo, wasn't she? I'm sorry he died the way he did, but he was rotten through and through. So, I guess that lets Elvira and Ethan off the hook?'

'It appears they were both in the pub when Ruby died. So that leaves Lucy, Ian, Richie and Joe.'

Jade sighed. 'Have you any new ideas on them?'

'Actually, I do.' Nia told her about what she'd realised at the pool and then what Richie had told her.

Jade sat up, excited. 'Ian paid Richie to make up some stupid story just to stop the police questioning him? I can't believe it, what an idiot – unless of course this is more serious, and he was on the beach killing Ruby. But why? We always come back to that.'

'Ah, I finally think I have got to the bottom of what happened the night of Ruby and Ian's car accident.' Nia pulled out her phone and found the photo. 'Can you see it?' she asked.

Jade shook her head. 'No, it all looks perfectly straightforward.'

'That's what I thought and then I looked more closely. Look at the car seat.'

Nia watched Jade's face change as the truth dawned on her. 'Oh my God.'

Nia nodded and then, from her pocket, she produced the candle she'd taken from Wight's and placed it on the table. 'And that is another piece of the puzzle. The number of times I walked past this, and I never saw it.'

Jade frowned, but Nia smiled and slowly she explained everything she knew.

By the time she'd finished Jade was shaking her head in disbelief. 'I'm so shocked, you know, you could be right. But if you are, Nia, then the killer will know you are getting close now. You need to go to the police; you can't hold on to this any longer.'

'I will go soon; I just need to be sure of one or two more things.'

Jade stood up. 'I have to go, but be careful, now, won't you?'

Nia watched Jade leave and then sat alone with Romeo snuggled up next to her. She felt as if she'd lit a touchpaper; all she could do now was wait and see what happened. She was aware of a stillness out in the close, but not a peaceful quiet, rather one heavy with expectation. The house grew darker as dark rain clouds gathered so Nia turned the lights on.

She slumped onto the sofa with Romeo beside her and before she knew it, she'd fallen fast asleep.

When she woke the rain had started as a steady drizzle.

'Well, that was a waste of three hours. When did I last sleep like that in the daytime?' she said to Romeo. 'Still, you need your walk, don't you? Come on, let's wrap up.'

Nia made her way down the road and onto the beach and to her surprise she saw Lucy was down there again. She was at the edge of the sea, tearing up paper, oblivious to anything around her.

41

Nia approached and touched Lucy's arm lightly. Lucy pulled it away in panic, starting to stuff the remaining paper in her pocket.

Lucy had made a poor job of trying to get rid of the paper and slowly the sea was returning it to the shore. Nia bent down and started to pick the pieces up and straight away she spotted that one had a small blob of red wax on it.

'My God, what are you doing with this letter?' she demanded.

'I found it in my pocket,' said Lucy, crying now. 'Someone must have put it there this afternoon. I promise you it's nothing to do with me.'

'But who would do that?'

'I don't know. I found it when we came back from Joe's. Oh, God, I'm so scared, Nia. Someone's trying to frame me for Ruby's murder, aren't they? But I didn't do it. I didn't kill Ruby.' She turned to Nia. 'You know about the accident, don't you?'

Nia led her away from the sea, back up the beach. 'I know you were driving the car that night. It was plain from the photograph Ruby had taken. Why else would the driver's seat have been that far forward?' she said simply.

Lucy nodded. 'You're right. I was the person driving. Ian was at home. I was driving back from my craft group. My mind was all over the place. I veered over to the other side of the road, collided with Ruby. It wasn't far from home. I panicked. I rang Ian and he came straight out. Unfortunately, Ruby had already rung the police, so he sent me home.'

'And that's when the lies started? He told the police he was driving, and he persuaded Ruby to do the same.'

Lucy nodded. 'It was all so stupid. It was such a minor bump. No one was hurt.'

'But Ian thought you'd been drinking – he was worried you'd be breathalysed.'

'He was, and that's why he sent me away. He took the blame for the accident.'

'It was a huge risk, lying about an accident. He could go to prison for that.'

'I know. We both knew the chance he was taking, but, as it was so minor, we didn't think any more would be said about it.'

'But Ruby didn't think so...'

'Oh, Ruby, she was so messed up. She kept saying she shouldn't have lied to the police.'

'She was right.'

'But none of it mattered.'

'It did to Ruby. What I don't understand is why didn't you tell Ian there and then you hadn't been drinking?'

'Because I didn't want to tell him about my illness. I was worried that maybe I shouldn't have been driving with the queries about my health. Ménière's is one of those illnesses you have to report to the DVLA.'

'But you hadn't been diagnosed then? Had you been told not to drive?'

Lucy shook her head. 'No, not then, but I knew I wasn't feeling right. When I was telling Ian about it all he was so cross with me. He said the police would have probably been lenient at the time but, as it was, we'd ended up lying to the police and it was all my fault.'

'Ian chose to lie as well,' said Nia gently. 'I have a feeling he was guarding his own reputation. This isn't all on you.'

'If only Ruby had kept quiet, stopped nagging us about owning up to what actually happened the night of the accident.'

'But she wouldn't give up.'

'No, but you have to believe me, as stressful as it was, I didn't kill her to silence her,' said Lucy. 'The problem is I think someone is trying to make it look like I did. That person who took the ring into the shop, drenched it in my perfume. And now this letter—'

'You could go to the police, explain—'

'I can't. I saw them, and I'm so scared.'

'What did you see?'

'I saw the person who pushed Hugo over the cliff.'

'Who was it?' Nia asked urgently.

But before Lucy could answer, Nia heard a crunching on the pebbles behind her, turned, and saw Ian striding towards them.

'There you are, Lucy; I was looking for you.'

'I came for some fresh air,' Lucy said hurriedly, and walked over to him. Turning to Nia, she gave a quick shake of her head to silence her, then added, 'I'll be off now. Good to chat. Don't worry about anything.'

Ian put his arm around Lucy and together they left the beach.

Nia looked down at the piece of paper in her hand, felt the red wax. Lucy said someone was trying to frame her: could it be Ian? Or was she simply a clever liar, and had she been trying to get rid of the evidence? And had Lucy really just told her that she saw someone kill Hugo? If she was right, then surely Lucy's life was in danger. Unless, of course, that was another lie.

Nia shook her head, called Romeo and together they made their way home. The rain was heavy by the time they reached the front door. She looked around, to see Joe running up the road, trying to keep dry by holding a leather jacket over his head. He needs an umbrella, she thought, but then so many young people didn't seem to like them.

She looked over at the postcard Safi had sent her. That worried her, but she couldn't think why.

'I might be going a bit mad,' she said to Romeo. 'TV and an early night for us.' Later, she gave Romeo his final meal and they went to bed. She was glad to draw the curtains and shut out the rain she could hear splattering against the window. It was cosy with her bedside light on, and she started to read. Eventually, sleep caught up with her. Her eyes closed. She reached over, turned off the light and lay down to sleep.

It could have been one hour later; it could have been six. She had lost track of time by then, but she was woken by the sound of her letter box and something falling onto the doormat.

She wrapped her dressing gown around herself and crept down the stairs nervously. On the doormat she could make out the outline of a small parcel. She picked it up and started to unwrap it. Her hands shaking, she knew immediately what it was.

Nia opened the front door, looked up and down the close but it was empty. Whoever had delivered this had been quick and was safe back inside their home.

She slammed the door, turned on the lights, and looked at the voodoo doll. It was similar to Ruby's: the same face, carefully sculpted, wrinkled, with mean, cruel eyes that glared at her. It was made of twigs, although the dress was made of blue silk. There were pins sticking in it. Most upsetting was the hair around its neck, which Nia knew instantly was her own hair. She remembered the hair taken from her hairbrush and knew the person who had broken in that day, who had rummaged among her things, was the same person who had made this. They had been planning this all that time ago.

Nia felt her stomach muscles clench. Ruby was right. It wasn't the stupid voodoo doll that really upset her, as unpleasant as that was; it was the intent, the thought that had gone into this. This person was deadly serious. Even if she didn't believe it could hurt her, they did, and their motivation was hate.

42

At the back of Nia's mind, a voice was trying to make itself heard.

'Calm down. This is just a stupid doll. They are trying to frighten you because you are nearly at the truth.'

Nia went upstairs and found her notes, the fossil with the red wax on it, the candle, and the postcard. Finally, she grabbed the voodoo doll. She laid everything in front of her on the coffee table and sat back.

She had all these clues, all this information. Now all she had to do was knit them together in the right way.

She decided to start back with Ruby. Ruby who knew everyone's secrets, Ruby who cared about the truth. Nia's eyes wandered to the voodoo doll, and she picked it up. She looked at the face, coldly, objectively now. It was the same face as the one on Ruby's voodoo doll and she was sure the same person had carved them both. She stared at the face. It was a mean, cruel face. The person who carved this had done it with hate.

She closed her eyes. Like a kaleidoscope, ideas and pictures appeared and the pieces started to make a pattern. The postcard, the candle, the funeral, Joe running in the rain without an umbrella, Lucy's perfume, Hugo's death, the funeral...

But all the time she was trying to think, Nia was aware that something was dragging her back to the voodoo doll. It was as if she couldn't let go. Her gaze was fixed on the eyes. They seemed to glare at her, burn hate into her.

Nia knew then she had to get the thing out of her house. She ran upstairs, threw on trousers and a jumper. Before she left the bedroom, she opened the curtains, and left the light on. She ran back down and put on her coat, grabbed a bag. Into it she threw a small towel, her aunt's torch that had been sitting unused on the side, the candle, the voodoo doll, and some matches.

Romeo had been following her, watching her, so she knelt down and cuddled him. 'I'm sorry. You can't come with me. You'll be safer here.' She gave him a handful of dog biscuits and left him munching happily.

Nia stepped outside and looked around the close. The rain had stopped; everything was still. The houses were in darkness, giving the impression that everyone had gone to bed, but she knew that was an illusion. In the last hour one person had left their house, posted the voodoo doll through her letter box, and she felt sure they must be awake. They'd have seen her lights being switched on; know she'd seen the voodoo doll. Were they enjoying thinking about how frightened she might be? Nia looked around. They would be watching her now, watching to see what she would do next.

Nia turned away and walked quickly out of the close just as the church clock struck two.

She headed for the steps beside the entrance to the pier, leading down to the beach. At the far end, she saw the light shining, but she couldn't make out any fishermen tonight; she was alone.

The pebbles on the beach were wet under her feet but she didn't care. She took off her shoes and socks and, using the torch, she carried the voodoo doll down to the water. Through the darkness she could see the white foamy tips of a troubled sea, but it didn't distract her. The sea could have this monster; the sea was big enough to swallow it whole, to make it disappear for ever.

She threw the doll as far out as she could, but she was battling the wind and the incoming tide. It didn't go far, but she saw a wave tumble over it and heard the sound of the sea sucking out the shingle, dragging the voodoo doll far out to sea. But just as she was about to go back up the beach she saw it again, wet, bedraggled but still in one piece. The sea was returning it. She picked it up. What did the sea want to tell her?

Slowly, she made her way back up the beach and huddled on the towel, further down from where Ruby had sat. She lit the candle. It wasn't easy, but once it was burning it seemed to take hold. Should she burn the voodoo doll? Then she remembered Ruby's words, 'The trouble is, the voodoo doll may have gone, but the hate remains.'

It was that hatred that Ruby believed was behind all of this. Nia went through the people in the close. All had their secrets; all were frightened of their secrets coming out. But who had hatred in their heart?

Nia picked up the voodoo doll the sea had returned to her. What was she meant to be seeing? She held it close to the flame, looked into its eyes. As horrible as they were, why did they look so familiar? She stared at them and then suddenly she saw it. She knew who had created this voodoo doll, who had killed Ruby and Hugo.

'Not a good time to be down here on your own, is it? Anything could happen to you. There's no one else here, not even fishermen tonight.'

Nia looked up at the tall figure looming over her; she felt very small and vulnerable. She tried to stand up, but the man pushed her down. She started to struggle to get up, then realised he had a syringe. Before she could move, he held it against her neck, the needle resting on the skin, not yet breaking the surface. She froze, too petrified to move.

'I can do it in your neck but, I promise you, you'd prefer the injection in your arm.' He gave a nasty smile. 'It's so tragic, another death on the beach, another overdose. This time an unstable woman whose marriage was falling apart, with a history of drinking.'

'But not drugs.' Her voice cracked as she spoke.

'Ah, but they will find enough back at your house to convince them you've hidden it well. Look, I've got this ready as well. Do you want to read your final words?'

He threw the letter down to her. She opened it and read.

I couldn't go on. I'm so sorry. I've accused good people of terrible things. It was all in my head. It's better for everyone that I go this way.

He leant down and snatched the letter from her. 'I don't want that to get wet. I'll tuck that safely in your bag when I've dealt with you.'

'I worked it out, you know, and, if I have, others will – you can't kill everyone.'

His mouth twisted into a horrible snarl; his eyes glinted cruelly. He bore a terrible likeness to the face on the voodoo doll and to his father.

Richie slumped down next to her, but he kept the syringe against her neck. Could this be her chance? Throw the candle at him and get away? But she doubted she could do it before he thrust the needle into her skin.

His face was close to hers now, his eyes burning with anger. 'I don't believe you. I've been watching you floundering around. You're just guessing.'

She swallowed hard and answered, 'I admit it took time. I had to start by trusting myself, believing what I'd seen on the beach. Once I'd done that and I was sure someone had killed Ruby, it was clear that that person had to live in the close.'

'You may have got that far, but after that you were lost.'

'Not quite. I had to keep digging, keep looking. I've suspected everyone at one stage. You all had reasons to want to silence Ruby, but the others were all missing one thing. None of them had hate in their heart.'

He glared at her. 'What do you expect? I've been angry since I was a child.'

'Maybe your upbringing excuses some things, but you've made

choices to let that anger stagnate inside you and poison you. I think you have been very angry for a long time that you were dependent on your father, a man you hate, to fund the gallery. But you knew it was the only way you would ever get established. Then one day you and Ruby were offered a way to be free from him. Ruby was left a large sum of money by her mother. This was your chance to pay off your father, to be free.'

Richie nodded. 'It was like a miracle; you have to understand how awful it was to be tied to him.'

'Yes, I can understand that at least. I met him. I could see instantly that he is a cold, cruel, unfeeling man who has no respect for what you're doing.'

'Exactly. You do see that. You can see why I hate him.'

'I see it, yes. I saw it in that portrait in the bungalow. It's him, isn't it?'

Richie smirked. 'It was worth every penny to have somewhere I could go and paint that – every time I add another layer of hate to him.'

'You're obsessed with him, aren't you? Instead of distancing yourself from him, you let him possess you. He started to come out in your work. I saw it in the voodoo dolls, the face. It's him, isn't it?'

Richie looked down at the voodoo doll lying next to the candle. He stared at it, loosened his grip on the needle. 'I hadn't noticed that. I had no idea my father had got into my head like that. I'd no idea I was carving him.' Suddenly, he seemed to come to himself and flipped a hand at the voodoo doll. 'This is all rubbish, though, isn't it? I can't believe it bothered you. It was Elvira who made me think of them when we were collecting bits for her wedding bags. She'd seen something on social media about them. I thought it would be fun.'

'Fun? You thought it would be fun to send one to Ruby and then to me?'

'It was. I found the whole thing very satisfying. Collecting the wood, carving the face, using the blue silk material from Lucy's display. A nice bit of misdirection, I thought. But I did it all properly. I followed all the instructions for the curse. There's something satisfying about ritual, isn't there? Made me feel powerful. And then there is the curse itself. You know, I actively tried to summon up as much hate as I could.'

'The hate you then felt for Ruby?'

'I used to love her; you know. She was so different from my father: gentle, kind, so I thought. What I'd not factored in was the fanatical side to her. It's her fault, all of this, you know. If she hadn't been stupid and given that money away, she'd still be alive.'

'But you didn't kill her then.'

'No. But I was so angry, and I made these other plans. If she'd kept out of it—'

'But she didn't. The night she gave me a lift to the Red Jet she followed you and saw the bungalow.'

She saw his eyes shift. He looked away.

'It was ridiculous to get so upset. I told her I wasn't having an affair, and yet she went on and on about telling lies, demanded I give up the bungalow. You have to see how unreasonable she was.'

'But that wasn't what she was so angry about, was it? She used words like betrayal to me. The truth is she knew exactly what you were doing at the bungalow, and it was nothing to do with finding your own style.'

'I don't know what you mean.'

'I mean, Ruby went into the bungalow that night.'

'No—'

'Yes, she did. It was her umbrella hanging up in the hallway. You hate them, like Joe. I should have noticed that at the time. She came in, went upstairs and into your studio and she saw, as I should have, exactly what was going on in there.'

He sneered at her. 'Oh, yes, and what was that?'

'You were forging paintings. The old frames, the assortment of styles. That should have told me. You are so talented, and you realised there was money to be made. My guess is that you went for smaller names. You weren't trying to make millions. No, smaller names, selling on eBay, with a carefully hidden clause saying you are selling it as "attributed to the artist" rather than by the artist.'

'You know a lot about this.'

'I know what to look for. When I was buying my daughter an original print online, I looked very carefully into provenance because I know it's very easy to get scammed. In fact, it was a postcard from her that set me thinking.'

'I may have the talent to produce the work, but I've no idea how to set anything like that up.'

'Maybe you didn't, but Hugo did. He was involved in so many dodgy schemes. He would know how to post forged paintings on the web and that is what Ruby worked out. She threatened to tell your father, maybe even go to the police, and so Ruby had to die.'

'She would have done exactly that. She had no mercy. She'd pushed me into all this. She made me do it. It was all her fault.'

'You always blame everyone else, don't you? You could have walked away from your father and that gallery any time. Ruby would have stood by you, but the reason you stayed was greed. The reason you were forging paintings, something that must have gone against everything you thought you stood for, you did that because of greed. You are the only one to blame for all of this, Richie, no one else.'

'You're wrong, none of this is my fault. You know, you may think you are clever working things out, but you have no proof at all.'

'Well, let me think.' Nia looked out to sea. 'You have no alibi now for the night Ruby died.'

'I told you my car was over there. I took the photo of the picture.'

'But you ride a bike, you could have taken that over with you. And the photo was taken late, well after you'd had time to kill Ruby.'

Richie looked around, seemed once more to be lost in thought. 'It shouldn't have been that easy, should it? I was up there watching you, waiting for you to go. Then I came down. Ruby thought we'd made up, sharing a drink together. I did hold her while she died, you know. After that I cleared away the dregs of red candle and lit the green one I'd taken from the cafe. Then I took the ring and sealed the letter. I nearly put the ring back on her finger, but it seemed a waste. Typically, my father had spent a fortune on her in a way he'd never done on me. But no one saw me. You have no proof.'

'If you'd left it at that, maybe you'd have got away with it. But of course, when Ian started being vague about the alibi, you panicked. It was stupid, all that business in the pawnbroker's, all to try and set up Ian or Lucy. There'll be CCTV. Then there's the charity shops where I guessed you bought the clothes. And, of course, you were seen killing Hugo.'

For the first time she saw alarm in his eyes. 'What do you mean?'

'You'd stopped thinking straight, hadn't you? Hugo knew too much about you, the art forgery. I guess he supplied you with the ketamine to kill Ruby, and all you could think was that he needed to die.'

'It was dark. No one could swear to what they saw, and anyway—'

'You could kill them as well? It doesn't ever come to an end, does it? Killing, hating – is that all you can think about?'

A wave crashed onto the stones.

Richie crept closer to her. 'Enough. Roll up your sleeve. No more talking—'

Nia looked down the beach. With the tide coming in, the sea was very close to them now.

'If you kill me here, the sea will take me.'

'I know, we're further down the beach than Ruby was. It's handy. No one will find you for days... maybe you will be lost for ever—'

Nia heard a scrunching on the shingle behind her.

'That's not going to happen.'

Jade came and stood in front of them. 'It's over, Richie. The police are on their way. It's finished – let Nia go.'

Nia froze, Richie was still holding the syringe to her neck, he could easily plunge it in.

However, she felt the pressure of the needle ease on her throat. He pulled away but then, without warning, he plunged the needle into his own neck.

The moon crept from behind the clouds and flooded the beach in light. For a second even the sea seemed to still.

Nia started to shake uncontrollably; her teeth chattered. She felt Jade's arms around her.

'It's over, shush now.'

'You came,' Nia whispered.

'It took me a while to wake up and see the light on in your room, but as soon as I did I knew something was up.'

Nia heard the ambulance, saw the blue lights flashing. Saw the paramedics hurtling onto the beach.

* * *

It was a long cold night, first at the hospital, then at the police station, but eventually Nia was allowed home. She'd given the house keys to Jade to enable her to look after Romeo and so Nia messaged Jade when she knew she was returning home. Jade and Romeo were on the doorstep waiting for her when she arrived home.

Romeo jumped up at her and she cuddled him.

'Are you ok? You must be shattered,' said Jade.

'I am, but please, come and have a coffee and a slice of cake. I want to tell you everything that's happened.'

43

MONDAY 14TH MAY 2018

Nia stood on the deck of the ferry, rucksack on her back, the handle of her case in one hand, Romeo's lead in the other. The announcement had come, and they were about to disembark.

She'd been away for a month. It felt a lot longer, but she had sorted out the house, packed up her life back on the mainland. Chris had moved in with Sian. The house was now up for sale.

She'd spent the day seeing Safi in Bristol, where she was studying. She had turned down Safi's invitation to stay in her chaotic student house because she'd promised Jade she'd be back, that they would be together this evening.

As always, Nia felt her shoulders drop slightly, her jaw relax, as she walked onto the island. Her senses were alert to the things she'd missed: the sound of gulls, the smell of salt air, the masts of the white yachts against the blue sky, the narrow streets.

She trod the familiar route to the close, stood in front of what was now her own front door.

Although it looked as deceptively snug and cosy as the day she'd arrived, there had been changes. Different plants and pots stood outside the houses. Different curtains hung in the windows.

Elvira's and Ethan's cars were parked beside the surgery, but they no longer lived above it. They had bought a run-down cottage in the middle of the woods; another vet had joined them and lived above the surgery now. To the left, Joe still lived and worked at Wight's. Opposite, the gallery no longer displayed Richie's paintings. The paramedics had saved him and now he was in prison, awaiting trial, and the gallery was occupied by a photographer.

The salon, of course, was still there. Jade, however, had sold her flat in Cowes and had bought Lucy and Ian's house. They had moved to Surrey, which was much easier for commuting to London. The spot on the morning breakfast show was proving a great success. Lucy in particular was hugely popular. Nia wasn't too sure how Ian really felt about that, but he was putting on a good show of being pleased for her.

And now Nia herself called her aunt's house home properly. Gwen had decided to move out to be with her daughter in San Francisco, and so Nia, until the divorce settlement went through, was renting her house. However, soon she would be buying the house for herself.

Nia opened the door and went straight through to the kitchen to let Romeo out and she went out into the garden with him. She saw Jade carrying baby Pearl around the garden, showing her the flowers.

'Hi,' Nia called.

Jade rushed over. 'You're back,' she exclaimed.

'It's wonderful to be home. And how are you, Pearl?' Nia turned to Jade. 'Her hair is even longer. It's amazing.'

Jade touched the glorious white-blonde curls on her daughter's head. 'You know, she looks so like my sister, but I think it's as well I didn't call her Ruby. That seemed too much of a burden. I didn't want her growing up thinking she had to be Ruby. No, she must be herself. But I'm glad she looks like her, I think it is nature's gentle reminder and I'm grateful for that.'

'So, what's the news?'

'You'll be glad to know we survived at the salon. The student did a brilliant job of standing in for you, but everyone has missed you. Oh, and Richie's father died. It was all very sudden.'

'No. What happened?'

'Yes, he had a heart attack. He never went to see Richie, but then I'm not sure what good that would have done either of them. He'd left a will, though, and guess what he did with the money?'

'Left it to Richie?'

'No way. He left it to the charity Ruby worked for. It might be the one decent thing he did with his life.'

'And how is this little one?' said Nia, smiling at Pearl.

'Getting spoiled rotten. Joe's parents come over so much. But I shouldn't moan. They're the reason I can keep working. They adore her.'

'You never regret telling Joe?'

'No. I would never have guessed how things would change once he came out to his parents. It was like he came alive, grew into himself.' She smiled. 'Anyway, we are very lucky. It's all working out well at the moment. And, surprise, Joe is bringing round his new partner to meet Pearl later this evening. I've met him a few times. He's lovely and Joe looks smitten.'

'And how are you finding today?' Nia asked more gently.

'Well, of course, it's sad, isn't it? When Pearl woke me up, my first thought was that she would never meet Ruby. And then I looked at her hair, and I felt in a way Ruby is still with me.'

'Is it any comfort knowing Richie is going to be punished for what he did?'

'It means a great deal to me to know the truth about Ruby's death and I know it would have mattered deeply to her. What Richie did was so wicked. I won't forget he took my sister away from me. But I'm not going to spend my life hating him either.'

'I've already been down to the beach, but I'd love to go with you this evening if that is what you are planning.'

'Of course. It's the reason I got back today.'

* * *

As the church clock struck ten, Nia settled Romeo and left the house. In her bag she had a candle and some fossils. As Nia stood waiting for Jade, she had the feeling that peace had been restored to the close.

The night was dark and still as Nia and Jade walked down through the close in silence until they reached the beach.

Nia was relieved to see it was empty. The sea was quietly rolling in, watching them. She lit the candle and put it in the place where, a year ago, she'd sat with Ruby. After a few moments Nia picked up the candle and used the wax to draw hearts on three different fossils she'd collected over time.

One she gave to Jade, one she kept but the third she took down to the sea. She placed it where the waves met the shore, watched the sea wash over it and said, 'For Ruby. I send you love, and I send you peace... dance with the waves... whisper with the waves.'

As she said the words, she saw the moon was shining down on the fossil and as she watched it started to glow. Slowly the darkness was driven back until finally all that remained was light.

ACKNOWLEDGMENTS

Firstly, an enormous thank you to you, my lovely readers, for taking the time to read *Good Neighbours*.

There are of course many other people to thank.

A huge thank you to my publisher Boldwood, to the whole team including Nia Beynon and Claire Fenby, who work incredibly hard and are always kind and helpful. A very special thank you to Sarah Ritherdon, for her belief and faith in my writing, for yet again taking the tangle of a first draft and working with me to craft this story. Thank you also, Sue Smith and Shirley Khan for your exceptional work editing, the cover designer and everyone involved in bringing this novel to life.

Thank you, Krissy Lloyd and all the staff, at Medina Books in Cowes, for your unending support of writers on the island. Your bookshop is a very special place, a treasure trove on our lovely island.

Thank you so much Maureen Parr for allowing me to use the name of your beautiful Cocker Spaniel, Romeo, and to everyone in one of the best ever groups: Cocker Spaniels On Facebook.

I would like to thank Isle of Wight photographer Steve Gascoigne of Available Light Gallery and Gifts for again generously donating a beautiful photograph to our competition. Thank you everyone on Facebook, Twitter and Instagram, bloggers, writers and friends. Your kind words and reviews mean more than you can know.

Thank you so much Karen Cass for again adding a touch of magic with your wonderful narration of the audiobook.

On a personal note, I have, as always, to thank my wonderful husband and children, Thomas and Emily. You, more than anyone, see the highs and lows and are always there for a hug and coffee when I need it.

MORE FROM MARY GRAND

We hope you enjoyed reading *Good Neighbours*. If you did, please leave a review.

If you'd like to gift a copy, this book is also available as an ebook, digital audio download and audiobook CD.

Sign up to Mary Grand's mailing list for news, competitions and updates on future books.

https://bit.ly/MaryGrandNewsletter

The House Party, another gripping thriller from Mary Grand, is available to order now.

ABOUT THE AUTHOR

Mary Grand is the author of five novels and writes gripping, page-turning suspense, with a dark and often murderous underside. She grew up in Wales, was for many years a teacher of deaf children and now lives on the Isle of Wight.

Visit Mary's website: https://marygrand.net/

Follow Mary on social media:

twitter.com/authormaryg
instagram.com/maryandpepper
facebook.com/authormarygrand
bookbub.com/profile/mary-grand

ABOUT BOLDWOOD BOOKS

Boldwood Books is a fiction publishing company seeking out the best stories from around the world.

Find out more at www.boldwoodbooks.com

Sign up to the Book and Tonic newsletter for news, offers and competitions from Boldwood Books!

http://www.bit.ly/bookandtonic

We'd love to hear from you, follow us on social media:

 facebook.com/BookandTonic

twitter.com/BoldwoodBooks

 instagram.com/BookandTonic